BROKEN SILENCE

ENDORSEMENTS

Jane Daly dazzles the reader with the sequel to *Broken*, by skillfully weaving together complex plots—secrets which could tear any family apart. In *Broken Silence*, she knits the lives, secrets, and lies of three people in one family, who ultimately surrender their secrets to one another. I was unable to put *Broken Silence* down. Non-stop mystery and drama!

—**Claire O'Sullivan**, author of *Romance Under Wraps*, and *Rules of Engagement*.

I've added a new favorite author to my list: Jane Daly. *Broken Silence* is a wonderful blend of action and adventure, emotional impact, and memorable characters. Reading this story was like enjoying smooth chocolate and fine wine. I've already reserved a space for it on my Keepers shelf!

—**Loree Lough**, *USA Today* bestselling author of nearly 150 award-winning books, including *The Preacher Wore Black Leather*, Book 1 in The Sundown Diner series.

Broken Silence explores the mindset of a young woman living one step ahead of the authorities and two steps behind her shame. Pain, betrayal, and guilt meet grace and love in a story beautifully crafted with real people and real issues. I highly recommend this chronicle of restoration, healing and forgiveness.

—**Deb Potts**, author of *Love on Life Support*, speaker and marriage mentor

This is real life struggles and challenges we all face in this mixed-up world in which we live. Jane S. Daly depicts the down-trodden and "messes" we all find ourselves in, by choices or not. She helps us to realize this fact: We are all lovable—and deeply adored by our Heavenly Father. I couldn't put this down but found the whole piece satisfyingly real for Young Adult, Light Suspense, or Contemporary Romance audiences.

—**Chris Daniel**, author, peer-reviewer RN, BSHS, CCM, CNLCP, MSCC, LNC, CBIS California Nurse Life Care Planning, Inc.

Surprises. Secrets. Suspense. From the first page to the end, Jane Daly keeps you turning the page wondering what will happen next and if situations will ever be resolved.

—**Diana Leagh Matthews**

When we keep silent about our pasts, our pasts control and haunt us. Jane S. Daly has written a must-read novel about secrets kept and the tangle of guilt waiting to destroy.

—**Carol McClain**, author, *Borrowed Lives, Prodigal Lives*

BROKEN SILENCE

Jane Daly

PUBLISHING THE POSITIVE
Plymouth, Massachusetts
A Christian Company
ElkLakePublishingInc.com

COPYRIGHT NOTICE

Cover and Interior Design:
Editor(s): Mary W. Johnson, Cristel Phelps, Deb Haggerty
Author Represented By: Credo Communications LLC

PUBLISHED BY: Elk Lake Publishing, Inc., 35 Dogwood Drive, Plymouth, MA 02360, 2023

Library Cataloging Data

Names: Daly, Jane (Jane Daly)
Broken Silence / Jane Daly
388 p. 23cm × 15cm (9in × 6 in.)
ISBN-13: 978-1-64949-852-6 (paperback) | 978-1-64949-853-3 (trade hardcover) | 978-1-64949-854-0 (trade paperback) | 978-1-64949-855-7 (e-book)
Key Words: Romance; Drugs; Goth; Police; Family Relationships; Honesty; Salvation
Library of Congress Control Number: 2023935010 Fiction

But everything exposed by the light becomes visible—
and everything that is illuminated becomes a light.

—Ephesians 5:13

DEDICATION

I've discovered family is more than blood. This is for my adopted family in Oregon. You hold a special place in my heart.

ACKNOWLEDGMENTS

Mark 4:22 (CSB) says, "For there is nothing hidden that will not be revealed, and nothing concealed that will not be brought to light."

I had a secret I didn't want anyone to know. I thought if my friends found out, they'd turn their backs on me. Like Jinxi, I was afraid. What I discovered, though, is once something that is kept in darkness is revealed in the light, it loses its power.

I'm grateful for so many people who have encouraged me during the process of writing this story:

Robin—my BFF who read the draft and loved it.

Hubby—who encourages me every day to "get some writing done."

Mary—Editor extraordinaire. You fixed, sharpened, and encouraged me. You're awesome!

Elk Lakers—my beloved publishing family. What a fabulous support system.

Readers—if you read *Broken*, then you get this gift of reading about the rest of Jinxi's and Dean's story. Thanks for taking the time to read this, and (hopefully) leave a review.

You can connect with me on my website www.JaneSDaly.com

I have a monthly newsletter and a blog, and I answer every email from friends and readers.

Facebook: www.facebook.com/janedalyspeakerandauthor
Twitter: @JaneDal26031324
Instagram: www.Instagram.com/thejanesdaly
Linkedin: Jane Daly | LinkedIn

CHAPTER ONE

Jinxi Lansing stopped at the bottom of the stairs, listening to the silence. The old house seemed to be holding its breath, waiting. Even the normal creaking and groaning had ceased.

Goosebumps broke out on her arms. She jumped when Ted woofed from behind. "Sorry, buddy. I know you need to go outside."

She dumped her backpack on the wooden kitchen table and then opened the back door. Ted dashed out, making a beeline to his favorite tree. Rubbing her hands up and down her sweatshirt-clad arms, Jinxi couldn't shake the feeling something was wrong. Two-plus decades of vulnerability made her hyperaware of the smallest change in the atmosphere.

Why wasn't Janice up yet? Jinxi's friend, mentor, and spiritual mom usually woke with the sun. A cursory glance around the kitchen indicated nothing had been disturbed, plus the fact the coffee maker sat dark. Jinxi pushed the button to start the morning's brew, then headed down the short, dark hall to Janice's bedroom.

"Janice?" Jinxi's voice echoed in the silence. Sheets and blankets formed a messy wad at the end of Janice's bed. "Janice?" The bathroom door was open and the room empty. Only the faint smell of Janice's citrus body lotion remained of her presence.

Nerves skittered up Jinxi's spine. She returned to the kitchen, then stomped into the living room. Fear and anger bartered for position. Janice never went anywhere without leaving a yellow sticky note.

Gone to WalMart—back soon

Coffee is ready to brew—just turn it on

Sandwiches in fridge—Help yourself

Janice's car was absent from the driveway. The Queen of Sticky Notes had left without letting Jinxi know. Of course she did. Janice didn't owe Jinxi a thing.

Old feelings like knife jabs pierced Jinxi's heart. After six months of having Jinxi in her home, Janice probably tired of having to constantly let Jinxi know where she was. Maybe it was time to move on. It wasn't like she was family. Her stay at Janice's was only due to the older woman's hospitality. That could change at any time.

One thing Jinxi knew for sure—relationships were transactional. You do this for me, I do that for you. Maybe letting Jinxi know where Janice had gone wasn't part of the agreement.

Jinxi returned to the kitchen and poured a cup of coffee. As she sipped, she eyed the knife rack on the counter. A familiar craving crawled over her skin. Pulling the paring knife free, she tested it against her arm. One little slice and she'd feel better. Or would she?

Ted interrupted her thoughts, clawing at the back door. Jinxi tossed the knife on the counter and let him in. The sound of a car door slamming had her heading back to the living room.

"Where were you?" Jinxi demanded when Janice unlocked the door and stepped into the house.

"I, uh ..." Janice pushed the door closed with tear-filled eyes.

Alarm bells sounded in Jinxi's ears, drowning out everything except Janice's ragged breathing. Janice's short gray hair was a tangled mess, and her sweater was buttoned wrong.

"You should have left me a note." Jinxi's words fell into the empty space between them like shattered glass. She crossed her arms, determined to hold onto the hurt.

"Merciful heavens. I'm sorry." Janice set her purse on an end table, then shrugged out of her sweater, tossing it onto her favorite chair. "I got a call. I left in a hurry."

Leaves chattered against the living room windows, blown from the trees by a gust of wind. Jinxi watched them swirl. A rock of fear in her stomach pulled her down to slump onto one of the dining room chairs.

"What kind of call?"

"Dean ..." Janice choked back a sob, one hand fisted to her trembling lips.

Jinxi's world tilted. Images flew through her mind. Scenes of Janice's son, Dean, teasing her, chasing Ted around the yard, tossing his niece Hannah into the air. She heard him yelling at her, their argument, she trying to get him to forgive her.

"Is he—" She bit her lip hard enough to draw blood. "Is he dead?"

Janice's breath caught. "Goodness, no. But he's in a coma. He fell and hit his head."

In her mind, Jinxi saw herself run to Janice and hug her, giving and receiving comfort. But her legs were wooden, her body frozen to the seat. How could she extend comfort when she'd never received it?

"You should have left a note," Jinxi said, sniffing away the tears threatening to push their way past her burning eyelids.

"I'm sorry," Janice repeated, her voice a monotone. "I have to call Brian. And Robin." Her hands dropped to her sides as she dragged herself toward her bedroom.

Of course. Family first.

"Wait." Jinxi stood, shoving the wooden chair back under the table. "Where is he? Can I see him?"

"Sacramento General, downtown. I don't know if they'll let anyone in who's not family."

Family. Which Jinxi was not. She heard the finality of Janice's bedroom door clicking shut.

The grandfather clock in the living room chimed, a sharp reminder she'd be late for work. She retreated to the kitchen for a drink of water to wash away the metallic taste of her blood. The coffee mug she'd used sat in the sink. After gulping some water, she slammed the cup down hard enough to crack it. Not satisfied, she banged the cup down again and again. It shattered into jagged pieces and the handle slipped off her fingers and clattered into the sink. She rested her arms on the counter, gripping the edge of the sink with bloodless knuckles.

CHAPTER TWO

Officer Raul Hernandez steadied himself against the hospital wall as he made his way toward where his partner Dean lay in the emergency room. He pulled his bandaged arm against his body to avoid bumping against any of the people coming and going.

The broken skin across his knuckles stung, a small price to pay for the satisfaction of smashing his fist into the older guy's face.

You gotta have your partner's back. Always.

That old man should've never touched Dean. Too bad the guy got a few blows in before Raul could stop him.

The pain pill finally kicked in, its familiar warmth spreading through his body. The scuffle with the loser at the apartments would be just the thing to keep him in meds for the next few weeks.

The nurses paid him no attention as he peeked into each room. His police uniform lent him authority he wouldn't otherwise have.

Dean lay on a high gurney, one of many patients waiting to be admitted. Raul stepped through the curtained area.

"Hey, bro, it's me."

No response.

"I hope you wake up soon. You need to know what happened tonight." Raul lowered his voice, but not the intensity. "I need to talk to you before they do."

He jumped as the curtains parted, and an older woman entered. She appeared equally surprised.

"Goodness, you startled me. Who are you?" she asked, her hand flying to her throat.

"I'm Dean's partner. Raul Hernandez."

"Oh! You were there when it happened. I'm Janice, Dean's mother."

"Sorry to meet you like this." Raul held out his bandaged right arm with a reflexive motion. With a grimace, he extended his left hand instead to shake Janice's. "Your boy's a good partner. Solid."

They stood on opposite sides of the bed, staring down at Dean's unconscious form.

"Can you tell me what happened?" Janice whispered.

Raul cleared his throat. "It was a domestic disturbance call. It shouldn't have gone down the way it did."

"What do you mean?" Dean's mother stroked her son's forehead.

"The kid, he reached in his pocket right as the dad rushed at us. I got a shot off, but it went wild." Raul shrugged, breaking eye contact. "The dad fired first."

"What about the young man?"

Raul shook his head.

"Oh, dear." Janice's voice quavered. "What happened to Dean?"

"After the dad shot, he came at Dean and me like a linebacker. Dean got knocked backward, and I was hit. I still had my weapon, and I was able to take control of the situation until backup arrived."

The curtains parted again, and a nurse appeared. "No visitors allowed. Unless you're here in an official capacity ..." She glared at him over her reading glasses.

"This is my partner." His voice challenged her to dispute him.

The nurse shifted her gaze to Janice. "And you are?"

"His mother."

Raul held his breath, hoping to speak again to Dean's mom.

The nurse spoke to Janice. "We're going to do an MRI, so we prefer all family wait in the waiting room. We'll let you know as things progress." The nurse clutched a blanket against her ample bosom and indicated the door with her head. "Both of you. Out."

Lunch at the Sacramento Food Bank came and went, and still Jinxi hadn't been able to slip away to ask permission to leave early. Indecision pulled her, a rubber band expanding and contracting. She should go to the hospital, but would they let her see Dean? And what about the rest of Janice's family? Dean's sister, Robin, made it clear she hated Jinxi's guts. Their brother Brian gave her the creeps, always staring. Brian's wife, Courtney, was her only ally. Perhaps Courtney would give her the info on Dean.

Jinxi and Dean hadn't spoken more than a few words since their argument a few weeks ago, around the same time he began working patrol. Maybe he'd wake up and wouldn't want to see her. His rejection still stung. What could she expect, anyway? Rejection, dismissal, a backhand slap, it was all too familiar.

Still, they'd been friends once. Her first real friend.

The food bank director, Padish Singh, shooed her out the door when she finally got him away from the homeless lunch crowd.

"You must go," Padish said, without his habitual smile. "Please give my regards to Mrs. Janice."

People jostled for seats on the bus heading downtown. Jinxi used her elbows to shove her way down the aisle, dropping her backpack on the seat next to her to discourage anyone wanting to sit. Her fingers patted the pocket of her jeans, searching for the lighter that wasn't there. Bad time to quit smoking.

She pulled a book from the backpack, staring at the pages with blurred vision. The book dropped to her lap. She sucked the stud in her lip against her teeth, clicking it back and forth. Would Dean wake up and tell her to bounce? How badly was he hurt? Was he going to die? A sharp inhale attracted the attention of a nearby passenger. Jinxi quickly lowered her head, wishing her hair were long enough to cover her face.

This might be a good time to pray. But God was probably mad at her for the near slip-up this morning with the knife. She'd promised no more cutting, tattoos, or piercing. Her transaction with God seemed to be one-way. She promised not to cut, but what was he doing in return? Even a deal with the devil was quid pro quo. Maybe this whole Christian thing was overrated.

Jinxi stared out the bus window, watching the passing scenery. How did Janice stay so calm? What was her deal with God that kept her from freaking out over every little thing? How would Janice handle this issue with Dean?

The bus traveled through midtown Sacramento, jerking to a halt at each stop. Businessmen pulled out smartphones or newspapers, ignoring the rest of the occupants. A few high school kids got on, ear buds dangling, tethered to a hidden phone or music source. Their loud voices grated at the edge of Jinxi's consciousness as she counted the street numbers they passed.

One-story buildings became multi-storied medical offices, filled with doctors, nurses, and sick people. She sucked in a breath, thinking about Dean in a room somewhere in one of the towers.

Sacramento General Hospital loomed tall and dark, hugging the sidewalk. The bus dropped her at the front doors, along with half the other occupants. The hospital doors whooshed open as they trooped en masse into the lobby. Some decorator had tried to make the hospital welcoming, but failed just short of success. The teal and brown faux leather chairs had been designed to look comfy, but to Jinxi, they appeared as hulking figures wanting to take her captive.

A feeling of déjà vu swept over her. The last time she'd been in a hospital was during the summer when Janice's granddaughter Hannah was sick. Hannah's unabashed declarations of love had created a child-sized crack in Jinxi's armor-plated heart.

Jinxi remembered how she'd gone to Hannah's room, not seeking to comfort her, but rather for assurance Hannah would be okay.

Until Robin screamed at her to get out or she'd call security.

"Where's the ER?" she asked one of the volunteers at the front desk when it was finally her turn. The volunteer looked her up and down, from the heavy Doc Marten boots to her dyed black hair. Her gaze finally settled on the stud in Jinxi's lip.

"Who are you trying to locate?"

She wanted to say, "My best friend in the whole world. The only man who's ever shown me respect." Instead, she gave Dean's name.

"He's been transferred to Room 1319 in the Trauma Unit."

The volunteer handed her a visitor's badge and pointed her to the elevators. The smell of disinfectant couldn't cover what Jinxi thought of as the stench of death. She gagged, trying to cover it up by coughing into the sleeve of her sweatshirt. She felt the side glances of the others in the elevator.

The elevator doors opened, and Jinxi stepped into a tiled waiting area. Chairs and tables, cozily arranged, gave the impression of an oversized living room. A sign on the wall pointing down a hall directed her to Trauma, its bold letters shouting the magnitude of its seriousness. She took a hesitant step forward as the doors to a second elevator opened. Dean's sister-in-law Courtney rushed through the sliding doors.

"What happened?" Courtney demanded. "Where's Brian? Is he here? And Janice?"

"I dunno. I just got here." Jinxi shrugged.

"Do you know what happened?" Courtney gripped Jinxi's arm as she propelled them toward the waiting area.

"Not yet. Dean's in a coma. No one really knows what happened."

Courtney brought her fist to her mouth as tears trickled out of her eyes. Jinxi braced herself as Courtney leaned heavily against her.

They'd taken only a few steps when Brian and Janice turned a corner and headed toward them. Courtney rushed to her husband, and he gathered her into his arms, staring at Jinxi over Courtney's shoulder.

"No change yet," Janice informed them, waving them toward the chairs.

Jinxi settled into a chair in a corner while everyone else chose a seat. Janice murmured words of comfort to Courtney, patting her on the back.

After a few minutes, Dean's sister Robin, her husband Carlos, and four-year-old Hannah burst through the doors of the elevator. Robin carried her newborn in a baby carrier, setting it down to give her mother a quick hug.

"What's going on?" Robin glanced at the others' faces, her stare resting momentarily on Jinxi, who shrank back against the chair. Hannah pulled away from Carlos and rushed to Jinxi, eyes bright.

"Hi, Jinxi!" she said, throwing her arms around her. "Will you play with me?"

Robin's mouth was set in a straight line. "Not now, Hannah," Robin snapped, turning her attention back to Janice.

"There was an incident ..."

Brian laid a hand on his mother's arm. "Relax, Mom." He turned to his sister. "Dean was on a call and was shoved by some punk. When he went down, he hit his head on one of those concrete parking lot pylons. He's got a bad concussion, and they have him in a medically induced coma to reduce the swelling in his brain."

Jinxi watched the family from her seat in the corner of the waiting area. Janice was the sun, drawing the others into her gravitational pull. If everyone were a planet, Jinxi would be Pluto, not sure where she fit.

The Raffertys pulled together in times of celebration and times of crisis. Everyone had gathered around Janice a few weeks ago when she'd gotten bitten by a black widow spider. They'd celebrated Dean's transfer from jail to patrol duty at their weekly pizza night. Jinxi bet they weren't happy about his transfer now. Especially Janice.

Janice and Brian took turns giving what little information they had about Dean and speculating on the rest. Jinxi alternated between chewing on a fingernail and sucking on the stud in her bottom lip. As she watched the family, she was transported back to her release from Girls' Ranch after her three-year incarceration. Her mother had showed up, clearly inconvenienced at having to take a day off work. When they'd gotten home, her mom headed straight to a bottle. She never asked about the years Jinxi spent there. Never a lecture about what she'd learned, blah, blah, blah. It was as if it never happened.

Hannah reached the end of her ability to be still and hopped up and down on one leg. "Can I see Unca Dean?" she asked, pulling on Jinxi's hand. "Can I? Pleeeeeese?"

Janice stood and motioned to the child. "Come on, Princess, let me take you downstairs to the gift shop. We'll find something nice to give to Uncle Dean, okay?" She turned to Robin and Carlos. "They'll only let two people in at a time, so why don't you two go first."

They headed for the elevator, Hannah bouncing on one leg. Janice never glanced Jinxi's way.

After an hour of no updates on Dean's condition, the family trooped downstairs to the cafeteria. Jinxi was finally alone. A quick glance down the hall showed the empty nurses' station. She tiptoed toward Dean's room, heart pounding. If someone in the family saw her, she'd be busted for sure. Kicked out with no chance of seeing Dean.

The head of the bed was elevated, and Dean's arms rested outside the sheet. An IV tube connected to a bag was inserted into the back of one hand. Jinxi's stomach lurched. The bandage surrounding his head gave him an alien-like appearance. One eye was swollen shut, the lid purple, the bruise spreading to his broad nose. Stubble darkened his cheeks. A machine beeped in a regular cadence.

She pulled a hard plastic chair close to the bed. Resting her arms on the side rail, she laid her chin on her hands.

Wake up, Dean.

Maybe if she concentrated hard enough, he'd open his eyes. Her gaze traveled down to his muscular arms, protruding incongruously from the skimpy hospital gown. She stared at his forearm until she could focus on each individual hair.

Jinxi thought back to a few weeks before, when something had shifted between them. He'd accused her of stealing a pair of earrings from his mom, when in fact it was Hannah who'd hidden the jewelry in Jinxi's room. Then there was the other thing with the money. Janice had forgiven her. Dean hadn't been quite so understanding. When he came to his mom's house, and Jinxi was around, it was an elaborate dance where he went out of his way to avoid touching her, even to brush past her in the hall.

She missed his teasing. He joked about her cooking, about the blonde roots starting to show in her hair, the way she let his dog sleep in her room. He'd even tried to kiss her once, before he thought of her as a thief.

Jinxi reached through the rails to rest her hand on Dean's arm, then jerked back her hand and stood as Janice opened the door and stepped in. Janice circled the bed and stood next to her, their shoulders touching.

"Any change?"

Jinxi shook her head as the door opened again and a doctor entered. He looked at the two women and asked, "Are you both family?"

Janice and Jinxi answered at the same time.

"Yes."

"No."

They glanced at each other, then back at the doctor.

He didn't speak as he logged onto the computer at the foot of Dean's bed. "We're going to do more tests. If he responds well, we'll talk about decreasing the medication and see if he wakes up on his own."

Jinxi grabbed the bed rail as a swoop of vertigo turned her legs to jelly.

The doctor looked up from studying the file. "Any questions? No. Then I suggest you both go home and get some rest. There's nothing else you can do right now. I'll talk to you tomorrow."

Janice put her arm around Jinxi's shoulders. Jinxi stiffened but didn't move away. They stood like that for several minutes, each lost in their own thoughts. How much more could her life change in such a short time? She didn't know what Janice was thinking, but hearing her sniffle, she bet Janice was thinking the same thing.

CHAPTER THREE

"I have good news."

Janice, Brian, Courtney and Jinxi stood as a unit when the doctor found them in the waiting area. Janice and Jinxi had returned to the hospital early the next day. Jinxi's boss, Padish, had given her the day off.

Janice exhaled with a whoosh as the doctor spoke to her.

"We've backed down on the meds. The swelling has gone down inside your son's head, and it looks like structurally he's okay." His smile was reassuring as he touched Janice's arm. "Your boy has a very hard head."

Janice made a noise that could have been a chuckle or a sob.

"When he wakes up, we'll transfer him from Trauma to a regular room."

"How soon do you expect him to wake up?" Brian asked, always the numbers person.

The doctor paused for a beat. "We hope in the next four to eight hours. I need to tell you, we have no way of assessing the extent of damage to his brain until he wakes up. The MRI and CT scans show normal activity, but sometimes there are behavioral or cognitive changes which aren't evident until the patient reaches full consciousness."

When the doctor left, Janice pulled out her cell phone.

"I need to call Robin."

She found a quiet corner. Jinxi heard her choking back tears as she relayed the news to her daughter.

Jinxi waited, pointedly ignoring Brian's piercing gaze, until Janice completed her call. "Are you going to go to Dean's room?" Jinxi asked the older woman.

"Yes, I think I'll go see him before I go down to the business office. I was told there's paperwork to fill out. Goodness gracious, can you believe they're already pestering me for payment?" Janice shook her head as if they'd asked her to chug a can of beer. "I'd love to go home and rest a bit. I'm exhausted. How about you? Do you want a ride home?"

"Courtney and I are going home," Brian announced.

Jinxi chewed her lip, the stud clicking back and forth. She wanted to stay at the hospital, to avoid the temptation to cut herself. Anything to relieve the pain of Dean's accident. Even though she'd gotten rid of her personal knife, there were all kinds of sharp instruments at Janice's house, waiting to take her captive again. Sometimes it was a battle of wills between her need and God's deliverance.

"I think I'll hang out here for a while."

"All right. I'll be back in a jiffy."

Brian took his mother's arm as they walked toward the elevators.

Jinxi fingered the cell phone in her sweatshirt pocket. Her link to the world outside. Who should she call? Aneesa, her supervisor and accountability partner, or maybe her boss? With a start, she remembered she'd promised Padish she'd phone him with an update.

She scrolled through the few names in the address book and called Padish's phone, leaving a brief message. "Dean should wake up in, like, four to eight hours. The swelling's down, but the doctor doesn't know if there's been any brain damage."

Jinxi pushed the END button with a sweaty finger. Brain damage. She shouldn't have said the words. As if saying them would make them come true. She took a breath, lungs pressing painfully against her ribs. I take it back. Her words turned into a prayer. Please don't let there be any brain damage.

The phone vibrated to life in her hand. The caller ID showed Consuela Lopez. Jinxi pictured Connie standing in the food bank kitchen, stirring something on the stove. It was only yesterday she'd stood beside her, helping prepare the noon meal.

"How is Señor Dean?"

"He's about the same, I guess. Still asleep, but the doctor said he should be waking up soon."

Connie's voice was stern, her Spanish accent even more pronounced. "Then he will be fine. I will pray that it is so." Jinxi pictured Connie making the sign of the cross and kissing her thumbnail. "You remember when mi esposo was taken by the INS? We pray and pray, and now he is return to me. You must pray too."

Jinxi felt Connie's urgency through the phone.

"You must also talk to him. I have a friend, her son have a bad fever, and he not wake up for three days. Every day, she talk and talk. When he wake up, he tell her he hear her. It is true. Talk to Señor Dean."

After the family left the waiting area, Jinxi crept into Dean's room and sat by his side. She reached out and laid her hand on his arm, jerking when he exhaled noisily. His skin was cool to the touch, and his hair was dark and coarser than she expected. She moved her hand down to cover his, then clasped his fingers in hers, looking for any reaction. It was the first time they'd touched since they'd sat in the swing at his mom's house. He'd brushed her shoulder with his hand, sending a bolt of electricity through her.

She put her hand on his bicep, testing its strength, then moved her hand up to lay it on his cheek, feeling the sharp nettles of days-old beard scrape her palm. Dean stirred, and she pulled away.

"Um, hi. It's me, Jinxi." Shoulders hunched, she stared down at her hands clenched in her lap. "I don't know if you can hear me or not, but here goes." She looked at his closed eyes, reassured he hadn't awakened and was getting ready to tease her. Or be angry. "I can't remember if I told you, but remember Connie, the lady I work with? Well, Padish has been helping her with all the legal stuff, and her husband came home from Mexico last week. You should've seen how psyched the kids were. Remember Miguel and Rosa? They came by the food bank last week to pick Connie up, along with her husband and they were, like, jumping all over the place."

Jinxi paused, racking her brain for something else to say.

"Um, I know you're probably still mad at me, but I hope you're over it. I'm really sorry about the mess with your mom's earrings." She gulped. "And the money thing. She said I didn't have to pay her back."

Jinxi reached out and put her hand over his again. "You have to wake up, okay?" She choked down a sob. Don't cry. Don't cry.

Hating herself for her weakness, she continued. "Please be okay." Her eyes blurred with tears. "You have to be okay." She rocked back and forth, unable to express the tangle of emotions surging through her.

"Mom?" His voice was hoarse, barely audible.

Jinxi held her breath as Dean's eyes slowly opened. He looked around, then his eyes settled on her face.

"I thought you were my mom," he whispered. "I felt her hand."

"Hi." She was finally able to force the word past her swollen throat.

"Hi." Dean licked his dry lips. "Can I have a drink?"

"I'll get the nurse." Jinxi sprang from her seat and ran to the door, signaling to the on-duty nurse.

The nurse bustled in. "How's our patient?" she asked, but he had already fallen back asleep.

Mariachi music exploded into the thick silence. Raul lunged for the cell phone, glanced at the name on the screen, then answered. "Bueno."

"He's awake."

"Has he said anything?"

"No."

"Gracias, esse."

Raul disconnected and tossed the phone on the sofa. The TV was on, its sound muted. Curtains kept the midday sun at bay except for a single crack. Dust motes hung lazily in the sliver of light, finally settling onto the worn carpet. Raul drummed his fingers on his thigh. Should he go to the hospital now and risk running into Dean's family, or wait until tonight?

He needed to see Dean before Internal Affairs got to him. They'd already been in Raul's face with their relentless questions.

Raul lit a cigarette with shaking fingers. At least they hadn't done a drug test after the shooting. This was already a hot mess without having to deal with that. He reached for the prescription bottle and shook out two pills. He grimaced as he swallowed them with the half cup of stale coffee sitting on the scarred wooden table. After the pain meds kicked in, he'd think more clearly about what to do.

The blood on his knuckles from his scuffle with the shooter had dried and begun to scab.

No one messes with me and gets away with it.

He'd have to make sure Dean got the message too.

CHAPTER FOUR

Anxious to see Dean again, Jinxi got up early the next day and headed for the bus stop before Janice emerged from her bedroom.

She exited the elevator at the trauma floor and made her way past the nurses' station to Dean's room. It was empty.

Panic surged through her, tingling her fingers. Thinking the worst, she ran back to the nurses' station and drummed the counter until someone saw her there.

"Oh, hi. Sorry about that," a young nurse said. "You're Mr. Rafferty's sister, aren't you?" She didn't wait for Jinxi to respond. "He's been moved to Room 5110."

Jinxi spoke through stiff lips. "Why? What happened?"

The nurse laughed. "Being moved is a good thing. He's in a regular room because he's not welcome here anymore." She smiled at her own attempt at humor, but sobered at Jinxi's frown. "He's awake and talking, so we don't need to monitor him twenty-four seven."

Jinxi turned wordlessly and marched back to the elevator, black boots stomping. Someone should have told her. Her need to pick a fight with someone, anyone, melted away at the sight of Dean sitting up in bed, eating a carton of green gelatin.

"Hey," Dean greeted her. He waved the spoon. "This restaurant has lousy food."

She set her backpack on a chair and walked over to stand by Dean's bed. He still had an IV line attached to the back of one hand, but all the other tubes and wires had been removed.

"How're you feeling?"

Dean appeared to think about it for a minute. "Well, I have a monster headache and my brain feels like it's been in a blender, and I'm starving for some real food. But other than that, I'm okay, I guess." He watched her eyeing him. "You should see the other guy," he said weakly. He brought his hand up, touching the bandage.

The tray next to the bed moved sluggishly as Dean set his carton aside, pushing it away. "Hey, I'm sorry to ask this." He rubbed the back of his neck, and Jinxi was cheered by the familiar gesture. "You're not a nurse, right?"

Jinxi shook her head.

Dean's eyes slid to her face, then away. "Well, um ... do I know you?"

Blood rushed to her face, leaving it itchy and hot. He didn't remember her? Oh, snap! What should she do?

"I'm Jinxi."

"Jinxi? What kind of a name is that?"

"It—it's, like, my nickname."

"We're friends?"

Jinxi nodded. Her throat thickened, like the time she'd had strep as a kid and hadn't been able to swallow. What was going on? What had happened to the Dean she knew?

"I'll be right back." She darted for the door.

The restroom down the hall from Dean's room offered a refuge. After locking the door, she splashed cold water on her face, patting it dry with a rough paper towel. He didn't remember her. She bit back a sob. No, she wouldn't let herself cry. She'd go back into Dean's room and tell him they were friends. She wouldn't mention he was mad at her. Maybe he'd never remember. But if he did … what then? Would he be doubly mad because she'd held back that bit of information?

They'd been on one official date. She'd tell him that. What she wouldn't say is he almost kissed her. That was before. He didn't need to know everything. Some secrets were okay, even between friends.

By the time she'd composed herself enough to return to his room, Janice had arrived. Jinxi's shoulders slumped at the sight of Janice's familiar figure leaning over to kiss Dean on the good side of his face, the cheek with less swelling. Oh, snap! Now she'd have to wait.

"Mom?" Dean looked up at Janice, as if waiting for her response.

"Yes, dear?"

Dean nodded, his relief palpable. "My head hurts."

"Of course it does, son. You fell and hit your head."

Dean touched the bandage. He turned and saw Jinxi, eyes brightening with recognition. "Jinxi. Right?"

Janice turned toward the door. "Oh, hi. I thought I might find you here. You got an early start this morning." She smiled. "You didn't even make coffee."

Jinxi's smile was close-lipped.

"Coffee? Did someone say coffee?" Dean's eyes lit up. "Can I have some?"

Jinxi and Janice looked at each other and shrugged.

"I'll go ask." Janice bustled toward the door, seeming relieved to be able to do something for her son.

Dean watched her leave. "Do I like coffee?"

Jinxi took a deep breath, her bangs lifting as she blew it out. "Yes. You like it with cream and sugar."

"Okay. Good." He shifted on the bed. "Why can't I remember anything?"

Jinxi was saved from answering by the doctor, who strode into the room and headed for the computer. He glanced up at the two of them after logging on. He used one index finger to tap the keyboard, using the other to push up his glasses, which had slipped partway down his nose.

"How are you feeling, Dean?"

"Fine, except that I can't remember anything, and my head feels like someone's pounding on it with a ball peen hammer." Dean crossed his arms and turned his head away from the doctor.

"That's pretty typical with a head injury." The doctor took out a small flashlight. "Turn toward me, please." He shined the light in Dean's eyes without comment. He listened to Dean's breathing, moving the stethoscope rhythmically around his chest and back.

"Head injuries are tricky things," the doctor said. "It's not like a break or a sprain, where we know exactly what happened, and we can see the extent of the damage. When you fall like you did, the brain literally shifts inside your skull. There are protective layers of tissue and fluid between your brain and your skull, but you hit so hard your brain collided with the bone, causing it to bruise. Many little synapses, or pathways, were broken."

He put the stethoscope earpieces down around his neck and continued. "We have no way of knowing how many pathways are broken in an injury like yours except by observing your behavior. When those pathways are broken, the brain has to find a new way to get from point A to point B, kind of like a detour around a bridge that's flooded out. How long the detour takes depends on a patient's age, general health, and the number of synapses involved."

He paused. "Do you understand?" Dean sat silent. Jinxi nodded at the doctor to continue.

"You must realize—with a brain injury comes some unfortunate side effects. You may get angry more easily and experience personality changes. You may get dizzy or weak, or as you've indicated, get frequent headaches. You may forget how to do things that used to come naturally to you. Some of these may go away with time, or they may not. You have to remember to be patient with yourself." The doctor pushed up his glasses again from their precarious perch near the end of his nose. "We'll run you through some tests. If everything looks okay, we'll send you home in a day or so."

Dean glared at the doctor. "When can I go back to work?"

The doctor's glasses had slipped down again. He peered at Dean over the top as he moved to the side of the bed. "I won't release you to work until your memory returns and the swelling is completely gone."

"When will that be?"

"It depends on your body's ability to heal. At least six weeks."

"Six weeks!" Dean threw up his hands. "You've got to be kidding me."

"You need time—"

"No. What I need is to get out of here." Dean crossed his arms and slumped against the pillows.

The doctor laid a hand on Dean's arm. Dean threw his hand off and uttered a curse. Jinxi's eyebrows shot up. She'd never heard him say anything near a swear word.

"I know this is hard for you. But you're in good health, you're young, and I have every reason to believe you'll be fine. The symptoms you're experiencing are mild compared to car accident victims with traumatic brain injuries. Some have to learn to read and write all over again. We won't know the extent of your cognitive abilities until we run the tests."

"Is that supposed to make me feel better?"

The doctor continued as if Dean hadn't spoken. "I'll be releasing you to go home in a few days. I don't want you to be alone, though." He looked at Jinxi. "When you get him home, I hope you can take some time off work to help care for him. He shouldn't be left alone for very long, in case there's some residual weakness or fainting. You may have to help him shower, or at least be available if he should experience any dizziness."

Jinxi's face grew hot. "We're not, I mean, like, we don't ..." She prickled with embarrassment at the thought of helping Dean shower.

The doctor peered at her over his glasses. "Well, maybe you can stay with him for a few days to help him get acclimated."

Jinxi felt a bubble of hysteria in her throat. What would the doctor think if she burst out laughing? She bit her lip. Hard.

"I'll give you a set of discharge instructions when you leave. Things to avoid, like strenuous exercise, excessive reading, that sort of thing." As he turned to go, he added, "Remember, be easy on yourself. You have a very real injury, and you need to have patience as you heal. See you tomorrow." The doctor strode out of the room.

"Well, that really bites!" Dean mimicked the doctor's voice. "No strenuous exercise, don't think too much, don't go to work, don't be alone." His fingers plucked at the blanket around his legs. "Just shoot me now."

He closed his eyes. "Go away. I want to be alone."

Jinxi slunk out of the room.

The throbbing in Dean's head matched the pounding of his heart, each beat a bass drum.

Who am I?

He glanced around the hospital room, searching for clues. Someone had written the date on the white board on the wall next to the door. "Today is Saturday, October 24, 2021. Your nurse today is—" There was a black line, over which was the name Salvatore.

The doctor had called him Dean. His name was Dean. The thought popped into his head. He breathed a sigh of relief. I'm Dean Rafferty. If he could just get rid of this headache, maybe he'd figure out the rest.

He jabbed the button to call the nurse. Where was everybody? A person could die in here, and no one would notice.

A nurse's assistant breezed through the door. "What can I do for you, sir?"

He glared at her. When did they start hiring fifteen-year-olds?

"My head hurts, and I want some water."

Her smile faded by a few degrees. "Of course. I'll ask your nurse for your pain meds."

"You do that, honey. Get someone who can actually help me, okay?" He shook the empty water pitcher. "In the meantime, you think you can get this filled?"

She snatched the pitcher from him and disappeared into the hall, shoes squeaking.

What happened to him? How did he wind up in the hospital without a clue about his life? Who was the strange-looking Goth girl, and what was she to him? He didn't even know what job he had. Dean squeezed his temples with the heels of his hands, pressing into the pain. The answer was in there somewhere, but he was clueless about how to get it out.

Jinxi caught Janice in the hall as she returned from the cafeteria. The older woman carried a lidded Styrofoam cup that gave off the smell of fresh-brewed coffee. Jinxi's senses went on alert. She'd missed her morning caffeine jolt.

"I thought I'd never get back up here. The line was unbelievable."

"Be careful going in there," Jinxi cautioned, indicating the door with a wave of her hand.

"Why? What's going on?"

Jinxi tugged at Janice's arm, pulling her toward the waiting room. "The doctor came while you were gone."

Janice's face fell. "Oh, dear. I wanted to talk to him."

"Dean's ticked off about what the doctor said. He can't go back to work for, like, six weeks. He's gotta be watched for a few days after he goes home."

Janice picked at the lid of the cup, opening and closing the flap. "Oh, my. No wonder he's upset."

Jinxi leaned toward Janice, speaking in a low voice. "The thing is, he can't remember anything."

The cup trembled in Janice's hand. "Nothing?"

Jinxi's voice was a whisper. "No."

Janice's face turned white. "Does the doctor think his memory will return?"

Jinxi leaned back and shrugged. "I think so. They're going to run some tests. But he said there could be personality changes."

Janice set the cup down on a nearby table, careful not to spill its contents. Her eyes were bright with unshed tears. "Will you pray with me?"

Jinxi's head swiveled around, checking the waiting room to see if anyone paid any attention to them. Satisfied they wouldn't be noticed, she nodded and took Janice's outstretched hands. They sat with shoulders touching as Janice prayed for Dean's full recovery.

CHAPTER FIVE

Dean woke with a start. He must have dozed off after the nurse brought the pain meds. He turned his gaze left and met the eyes of his mother, who sat in a recliner, knitting needles flashing. To his right was that girl with the strange name.

Jinxi.

She looked at him and smiled. She straightened up from the couch, stretched her arms above her head and yawned. The book she'd been reading fell to the floor with a soft thud.

"I guess I fell asleep for a few minutes," he said.

His mother laughed. "I'll say. You've been out for two hours."

Like a strobe light, images flashed in his brain. "I'm in the hospital, right?" He saw his mom and Jinxi exchange a look.

"Yes. You took a fall and hit your head. You've had a concussion." His mother leaned forward in the chair. "Remember?"

"Could I get something to eat?" He hoped to distract her from any more questions. His head hurt with the effort of trying to remember anything.

Janice dropped the knitting and sprang to her feet. "Sure, honey. Your tray is right here." She pulled the rolling lap tray toward the bed. Jinxi pulled her feet back to avoid blocking the wheels. Janice removed the covers from the food, stacking them with efficiency on the side of the tray. The cellophane covering the sandwich went into the trash, along with the beverage lid. "Here you go. All set." She sat back down with a hopeful glance.

"Uh, could you not watch me eat?"

His mother's smile froze. "Sure. We'll just go to the waiting room. Come on, Jinxi." She motioned to the girl, and they walked toward the door. Jinxi glanced at him over her shoulder, throwing him a smile.

He'd barely had time to swallow the first bite when a male nurse entered. His dark skin stood in contrast against the white scrubs. "Good afternoon, Mr. Dean. My name is—"

Dean held up a hand. "Wait. Don't tell me." He glanced at the white board for confirmation. "Salvatore."

The nurse smiled. "That is correct. However, most people call me Sal."

Dean rolled his eyes. "I don't have a clue what most people call me."

Sal barked out a laugh. "Do not worry. Your memory will return in due time." He set some equipment on the end of Dean's bed. "Now I must take your vital signs." Sal's movements were quick and efficient. "Now I must check your wound."

Dean winced as Sal pulled the tape free from his head. Sal's fingers probed, eliciting a hiss from Dean.

"I am sorry for the hurt." Sal continued to probe, until Dean was sure he'd pressed every sore spot in his entire head.

"I will have someone replace the bandage with a fresh one. Thank you for your patience." Sal grinned. "You are a patient patient."

Dean took a bite of sandwich to block a snarky response. As the nurse prepared to leave, Dean stopped him with an outstretched arm. "Hey, can I ask you something?"

Sal stopped gathering his equipment. "Of course."

Dean's legs twitched, jarring the tray. Some juice spilled onto the plate holding the other half of his sandwich. He reached for it, moving it to safety. "Where am I? I mean, I know I'm in the hospital, but which one?"

"This is Sacramento General."

Dean looked away from the sympathy in Sal's eyes. "Do you know what happened to me?"

"Have you not seen the newspaper?"

Dean shook his head, then winced from the resulting stab of pain.

"There was an incident, a shooting, and the man who shot the gun knocked you down. Your partner killed the man's son."

Dean rubbed the back of his head. "Partner?"

Sal nodded. "Yes. Your fellow officer."

"I'm a cop?" Dean's fists clenched and unclenched. Why couldn't he remember? He closed his eyes, willing his brain to cooperate.

He felt the warmth of Sal's hand on his shoulder. "Get some rest. You will feel better tomorrow."

He was a cop. He was hurt in the line of duty. He repeated the words, like a mantra until sleep overtook him.

"He's asleep again." Janice's shoulders drooped. She and Jinxi had returned from the cafeteria. Janice stifled a yawn. "Maybe I'll go down to the gift shop and find something to cheer him up."

Jinxi shifted her weight from one leg to the other as she watched Dean's chest rise and fall. The clicking of the stud in her lip against her teeth sounded loud in the room. "I, uh, I'm gonna stay here." She glanced sidelong to gauge Janice's reaction.

"Are you sure?" Janice gathered her knitting, stuffing it into a cloth bag.

"Yeah. I'll hang out here for a while." Jinxi shoved her hands into the back pockets of her jeans.

"All right. I'll come back in a bit. Can I bring you anything?"

Jinxi shook her head. "No, I'm good."

Janice patted her on the shoulder as she passed. "I'll see you in a little while."

Jinxi settled onto the sofa and picked up her book. After she'd read the same page three times, she gave up and stretched out, resting her head on the arm of the sofa. Runaway thoughts pinged through her head like an out-of-control hose spurting water in every direction. What if Dean woke up and remembered he was mad at her? Would he give her the chance to ask for forgiveness yet again? Would this near-death experience give him grace toward her?

Tension knotted her stomach as she considered every possibility. Maybe he wouldn't remember, and they'd be able to go back to being friends again. But if he remembered later, then what? She turned on her side, searching for a comfortable position.

A small voice spoke to her spirit.

Trust me.

Right. How to do that when everyone she'd supposed to be able to trust had hurt her. How could she trust in someone she couldn't see? She knew she'd been forgiven of all her past sins. But what did that have to do with her life now?

Dean stirred and opened his eyes. "You're still here." He rubbed his face and yawned. "Where's my mom?"

Jinxi sat up, hoping her baggy sweatshirt disguised the frantic beating of her heart. "She went down to the gift shop." She held her breath, waiting to see where the conversation would lead.

Dean slid his legs over the side of the bed. "I need to use the restroom."

"Shouldn't you wait for the nurse?" Jinxi shot to her feet.

"I'll be fine." He stood, bracing himself with one hand on the footboard.

"I'm getting the nurse." She bolted for the door.

When Jinxi returned with Salvatore in tow, they found Dean slumped on the side of the bed, holding his head in his hands.

He waved them away. "I'm fine. Just a little dizzy."

Salvatore helped him to his feet, bracing his shoulder under Dean's arm, and they made their way to the bathroom. Jinxi sank down on the sofa, fingers patting her jeans pocket, searching for the missing cigarette lighter. She chewed on a nonexistent fingernail instead.

When the men returned from the bathroom, Salvatore helped Dean climb back into bed. "Use the call button next time."

Dean laid his head back and closed his eyes, grimacing.

"Do you want me to leave?" Jinxi asked.

"No. Stay for a minute. Talk to me."

"About what?"

"Anything. Tell me about you. Like, how old are you? How do we know each other?"

"Why are you asking me all these questions?"

"Because I feel like it's stuff I knew before I hit my head, but I can't remember. I want to know, okay?"

Jinxi took a deep breath. "I just turned twenty-two last month. Remember, you and your mom came to my birthday party at the food bank. You gave me this necklace." She reached inside her sweatshirt and pulled out the cross.

He leaned over and took it between his thick fingers, turning it this way and that. He closed his eyes for a moment. "Right." He nodded. "Your birthday." He opened his eyes and dropped the necklace. "Are we, you know, together?"

"No."

Was he relieved or disappointed at her answer?

Dean gave a brief laugh. "Good. I'd hate to forget something like that." He folded his arms across his chest. "Tell me more. How did we meet?"

Jinxi took a deep breath, then let it out. Where to start?

Dean closed his eyes and listened to Jinxi's version of how they met. Fragments came together to form patterns of returning memory. It was like the quilt on his mother's bed, small squares stitched together to make a design. Pieces clicked into place as she spoke. Their meeting outside the jail. Remembering how starved and scared she'd looked. Offering to buy her breakfast. Her suspicion. Then surprising himself by taking her to his mom's house.

A stab of pain in his head made him wince and grab the covers in his fist.

"What is it?" Jinxi voice, filled with concern, sounded far away.

"Pain," he gasped. He opened his eyes and lunged for the call button. The response was immediate.

He swallowed down the pain medication with a gulp of water. "Keep talking," he urged.

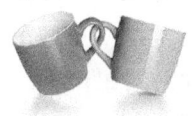

Jinxi talked until Dean's breathing calmed. She told him how he'd gotten Ted from the SPCA, partly for his niece Hannah and partly to guard the house. She left out how angry he'd been about Ted sleeping in her room. She told him about their day at Folsom Lake with his friends, and when they went out to play pool.

Jinxi stopped talking when she was sure he was asleep. She pulled her book and an apple out of her backpack. The words blurred as her concentration wavered. Dean was like a stranger. Weird, him asking her all the personal things. She thought back to the day they'd met outside the jail. She'd come to the end of herself. With only five dollars left in her pocket, she tried to sell herself to a man on a street corner in downtown Sacramento who turned out to be a cop. After spending the night in jail, she'd been hungry and dirty. And angry. She remembered how she nearly bit Dean's head off when he offered to buy her breakfast.

The rest was a miracle. Janice took her into her home and showed her the love of God. After two years of bouncing around from motel to motel with her drug-dealing boyfriend, Jinxi loved having someplace she could call home.

"God, I'm still new to this praying stuff," she whispered, "but could you please make Dean better? Thanks."

Sun streamed through the blinds in Dean's hospital room. He'd eaten breakfast and waited for the nurse to help him to the bathroom to shave off the three-day forest darkening his face. He rubbed the stubble, eyeing the bathroom, only a few feet away. Why wait for the nurse?

A knock on the door, and a dark-skinned man entered. Recognition flashed, images of the man in a police uniform.

Today, he was dressed in jeans and a dark Tee shirt. Stale cigarette odor floated around him.

"Raul."

Raul grinned, his perfect teeth like Chiclets against his bronze skin. "Amigo, I'm glad to see you awake." He crossed the room and stood next to the bed. "I came here last night but you were dead asleep."

"I'm glad to be awake." Dean's head felt fuzzy from the pain meds. "So what happened?"

Raul's face sobered. He shifted his weight from one foot to the other, his hands trying to find a place to stay, first in his pockets, then on the bed rail. "What a disastre. Do you remember anything?" He leaned forward, the intensity radiating from him like summer heat off asphalt.

Dean shook his head.

"It went down like this. We responded to a 415-F. It was a guy and his kid. The guy shot first, then I got a shot off, but it hit the kid. The dad rushed us and tackled you like a linebacker." Raul pulled at the neck of his Tee shirt, bunching it in his fist. "Internal Affairs is involved."

He looked at Dean, then broke eye contact. "You gotta remember to tell them the guy shot first."

"But I—"

"Bro. Get real. The brotherhood sticks together. You know that."

Both of their heads swiveled toward the door as a nurse's assistant entered. "I brought you a razor, if you want to shave."

Raul slapped his palms on the bedrail. He leaned down to whisper, "The guy shot first."

Dean swallowed hard as he watched Raul's retreating back.

CHAPTER SIX

Dean squinted at the sunlight streaming through the window. Where was he? Why was he in a hospital room? Then he remembered. He'd been injured on the job. He was a cop. Something about a gunshot.

His head pounded as he pushed the button to raise to a sitting position. A knock sounded on the door as he reached for the cup of water on the nightstand. The door opened and two men in dark business suits strode into the room.

"Officer Rafferty, we're here from the Office of Professional Standards. We'd like a moment to talk with you."

Internal Affairs.

Dean choked on his sip of water. "Okay."

The first man pulled out a business card and handed it to him.

JAMES FREEMAN
Office of Professional Standards

The second man didn't offer a card or his name.

"We'd like to go over the details of the incident of October 22, 2021," Freeman said. "You're entitled to have your union advocate present. I would encourage you to do so. We'll be taping the conversation. Is this afternoon convenient?"

Dean nodded. "Yes, sir." He resisted the urge to salute by crossing his arms over his chest.

"We'll be back in about two hours to set up. Please do not contact anyone in the meantime. We need to hear about the incident from your perspective."

As soon as they turned their backs to leave, Dean let out the breath he'd been holding. His hand shook as he reached for his water cup. He was so screwed. His partner wanted him—no, needed him—to lie, to say he remembered what happened.

His lunch tray had been delivered while he slept, but he shoved it away, his stomach in knots. He envisioned several scenarios. One where he told the truth, that he couldn't remember anything. And one where he said what Raul wanted him to say. Neither outcome was good. Either he betrayed his partner, or he lied under oath. He felt trapped, locked into a cage with hungry pit bulls at each corner.

Raul pulled his cell phone from the pocket of his jacket. He leaned against the outside wall of the hospital, oblivious to the crowd entering and exiting the main doors. He punched a number and waited.

"Bueno."

"It's me. He can't remember squat."

"And?"

"I told him what to say."

"Think he will?"

"He will."

"Do you think he's awake?" Janice asked.

Jinxi bit back her irritation. Janice asked the same question a zillion times. They stepped into the elevator with several other visitors, some with faces drawn with concern, others smiling, carrying pink or blue packages.

The door opened, and they stepped out, heading straight to Dean's room. A basketball game danced across the muted television. Dean lay motionless. His eyes fluttered open as the women entered.

His relief at seeing them was palpable. "Oh, it's you."

"Were you expecting someone else?" Janice went to him, resting her hand on his shoulder. Jinxi watched from the door.

"Actually, I was." Dean gulped. "Some guys from Internal Affairs are coming over today to take a statement."

"Statement?"

Jinxi crossed the room, taking a seat on the sofa. What was going on? What was Internal Affairs?

"Why do they need to take a statement?"

Dean shrugged, nudging Janice's hand off his shoulder. He rubbed the back of his neck. "It's what happens when there's an officer-involved shooting. IA takes a statement to make sure the discharge of weapons was justified."

Janice's hand flew to her chest. "Goodness. And in your case, was it?"

Dean chewed on his lip. "I dunno. I can't remember."

"Well, then you should be fine." Janice's voice held a note of forced cheerfulness. "Right?"

Dean answered slowly, as if talking to a child. "Like I said, I can't remember. It's a blank."

Janice sank onto the recliner. Jinxi watched the interplay, afraid to open her mouth.

"What do you remember?" Janice pressed.

Dean squeezed his eyes shut. "It's like a jigsaw puzzle with pieces missing. I can remember some things, but not other stuff." He groaned. "I hate this."

Jinxi cleared her throat. "The doctor said your memory should come back."

Dean spoke through clenched teeth. "He also said some things may never come back." His voice rose in intensity. "What if I can't remember how to be a cop? Then what?" He made a fist and struck the bed.

Janice's eyes filled with tears. She leaned toward the nightstand to grab a tissue.

Jinxi shrugged. "I guess you'll have to face that when it comes."

Dean's eyes glittered with anger. "Easy for you to say. You have no idea what you're talking about. You know what? You need to leave. Now." He pointed toward the door.

Jinxi stole a glance at Janice as she slunk toward the door. Janice's mouth hung open.

Jinxi sat in a turquoise-colored chair in the empty waiting room. The hospital had made every attempt to make the area warm and inviting, but it missed the mark. The chairs were made to resemble leather, but were uncomfortable and stiff. The still life paintings on the walls looked like cast-offs from a cheap hotel.

Jinxi leaned back and indulged in her favorite daydream. Learning to cook from Connie had been a lifesaver. One day she'd be a chef, working in a high-end restaurant. She'd have her own tools, the best knives on the market. And pans—crepe pans, saucepans, maybe even a cast iron skillet. People would come from all over to enjoy her one-of-a-kind recipes.

Until then, she'd hone her craft by learning all she could.

Jinxi made a mental inventory of what Janice's refrigerator contained. There might be some leftover roast from two nights ago. It would make a great beginning to burritos.

When she got to the dessert-planning stage, Janice's footsteps broke into her concentration. She dropped into a chair next to Jinxi.

"I'm so sorry he talked to you that way," Janice said.

Jinxi shrugged. "Whatever. The doctor said he'd be, you know, crabby."

Janice wrung her hands in her lap. "I've never heard him be so rude. Dean was always my sunshine boy. Easy-going. What are we going to do?"

One thing Jinxi wasn't going to do was say anything to annoy him again.

The men arrived in Dean's hospital room carrying briefcases and recording equipment. They were accompanied by a woman and man, also in dark suits. The woman introduced herself as Marion Brown, his union representative.

"I need a few moments to confer with Officer Rafferty in private," she said. The dark-suited men retreated, grumbling.

"Officer Rafferty, you have the right to ..." Her words dissolved into white noise while Dean's head pounded with each beat of his heart.

Ms. Brown stepped to the door and motioned the others back into the room. Sweat trickled down Dean's chest as the sound equipment was set up. He stared at the ceiling, concentrating on a water spot.

"Okay, we're all set. Let's get this started."

The man named James Freeman took a seat by the bed. "Lieutenant James Freeman. October 24, 2021, one-thirty p.m. Officer, please state your name for the record. Let me remind you that you are under oath, and you have agreed to be recorded."

Dean unglued his tongue from the roof of his mouth. "Dean Rafferty."

"Would you please describe the events that occurred on October 22, 2021, beginning with signing in for duty?"

Dean closed his eyes as images flashed through his brain like a crazed strobe light. "Well, let's see. I checked in at 1500 and met up with Raul."

Freeman interrupted. "That would be Officer Raul Hernandez?"

"Y-yes. Raul Hernandez." Dean rubbed his hand across the back of his neck. "We, um, we checked out our vehicle and began our patrol." Dean explained every stop and every call that had come in with as much detail as he could remember.

"There was a traffic stop about 2330 involving a DUI, so we were late coming back from our shift. We had to wait for the tow truck. We were headed back to the station when the call came in."

"Which call was that?" Freeman asked.

Dean licked his dry lips. "The call. You know, the one."

"Please state which call you are referring to."

Dean spoke through clenched teeth. "The 415-F came in when we were on our way back to the station. We—"

"What time was that?"

"Um, I'm not sure—"

"Was it after twelve o'clock midnight?"

"I think so."

"Was it before 0100?"

Dean scrunched his eyes closed, trying to think past the congo drums in his head. Freeman's chair creaked as he shifted in his seat. The silence lengthened.

"I can't remember."

Freeman consulted his notes. "What happened then?"

Dean took a deep breath. He heard Raul's voice in his head.

Just tell them the dad shot first, bro. You gotta back me up.

His hands clenched and unclenched around the sheets as he fought with the demon hammering inside his skull.

Freeman was like a K-9 cop with a cornered suspect. "What happened after the radio call, Officer Rafferty? It's a simple question. Just tell us what happened."

Dean rubbed his temples with the heels of his hands. His union representative laid a hand on his arm. He shook it off. Finally, he opened his eyes and focused on a spot on the far wall.

"I can't remember what happened." Relief washed over him. His gaze shifted to Freeman, who held his gaze for several moments before looking away.

Freeman cleared his throat. "Well, Officer, that's not very helpful."

Dean's voice rose. "It's the truth. Ask my doctor. He said that short-term memory loss is normal after a head injury."

Freeman's lips formed a straight line. "I'm sure it is."

After the group gathered up the equipment and all the paperwork, Freeman addressed Dean. "Here's my card. If you should happen to remember, call me. We'll schedule another interview."

Ms. Brown laid her business card on Dean's tray. "If you remember anything, call me prior to them, okay?" She gave Dean a reassuring smile.

After everyone left, Dean rubbed his sleeve across his forehead to wipe off the sweat. His heart raced as if he'd run five miles on his treadmill. He leaned back in the bed and closed his eyes, willing the pain in his head to stop.

He'd betrayed his partner. How could telling the truth be so hard? What ramifications could he expect from his admission that his mind blocked every bit of the call? Raul would tell the force Dean didn't have his partner's back. No one would want him as a partner. His career would take a dive, and he'd be back working in the jail, processing paperwork for thugs and prostitutes. He'd be one of those cops on the outside of the brotherhood. Hot acid brewed in his gut as he continued down the path of worst-case scenarios.

The walls of the hospital room seemed to narrow around him. Desperate to escape, Dean threw his legs over the side of the bed and stood, then shuffled to the door, using the edges of the doorframe to get his balance. A window at the end of the hall looked down to the hospital parking lot, offering a glimpse of the street below.

Dean's life was over. His career was history. Why was God messing with his life?

A verse came to him, something he vaguely remembered from Sunday school years ago.

My thoughts are not your thoughts, neither are my ways your ways.

Was that how it went? What did that mean, anyway. Big deal, so God's thoughts weren't his. Dean sure wouldn't be messing with God's life the way God was messing with Dean's.

Rain spattered on the hospital window, blurring the view. Old memories tumbled around in Dean's brain like marbles in a dryer. Maybe God was punishing him for getting angry with him about his father's death. Or punishing him for something else.

A fleeting thought of a girl teased the edge of his mind, refusing to become clear.

If his head didn't hurt so badly, he'd bang it against the window.

CHAPTER SEVEN

Dean dragged himself back down the hall. A few feet away from his door, he spotted a man exiting his room. He wore a pair of khaki pants and a brown patterned sweater vest over a white shirt.

"Hey! What're you doing in my room?" Dean approached him on rubber band-like legs.

"Here, let me help you." The man gripped Dean's arm, supporting him as he assisted Dean into the bed.

"I'm fine," Dean said through clenched teeth.

The man smiled. "Yes, I can see that. I'm Mike Zannakis, the hospital chaplain. Most people call me Chaplain Z."

Dean looked him up and down, then leaned back on the bed and turned on the television. "What do you want?"

The older man pulled a chair closer to the bed and looked up at the television. "Basketball. Who's playing?"

Dean didn't bother to answer.

"Great! Looks like our Kings might win one." The score was Kings, sixty-five, Lakers, fifty-nine.

"Ha!" Dean snorted. "Fat chance. The Lakers will take this one." He looked over at the chaplain. "What do you want?"

Chaplain Z spread his hands, palms up. "I like to visit folks to see if they have any needs I can help them with. Lots of times people end up in the hospital due to a trauma—something that catches them by surprise, like a heart attack or a car accident. They have questions. Why did this happen? How did God allow this? Did I do something wrong? My job is to help point them in the right direction if I can." He smiled.

"I'm not sure what I believe about God. Or even if I believe in him."

Chaplain Z raised an eyebrow. "Really? Why not?"

"Because my dad believed in God, went to church, the whole nine yards. He was a very spiritual man, you know what I mean? Then, poof, he was gone. Killed in a freak accident at work. If God is so loving, why did he take my dad away from us?"

The chaplain's smile took the sting from his words. "God didn't take your father. I'll share some Scripture–"

"No. Don't."

Chaplain Z stood. "Look," he said, laying his hand on Dean's arm. "You'll be going home soon, back to your life, your routine. Use this time to really think about your life. What you believe and why you believe it. God wants you to know him."

Dean laughed mirthlessly. "You mean, 'God loves you and has a wonderful plan for your life.'"

Chaplain Z chuckled. "I wish it was that easy. No, what I mean is, going home will be hard. You've got some recuperating to do, and it'll be difficult. Life is hard, but it's easier knowing you're in the Lord's hands, and he's taking care of things." The chaplain pulled a business card from his shirt pocket and held it out. Dean kept his hands by his side, so Chaplain Z laid it on the hospital tray. "Here's my card. Call me if you want to talk, or if you want to yell." He smiled. "Or if you want to pray."

"Don't hold your breath."

"Great news," the doctor announced, startling Dean from sleep. "We're sending you home today."

Dean rubbed his eyes. "Hmm."

The doctor sat on the edge of the bed and put the stethoscope into his ears. He leaned forward and placed it on Dean's chest. "Breathe in for me." The doctor was close enough that Dean could smell the breath mint he sucked on.

"I'm going home today?"

The doctor nodded, crunched the breath mint, then turned to the computer. "We'll get the paperwork processed, and you should be out of here this afternoon." He stood and shoved the stethoscope in his pocket. "Remember, we talked about you not being alone for a few days."

Dean nodded.

"You may be a bit shaky at times, so I want you to be careful. No driving. No strenuous exercise. I'll send you home with some pain meds for the headaches. I would advise you to avoid a lot of reading. Watching TV is okay, but only a couple of hours a day. Eyestrain and movement can exacerbate the headaches."

Dean barely listened as the doctor rattled off a bunch of other instructions, including something about rehab. He was anxious to be home, away from the constant noise and interruptions of the busy hospital. Especially away from people watching him eat, sleep, and use the bathroom.

The doctor left as Dean's breakfast tray was delivered. He glanced at it, then reached for the phone to call his mom. Instead he searched for Jinxi's number on his cell phone.

"It's me. They're releasing me from prison today."

"Sweet! What time?"

"I don't know exactly, probably this afternoon. Will you come with my mom to get me?" Why was he so anxious to see her?

"'Kay. How about I make some cinnamon rolls to celebrate?"

Dean practically melted through the phone. Homemade cinnamon rolls. The memory of the smell of rising dough swept him back to a picture of a warm kitchen filled with laughter. He smiled, thinking about all of Jinxi's cooking he'd enjoy while recuperating at his mom's.

Dean breathed in the familiar smell of his mother's house. Furniture polish, old wood, and wet dog. A dog rushed at him, barking a greeting. His curly tail quivered with excitement as he sniffed every inch of Dean's legs. Dean sank onto the couch, rubbing the dog's wiry head.

"Hey, Red-Head Ted. Good dog. Good boy." Relief flooded him. He remembered the dog's name.

"I think Ted's smiling." Janice dropped her purse on the piano bench, Jinxi on her heels. "Can I get you anything? Water? Something to eat?" Motherly concern radiated toward him.

"How 'bout one of Jinxi's cinnamon rolls." He gave Jinxi what he hoped was his best attempt at looking pitiful.

Jinxi rolled her eyes as she turned toward the kitchen. He thought he heard her mutter "Baby," under her breath.

Jinxi and Janice bustled around the kitchen in what Jinxi called their kitchen dance. They moved in harmony, each moving out of the other's way, smoothly executing their tasks.

Janice prattled on and on as she started a fresh pot of coffee. "I hope Dean manages the stairs okay. I thought about giving him my room, but I don't think I can manage the stairs, not every day. Goodness, are we out of cream? I know how Dean likes his coffee. Lots of cream and sugar. Do you mind sharing the bathroom with him? You could ..."

Reality check. She'd be sharing a bathroom with him. Oh, snap! She hadn't thought about being in the same house, much less sharing her personal space. How long had it been since she'd had her own bedroom and bathroom? Not since she'd left her mother's house. At the Girls' Ranch, she'd shared a dorm-like bathroom with nine other girls. Then the time she and Skeeter were together. She pinched her lips together.

This would suck big-time.

The Sacramento Food Bank was comprised of an administration office, cafeteria, kitchen, and two warehouses. The food used to prepare lunch for the homeless was kept in the smaller warehouse. The larger one had floor-to-ceiling shelves, two walk-in refrigerators, and several long tables used to box or bag groceries for the needy people who lined up for food to help them get through the month. Volunteers handed out groceries every two weeks to people who had proved to the organization they were truly in need of help. The administrator, Padish Singh, ran the food bank with a combination of mercy and justice.

Jinxi liked working in the kitchen, helping the head cook, Consuela, or Connie. Sometimes she had to help in the office, filing and keeping inventory records up to date. Today, however, she helped their maintenance guy, Hank, sweep the big warehouse. Even with the steel doors rolled down and bolted, dust and leaves managed to blow in.

She and Hank worked in companionable silence. Jinxi liked that Hank's mental disability kept him from chattering while they worked. Unlike the volunteers who regularly came to help, he never asked questions about the scars on her arms, or the meaning of the tattoo on the back of her neck.

Hank whistled a tuneless melody while they swept. The door to the small warehouse opened and Aneesa stepped in, energy crackling around her.

"Hey, guys. I have a favor to ask you."

They stopped sweeping to gape at her. When Aneesa had a favor, it usually meant more work.

"Padish said the food delivery from Raley's will be a little late, probably not until around five o'clock. Can you guys stay and help unload?" Jinxi and Hank looked at each other without answering right away.

"He'll pay overtime."

They grinned at each other and nodded.

"I'm ordering pizza," Aneesa said, over her shoulder. She strode out the door, closing it with a thunk behind her.

"Sweet!" Jinxi said, as they hastened their sweeping in preparation for the delivery.

When they were done, Jinxi made her way through the quiet cafeteria and headed to the restroom to wash her hands. When she emerged, Aneesa caught her in the hallway outside the office.

"Sorry to ask this, but do you have a couple of bucks I could borrow? I only have enough cash for the pizza, and none for the tip. I don't know where Padish is, but if he doesn't make it back before the pizza comes …."

"Sure. Let me get my backpack." They walked into the office together. Jinxi retrieved her backpack from the shelves in the corner, pulling out her wallet and digging into the zippered pouch. "Nope, all I have is a twenty. Sorry." She looked up anxiously at Aneesa. "You can have it, though."

"Don't sweat it. I'll figure something out."

Jinxi snapped her fingers. "Wait. I just remembered. I keep a five hidden just in case I ever get stranded." She didn't tell Aneesa it was the same five-dollar bill that had been in her purse the day she hit bottom. The day she was arrested and spent the night in jail. The day she met Dean and Janice, and her life changed forever.

Aneesa bent over as Jinxi held out the bill.

"I think you dropped this." Aneesa held what looked like a folded newspaper article.

A shot of adrenaline hit her like a lightning bolt.

"Give me that!" Jinxi snatched the paper out of the other woman's hand. She shoved the five dollars at Aneesa, turned on her heel and stumbled into the darkened cafeteria. She sat at one of the tables and willed her pulse to return to normal. She didn't need to unfold the paper to know what it said.

CHAPTER EIGHT

The rain had stopped sometime during the night. Drops clinging to the leaves of the oak tree outside Janice's bedroom window spattered against the house with each gust of wind. Janice hummed along with a song on the radio as she readied herself for the day.

She chose a blue sweater instead of a blouse, knowing the blouse buttons would give her trouble. Welts from the black widow spider bite a few weeks ago had faded, but the effects still lingered. What would have happened if Jinxi hadn't found her, collapsed outside her gardening shed? What if Dean hadn't been there to put ice on the bite? She shuddered, pushing those thoughts away.

Today, she must think about Dean. Was it wrong to have a favorite child? Brian's analytical nature made him distant at times, while she and Robin regularly clashed. From her early childhood, Robin had been a handful. Red-haired and tempestuous, she and Tom nicknamed her Mercury. With a guilty pang, Janice realized she hadn't thought about Tom for over twenty-four hours. Her glance rested on his picture on top of the dresser. It was her favorite, the one of him throwing his head back in laughter. She couldn't remember the occasion, bringing on another shot of guilt.

The phone's shrill ringing jolted her from the memories.

"Mom, I'm coming over to visit you and Dean this morning."

Robin never asked if it was okay to come over. She assumed Janice had nothing else to do.

"What time?" Janice asked with a sigh.

"Why are you sighing? Do you want me to not come?"

"No, it's fine. What time do you think you'll be here?" Janice wanted to see her granddaughter and grandson, but running back and forth to the hospital the past few days had worn her out.

"About ten. I want to ask you some questions about our ancestry. Hannah has to do a family tree for her preschool class."

Janice's heart quickened. "Family tree?"

"Yeah, you know, names of her grandparents, great-grandparents, stuff like that."

Janice exhaled a short puff of breath. "Oh, all right."

The call concluded. Janice sank onto the bed and stared at her feet. Oh dear. What if Robin started asking more questions than Janice was willing to answer?

She was saved from her thoughts traveling down that path by the sound of Dean moving around upstairs over her head.

"Anybody home?" Robin's voice carried from the living room into the kitchen where Janice and Dean sat at the table, sharing the morning newspaper.

"Don't you lock the door?" Dean glared at Janice over the top of the sports section.

Janice shrugged. "Not unless I leave."

"It's not safe to leave your doors open."

Robin turned sideways to make room for Owen's baby carrier as she navigated through the door into the kitchen.

"Where's Hannah?" Janice asked.

"Preschool." Robin set the carrier on the floor, then looked at Dean. "Hey, little brother. Glad to see you looking better." She leaned down to give Dean a peck on the cheek. "There are easier ways to get attention, you know."

"Jealous?" Dean asked, grinning.

"Uh-huh. Just goes to show you really are hard-headed." Robin turned toward the cupboard where the mugs were kept. She stood on tiptoe and pulled a mug down from the middle shelf. "Got any tea?"

"Of course," Janice answered. "Let me warm up some of Jinxi's cinnamon rolls too."

Janice got up to bustle around the kitchen, putting water on to boil, taking a few rolls from their foil wrapper. Robin took her place at the table, leaning over to be sure Owen still slept.

Janice watched the interplay between brother and sister, wondering how much time she had before Robin started asking questions about their heritage. She should have known it would come to this someday. Questions, answers, secrets. She and Tom had agreed the best course of action was not to say anything. But now he was gone, leaving her to face the consequences of their decision made so many years ago.

She tuned back to her kids' conversation.

"Every half hour or so, they come in and ask, 'Can I take your vital signs, please?' I mean, really, every half hour. Then they continually want to take blood and whatever other bodily fluid they can get their hands on. Bunch of vampires." Dean frowned.

"You had everyone worried." Robin reached across the table to touch Dean's arm.

"Oh, come on. It takes more than a little head injury to keep me down. I'll be back at work in no time." His voice held a hint of false bravado. "They're saying six weeks, but I bet it'll be sooner."

"You better listen to the doctor," Janice warned. "You still haven't gotten back all of your memory."

"I'm fine." Dean shook off Robin's hand and sprang to his feet. "I wish everyone would leave me alone." The chair scraped on the linoleum as he shoved it back with his legs. He strode from the room. Seconds later, Janice heard the television.

Robin looked at her, eyes wide. "What was that all about?"

Janice sighed. "The doctor said he might have personality changes."

Robin grimaced. "You better hope it's temporary."

Owen stirred in his carrier. Robin smiled at her mother. "Want to hold him?"

"Of course." Janice undid the buckles and gently lifted her grandson out of his seat. He nuzzled her neck as she cuddled him to her chest. He smelled of baby shampoo.

Robin reached into her diaper bag and pulled out a manila folder. "Mom, here's what I need to know."

Janice looked over Owen's back to the form Robin pulled from the folder. It showed a drawing of a tree, with spaces above the upper branches for the names of Hannah's parents, grandparents, and great-grandparents, along with their birthplaces. Janice released the breath she'd been holding.

This shouldn't be too hard.

They worked on it together, Janice dictating and Robin writing. The baby fussed, and Janice handed him to Robin so she could nurse him.

Janice busied herself putting away the remains of their snack. She stuck her head out the kitchen door. "You okay in there?" she asked Dean.

"Yeah. Fine," he answered, not taking his eyes away from the TV.

"Didn't the doctor say not to strain your eyes?"

Dean pointed the remote toward the television and punched the OFF button. He stood and stomped toward the stairs without answering. Janice heard his bedroom door slam a few moments later.

Mercy. Maybe I should just keep quiet.

"Sounds like my brother needs an attitude adjustment," Robin said with a grin. "Isn't that what you used to tell us?"

Janice turned toward her with a wry smile. "He's a little too old for me to spank."

Robin lifted Owen to her shoulder to burp him. "Not to change the subject, but I heard about a DNA test that shows markers for certain types of illnesses. I'm interested because of Hannah's arthritis. Does anyone in our family have a history of RA?"

Janice's hand flew to her chest as she turned toward the sink, clearing her throat. "Um, not to my knowledge."

Satisfied Owen was ready to return to nursing, Robin continued. "It looked interesting. We could all have the test done, then we'd find out if there are any other conditions we should be aware of. What do you think?"

Janice took a deep breath, willing her voice not to shake. "I ... I'm not sure."

"If you're worried about the expense, Carlos and I can take care of the cost."

"N-no. Not that. It's just that ... maybe you should leave well enough alone."

"Oh, come on, Mom. DNA testing is the latest technology for preventing illness. What are you afraid of?"

Indeed.

She was afraid of her world crashing down around her.

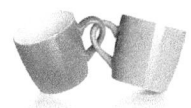

Miles away, a woman sat at her computer and Googled the name "Dean Rafferty." Nothing new had been added since the last time she checked. Just the briefest mention in the Sacramento Bee from a few years ago about his graduation from Sacramento State after playing football for four years and his entry into to the police academy. Her fingers hovered over the computer, wondering what to do next. How could someone be hidden in today's information hungry world? He had no Facebook page, no Instagram or Twitter, and he wasn't on Linked In. He wasn't a member of the Alumni Association. There was nowhere else to search.

Unless he was dead. Quickly, she began a search of online obituaries.

CHAPTER NINE

Dean dry-swallowed a pain pill. His mother's hovering was getting on his last nerve. The cell phone vibrated on the nightstand, fully charged after being unused during the time he'd been in the hospital. Eleven voice mails, a hundred and twenty emails.

First the voice mails. Three from Patrice, two from Damaris. His mind flashed on the faces of his friends from Sac PD—one more thing he remembered. One message from Freeman, the Internal Affairs guy, wanting to meet again. One from Sommer, Damaris's wife. His head hurt with the effort of recalling her face.

Four from Raul, each one rising in intensity.

"Call me back, bro. We need to talk."

"What did you tell IA? They're all over me."

"Call me, partner."

The last one held the note of a threat. "You better call me back when you get this."

Dean's stomach sank as he rubbed the back of his neck. Bottom line, Raul wanted him to lie to Internal Affairs. Why did it matter so much?

His head ached from trying to figure it out. If he couldn't remember what happened that night, it would be Raul's word against the word of the dead kid's father. Easy enough to figure out who was telling the truth. So why was it so important for Dean to lie, to say the father fired his weapon first. Maybe there were witnesses who'd said something different. Maybe Raul had fired first by mistake. What if he did? There was always an investigation when deadly force was used by an officer.

The cell phone rang, interrupting his circular thoughts. It was his friend Patrice.

"Hey, Dean. I'm glad I caught you. I'm getting ready to start my shift."

A jolt of jealousy hit him like a sucker punch. He should be working, not lying in bed like an invalid. "Hi, Patrice," he said, voice flat.

"I called to see how you're feeling."

"Lousy. My head hurts all the time. I can't remember things."

"That stinks." Her voice took on a tone of forced cheerfulness. "You'll be back at work before you know it."

Dean didn't answer.

"I saw your partner yesterday. He came in to talk to Sarge. He didn't look too happy when he left."

"He wants me to lie to IA," Dean blurted.

"What? That's crazy. Talk about career suicide."

"Yeah." Dean pinched the bridge of his nose. "He says I've got to keep the brotherhood or something like that."

Patrice's response was instantaneous. "No way, Dean. You know the right thing to do, and it isn't to lie to IA."

Did he know the right thing to do? He couldn't remember. His dad's voice came to him, a whisper above the roaring in his head. "Always tell the truth, Deano. The truth will set you free."

Yeah, right. The truth would make him an outcast. No matter what Patrice said.

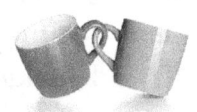

Darkness fell as Jinxi dragged herself from the bus stop down the street to Janice's house. Although the calendar said autumn, the weather seemed reluctant to surrender the summer's heat. She shifted the backpack on her shoulder, anxious to reach home, drop her burden, and take off her heavy boots. She swung her gaze from right to left as she walked, making sure no one was going to cause her trouble.

This wasn't the best neighborhood to be walking in, especially given her small size. Dean had told her no one would bother her because of some street agreement, but she was still careful. There was a reason why the windows on almost every house were barred. Janice's carelessness about keeping her doors locked caused a grip of stress to Janice's family. And to Jinxi.

The ache in her arms from unloading the semi-truck full of food was nowhere near the ache in her soul. Had Aneesa seen the newspaper article that dropped from her wallet? If so, she'd want to ask why Jinxi carried it around. The headline shrieked accusation, even after seven years.

Her mind swung to the chef's knife in her backpack—to the release it would bring. Bright red blood, physical pain in place of ... No. Not that. Never again. When God became real to her for the first time, she'd promised to give up all addictions. Smoking, drinking, tattoos, and cutting. Where else could she find relief?

There wasn't anyone Jinxi could talk to about it. Her sin was too great, her actions too heinous. All her new friends would shun her because of what she'd done. She rested her hand on the gate at Janice's house, took a deep breath, then pushed through the gate, forcing a smile onto her face.

"Hi. You're home late," Janice greeted her. She slid her glasses off and set them on top of her Bible. "You look tired."

"You got that right. I'm whipped. Would you mind if I didn't cook dinner? We had pizza at work."

"Of course not. I'll just make a sandwich or something for Dean and me."

Jinxi let the backpack slide off her shoulder as she mounted the stairs. She was greeted at the top by a grinning Dean.

"Hi! I thought I heard you come in. I'm glad you're home."

He moved aside as Jinxi reached the last step. Her arm dropped from the weight of the backpack. It hit the floor with a thump.

"How was work? You work at the food bank, right?" Dean's face clouded over, his forehead wrinkling in concentration.

"Yup." Jinxi turned right, down the hall toward her bedroom, Dean on her heels. She reached the bedroom door and turned around to face him. "Could you give me a couple of minutes?"

"Why? What're you going to do?"

He reminded her of Ted, anxious for a pat on the head. "I'm gonna take off my boots, then wash my face and hands."

"Oh. Okay."

Guilt rose inside her as his face fell. "Wait for me downstairs, okay? I'll just be a few minutes."

By the time she padded downstairs in her stocking feet, Janice had already started on the sandwiches. She'd opened a can of soup, warming it on the stove.

"Why don't you go sit down with Dean? I've got this."

Jinxi grabbed a soda from the fridge. "You sure?" she asked, even as she headed into the living room. She plopped down on the sofa at the opposite end from where Dean sat. "What'd you do today?"

He shrugged, eyes never wavering from the TV. "Talked to my sister. Played with Ted. Answered some phone calls. Deleted a ton of emails."

She tucked her legs under her. "Sounds great."

"Yeah, right. Bor-ing." He waved his hand in the air in dismissal.

"I dunno. Beats having to do manual labor every day." She winced as she rubbed her sore arm muscles.

Dean snapped his fingers. "Oh, yeah. I forgot. I also made my partner mad at me."

Jinxi was about to ask him what he meant when Janice called out, "Dinner's ready."

CHAPTER TEN

Dean woke with another blinding headache. He turned over on his back, shifting on the twin bed. He wished he was sleeping in his apartment, on his comfy futon. Instead, he was sleeping in his old room. He cursed the doctor who'd instructed him to stay with his mother for a week or until the dizziness passed. Then he cursed the man who had caused the fall and the subsequent head injury. Pressing the sides of his head with his palms, he pushed until he felt like his brain would squeeze out his eye sockets.

God, why are you doing this to me? What did I ever do to deserve this? I'm slowly losing my grip.

He heard Jinxi moving around in his sister's old room at the other end of the hall. Was his relationship with Jinxi more than friendship? She denied it, and he couldn't remember what they were supposed to be. There were too many gaps.

His cell phone buzzed on the nightstand. "What."

"Bro, this is Raul."

"Yeah."

"IA talked to me yesterday." Raul's voice was harsh. "They said you couldn't remember what went down."

Dean sat up, swaying from the pain in his head. "Uh, yeah."

"Man, you said you had my back. We were gonna look out for each other. You let me down, bro."

"Raul, look, I—"

"No, you look. I needed you, y'know. That little punk's dad is suing the department. You know, the one I took out."

Dean murmured something like an assent.

"He's saying the kid had a cell phone in his pocket, and he didn't even have a weapon."

"But the dad had a gun, right?"

"Yeah. But he's saying we came in and fired on them first before we did anything. Before announcing who we were and all that. It's bull, man. Pure bull."

"What's gonna happen?"

Raul's tone went from harsh to strained. "I'm on leave, man. I can't work. They're making me stay home like I did something wrong. I gotta wait for the hearing."

Dean stared at the floor, fighting vertigo.

Raul's voice continued like hammers tapping behind his eyes. "You gotta go to IA, bro. Tell them what happened. You gotta help me."

Dean muttered something, he wasn't sure what, but it was enough to get Raul to end the call. His hand shook as he set the cell phone back on the nightstand. Maybe a shower would help clear his head. He shook out a pain pill from the prescription bottle next to the phone and downed it with a sip of water.

He padded down the upstairs hall toward the bathroom, steadying himself with one hand on the wall. Jinxi's door was open, but the bathroom door was closed. He heard the shower running.

"Dang!" He slammed his fist into the wall, then turned and headed toward the stairs. Maybe a cup of coffee instead of a shower would help.

His mom was in the kitchen, scooping beans into the coffeemaker as he rounded the corner. Her smile was bright. "Good morning, sweetie. Did you sleep well?"

"Why isn't the coffee ready?"

Her smile faded. "It should be ready in about five minutes."

"In five minutes, I could be dead." He threw himself down at the kitchen table and rested his head in his hands. Ted, who had risen to greet him, slunk under the table and lay down with a whimper.

Janice turned the coffeemaker on, the sound of the grinder like a chain saw in his head. "Bad night?"

"Bad everything. Bad headache, bad sleep, bad life."

Dean heard her sigh. "As much as I love having you back under my roof again, I can see this isn't going to work for very long."

Dean swung his gaze to her, then regretted it when a wave of dizziness hit. "What?"

"You're like a grouchy bear, snapping at everyone who comes near you."

Dean sighed. "I'm sick, remember? I have a head injury, and I hurt."

His mom's words were like blows to his head. "That doesn't give you the right to treat everyone around you like dirt. I know you hurt. I know you don't feel well. But we're trying to help you, honey. You need to act nicer."

Dean didn't answer. He stood and picked up an empty mug. He pulled the coffee pot out from the machine as it brewed and quickly splashed some coffee into his cup.

He grabbed a paper towel as Jinxi appeared in the doorway.

"Good morning. Is the coffee ready?"

Dean didn't answer. Neither did his mom.

"Um, what's going on?"

Dean sat at the table, hunched over his mug.

"I was just telling Dean he needs to stop snapping at everyone just because he's miserable."

"You're miserable?"

No one spoke as the last of the coffee dribbled into the pot. Dean watched Jinxi pour herself a cup and fill his mom's mug. The fragrant smell of fresh coffee that once filled his morning with hope now made him want to puke.

"You don't feel good today?"

Jinxi reached across the table and laid her hand gently on his arm. Was this a friendship touch? He looked at her hand, small and white on his arm, but didn't shake it off. His throat filled with emotion, making it difficult for him to speak. Jeez, he was turning into a crybaby. Next thing he knew, he'd be binge-watching The Bachelorette.

"I, uh, have a headache," he said, staring at a crack in the ancient wood table.

"Did you take a pain pill?"

"Yeah. But it hasn't kicked in yet."

"You need to give it some time," Mom said.

"I know!" Dean exploded. He shot to his feet, swaying from the sudden movement. Ted yelped from under the table. "Just leave me alone." He grabbed the coffee pot and sloshed coffee over the sides as he hastily filled his mug. He stomped out the door and up the stairs.

Jinxi and Janice looked at each other, speechless. Jinxi reached down to pat Ted. "It's okay, boy. You're all right." He gazed up at her, tail thumping on the floor.

"I'll go talk to him," she told Janice.

"But you'll be late to work."

Jinxi took a sip of coffee and nodded. She took the hour-long bus ride every day to the food bank. "I can take the next bus."

"I could take you to work."

Jinxi stood up and gave Janice a tight smile. "That would be great." Jinxi took the creamer from the fridge, juggling it with the sugar and her own cup of coffee.

Jinxi had no idea what she was going to say to Dean as she trudged up the stairs. She found him sitting on his bed, back against the wall. He looked up as she stepped tentatively into his room.

"Hey," she said. "I brought the poison you put in your coffee." She pulled his desk chair around and sat to face him. "Head any better?"

"A little."

Jinxi closed her eyes and sent up a quick prayer. "What's up?"

"What do you mean?"

"I mean, what's got you so twisted up?"

"Twisted up?"

"Yeah. You're walking around here like everyone's out to get you. You remind me of me when I first came here." She smiled at the irony.

Dean grinned. "You were kind of a snotty little witch."

"Hey, watch it." The tension gripping her stomach eased a little. They were back on familiar ground. "So why the dark cloud? I thought you liked having someone to take care of you. Like, you don't have to cook, your mom does your laundry. All you have to do is lie around and be pampered."

Jinxi jumped when Dean smacked his hand down on the bed. "You don't get it! I'm sick of lying around. I'm sick of not being able to go to work. I can't read too much, can't watch TV too long, no exercise. I'm going nuts. Plus my head feels like it's in a vise."

Jinxi heard Ted's nails clicking on the floor as he came upstairs. He jumped up on the bed next to Dean and laid his head on Dean's leg.

"I thought you didn't want him on your bed."

"I don't." He shoved the dog. "Down, Ted. Off the bed. Now!" Ted jumped down and padded to Jinxi, nudging her hand.

"What else?" she asked, petting Ted's coarse fur.

"Isn't that enough?"

"You're bored. Big deal. There's other stuff you can do."

"Like what?"

"You could come to work with me for a couple of hours. There's always something to do at the food bank." Jinxi watched him over the rim of her mug to gauge his reaction.

Dean shook his head. "I don't know. Maybe." He shrugged. "It's just that Raul—"

"Raul, your partner?"

Dean set his mug down on the nightstand and rubbed his face with both hands. "Never mind."

Jinxi's eyes narrowed. "What did you tell Internal Affairs?"

Dean gestured impatiently. "I told them the truth. I told them I can't remember anything."

Jinxi tilted her head to one side. "Okay, so? Like, what's the big deal?"

Dean leaned his head back against the wall. "The department is getting sued," he said with a sigh. "The department in general, and Raul in particular. If I could remember what happened, it could help him out."

Jinxi blew out a breath through pursed lips. "That's heavy."

"Tell me about it," Dean said, eyes closed.

Jinxi grabbed his cell phone off the nightstand, checking the time. "I've gotta go to work." She stood, nudging the bed with her hip. He opened his eyes halfway. "I'll, you know, pray for you, okay? And think about coming down to the food bank. It might help to get out of the house for a while. Oh, and by the way, you're welcome for the cream and sugar."

"You feeling better today?" Aneesa greeted her as Jinxi dropped her backpack in the office.

"What do you mean?"

"You grabbed that piece of paper from me yesterday and took out of here like a shot. What was that all about?" Aneesa tapped a pen against her wooden desk.

Jinxi glanced over her shoulder to find Aneesa staring at her, face full of concern. Even her wild corkscrew mane of hair seemed to lean toward her. Jinxi concentrated on pulling the chef's knife and apron from her pack. "I'm okay." What else should she say? That she was afraid if Aneesa found out, she'd immediately fire her?

She felt Aneesa's impatience as she turned around.

"Let me see your arms."

Jinxi dutifully pushed up her sleeves. Aneesa nodded in satisfaction to see there were no new wounds. They'd made a pact to hold each other accountable. They both shared the same temptation.

Aneesa put a hand on Jinxi's shoulder. "You know you can talk to me, right?"

Jinxi nodded, head down.

Aneesa gave her a little shake. "When you're ready, I'll be here. Now get to work."

All morning, Aneesa's words rang in her ears. Would this burden be lifted if she told someone? She'd kept it a secret for so long, burying it deep inside a hard shell of protection.

She'd memorized the newspaper article. It screamed in her head. The accusation still made her cringe. Jinxi and her friends thought it would be fun to set a vacant lot on fire, then watch the fire department zoom in and put it out. It hadn't happened that way.

"Yinxi." Connie's voice interrupted her thoughts.

Jinxi glanced up from the box she was unloading. "Huh?"

"You are needed in the kitchen, chica." Connie pointed to the clock.

She'd completely lost track of time. She looked over to where Hank was working. He waved her away.

Jinxi scuttled to the kitchen behind her friend. "Sorry," she mumbled.

She worked alongside Connie and the day's volunteers, preparing the meal. Afterward they stood in a row, dishing out food to over a hundred people. Jinxi recognized the regulars. Some greeted her with a smile, while others kept their heads down.

At the very end of the line were a mother and son. The mother gently pushed the boy, urging him forward. Jinxi looked up to see what was taking them so long. The boy raised his head briefly, but it was long enough for her to see the scars. One side of his face was misshapen, grotesque. He'd been burned.

Jinxi's hand shook as she dished corn onto his plate. Bile rose into her throat, burning and clawing. She served the mother, then let the metal spoon clatter into the tray. She dashed for the bathroom, closed herself in a stall, and retched into the toilet.

CHAPTER ELEVEN

The phone rang, a welcome interruption to Janice's morning chores.

"Hello, Jan, dear. It's Emma."

Janice sank onto the partially made bed. "Oh, Emma, I'm so glad you called. I'm at my wit's end."

Like a burst dam, the words poured from her regarding Dean's personality change. "I feel so helpless." She stood and walked to the bedroom door, peeking down the hall to see if Dean had returned downstairs. "I don't even like him anymore," she whispered.

To her surprise, Emma laughed. "If we liked our children all the time, we'd be lying." A chuckle rippled behind her words. "I've heard it said we only like our children fifty-one percent of the time. When they're little, I wonder if it even gets to fifty-one."

"But—"

"Jan, you may not like him, but you love him. Just keep praying, dear. It'll all work out in God's time."

Janice murmured her agreement. As Emma prayed for her and Dean, Janice's mind drifted to the DNA test Robin had mentioned. Should she confess her secret to Emma? Would it change their relationship? At the time, she and Tom had agreed it was for the best, but now the secret threatened Janice's idea of the perfect family. Would she be relieved of the burden of silence, or would exposing it only make things worse?

She and Emma ended their call without her admitting anything else to her friend.

Janice knew it was wrong to have a least-favorite child. It wasn't Robin's fault. They'd been at odds with each other since Robin learned to talk. This latest DNA thing was another example of how she managed to get under Janice's skin.

The grandfather clock in the hall chimed, reminding Janice of her unfinished chores. She stood and pulled up the covers on the bed, plumping the pillows with more force than was necessary. Her knees protested as she bent down to retrieve a decorative pillow from the floor. She should get that knee replacement scheduled. Maybe she'd have it done while Dean was around to help.

Tears of frustration burned behind her eyelids. She didn't know what to do anymore. Just when she thought things were smoothing out, bam, Dean had an accident.

I want to escape my life.

The thought came unbidden from the depths of her being. Hadn't she suffered enough? She'd lost her husband, taken in a homeless girl who stole from her, and watched her granddaughter suffer with juvenile rheumatoid arthritis. How much could a body take?

Janice hobbled into the living room, sank into her rocker and pulled her Bible onto her lap. Tears overflowed as she poured out her heart to her Lord.

Jinxi skidded to a stop in the kitchen doorway, her eyebrows raised enough to approach her hairline. Dean sat at the table, reading the paper, a steaming cup of coffee by his hand.

"What's this? Why are you up and dressed?" She turned to pour her first cup for the day. "Do you have a doctor's appointment or something?"

"No."

Hugging the cup with both hands, she sat down across from him. "Do I have to guess?"

"Well—"

"Wait! Don't tell me. Let me try." She tilted her head to one side and chewed her lip. "You have an appointment with your attorney."

He shook his head.

"Internal Affairs?"

"No."

"Raul?"

"Nope."

By now Jinxi was hiding her smile behind the coffee mug. "Um, wait, it's coming to me. Here it is. I've got it!" She held up one finger. "You admit I was right, and you're coming to work with me today."

Dean shook his head. "No way. I will not admit you were right. But I am coming with you to work."

One corner of Jinxi's mouth turned down. "Just one problem, though. You'll have to ride the bus with me."

"No way. We'll take my truck."

She got up to make herself a piece of toast. "But you can't drive yet, remember?"

Dean brought his fist down on the table. "Shoot! I forgot about that." He shoved his chair back as he sprang to his feet.

Jinxi stuck out her hand, palm toward him. "Wait. I could drive your truck, then bring you back home when you get tired."

Dean was shaking his head before she even finished the sentence.

"No. Not in a million years. Nobody drives my truck. Besides"—he leaned toward her—"you probably couldn't even reach the pedals."

She wanted to slap him, but stopped just as her toast popped. Dean reached over and grabbed it out of the toaster before she could react.

"Hey! That's mine!" she protested, but he was already spreading peanut butter on it and taking a huge bite.

Resigned, she put another piece of bread in the toaster and shoved the lever down. "So, any suggestions?"

Janice came into the kitchen rubbing her eyes. "Any suggestions about what?"

Dean drummed his fingers on the table and didn't answer.

Jinxi indicated Dean with a wave of her mug. "We were trying to figure out how Dean was going to get to the food bank with me. He refuses to ride the bus, and he won't let me drive his truck. We're stalemated."

"I don't mind driving you."

Dean looked up and snorted. "I'm twenty-five years old and I'm being driven around by my mother." He shook his head in disgust.

"Oh, good grief," Jinxi exploded. "Get over yourself. It's only for a couple of weeks."

Her toast popped, and she snatched it up and threw it on a plate.

Janice and Dean looked at her with surprise. Janice glanced back at Dean and shrugged. "She's right. If you want to get out of the house, I'll take you. When your doctor releases you to drive, then you can drive yourself. In the meantime, it's either that or stay home." Janice filled her coffee cup and disappeared down the hall.

Jinxi and Dean glared at each other without a word. Dean finally broke eye contact. "Fine," he said, as he hunched over his cup.

"Fine what?"

"Fine, I'll let Mom drive," he exploded.

Jinxi smiled sweetly. "Good. I'll go get my stuff. We should leave in about twenty minutes." She didn't wait for an answer but hurried up the stairs, Ted at her heels.

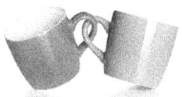

At the food bank, Jinxi was immediately pulled into the maelstrom. Dean was left on his own to figure out what to do. He opened the door to the office and was greeted enthusiastically by the office manager, Aneesa.

"Dean! What an awesome surprise." She reached for the radio blasting out gospel music and turned it down to a normal decibel level before grabbing Dean in a bear hug. "I heard you were hurt on duty." She held him at arm's length and looked him up and down. "You don't look hurt to me, baby. Well, except for that bandage on your head."

When Dean regained his breath, he answered, "I fell and cracked my head open, but the doctors fixed me up again. Just like Humpty Dumpty."

Aneesa laughed with her usual shout. "Ha! That's great. May I ask what you're doing here?"

Dean gave her a sheepish look. "I'm really bored. The docs won't let me do anything fun. No reading, no watching TV, no exercise. And no work for six weeks."

"Oh, child, that's gotta be rough." She clicked her tongue and shook her head, the wild spiral curls bouncing. "Don't you worry. We'll set you right up."

"Actually, Jinxi suggested I come down and see if I could help."

Aneesa nodded. "Mmhm. That girl's come so far. She's like a flower, opening up to the sun. She's a hard worker, that one."

Aneesa grabbed his arm and pulled him toward the door. "Come on, boy, we've got lots for you to do." She stopped in the hall. Turning back to eye him again, she asked, "Can you do any lifting?"

Dean nodded. "A bit. Just don't ask me to push-start one of your old junkers."

Aneesa shouted with more laughter.

Dean's memory flashed with new images. One day when Janice had volunteered to work at the food bank, Aneesa's car wouldn't start. No one had any jumper cables, so Dean had offered to push the car until she could jump-start it with the clutch. Several sweaty tries later, they'd called it quits. Dean had given the car one last shove, lost his footing, fell and scraped holes in his jeans.

Why could he remember stupid stuff like pushing a dead car, but not the most important things—the events leading up to the shooting, his accident, Raul's craziness?

Aneesa steered him past the kitchen, where Jinxi worked with the cooking staff, into one of the massive storerooms. He was glad he'd worn his jacket. The concrete floor radiated the chill from the dampness outside.

"I'll get Hank. We've got some boxes to fill for the women's shelter. You can give him a hand." She pointed to a stack of cardboard that needed to be made into boxes. A few seconds later, a tall black man sidled into the warehouse.

He waited in silence until Dean felt his presence and turned around. Then the man was all smiles. He bobbed his head as he held out a hand. "Mr. Dean," he said softly. "It's g-g-good to s-s-see you."

Dean grabbed Hank's hand and pumped it up and down. "Hank, my friend. Good to see you too." His brain registered the man and his name as the memory returned. He waved toward the pile of cardboard. "I guess we have work to do."

He and Hank set to work, shaping the boxes and taping the ends. Despite the older man's disability, he nimbly formed each box, taped it, and moved on to the next. He soon outpaced Dean two to one.

When the boxes were spread around the floor, Hank motioned to Dean to begin the task of filling them with the canned and bagged goods on the long tables. A couple of volunteers showed up and they all formed an assembly line, filling each box with the exact same combination of beans, rice, and canned goods. By the time they'd filled about twenty boxes, Dean had removed his jacket and was wiping the sweat off his forehead. His legs threatened to collapse beneath him. He saw Hank watching him.

"Mm-Mr. D-d-Dean, go in-into the cafeteria and s-s-sit down." Hank grabbed Dean's arm and pulled him through the doors of the storeroom and into the big cafeteria, already filling up with homeless people. Dean tried to pull away, but Hank was undeterred. After he settled Dean at one of the tables, Hank disappeared into the kitchen. He reappeared a few moments later with a plastic cup filled with water. He handed it to Dean wordlessly and watched while Dean took several deep gulps.

"You okay?" Jinxi demanded, coming through the kitchen door. "You look awful."

"Well, thanks." Dean felt as if a hatchet was trying to split his head in two.

Jinxi approached him, her face a mask of concern. "I'm calling your mom. You need to go home and rest." She pulled her cell phone out of her pocket and spoke to him as she began to dial. "You probably did too much on your first day out. What were you thinking?"

"You don't need to call my mom. Apparently, she's already right here."

She looked at him sideways. "Ha. Just be quiet." Janice answered the call, and Jinxi explained that Dean was ready to go back home. "She'll be here in a bit. Sit. Don't move."

Dean wasn't sure he had the energy to fight, so he sat on the bench with his back against the table. A few minutes later, Jinxi reappeared with a plate of steaming food.

"This is what we're serving for lunch. Go ahead and eat while you're waiting for your mom."

Dean's stomach rumbled as the smell of lasagna assaulted his nose. He turned around on the bench and swung his legs over to face the table, fighting a swoop of vertigo.

"You going to join me?"

But she had already turned back toward the kitchen. "Heck, no. I have tons of work to do."

Some of the people in the big room looked longingly at Dean's plate, but he pointedly ignored them and ate, quickly downing the lasagna, a piece of bread, and the salad, clearing the plate as if he hadn't eaten for a week. The food took away some of the feeling of shakiness. He stood to throw away his plate and had to catch himself with a hand on the table. His head spun, but he refused to give in to it, raging inwardly at his weakness. He sat back down, hands clenching and unclenching in his lap. He wanted to hit something or someone, to lash out against this helplessness. Where was his control, his strength? Had it all leaked out of his head wound when he fell?

He was weak as a kitten and stupid as Hank. As the thought came, he squirmed in shame. Hank was a good man who'd suffered injuries in the Vietnam War, injuries causing him permanent disabilities. What if he was going to be like Hank for the rest of his life? His breath caught in his throat. No. Please, God. Let me get well. Let me get strong again.

Wait. Was he praying? To a God he didn't believe in?

CHAPTER TWELVE

Dean rested his head in his hands, examining the nicks and scratches in the green-laminated cafeteria table. His head jerked up when he felt a hand on his back.

"Dean Rafferty! You are a sight for sore eyes, yes?" It was Padish Singh, the executive director of this branch of the food bank. He was a tall, East Indian man with a perpetual smile on his dark face.

Dean rose to stand, but the older man gently pushed him down and seated himself on the bench.

"It's good to see you too, Padish." Dean despised the weakness in his voice.

"Aneesa tells me you are helping out here, yes? We are honored." He clapped his hands together.

"I don't know how much help I am."

"Many hands make light work, my friend. Anything you can do helps." Padish's face turned serious. "You had a bad injury, yes?"

Dean nodded, then regretted the action.

"My friends at the police department tell me there is a lawsuit, yes?"

Dean shook his head, slowly this time, amazed as always at the small-town atmosphere of this city, the capital of the state of California.

"Something like that," he said. "I guess they're waiting for the mush in my brain to remember what happened."

Padish's hand tightened on Dean's arm. "Whatever you remember or don't remember is not important. Where you came from and what your father lived by are the only important things." He sprang to his feet before Dean could respond. His normal smile split his face. "Good to see you again, Dean."

Then he was gone, opening the metal rolling windows to the kitchen and rounding up the people into an orderly line for lunch.

What was that all about? Dean didn't have too much time to ponder Padish's words. Janice appeared at his side, concern etching her face.

"Are you all right?"

"I'm fine, Mom, really." Dean waved his hand impatiently. "Jinxi overreacted. I'm just a little tired, that's all."

Janice reached toward him. Dean ignored her help and forced himself to his feet, struggling to keep from swaying.

"Let me help you."

"No. I said I'm fine. Just leave me alone." Dean began walking toward the door, ignoring the stares of the people gathering for lunch. "Let's just go."

Before they got to the entry between the front door and the cafeteria, Jinxi was on their heels. "Hey, aren't you going to say goodbye?"

"'Bye."

"I'll see you tonight, okay?"

He didn't answer.

Dean ignored the silent tension in the car. He leaned the seat back as far as it would go and closed his eyes. When they arrived at the house, Dean headed upstairs to his old bedroom. His head had just hit the pillow when the doorbell rang. Ted's frenzied barking further dispelled any chance of sleep.

A few minutes later, Janice called up the stairs. "Dean, some men are here to see you."

Dean took a deep breath and blew it out again. He threw his legs over the side of the twin bed and rolled to a standing position. Before heading down the stairs, he tapped out a pain pill from the prescription bottle on the nightstand and swallowed it with a bit of leftover stale morning coffee. Grimacing, he walked down the hall.

He heard his mother offering the visitors coffee, which they refused. As Dean's foot hit the last stair, he almost turned around and hurried back to the safety of his bedroom. The men were Freeman and his partner from Internal Affairs. Their relentless questions would be exhausting.

Dean made his way into the living room and sat down. Freeman addressed Janice. "Mrs. Rafferty, would you excuse us, please?"

So formal and polite. Were they waiting to bring him down? Dean knew he was being paranoid but couldn't stop his brain from twirling around various scenarios where he was somehow held to blame for the shooting incident.

Janice excused herself. Dean heard the determined click of her bedroom door closing. Freeman waited a beat before addressing him.

"Officer Rafferty, I don't suppose you've had any convenient return of your memory of the shooting incident?"

Dean searched the man's face for sarcasm. Finding none, he responded, "Not yet." He wanted to yell at them to leave him the heck alone. His jaw clenched with the effort of holding back the words.

Freeman continued. "We just wanted to ask you a couple of follow-up questions. Okay with you?"

"Yeah." Dean crossed one leg over the other with seeming indifference.

"Do you wish to have your union representative present?"

"No. Let's get this over with." Dean hoped he wouldn't regret that decision.

Freeman's next question was tossed like a grenade. "Were you aware of your partner's drug use?"

Dean's foot thumped to the ground as he uncrossed his legs. "What? No!"

Freeman looked at him without blinking. "We have reason to believe your partner Raul Hernandez is a habitual drug user."

Something in Dean's head went clunk, like a fishing lure hitting the surface of a lake. He closed his eyes and tried to concentrate. A snippet of memory hovered at the perimeter of his consciousness. What was it? Fragments of a scene flashed like a strobe light.

Freeman's voice cut through his concentration. "We need to know if he was using on the night of the shooting."

Dean put out a hand. "Hold on one second. Just wait." He leaned back in his chair and closed his eyes again. The thought was gone like a vapor. He shook his head. "I'm sorry, guys. I don't remember."

Freeman's partner shifted impatiently on the sofa. He and Freeman exchanged a look. The man finally spoke, his voice low and harsh.

"An officer who lies is immediately terminated. You'd better think long and hard about your answers from here on."

An arrow of fear shot through Dean's stomach. "I'm not lying. I thought I remembered something, but it's gone."

Clearly, Freeman was playing the good cop in this interview.

"Officer Rafferty, we need to be the first ones you call if and when you remember anything about that night. We know you want to protect and support your partner. I understand about the loyalty and the brotherhood and all that. I've been in your situation, too." Freeman's voice took on a sympathetic tone. "But this is important, okay? You have my card. Call me if anything comes to you."

Both men stood but didn't offer to shake Dean's hand. Freeman's unnamed partner glared at him as they made their way to the front door. Dean didn't show them out. When the door closed behind them, he sat forward, his elbows resting on his knees.

His head hurt from the effort of trying to remember something, anything. He stood wearily and dragged himself upstairs. He was asleep the instant he lay down.

Two hours later, he woke with a start. His cell phone was vibrating on the nightstand. He grabbed for it and answered before looking at the screen to see who was calling.

"Hullo?" He sat up and shook his head to clear the sleep.

"Bro, it's me." It was Raul, his voice urgent. "What did you tell IA? They're all over me like a swarm of ants."

"Umm, what?" His head was fuzzy from sleep and the pain pill he'd taken.

"You must've said something, dude. IA wants to see me again. I think they're trying to take me down."

Even in Dean's groggy state, he sensed paranoia in his partner's voice. "They were here today. They just asked if I remembered anything," Dean said, hedging.

Something flashed in his brain, like a light turning on and then off. He saw Raul smiling at him and saying, "Showtime!" Was that the night of the shooting? He tried to concentrate on the memory.

Raul's voice was strident in his ear, bringing him back. "Listen, bro. If they take me down, don't think I'm gonna go down alone, comprendas? We were both there. Just remember that."

The line went dead. Dean slumped over on the edge of his bed and carefully set the cell phone back on the nightstand, his hands slick with sweat. Was it because of Raul's warning or the memory that was coming back? He concentrated on the picture he had in his mind of Raul. He rubbed his hands across his jeans and forced himself to think. They were in the squad car on the way to ... where? Distorted images flashed through his head. He and Raul laughing. Reaching for the switch to turn on the lights and siren. Raul with something in his hand. A gun. No, an envelope. Not an envelope, a folded piece of paper. Raul shaking something out into his mouth.

Reality hit him like a brick. Raul was shaking some pills out of a small white packet and tossing them into his mouth.

"What are you doing?"

"Just a little something to keep me awake."

Was that before they got the domestic disturbance call? Bile rose in his throat. He swallowed and focused on breathing.

Lying back on the bed, he covered his face with his hands. What now? Was the memory real, or something caused by Freeman asking about Raul's alleged drug use? If his brain wasn't like scrambled eggs, he'd know. If it was real, then what? Should he run to Internal Affairs and blab that he remembered some isolated incident? Maybe he should just keep quiet and continue to insist he couldn't remember anything. If he told IA he remembered Raul taking some pills, they might not believe him. Did he even believe it himself? Should he get his partner in trouble because of something he thought he remembered?

He silently cursed the whole situation.

CHAPTER THIRTEEN

The door to the food bank's cafeteria opened precisely at twelve o'clock, Monday through Friday. People lined up outside as early as an hour before, since the cafeteria's seating capacity of sixty-five meant latecomers might not get in. One church volunteer group, when it was their turn to serve, brought sandwiches to hand out to those denied admission.

As people filed in, the noise level increased. The aroma of Connie's cooking mingled with the smell of dirty bodies and human misery.

Jinxi kept one eye on the aluminum tray of vegetables and one eye watching for the mom with the scarred boy. She'd managed to avoid serving them the past few days. She spotted them toward the end of the line.

"Mark, could you take over for me? I need to run to the restroom," Jinxi said to one of the regular volunteers.

Mark took the serving spoon from her as she scooted out the kitchen door. She got as far as the hall leading to the restrooms when Aneesa appeared in her path.

"Hold on a minute."

Jinxi stopped midstride, her eyes shifting from the restroom door to Aneesa and back again. Nerves prickled on her arms and the back of her neck.

"What's going on, girl? You feeling all right?" Aneesa stood with her hands on her hips and a frown on her face.

"Yeah. Fine."

"Then why are you running to the bathroom every day at the same time?"

Jinxi's face burned. "None of your business."

"Now that's where you're wrong. It is my business when you're not doing your job."

Shoulders hunched, Jinxi looked down at the floor.

"If you're not going to talk to me, then I suggest you get a move on and get back to the kitchen."

Jinxi stomped back to the kitchen, anger brewing like a boiling tea kettle. Ignoring the few people who hadn't been served lunch, she grabbed a pot from the counter and slammed it down in the sink. As it filled with hot soapy water, she scrubbed the inside with angry strokes of a brush. She should have the right to go to the bathroom whenever she darn well pleased. Why was Aneesa hating on her? She hadn't done anything wrong.

At the sound of Connie's voice, Jinxi turned.

"Todo bien, chica?"

"I'm fine." That is, until Aneesa gets up in my business.

Connie smiled, teeth white against brown skin. "I think the pot is clean, chica."

After hours of flopping like a fish in the narrow bed, Dean fell into an uneasy sleep. Dreams of people chasing him with guns and knives woke him up, leaving him sweating and panting. Through the open bedroom door, he saw a wraithlike figure gliding down the hall toward him. He sat up with a start, his heart hammering.

"You okay?"

It was Jinxi, pulling a throw around her.

"Yeah." His breathing slowed. "You scared me," he whispered fiercely.

"You scared me. I heard you moaning, then you yelled something," she whispered back.

"I did not," he insisted.

"Want to talk about it?"

Dean motioned for her to sit down on the end of the bed, scooting over to make room for her. Jinxi settled herself, tucking her legs up under the throw. The glow from the streetlights created a halo effect on her hair.

Sitting in the semi-darkness, Dean relaxed into the intimacy of the moment. Was there more to their relationship than just friends? If so, why hadn't she said anything? Letting his mind drift, Dean grasped onto a thread of memory. It tickled at the edges of his mind, swirling just out of reach, like a helium balloon released on a windy day.

Jinxi's voice jolted him back. "What are you thinking about?"

Dean took a deep breath, then blew it out through pursed lips. "I think I remembered what happened that night."

"The night of the shooting?"

"Yeah." He rubbed the back of his neck. "It's kind of disjointed, but it's starting to come back in pieces."

After a few seconds of silence, Jinxi waved her hand for him to continue, but he shook his head. "Not yet. I need to think it through."

She pulled her legs up and rested her chin on her knees. "Okay."

Anxious to keep her there a few more minutes, he searched for something to say. "What's your earliest childhood memory?"

"I don't know," she shrugged. "Haven't ever really thought about it."

"Mine is from when I was about three years old. My dad was holding me, and we were in the back yard."

"You remember that far back?"

"Strange, huh? It's like Swiss cheese. Some things are super clear, others a blur. Anyway, he threw me up in the air and caught me. I remember it felt like I was flying."

"You're lucky."

"What do you mean?"

"You're lucky to have a dad. Mine bailed when I was really little. Your dad taught you to fish and stuff." She picked at a thread in the throw. "That must have been cool. I always wanted a normal family."

Memories flooded back—of time spent with his dad, backpacking in the mountains and catching enough fish to feed them as they sat by a cozy campfire. Hours spent throwing the football. The tire his dad hung from the tree to teach him accuracy. The family vacation they took to Disneyland and how Robin had gotten sick. His parents took turns nursing her in the hotel room so he and Brian could go on the rides.

Maybe he was lucky to have had his father for as long as he did. He'd been angry for a long time about his father's death.

"I think my earliest memory was of kindergarten," Jinxi said. "I sort of remember we had to draw a picture of our family and I drew my mom and me. Some kid looked at my picture and told me that you couldn't be a family with just two people. The teacher came over and told him to be quiet, but I knew he was probably right."

Dean scooted closer, arm poised to put it around Jinxi's shoulders. Would she jump and run? Or would it be a natural part of what they'd shared in the past? Too confusing. Instead, he laid a hand on top of hers. "I'm sorry."

She shrugged. "It's okay. I'm over it." Yawning, she said, "I better get back to bed. Some of us have to work tomorrow."

Dean released her hand reluctantly. "Okay. Sleep well."

She stood and stretched. "You coming to the food bank with me tomorrow? Or rather, today?" she asked, leaning toward the clock on his nightstand.

"Maybe. Depends on what the doctor says. My mom is taking me for my appointment, and if he releases me to drive, then I'm there."

"That'd be cool. 'Night." Jinxi slipped down the hall to her room. Dean heard the door close behind her. He lay back and crossed his arms under his head. Melancholy shrouded him like a heavy wool blanket. The brief moment of shared intimacy teased like a drop of water to a man dying of thirst. He was ready to open his heart, baring everything to a woman, to someone who would know him and love him in spite of himself. For that spiritual connection like his parents had shared.

Could Jinxi be the one? Or were they too different? Her baggage could drag them both down.

Turning on his side, he tucked the pillow more comfortably under his head. Good thing I don't have any baggage.

Rain rattled like pebbles on the windshield of the truck. Bits of wind-driven leaves stuck to the wipers, smearing Dean's view. He was driving again, thanks to the doctor's release. Pulling into the parking lot of the police station was like coming home. He dashed through the driving rain and up the cement stairs to the main doors.

The station was a hive of activity, a typical day at the office. Desks clustered together in groups of two or four filled the cavernous room. The more senior officers had the desks along the back wall, away from the frenetic activity.

The constant ringing of the phone added to the cacophony. A few poor souls sat with their heads down in hard chairs while an officer processed their paperwork. The room smelled of unwashed bodies and disinfectant spray.

The receptionist looked up as he approached. Dean looked past her to some of his friends who were standing together near the table that held the world's worst coffee. One of them glanced his way, then said something to the group. Everyone turned to look at him before huddling back together. Dean felt the hairs on the back of his neck tingle.

"Hey, Marsha," Dean said to the receptionist.

"Who are you here to see?"

"Oh, um, I'm here to see my sergeant." Dean rubbed his hand through his hair, brushing off the moisture. He was saved from further scrutiny by the appearance of his sergeant, striding through the room. He stopped when he saw Dean.

"Rafferty," his boss greeted him.

"Hey, Sarge. Do you have a minute?"

Sergeant Cavanaugh took a couple of chews of his ever-present gum before answering. He was a big man, over six feet, habitually hunched over as if the weight of the world rested on his shoulders. The officers under his command respected him, but none knew him well. He turned back toward his office and motioned for Dean to follow him.

Dean nodded at the group near the coffee. They nodded back but didn't smile. There was a moment when the phones were silent, and all conversation ceased as Dean followed Sergeant Cavanaugh. The silence was broken by one of the arrestees, who scraped his chair back on the bare linoleum floor.

Sergeant Cavanaugh's office was in the rear of the building. Awards and recognitions covered the dark walls. A low credenza behind the desk held a photo of a smiling family and another of two children in front of a Christmas tree. The sergeant's desk was a flurry of papers, reports, and file folders. The government-issue chair groaned as he sat down.

Dean sat in one of the hard metal chairs facing the desk. He shifted uncomfortably before speaking. "The doctor says I should be able to come back to work in a couple of weeks."

His sergeant looked at him, expressionless. "Has Internal Affairs been in touch with you?"

Dean broke eye contact, glancing at the wall of certificates. His head began to pound. "Um, yeah. Yes, sir."

"Did they happen to mention that until this mess is cleared up you and your partner will be on administrative leave?"

Dean's stomach dropped. "Wh-what?" A roaring tsunami filled his head.

Sergeant Cavanaugh turned his chair toward the credenza with a loud squeak. He turned back to face Dean and plopped down a bulging manila file. Dean could just make out the label and thought he saw his name and Raul's.

"According to IA, as soon as the doctor releases you, you're to be notified that you are relieved of duty until further notice."

Dean opened and closed his mouth a few times, trying to get some moisture back. Sarge glared at him, an indecipherable look in his eyes. "Is there anything you want to tell me, Rafferty?"

"I—I'm not sure what you mean." Dean swallowed hard around the paralysis of his throat.

"The department has help for people with ... problems."

"Problems?"

The sergeant sighed heavily. "If I have to spell it out for you, Officer, then I will. There's help for employees with substance abuse problems."

Dean scraped his chair back in disbelief. "Substance abuse? You've got to be kidding."

"Oh, I assure you, I'm not kidding." The sergeant's demeanor was even more grave than usual.

"That's ridiculous," Dean exploded. "I've never touched the stuff."

Sergeant Cavanaugh pursed his lips. "Your partner says otherwise."

"Raul?"

"Unless you have another partner, then yes. Officer Hernandez."

"I don't believe it. Where would he get the idea I'm using drugs?" After all that talk about partners sticking together and having each other's back, why would Raul tell his sergeant that he was a drug user?

Raul wouldn't do that to him. Or would he? Like a lightning bolt, Dean realized bitterly why his so-called friends in the other room snubbed him as he walked by. Raul must have let everyone know Dean was the one responsible for the shooting because of some judgment error due to his drug use. With a sick feeling, he wondered how he would ever regain his reputation.

"So you deny it?" the sergeant said.

"Of course I deny it." Dean smacked his hand down on the edge of the desk. "It's not true. I don't even drink."

They looked at each other over the open file on the desk. Sergeant Cavanaugh tapped his index finger on the papers.

Sweat began to trickle down between Dean's shoulder blades. He forced himself to concentrate through the thunder in his head.

"I have your badge and your weapon," Sarge told him. "They were taken from you at the hospital. They'll be locked up here until you return to work. Until then, I suggest you get some rest. You look a little pale. See Marsha on your way out. She'll give you the consent forms to sign for a drug test."

Dean nodded.

"It would help if you could remember what happened that night. At this point, it's the victim's father's word against your partner's."

Dean hoped he didn't look guilty. "Yes, sir."

Rain pelted his bare head as he stumbled from the building and dashed to the parking lot. He sat motionless behind the wheel of his truck, hands frozen on the steering wheel. What just happened? How could he be accused of using drugs? His dream job of being a policeman was turning into a nightmare.

Dean jumped as his cell phone vibrated in his pocket. He pulled it out and looked at the screen with dread. Good, it wasn't Raul. The caller ID showed Patrice, his friend from the force. Dean flashed back to when he, Damaris, and Patrice had gone through the academy together.

"Hello?"

"Dean," she exclaimed. "You shot out of here before I could even say hi. What's going on?"

"I don't know what's going on, Patrice. One day I'm riding in a patrol car with Raul and the next, Sarge is asking me if I'm using drugs."

"You? Using drugs? That's a stretch."

Dean rubbed his hand across the back of his neck. "I know. This is madness."

"I heard the department is being sued by the father of the kid Raul shot. And I guess he's named in the lawsuit as well."

"Yeah. They're all saying if I could remember what happened, everything would be okay. But what if I remember and no one believes me because they think I'm a druggie?" Dean pounded the steering wheel in frustration. "I'd like to know who started that rumor."

"Calm down, Dean," Patrice soothed. "I'll talk with Damaris, and we'll see if we can get to the bottom of this.

Somebody's gotta know who started the rumor." She changed tack. "How're you feeling?"

"Like garbage. My head still feels like it's in a vise, but at least I can drive. I'm just so sick of this."

There was noise in the background and Patrice said, "I gotta go. My partner's here. I'll call you tomorrow, okay?"

Dean barely had a chance to say goodbye before she disconnected. He started the truck with wooden arms. As he drove, anger bubbled up like hot lava. Why was this happening to him? Was God out to get him? First the accident, then the whole IA thing, now this rumor that threatened to ruin his career.

His tires screeched in protest on the wet streets as he drove toward home. He deliberately drove over the speed limit. In his mind, he dared an officer to pull him over. He arrived home without incident, but instead of going back into his mother's house, he pulled up in front of his garage apartment.

The apartment door was wet and swollen as he shoved it open. A spider web caught him across the face, and he slapped it away. Stale, damp air clung to everything. After turning on the heat, he shed his wet jacket and hung it over a chair. Digging through his closet, he found a dry sweatshirt and pulled it on.

Anger spent, he sat down on the futon couch that doubled as his bed. His father had added the apartment over the garage several years ago. Rent they received from the various college students who'd stayed there throughout the years helped his parents raise three kids on a single income. After Brian and Robin left home, Dean had moved out there and paid his mother a small rent.

He liked being able to keep an eye on her, and she loved having her youngest son so close. He took care of most of the home improvement projects that came with having a house that was over sixty years old. His friends teased him that he still lived at home with his mom, but he just smiled and reminded them his rent was minimal compared to what they paid.

The apartment suited him just fine. The kitchen took up one corner, the bathroom one corner, and the living room the rest of the space. Downstairs in the garage was his workout room. His weights and treadmill competed for space with all the stuff that accumulated after living in the same house for more than twenty-five years. His mom preferred to park under the carport next to the house, so the situation worked out in his favor. Except sometimes, he felt a little crowded by his mother.

His cell phone vibrated again, and he heaved himself up to retrieve it from his wet jacket pocket. His mom.

"What."

"Hi, honey. I saw you drive by, but you didn't come in. Where are you?"

"I'm in my apartment."

There was silence for a moment. "Your apartment."

"Yeah. I'm moving back here. I don't need to be watched like a baby anymore."

"I didn't know you felt like I was babysitting you." When Dean didn't respond, she continued. "Well, if the doctor thinks you're okay on your own, I guess it's for the best."

He mumbled agreement.

"OK, then. Let me know if you need anything. I love you."

"You too," he answered.

He hung up and tossed the phone on the kitchen table. "People just need to leave me alone," he muttered.

Later that evening, persistent knocking woke Dean from a deep sleep. Someone was at his door. He dragged himself out of bed, rubbing his hands over his face. Pulling open the door, he saw Jinxi standing on the threshold with a plate wrapped in aluminum foil. Ted was already pushing past her into the apartment.

"Hey," she greeted him. "You okay?"

Dean moved aside to let her in. "Would everyone quit asking me that? Sheesh."

Jinxi made a face at him and headed toward the kitchen area. "I brought you some dinner." She set the plate down as he closed the door behind her. "Do you mind if I turn on a light?"

Dean flipped on the kitchen light without answering her.

"Thanks."

Dean yawned open-mouthed.

"Have you been asleep all afternoon?" Jinxi asked.

He shrugged. "I guess."

"Your mom is worried." Jinxi chewed a fingernail, eyeing him. "I thought you were coming over to the food bank today." She pulled out one of the stools that faced the kitchen counter and sat.

Dean sat next to her and pulled the foil off the plate. "Yeah, well, I didn't make it." He got up and went around the bar and dug around in a drawer. Pulling out a fork, he sat back down and began to eat.

"What did you do today, after the doctor's?"

"Went to the station. Came home. Fell asleep."

She sniffed, then gathered her sweatshirt around her and stood up.

"Well, I guess I'll go back." As she walked toward the door, she asked, "Do you want Ted to stay here with you?"

Dean shrugged. Jinxi called to the dog, who had curled up near the floor heater. He looked at her accusingly before getting up and reluctantly following her out into the cold night.

CHAPTER FOURTEEN

Wind blew leftover moisture from the trees like fake rain. The night was clear, and Jinxi could see a few stars through the stark branches. She hugged her sweatshirt around her as she trudged over the soggy lawn toward Janice's house. Light shone from the kitchen window, guiding her across the dark expanse of the yard. How comforting one little light could be.

She clung to the sliver of warmth represented by the light, smarting from Dean's rejection. Why was he so moody, so curt? Maybe he felt like they were getting too close. Last night he'd edged open the door of his heart, but today the door was shut and locked.

Jinxi recalled the phone call she'd made to her mother after abruptly leaving Bakersfield and traveling all the way to Sacramento. Her mother had said she was worried, and for a moment, Jinxi's heart leaped. She'd finally gotten her mother's attention. Then her mother had gone on to say she was worried about Ron, her boyfriend. That comment had cut as deeply as one of the self-inflicted wounds on her arms.

Dean was holding her at arm's length, pushing her away like her mother had done ever since Jinxi was born. In her head, she knew God loved her and wanted to be her father. But the reality was, she was unlovable. Janice cared for her.

But love? That was way beyond Jinxi's expectation. She set her feet firmly on the steps to the back porch—even as her eyes ached from unshed tears.

Dean knew he'd behaved like a jerk. He finished eating his dinner and mentally beat himself up. What was wrong with him? Jinxi and his mom cared about him. Why couldn't he tell them about his visit to the station? They might have some advice about what to do. Or he could call Patrice. He reached for his phone, then pulled his hand back. Did he really want to know who'd started the rumor? It could well have been Raul. What about all that stuff about partners having each other's back?

Dean wanted to retaliate. He wanted his reputation. He wanted his job. And he wanted to hurt whoever had started this rumor.

Maybe he should call Freeman and confess he now remembered what had happened that night. But did he remember? Was his brain working okay now? Maybe it was something he dreamed, but didn't really happen. He'd be ruining another officer's reputation. Maybe the other guys would judge him for being a snitch rather than a drug user. Could he ever win?

Maybe I should just go to work at Starbucks.

Dean pulled a bottle of water from the fridge and threw himself down on the futon. Too keyed up to stay down, he got up, shed his jeans and shirt, and pulled on his workout clothes. He made his way carefully down the wet stairs and opened up the garage for the first time in several weeks. The treadmill was dusty, but it hummed to life when Dean plugged in a thirty-minute workout at a reasonable pace. Turning on some energetic rock music, he began to run.

Ten minutes later, his head pounded in rhythm with his heart. Sweat dripped from his nose, wetting his Tee shirt He jumped off the treadmill and angrily punched the stop button as he struggled for breath. When did he become so weak, so fragile? His legs shook as he stumbled over to the weight bench and sank down. He rested his forearms on his thighs and stared at a crack in the concrete floor, wondering if he even had the energy to climb the stairs.

Back in his apartment, heaviness settled in like an unwanted guest. He slumped on the futon, fuzzy-headed, and brooded over how he'd ever get out of this mess. Since the accident, nothing was the same. He'd lost his department's respect. His partner had turned against him. What else could go wrong?

Distraction beckoned in the form of his computer. Maybe someone had emailed with some good news. It had been a while, and he had fifty-seven new emails. He quickly deleted all the junk ads for prescription discounts, then read through the few from friends asking how he was doing. An email from an unfamiliar name stopped him. Katie Edwards. He was on the point of hitting DELETE without opening it. Why was that name familiar? He racked his brain, wondering how many memories he'd lost in the fall.

Dean clicked it open and began to read. Two sentences into it, memories came flooding back in a flash flood of shame.

Dean quickly scanned the email, then went back and reread it slowly.

Dear Dean,

I don't know if you remember me, but we were both at Sac State together. I got your email from one of our mutual acquaintances. We met after I had just broken up with my boyfriend. There was a party at my sorority house, and we invited your fraternity. I was feeling pretty emotional, and you were kind enough to make sure I had a good time. Anyway, I guess we both had a little too much to drink. And, well, the thing is, I have a six-year-old son. He's been asking a lot lately about who his dad is. I hope you'll do the right thing and take a DNA test to prove things one way or another. I've attached the link so you can send for the test.

Thanks.
Katie

An ant crawled across the desk. Dean extended his hand to crush it. He wondered if the insect had any idea something big and bad was about to come crashing down on him. He was the ant, making his way unsuspecting through life, unaware that tragedy was about to hit him like a huge thumb from the sky.

Was it possible he had a kid somewhere? A six-year-old son? His world was rocked by the thought. Like falling dominos, one irresponsible night had far-reaching consequences. He'd taken advantage of a girl who was depressed over her boyfriend.

She was wrong, though.

He hadn't had too much to drink. No more than two beers. He knew exactly what he was doing when he took her up to her room to comfort her away from the crowd.

What was he going to do? He wasn't prepared to help raise a kid. Would she want back child support? Every other weekend visits? What if he didn't like the kid? How would he explain this to his mom and to Jinxi?

He sat back in his chair. Whoa, what about Jinxi? Here he was thinking about a relationship with her, and now this. He wouldn't blame her if she ran the other direction as fast as she could. Nobody would want to be with someone with so much baggage.

With a sinking feeling, he returned to the email and clicked on the link to the DNA testing company and ordered the test. Until the results came back, he'd keep Katie's email quiet. No sense in anyone getting the wrong idea. The guys at Sac PD called him 'the forty-year-old virgin.' He'd never hear the end of it if they found out he had a kid.

CHAPTER FIFTEEN

"I have wonderful news!" Padish's voice rang through the empty cafeteria.

Jinxi and Hank had just finished wiping down the tables with disinfectant. She rubbed an arm across her nose. Like Aneesa, Padish's news usually meant more work.

The staff and volunteers gathered to hear what their leader had to say.

"We will soon have a new helper. He will be doing community service hours here, starting tomorrow." Padish's face held its perpetual smile. "Jinxi will show him the ropes, yes?"

I knew it would mean more work. She'd started at the food bank doing court-ordered community service. She remembered how Hank and Connie had taken extra time to help her. Now she'd be stuck doing the same thing for some other loser.

Jinxi scrunched her face into what she hoped was a smile as she looked up at her boss. He touched her lightly on the shoulder.

"His name is Jared."

A guy? No way. She was a loser-guy magnet. She had to get out of this. "Um, I'm not sure I'll have time—"

"Of course you will." Padish's hand was a lead weight on her shoulder. "I will make sure it is so." He clapped his hands together. "Back to work, everyone!"

Jinxi narrowed her eyes as Padish turned to go back to his office. Then she stomped into the storage room, grabbed a broom, and began to sweep, muttering under her breath.

"W-what's wrong, M-m-miss J-jinxi?" Hank's dark face was a mask of concern.

She threw down the broom. It hit the concrete floor with a satisfying clatter. "I don't want to help some convict."

Hank limped to the broom, picked it up, and leaned it against the wall. He turned back to face her. When he spoke, it was without a stutter. "It wasn't that long ago you were the convict."

Her mouth dropped open as his words pierced her like a pin in a balloon. Anger deflated, she slumped onto a box and held her face in her hands.

"Y-you'll b-b-be fine."

She ground her teeth in frustration. Hank moved away to work in a far corner of the storeroom.

Maybe she should quit. Just leave here, say adios, and go somewhere else. Someplace where no one placed any demands, and there was no accountability partner and no kids with burned faces. Fat lot of good that did her last time. She'd run away from Los Angeles when her boyfriend Skeeter was arrested. She'd ended up in Sacramento, broke, and in jail. If it weren't for Dean's intervention and Janice's goodness, she'd still be hustling the streets.

If they knew everything about her past, they'd be disgusted. She pictured Janice's face, turning from her in revulsion. Dean would blow up and yell. At least he'd have an excuse to get rid of her.

Oh, snap! She's just have to make sure no one ever found out.

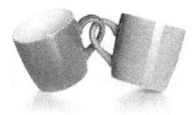

Time to help Connie in the kitchen. They bustled around, each in charge of two volunteers. Jinxi directed her older ladies to start the industrial-sized coffee pot and fill the creamer and sugar containers. She fiddled with her earring, worrying about what she'd have to do with the new guy. Jinxi hated him already. She even hated his name. Jared.

After the aluminum doors over the serving area were rolled up, Jinxi quickly scanned the line for the mother and what she thought of as the burn boy. Snap! They were chatting with Aneesa. She wouldn't be able to escape.

A familiar sense of doom lay across her shoulders.

"Yinxi? You okay?" Connie's warm voice breathed in her ear.

"Yeah. Fine." Her blue eyes met the other woman's soft brown ones. They were both the same height, but Connie outweighed her by at least twenty-five pounds. She blamed it on her having to cook for her family, but Connie had an unquenchable sweet tooth.

The line of people surged forward. Metal spoons clanked in aluminum trays and the buzz of conversation grew. Determined to keep her head down, Jinxi concentrated on slapping spoonfuls of green beans on paper plates.

A skinny brown arm holding a plate appeared in her peripheral vision. It was like trying not to look at a car accident. Jinxi looked up, and her eyes met those of the Burn Boy. She tried not to grimace as she placed the vegetables on his plate.

"Thank you," he murmured. Behind him, his mother urged him forward, hand on his back. Her gaze met Jinxi's with a look of accusation. The mother's lips tightened.

"Y-you're welcome," she stammered, breaking eye contact.

The mother thrust her plate at Jinxi with an air of defiance. "Something wrong?"

Jinxi bent her head over the serving dish and shook it. Could this day get any worse?

On rare occasions, traffic was light enough for the bus to arrive early at the food bank. Jinxi hopped down the steps and joined a small cluster of volunteers who gathered near the front door. The sharp smell of cigarette smoke drifted toward her. She reached in her right front jeans pocket for the lighter that wasn't there. A quick smoke would be nice before facing the new community service guy. Something to calm her nerves.

A thought came unbidden to her mind.

Pray.

She stopped in her tracks, did a one-eighty, and headed in the opposite direction. She stopped at the corner and looked both ways. Good. No one was coming.

"Uh, God, can you please help me today? I really don't want to go to work. So, um, maybe you can make that guy not show up. And the mom and …" She choked on the words. "Burn Boy. Thanks. I mean, amen."

She headed back to the food bank and pushed through the front door into the lobby.

"Hey, girl," Aneesa greeted her. Today the mass of curls was held back by an African print scarf. "You're early."

"Hi." Jinxi let the backpack slip off her shoulder. She swung it onto a shelf in a row of cubbies along the back wall.

"Ready to meet your new protégé?" Aneesa's smile did nothing to ease the clenching of Jinxi's stomach.

So much for praying.

"Padish is showing him around. You can catch up with them in the big storeroom."

The food bank had two storerooms. The smaller one served as the initial drop off point for donations from grocery stores, while the bigger one held massive refrigerators and freezers. Long tables cut the larger room in half. They were used as an assembly line to pack boxes and bags to distribute to the less fortunate. Those numbers had grown since the recession. Sometimes they had to turn people away. Jinxi hated to see the sadness in Padish's eyes when that happened. She was almost tempted to donate her paycheck so they could buy more food. Almost. Maybe after she'd saved enough for her second chef's knife.

She took a deep breath and steeled herself as she passed through the smaller room. She heard Padish's voice as she pushed through the door into the larger storeroom.

"Today you will help Miss Jinxi in here, yes? She will be here momentarily to show you what to do."

Jinxi wordlessly approached the two men. Padish addressed a shorter white man. He wore a white Tee shirt revealing a canvas of tattoos from his wrist up into the sleeves. His head was shaved, and his earlobes held ear gauges. She could see through the holes to the room behind him.

"Ah, here you are." Padish's smile didn't waver as he introduced them.

Jared didn't smile. He didn't put out his hand to shake hers. He just stared at her with eyes full of pent-up aggression.

Jinxi felt sweat break out on the back of her neck. She sucked the lip stud against her teeth, its click audible in the too-silent room.

Padish clapped his hands. "I'll leave you two to work."

Jinxi tore her eyes away from Jared to watch as Padish exited the room.

As soon as the door clicked shut, she whipped around to face him.

"What are you doing here?" Her words hissed through her teeth.

"Is that any way to greet a boyfriend?" He slouched against the table, arms crossed.

Jinxi felt her face flame. "Ex-boyfriend." She put her hands on her hips and glared at him. "And your name's not Jared."

He threw back his head and laughed. "It is now." He shrugged his skinny shoulders. "Isn't technology cool?"

"Again. What. Are. You. Doing. Here, Skeeter?" Her morning coffee threatened to explode from her stomach.

Jinxi glared at him, hiding her fear behind anger. The last time she'd seen him was when he rode away from her on his motorcycle, leaving her standing in front of Janice's house. A shiny bald head replaced his scraggly blond hair. The ear gauges were new, along with some of the tattoos. How did Skeeter drop back into her life like a flaming meteor?

Skeeter reached for his jacket and pulled out a pack of cigarettes.

"You can't smoke in here." Her voice squeezed out of a small space that used to be her throat.

"You gonna tell your boss?" Skeeter mocked. He took out his lighter and flipped it open and closed, open and closed, setting Jinxi's teeth on edge.

She hugged her arms across her chest, burying her chin in the neck of her sweatshirt. "I thought you were in LA."

Skeeter rubbed his head. "The heat was on, you know that. I met a guy who told me he could get me a new identity. Clean slate and all that stuff." He grinned at her. "It worked, too, until we were riding together in his car, and he got pulled over. Next thing you know, we're in jail, and I'm paying my debt to society." He waved his arm around the room. "Seeing you here is a fringe benefit." He pushed himself away from the table and approached her.

She took a step back.

"This'll be fun. We'll take up where we left off." His arm snaked out and grabbed her before she could move.

Skeeter's hand gripped her arm in a painful grasp. Jinxi's heart sped up, a pounding bass drum in her chest.

"Let me go," she said, with what she hoped was a warning tone.

"Or what?" His face was close enough she felt his hot breath on her cheek. "Do your new friends know about you? Do they know your little secrets?" He used his other hand to flick open the lighter and hold it near her face. "Do they know how much you love fire?"

She licked her lips with a tongue drier than sand.

Skeeter dropped her arm and shoved her away, barking out a laugh. "Poor little Jinxi. Scared like a rabbit."

Jinxi turned and dashed to the door, yanked it open, and ran to the alley behind the building. Her chest heaved, each breath a stabbing pain. Maybe she'd drop dead from a heart attack.

When her heart rate returned to normal, Jinxi considered her options. The temptation to run away warred against the feeling of belonging that had enveloped her at the food bank. Slow anger started like kindling, then grew to forest fire proportions. She wouldn't let Skeeter ruin what she'd worked so hard for.

CHAPTER SIXTEEN

The door to the food bank office was closed, but Jinxi tried the knob anyway. It turned easily in her hands. Dust motes floated lazily in the empty room. She glanced at Aneesa's desk for some indication of where Aneesa might be. Seeing nothing, she retreated, closing the door behind her. Her heart leaped to her throat when she almost collided with Burn Boy.

"S-sorry," Jinxi mumbled.

He smiled up at her, his mouth lopsided from the burns on his cheek. "It's okay. I'm not supposed to be here. My mom is talking to that tall guy. She told me to stay close."

Jinxi shifted her weight from one foot to the other, trying not to stare at the boy's crinkled skin as her stomach churned. As he walked away, her mind replayed the incident that had sent her to Juvenile Hall, then to the California Girls' Ranch for most of her high school years.

She and her friends laughed about throwing matches into the dry weeds of a vacant lot. They'd start a fire, then hide as the fire department arrived with their trucks to put out the blaze. They'd watch all the action and excitement from a safe distance.

Jinxi felt the heat in her face, as if she were standing next to the blaze. She wiped the sweat from her forehead with the back of one hand, expecting to see it blackened with soot. Just like that afternoon.

The rest of the morning passed in a blur. Stupid mistakes caused Connie to ask if she was okay.

Her answer each time was the same. "Fine."

Connie shrugged and stopped asking.

Skeeter ate in the cafeteria, grinning at her when their eyes met. Jinxi turned away. His gaze was a knife stab to her gut.

Aneesa bounced into the kitchen after the last person was served. "Great lunch, ladies." She included Jinxi, Connie, and several volunteers in her praise. Her brow wrinkled when her eyes landed on Jinxi.

"You feelin' okay, honey?" She reached out a hand to feel Jinxi's forehead. "You're even more pale than usual."

Jinxi shook her head. She couldn't explain to Aneesa this was one of the worst days of her life.

"Why don't you go on home," Aneesa told her. "We'll manage without you for the rest of the day."

"You sure?" Jinxi asked, even as she pulled off her hairnet and untied the apron.

"You bet. You go home and get some rest."

Jinxi didn't need to be asked twice. She scurried past the tables of homeless people and headed around the corner to the office. The door was open, and Padish sat at his desk.

His face widened into his habitual grin when he saw her. "Our little Jinxi. How are you doing?" His smile faded as he took in her appearance. "You are sick, yes?"

Jinxi nodded. "Aneesa said I could go home. If that's okay." She waited until Padish murmured his agreement before she shouldered her backpack and headed out the door.

The bus dropped her off a few blocks from the house. As she approached, she noticed Janice's car wasn't parked in the driveway. Jinxi heaved a sigh of relief. Better not to have to talk to anyone right now. She dropped her pack at the foot of the stairs. The kitchen beckoned her. Baking something sweet and chocolaty would go a long way toward helping her cope with the Skeeter situation.

Jinxi trotted up the stairs to her room to retrieve her cookbook. The personalized binder, created by Janice, held Jinxi's favorite recipes. She'd started with only a few pages, but after three months, it bulged with sheets downloaded from recipe websites. She'd added dividers to separate them into categories.

Jinxi propped the binder open on the table, supported by the napkin holder. She ran a finger down the list of ingredients for chocolate cake, then rummaged through the pantry until she had everything she needed.

Thirty minutes later, she shoved the two round cake pans into the oven and closed the door with her hip. She stood in the middle of the kitchen, surveying the mess. The peace she expected hadn't come. Maybe she should make something for dinner.

The dirty pans went into the sink. She turned on the faucet and added some dish soap. They could soak while she worked on a quiche.

As she rolled out the crust, her mind returned to the confrontation with Skeeter. She bit her lip, moving the stud back and forth against her teeth. She couldn't work with him every single day. What if he told someone her secret? She imagined Padish's face, filled with disgust. Aneesa would shake her head, horrified. Connie wouldn't ever let her near the kids again. Dean would never again speak to her.

She was a terrible person.

Why did that mom and Burn Boy have to turn up at the food bank? Why couldn't the past stay in the past? A siren wailed in the distance, drawing her thoughts to that day when she was fourteen. The fire started as something fun. When sparks flew to the house next to the vacant lot, things got bad. Who knew a house could burn so fast?

Jinxi brushed a strand of hair away from her face with a floury hand. After draping the crust across the pie pan, she pressed it down and started crimping the edges. The rote action calmed her spirit. A verse from her Bible bubbled to the surface like water beginning to boil.

For I know the plans I have for you, declares the Lord. Plans to prosper you and not to harm you, plans to give you hope and a future.

Jinxi's hands stilled on the crust. What possible plans could God have for bringing Skeeter back into her life? What was she supposed to do, pray for him? She barked out a laugh. That'll be the day. After the way he'd mistreated her. Though the visible bruises were gone, her spirit carried the scars of every blow.

"What smells so good?"

Jinxi jumped as Dean pushed through the back door of the house. She turned on him with a snarl. "You scared me."

He raised his hands in surrender. "Sorry. I let Ted out of my apartment to do his business and thought I saw movement in here." He turned toward the oven. "Whatcha cooking?"

The corners of Jinxi's mouth turned down. "Cake." She focused on the pie crust.

Dean pointed to the pie pan. "What's that?"

"Quiche." Finished with crimping the crust, she pulled a whisk out of a drawer and began to beat the egg mixture with more force than was necessary.

"You okay?" asked Dean.

"Yup."

"Why are you home so early? You didn't get fired, did you?"

Jinxi sent an angry glare in his direction.

"Nope." She poured the mixture into the crust, slopping some onto the counter. As she reached for a cloth to wipe it up, he stopped her by placing a hand on her arm.

"What's going on?" His broad faced wrinkled in concern.

"Nothing." Jinxi jerked away, crossing her arms against her middle.

He mirrored her, crossing his arms and leaning against the counter. "Nothing." One eyebrow raised. "First, you're home way earlier than normal. Second, you're cooking up a storm, which means that something has you twisted up. Third, you've clammed up like Mom's cellar door after a wet rain."

Sometimes Jinxi hated Dean's skill at observation. Why couldn't he just leave her alone?

Jinxi took a deep breath and blew it out. What if she told him everything? He'd been her best friend once, before he found out she'd stolen money from his mom. Which, she reminded herself, he didn't remember. Yet.

Her palms grew wet as she considered whether to tell him about Skeeter. Maybe she could start there, gauge his reaction, then see if it was safe to talk about the fire. She gnawed on her lip.

Trust me.

The voice spoke through the haze of indecision clouding her mind. Trust meant putting in jeopardy the security she'd found in Janice and in her food bank family. Trust meant putting it all on the line, hoping she wouldn't find herself back on the street, hustling for a buck. It meant allowing someone in, being vulnerable.

"There's this guy ..."

CHAPTER SEVENTEEN

Dean's arms ached as he pounded the speed bag hanging from the garage rafters. Fueled by rage, he pictured Jared's head as he landed each punch. Five minutes later, he wiped sweat from his forehead with the back of one arm, letting his hands drop to his sides. He shook his head with a disgusted grimace. Before the accident, he'd have gone at least twenty minutes, dancing and bouncing around the punching bag.

He sat on the weight bench and pulled off the gloves. He thought about what Jinxi had told him. What a life that must have been, moving from hotel to apartment to campground, always one step ahead of the authorities. If things had been different, their paths might have crossed sooner, and not in a good way.

Now that Jared, or Skeeter, or whatever the heck his name was, was here in Sacramento, Dean would have to keep an eye on him. Maybe ask one of his friends on the force, if he still had any friends, to watch for him.

When he thought of the kind of abuse she must have experienced at the hands of this jerk—well, it was a good thing Dean's gun was under lock and key with his sergeant. He wouldn't shoot him, but he might use the butt to knock some sense into him.

He threw the gloves against the wall of the garage, where they dropped to the cement floor. His cell phone vibrated on the bench beside him. The screen showed a number he didn't recognize.

"Rafferty."

"Officer Rafferty, it's Freeman. I have some information I'd like to bring to your attention. I'll be at your place tomorrow morning at eleven."

Adrenaline surged like an electric current through Dean's body. "Uh, couldn't we meet at the station?"

"No. I prefer to have this conversation away from prying eyes."

"Oh. Okay."

Freeman's voice took on a hearty tone, as if they were friends. "Great, then I'll see you tomorrow. Have a good evening."

The adrenaline melted away, leaving Dean trembling. With his cell phone in one hand, he scrolled through the contacts, sweaty fingers leaving smudges on the screen. He punched the number for his friend Patrice. Her voicemail notification blared through the tinny speaker with the theme from Bad Boys. She cheerily told him she was out arresting bad guys and to leave a message.

"It's Dean. I need to find out what's going on. IA is all over me. Call me."

He punched END and tossed the phone on the bench beside him. Dang. If he could only remember what happened that night. Really remember, not fish up some fragment of a dream. Maybe he was the one using drugs. If he couldn't remember, maybe narcotics had scrambled his brain, in addition to the head injury.

He touched the scab on his head, a grim reminder he was lucky to be alive. Too often good men died in the line of duty, men whose only desire was to protect and to serve their communities. Sure, there were stories about rogue cops, who took money or drugs from arrestees. But not on his team, and surely not him.

Hunger drove Dean to his mother's house, hoping Jinxi was done cooking the quiche she'd been making. And maybe he could score a slice of that chocolate cake. Pushing his way through the back door, he found her spreading the last of the icing around the side of the cake. Something flickered at the edge of his consciousness—a flash of memory, a pair of shining gold earrings in her hand. His eyes flew to her ears, but silver hoops dangled from her pale earlobes.

"What?" Jinxi asked, looking up from the cake, knife poised.

"Huh?"

"What are you staring at?"

Dean shook his head, grimacing at the resulting needle-stab of pain. "The cake looks awesome."

She smiled and straightened, rubbing her lower back. "It does, doesn't it?"

He closed his eyes for a moment, hoping to regain the memory. "Do you have a pair of gold earrings? With a row of diamonds?" When he opened his eyes, Jinxi had her back to him.

"No."

"Hmm. I'm trying to remember something." He slumped down on one of the wooden chairs and brought his fist down on the table. "Jeez, this is so frustrating. Some things I remember perfectly, while other stuff I can't."

Dean watched as Jinxi rummaged around in the refrigerator, tossing ingredients for a salad on the counter behind her. Lettuce, tomatoes, and cucumber, followed by a bottle of dressing, slammed down on the cracked tile.

He drummed his fingers on the table, watching her jerky movements as she assembled the salad. "You sure you've never had a pair of gold earrings?"

Jinxi stopped, shoulders rigid. "I said no."

Dean heard his mom's footsteps as she came down the hall toward the kitchen. Her gaze swept over Dean, then to

Jinxi, who attacked the cucumber with a knife like it was going to escape.

"Something smells good in here. I can't tell if it's cake or quiche, but I can't wait to try both."

Dean dragged his gaze from Jinxi's stiff back. "Hey, Mom. How was your day?"

Janice pulled out the chair opposite him and sat. "Pretty good. How are you feeling?"

Dean shrugged. "The same." He thought about his meeting tomorrow with Freeman but decided against bringing it up. What was going on with Jinxi?

Janice struggled to her feet. "Before I forget, some mail came for you today. Let me go get it."

Dean started to rise. "Want me to get it?"

Janice waved him back down. "No, it's just out here on the piano. Let me."

Jinxi still hadn't turned around. He wanted to go to her and touch her arm, ask her what was wrong. Maybe she'd turn to him, and he'd hug her …

"Here you go, honey." Janice plopped some mail on the table, disrupting his thoughts.

A thick envelope lay buried under miscellaneous bills. Dean pushed the bills aside, blanching when he saw the return address on the bulky envelope. Family Ancestry DNA. He plucked it off the table, but not before Janice saw it.

Her voice was tight when she spoke. "I see Robin got to you, too."

"Wh—huh?" He stared open-mouthed at his mother. How would he explain this? Nobody did random DNA tests on themselves. He needed to come up with something fast.

"Robin. Your sister."

Dean licked his dry lips. "What about her?"

Janice picked at a chip in the wooden table, her eyes downcast. "She asked me to take a DNA test, too. For genetic markers for disease. Because of Hannah's RA. I see she asked you to take one as well."

Dean snapped his fingers. "Right. I forgot." Convenient. He shot to his feet, anxious to take the offending and potentially accusatory test home. "I gotta go."

He took two steps toward the back door. As his hand twisted the knob, he turned and spoke to no one in particular.

"I'm not hungry." It was only then Jinxi spun around to look at him, questions shooting from her eyes.

CHAPTER EIGHTEEN

The bus rumbled through the city streets, disgorging women dressed in restaurant logo wear, dark-suited businesspeople, and teenagers with pants sagging below their exposed boxers. Stops became less frequent as they neared the river, where cardboard boxes served as homeless shelters. Jinxi barely noticed the X-rated bookstores, liquor stores, and the Gospel Mission where shabbily dressed crowds gathered daily in search of their choice of comfort.

The closer the bus got to the food bank, the tighter her stomach knotted.

Maybe he won't show up today. Maybe he got busted again.

If her usual luck held true, Skeeter would be there, a malevolent doppelgänger intent on destroying what she'd gained in the past three months. She couldn't—no, wouldn't—let that happen.

Jinxi jumped off the last step of the bus, automatically digging for the cigarette lighter in her front pocket. Oh, snap! Not there. Was there anything in the Bible about smoking? She'd have to ask Janice. She took a deep breath and pushed open the door to the food bank.

The familiar smells assaulted her—stale food, stale bodies, dead hopes. After greeting Aneesa and dropping her backpack into a cubby, she made her way to the kitchen. Connie stood in the middle of the room, hands on her ample hips, a frown on her face.

"Hola, chica." Connie slowly pivoted, surveying the kitchen with sharp eyes. "Something is not right."

Jinxi looked around the room, turning slowly in a circle. "What're you talking about?"

Connie shook her head and clicked her tongue. "Someone moved my things."

"What things?"

Connie opened and closed cupboards, grumbling. "Everything is moved around. My bowls, my mixer. All is not right."

Jinxi shrugged and headed toward the storeroom door. "I hope you figure it out."

So much for her plan to delay seeing Skeeter by wasting some time talking with Connie. No way would she be drawn into a search for missing implements. Connie was way too protective of her stuff.

She pushed open the heavy door and stepped into the cavernous storeroom, then jumped as Hank appeared out of the shadows.

"Is Skee—I mean Jared, here yet?" She held her breath, waiting for Hank's answer.

He nodded and jerked his thumb toward the rolling door leading to the alley behind the food bank. "Y-y-yes, M-Miss J-jinxi. I t-told him to s-s-sweep up the alley."

The corners of Jinxi's mouth turned down. What did Padish expect her to do? Make Skeeter shadow her every move? She couldn't tell him what to do every minute, every second. Why couldn't Hank do it? He'd been here longer than she had.

Hank laid a big hand on her shoulder. "You ok-kay?"

Jinxi froze, welcoming the warmth of his comfort, yet anxious to throw off his hand. She shrugged, and Hank's arm dropped down to his side.

"I'm good." She owed him more, but the story would suck too much of the energy she'd need to work alongside Skeeter. Taking a deep breath, she crossed the dimly lit storeroom and headed to the metal rolling door. The chain moved easily in her hand as she pulled the door up high enough so she could bend down and step outside.

"Check this out!" Skeeter called when he saw her.

Flames shot out of a metal barrel filled with trash. Skeeter was in the process of tossing leaves and other debris into the fire.

Shock and horror glued Jinxi's feet to the concrete. "No," she whispered, licking lips dry as sandpaper.

Skeeter smiled, his face an evil mask. "Oh. I forgot. You're afraid of fire."

He advanced on her. Jinxi took an involuntary step back, bumping into the metal door. He grabbed her arm, pulling her closer to the burning barrel. She shook her head, but no sound came out of her mouth.

That one day, everything had gone horribly wrong. A gust of wind threw burning leaves onto the roof of the house next to the lot. The roof caught on fire and quickly engulfed one side of the house. Jinxi and her friends watched in horror as a mother ran from the house, screaming about her baby trapped inside.

Skeeter dragged her to within a foot of the fire. Her face burned from the heat and smoke.

"Is this what it was like for you and your friends? Watching that house burn, not knowing a kid was inside?"

Bile rose in Jinxi's throat. She should never have told Skeeter her secret. A few years back, she'd mentioned to him her time spent in the Girls' Ranch. He'd badgered her until she finally confessed the whole sordid story. She'd made him promise not to tell anyone. She was a murderer.

"No ..." she moaned. If Skeeter hadn't been holding her arm, she would have sunk down on the dirty alley concrete. Her head spun, and she needed to throw up. When Skeeter finally released her, Jinxi stepped back, dropping her head between her knees. The wind shifted, and the smoke headed away from her. She breathed in several clean breaths. "What do you think you're doing?"

Skeeter shrugged and grabbed the broom leaning against the brick wall of the food bank. "Just doing what I was told." His face took on a sly look. "Do any of your new friends know about your little secret?"

Jinxi shook her head. Pushing the hair away from her face, she fanned herself with one hand. "No. And they don't need to."

Skeeter appeared to consider this. "What if I tell them?"

Panic shot through her like a hit of cocaine. "No! You can't."

Skeeter leaned against the broom handle, rhythmically tapping it with one hand. Then he idly put his finger through his ear gauge. "I'll make you a deal."

"What kind of a deal?"

"I won't tell anyone your deep dark secret," his voice mocked. "But you have to do something for me."

Jinxi crossed her arms. "Like what?"

"I'll let you know."

"When?"

He shrugged, then swept a few stray leaves toward the barrel. "I don't know. Maybe a couple of days. Deal?"

Like making a deal with the devil. What choice did she have?

"Okay." She turned to go back inside, speaking over her shoulder. "Put out that fire. Now."

Jinxi ducked under the metal door and strode across the storeroom. Someone, probably Hank, had turned on the lights. She pushed through the door leading into the cafeteria, hoping to duck into the restroom without being stopped. Volunteers milled around the lobby, waiting for direction, but no one sought her out.

Once she reached the refuge of the bathroom, she sat in a stall and considered her options.

Option one—pack up, move out, and go somewhere else.

Option two—do what Skeeter wanted her to do, then tell him it's over.

Option three—tell someone what she'd done and hope for the best.

She mentally crossed off option three. No way would she risk her reputation here with all these Christian people. Everyone thought she was wonderful. A good worker, great cook, responsible tenant. Even God might be a little pleased with her. Except for this one thing. The event that changed her from being just a loser into a killer.

Sure, Janice forgave her for stealing money from her investment account. But this? No way. If Skeeter said anything, everyone would know what she really was. A monster. A child murderer. Who could forgive that?

CHAPTER NINETEEN

The DNA test sat on Dean's kitchen counter, its presence an accusation. He stared at it from across the room as he slumped on his futon. If only ... if only he hadn't gotten that girl Katie drunk. If only he hadn't convinced her to go up to his room. If only he'd kept his pants zipped.

If only he could remember the shooting incident. His dreams last night had been filled with frightening images. Scenes where he pulled his weapon and fired at a six-year-old boy, one that looked remarkably like himself. Dreams of being led to jail in handcuffs, walking by his peers who threw DNA sticks at him.

Dean downed a bowl of cereal while standing at the window, watching rain drizzle onto the backyard lawn. His watch showed 10:45, late to be getting out of bed. Just as his body had finally adjusted to the graveyard shift, the accident threw off his inner clock. Splashing some coffee into his mug, he added cream and sugar and stirred it with a finger.

Rubbing a hand across his face, he felt the two-day old stubble. He should probably shave.

Why bother? You don't have to look clean-shaven if you've got nowhere to go.

The intercom connecting his apartment to his mom's house crackled to life. "Dean? Are you home? There's a Mr. Freeman here to see you."

Dean reached for the button on the intercom to answer, then stopped. He turned abruptly away and strode toward his closet. He pulled on a hoodie, grabbed his wallet, keys, and cell phone, and dashed out the door. He took the stairs two at a time, jumping off the second-to-last step.

His truck roared to life just as his cell phone rang. Janice. He held the phone to his ear as he made a U-turn and headed away from the house.

"Hey, Mom."

"Dean, there's a man here to see you. He says you had an appointment with him." Her voice was low, as if she covered the mouthpiece with her hand.

Dean thought quickly. "Tell him I'll have to reschedule. I forgot I have a doctor's appointment today. I'm late as it is." He maneuvered onto a main street without knowing where he was going.

He glanced up to his rearview mirror as his mother relayed the message to Freeman. Dang. A police cruiser pulled up close behind him. Sweat broke out on his forehead when red and blue lights flashed. A quick woop-woop of the siren indicated he should pull off the road.

Dean tossed the cell phone onto the seat with a disgusted grunt. His sweat-slicked hands gripped the steering wheel while he waited for the officer to approach.

The officer knocked on the passenger window. Dean hit the window control. A blast of rain dampened the interior of the truck and dripped off the man's hat.

"Need to see your license, registration, and proof of insurance."

Dean fumbled with the seatbelt, then leaned forward to dig his wallet out of his jeans pocket. As he reached for the glove box to retrieve the registration and insurance card, he realized he didn't have his police ID. No badge, nothing to help him get a pass. Should he even mention he was with Sac PD?

The officer took the proffered information. As he turned to head to his cruiser, he said, "Cell phone use in a vehicle without a hands-free device is against the law in the State of California. Were you aware of that?"

Dean nodded. "Yes, sir."

Dean watched the man return to his patrol car to run Dean's driver's license information through the system. He knew the drill. See if the violator has any outstanding warrants. Verify the VIN number of the vehicle with the registration. Check the expiration date of the insurance.

He drummed his fingers on the steering wheel. He didn't need this, in addition to everything else. A freaking ticket. If only he had his badge. That would've kept him from getting a citation.

An eternity later, the officer returned, handing Dean's information through the window. "I'm going to need you to sign this," he said, shoving a pad of traffic violations at Dean. The rubber band holding the used ones was stretched to its limit.

Dean read the sheet. Yup, he was getting a citation for using a cell phone. He scrawled his name and handed the mess back to the officer. He stared straight ahead, trying to control his urge to yell and pound his fist on the dashboard. The officer took his time tearing off Dean's copy of the infraction.

Finally, he handed the ticket through the window. "Have a nice day, sir."

Dean snatched the paper and waited until the window was rolled up and the officer had walked away before throwing it on the floor. It landed face down, revealing what looked like a handwritten line scrawled across the back.

He leaned over and retrieved the yellow paper. Sure enough, something was written over the printed information on the back of the ticket.

Watch your back, amigo.

Dean swung his gaze to his rearview mirror, but the officer had already driven away. His hand shook as he turned the ticket over. It was signed M. Cruz. Must be a friend of Raul's.

Dean shook his head to clear it and got a stab of pain for his effort. He swallowed, trying to find enough moisture to ease the dryness in his mouth.

How had his life become all kinds of bad? One day, he was living his dream of being on a patrol beat. The next, he had a massive head wound, he was running from Internal Affairs, his sergeant accused him of being a druggie, a girl he'd been with only once thought he was the father of her kid, and his partner was out to get him. Could life get any worse?

Dean gunned the engine as he pulled away from the curb. The tires spun on the wet pavement as he U-turned and headed back to his apartment. Angry thoughts bubbled like hot lava. How would he ever sort out the mess of his life? This wasn't fair. None of this was his fault. Everyone was out to get him. Even God.

He rubbed the back of his neck, wishing his dad was still alive. He'd know what to do. His advice was always right on.

Who could he talk to?

Not his mom. She'd be shocked he'd taken advantage of some girl in college. Although maybe she'd want to have another grandchild. He mentally shook his head. No, too much explaining to do. Too much risk his mom would be ashamed of him.

Damaris? Li'l D? He'd been a friend since the academy. Maybe he'd know what to do about the Raul situation. Or maybe Patrice. Although she'd be disgusted to know he was the perpetrator of a date rape.

What about Jinxi? Her past wasn't all that stellar. Maybe she'd be able to relate. A flash of memory, the mental picture of her holding a pair of gold and diamond earrings. His gut churned as he concentrated on the thought. Anger. Him yelling at her. Then shame. But his shame or hers?

He pulled up to a four-way stop, gripping his head with both hands. Every effort to remember was rewarded with a stab of pain. A car blew its horn behind him, urging him to move. As he accelerated, his phone rang again. He glanced in his rearview mirror, then picked up the phone. He didn't recognize the number.

"Rafferty."

"Officer Rafferty, I've rescheduled our appointment for tomorrow at three o'clock." Freeman's voice left no room for argument. "I trust you have no conflict with that time."

"Uh, no, sir."

"Good. Don't cancel on me again."

Freeman disconnected before Dean could answer. He tossed the phone back on the seat, then pounded the dashboard with his fist. Dang! This was so messed up.

CHAPTER TWENTY

The rain stopped sometime during the night. Janice woke to a blue sky dotted with puffy white clouds. She pulled open her bedroom blinds, blinking at the sharpness of the clear morning. Everything had been washed clean overnight.

If only her conscience could be washed as clean as the trees dotting the landscape of her yard. Her conversation yesterday with Robin sat heavily on her mind like a muddy bog, smelly and noisome.

"Why won't you take the DNA test?" Robin had demanded.

She couldn't come up with a reasonable excuse. She and Robin had argued, resulting in angry words on both their parts.

Janice thought they'd gotten beyond that point in their relationship. She held her tongue over Robin's lack of discipline over Hannah. She never criticized Carlos for the long hours he worked. She didn't comment on the way they seemed to spend money like water to buy the latest gadgets. She always agreed to babysit, even if it meant disrupting her plans. Why couldn't Robin see?

After showering and readying herself for the day, she stepped into the kitchen, hoping to be alone. Some coffee was left in the pot, so she poured herself a cup and reached for the phone.

"Hello, Jan dear." Her friend Emma's voice, scratchy with age, greeted her cheerfully.

"I know we'll see each other at the Widows' Club, but I wondered if you could meet me there a little early. I need to talk to you about something." Janice's words rushed out in a single breath.

"Why don't you swing by and pick me up? We can talk in the car."

Janice glanced at the clock on the microwave. "I'm ready to go now. I can be there in twenty minutes."

Emma chuckled. "Must be very important. I'll be waiting."

Janice downed the lukewarm brew, then grabbed an apple from the fruit bowl on the counter. Since Jinxi'd come to stay with her, they always had an abundance of fresh fruit. The girl couldn't seem to get enough. Janice shook her head ruefully, thinking of Jinxi's slight frame. Yet she never seemed to gain a pound.

True to her word, Emma stood in the entry of the senior assisted-living facility, leaning on her cane. Janice pulled up to the covered portico, and Emma walked the few steps to the car.

"What's so important that it can't wait for the Widows' Club?" Emma asked, once she was settled in with seatbelt fastened.

Janice's knuckles showed white as she gripped the steering wheel. She inhaled, sending up a quick prayer for the right words.

"Robin wants me to take a DNA test," she said with a whoosh.

Emma tilted her head. "I don't understand. Maybe you'd better back up and start from the beginning."

Janice nodded. "Of course."

She started on the safe ground of Hannah's rheumatoid arthritis. "Remember how Hannah was diagnosed a couple

138

of months ago with RA? Robin wants to know if anyone else in the family has genetic markers for diseases of any kind."

"Sounds reasonable. I hear they're doing some wonderful things with genetic testing."

Mercy, this isn't going where I want it to go.

"The problem is"—Janice gulped in a breath as she pulled up to the coffee shop and jammed on the brakes, jerking her and Emma against the seat belts—"Robin's adopted."

There, she'd said it. The awful truth blasted past her lips like the fire of a jalapeno pepper, burning tongue and throat.

Emma stared out the windshield at the street without speaking. People passed by them, rushing in and out of shops in the strip mall. The only thing Janice was aware of was her own breathing, rasping in the small space of her car.

Emma turned, confusion in her rheumy eyes. "She doesn't know?"

Janice shook her head vigorously.

"Oh, my. That certainly creates a muddle, doesn't it?"

"Tom and I thought it best not to tell her the circumstances of her birth. At the time, it seemed a good idea. Now I'm confused."

"Is it so terrible to be adopted? These days, there isn't the stigma attached like it used to be in our day." Emma chuckled, "Well, in my day, certainly."

Janice laid her hand on Emma's arm. "You don't understand. Robin was conceived as a result of incest. Her father and her grandfather are the same man." The words dropped into the air between them, charged with dynamite. "He's in prison."

"My heavens," exclaimed Emma. She put her hand over Janice's. "And her mother? Birth mother," she corrected herself.

Janice shook her head. "Disappeared. I've tried to locate her, but it's like she took on a new identity. I'm sure she wants to forget the whole situation." What Janice didn't say was how she wanted to keep tabs on the woman, for fear she'd show up on Janice's doorstep one day, determined to meet her daughter. She couldn't let that happen.

"What are you going to do, Jan dear?"

Janice slumped back against the seat.

"I don't know." She'd prayed about what to do, but her prayers echoed back with loud silence.

Emma's look was full of sympathy. "You need to tell her the truth."

Janice shook her head. "What if she gets so angry with me, she won't let me see my grandchildren?" A sob rose in her throat.

"Child, you know the truth shall set you free."

"Yes, but—"

"Your daughter deserves to know the truth."

What Emma said was true, but Janice's heart refused to connect with her mind.

When she arrived home, the red light on the answering machine blinked impatiently. Janice put her purse in the bedroom and hung up her sweater, smoothing out the sleeves. She detoured down the dark hall to the kitchen to fix herself a cup of tea, and brooded over what Emma said as she waited for the microwave to heat up the water. Her mind traced every possible outcome in telling Robin about her birth, most of them ending in disaster.

She jumped at the microwave's beep. She absently dipped a tea bag in and out of the cup as she padded into the living room to listen to the voice message.

"Mom, it's me." Janice's stomach clenched at her daughter's strident voice. "Look, I know you don't want to do this DNA thing, which I can't figure out why not, but it's important to me. I'm dropping off the test tomorrow. If you won't do it for me, at least do it for Hannah and Owen."

Robin knew just which buttons to push. She'd been that way her whole life. Always bumping against the boundaries, kicking and screaming to get her way, arguing against anything she thought was unfair. Intensely jealous of anyone who might take Janice's attention, especially Dean, and now Jinxi.

Janice closed her eyes, but the prayers that used to come as easily as breathing now felt forced. Had she come this far in her Christian walk to now feel rudderless in a choppy ocean?

Life had been easier when Tom was alive. He'd been the spiritual head of the family. He'd made all the decisions. Nothing bad had touched their lives. Janice's biggest ordeal was keeping one step ahead of Robin.

Since Tom died, life was fraught with disaster. Especially since Jinxi had come to live with her. Dean had taken pity on the poor girl, feeding her breakfast, then bringing her home to shower and get cleaned up. Janice could never have foreseen the events that followed. Jinxi getting sick, Janice offering her a place to live, Jinxi's salvation. Then discovering Jinxi had stolen money, big money, from Janice's investment account.

Janice absently rubbed her arm, remembering how Jinxi had been the one to find her when she'd gotten bitten by at least one and maybe two black widow spiders. She might have died if Jinxi hadn't been there.

Hannah's juvenile RA had come out of nowhere. Then Dean's accident. Merciful heavens. She should never have prayed that prayer on the day Jinxi showed up on her doorstep. God, my life is too mundane.

"Be careful what you pray for," she said to herself.

Now to figure out what to do about Robin and that DNA test.

CHAPTER TWENTY-ONE

People lined up in the food bank cafeteria, waiting patiently for the steel windows to roll up. Jinxi peeked out the door, scanning the crowd for Burn Boy and his mother. She spotted them halfway down, wedged between the guy with no teeth wearing a Forty-Niners jersey and a skinny woman in a tank top. Meth head. Nobody wore a tank top in this weather.

Jinxi ducked back into the kitchen, wondering how she could avoid the mom and kid today. With a flash of genius, she turned to Connie.

"Hey, I'll be back in a few minutes. I need to, you know, check on Jared. Make sure he's doing what I told him." She held her breath, hoping Connie wouldn't question her.

"Bueno, chica. I finish up here."

Three volunteers pushed through the kitchen door and headed for the cupboard where aprons and hairnets were kept. Jinxi nodded at them before stepping into the cafeteria, and then left through the steel door leading into the storeroom.

Jared had stripped down to his undershirt. It was dark with sweat. The muscles on his skinny arms stood out as he heaved boxes of food from the pallets stacked on the floor.

"Hey."

He turned at the sound of her voice. "Well, well, if it ain't little Jeanette Xaviera."

Her mouth turned down at his use of her full name. "It's nice to see you working. Finally."

He threw back his head and laughed, the light glinting off his bald head.

"It's nice to see you. Period." He pulled a long-sleeved Tee shirt over his head, then lounged against one of the tables. He reached into the back pocket of his jeans and pulled out a pack of cigarettes.

"I told you," Jinxi said. "No smoking in here."

"Since when did you become a rule-follower?"

She glared at him without answering.

"C'mere," he demanded. When she didn't move, he slowly straightened up. "I said, come here." His tone was low, menacing.

Jinxi slowly advanced toward him, bracing herself for a blow.

"That's better," he said when she was two feet away. "Let's talk about our deal."

An icy finger of dread crept up her spine.

"I need you to do something for me."

"Wh-what?"

"There's this guy, he's coming in from LA. I need you to meet him and take a package from him."

"What kind of package?"

"Don't be stupid. What do you think? Come to my place Saturday night, nine o'clock. I'll let you in, then I'll disappear. You take the stuff, then I'll be back after he leaves. Got it?"

Jinxi nodded dumbly.

She flinched as he reached out and grabbed her chin. "Not a word to anyone." His smile reflected the evil in his eyes. "Or I'll tell everybody you killed a kid."

Jinxi nodded again, unable to speak. She turned toward the outer doors and stumbled into the alley on wooden legs.

Oh God, oh God, what am I going to do?

The alley offered privacy, not comfort. Stained brick and concrete made up the warehouses on either side. The long expanse of windowless buildings rose like prison walls. Trapped. Backed into a corner by her past. Would she ever escape what she'd done? Not likely. Not in this lifetime.

The forgiveness she'd experienced a few weeks ago in Janice's backyard couldn't possibly extend to murder. If there were levels of sin, she'd scored a perfect ten. God couldn't overlook something that big, and she doubted any of her new friends would either. If anyone found out, she'd probably lose her job and be back out on the street. Or forced to hook back up with Skeeter.

A guttural cry rose up from her belly and forced its way out her mouth. She had no choice. She'd do what Skeeter asked, then hope he'd leave her alone. Without exposing her secret.

Lunch was ending as she made her way back to the cafeteria. Her stomach roiled as she glanced around the room. Padish sat across from Skeeter, their heads bent together as they talked.

He wouldn't, would he?

Jinxi crossed her arms against her stomach, pressing on the nausea threatening to overwhelm. She looked around wildly, her gaze coming to rest on her knife case.

No one looked her way as she edged toward the counter, then slipped the case into the pouch on the front of her hoodie.

"I'll be right back," she called out to Connie as she slunk toward the main foyer and the safety of the restroom.

She hesitated for a moment before pulling the chef's knife from the case. The knife represented her future, her dream. Using it on her arm would defile it somehow. But what future did she have anyway? Dreams of becoming a chef? She'd forfeited any right to a bright future when she'd deliberately set the fire that stole the future from that little boy. God was punishing her for her sin. Didn't she read in the Bible, 'an eye for an eye'?

She'd do what Skeeter demanded and continue to hold her secret close. She didn't deserve any better.

The knife slid easily across her bare skin. Blood quickly filled the cut, a red reservoir of pent-up emotions, finally released from the deep places inside.

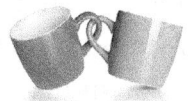

"Padish wants to have a staff meeting at four o'clock," Aneesa announced. Jinxi and Connie were finishing up the kitchen cleaning, while Hank swept the cafeteria in slow, measured movements. Skeeter had already left, fulfilling his daily six hours of required community service.

"Sí, senorita," responded Connie as Aneesa strode back to the front office, curls bouncing in rhythm.

Jinxi looked at Connie. "What's up?"

Connie shrugged, then smiled. "Maybe we all get a raise, no?"

Jinxi snorted. "Not likely. Better get ready for more work." She slung a towel over her shoulder.

At four o'clock, they gathered in the cafeteria. Jinxi, Hank, and Connie sat together on one of the benches as Padish paced in front of them. Gone was his customary smile. His face was grim as he began to speak.

"My friends, we have a serious problem."

Jinxi's heart thundered in her chest. Did Skeeter break his word and say something to Padish? Would his next words be, 'we have a murderer in our midst'? She leaned forward, resting her arms on her thighs, dizzy with fear.

"A few days ago, some money was missing from the office. As you know, Aneesa and I lock the door when we leave, not only to protect the food bank's valuables, but also to protect the privacy of our donors and volunteers."

Missing money. Jinxi drew in a ragged breath. This had nothing to do with her.

"Either Aneesa or I neglected to latch the door properly one day last week. She was called away to an emergency with one of our recipients while preparing a cash deposit. When Aneesa returned, the money was gone."

There was a collective intake of breath from all of them. Everyone knew the food bank operated on a tight budget. Every dollar, every cent counted.

Padish continued. "I wish to talk to each of you privately to see if you have any ideas about the missing money." He frowned, his eyes filled with sadness. "If any of you needed the money for something, this would be the time to say. You have my word I won't involve the authorities."

Jinxi looked at Connie, then at Hank. Surely her two work friends wouldn't have stolen from Padish.

"Miss Jinxi, I will start with you." Padish gestured that she should follow him to the office.

She wracked her brain as she followed his stiff back. Had she seen anyone sneaking around the office? Before she could make sense of everything, she was sitting in a hard chair across from Padish's desk.

He steepled his fingers in front of his face, staring into her eyes. "Is there anything you want to tell me?" he asked softly.

Jinxi pursed her lips and shook her head.

His sigh was deep and seemed to fill the room with sadness. "Someone saw you exiting the office on the day the money went missing."

Padish's words dropped like a boulder into a lake of lava. Hot waves splashed over Jinxi as she realized the intent of his words.

"I—I—" Shocked to her core, she couldn't form a complete sentence. As reality settled in, her heart hardened. Of course they suspected her. Why wouldn't they? Should she even try to defend herself?

"I didn't take the money." Her words, flat as a slab of concrete, fell between them.

Padish's silence spoke volumes.

"I didn't take the money." Her voice rose in pitch and intensity.

"Can you explain to me why you were in this office?"

Jinxi stared down, absently noting the stained carpet beneath her boots. How many losers had sat in this same chair, pinned by Padish's words?

"I was looking for Aneesa, and the door was unlocked." Her words tumbled out, spinning like a combination lock. "I went in, expecting to see her, but, like, no one was in the office. It was weird the door was unlocked. So I left." She remembered running into Burn Boy. Was he the snitch that had ratted her out?

"Did you see the money on the desk?" Padish probed.

Jinxi forced her mind back to that day, trying to picture Aneesa's desk. Was the deposit there or not? What did it matter anyway? They'd always suspect her. She was the strange one, the outcast. The murderer.

"I can't remember."

Jinxi dragged herself home from the bus stop on aching legs. Padish's unspoken accusation left her feeling physically pummeled. Just as she thought her life was on a good track, moving toward a brighter future, everything seemed to crumble. Burn Boy showed up at the food bank, reminding her of her past. Aneesa had probably gotten a good look at the newspaper article and was suspicious. Then Skeeter showed up unexpectedly in her life, forcing her to do something illegal. Again. Now her boss thought she'd stolen money from him. How much worse could it get? At least Dean didn't remember about the money she'd taken from his mom.

How ironic that she'd be accused of doing something she didn't do, after being forgiven for doing the very same thing to Janice.

Ted jumped up from his spot on the porch and greeted her with a woof. His curly tail swung crazily as he expressed his excitement at seeing her.

"Good boy, Teddie, good boy. Let's get you a treat." The bright spot in her otherwise miserable day.

Jinxi circled around to the back of the house. She entered through the back door, hoping to avoid Janice, who would be either in her bedroom or the living room. She pulled out the package of dog biscuits and shoved two in her sweatshirt pocket.

"That you?" Janice called from the living room.

Jinxi peeked around the corner of the stairwell. Janice had the news on the television, the sound muted. "Yeah, it's me. I'm sick, so I'm not cooking."

She turned toward the stairs, Ted at her heels.

"I'm sorry to hear you're not feeling well. Is there anything I can get you?"

"No," Jinxi called over her shoulder. No way did she want to get into a discussion. She hurried up the stairs, boots clomping. At the top, she turned right down the hall toward what she now called her bedroom. It used to be Robin's when she lived at home. Jinxi had added some of her own things, gradually pushing aside Robin's personality.

She slung her backpack onto the bed, then sank down next to it. She smiled to herself grimly, remembering how she used to pack up all of her things every morning when she left for work. It was a habit born of bouncing from place to place with Skeeter, always one step ahead of the police. Now her backpack was lighter to carry. She hoped she wouldn't have to return to the constant worry of where she'd be the next day. If she got fired over the money thing, no one would believe she didn't steal it. Even Janice would suspect her, and with good reason. She was sunk.

Ted nudged her hand, impatient for his treat.

"Sit. Sit."

He sank to his back haunches, barely resting on the floor. His body shook with excitement. Jinxi tossed one of the biscuits and he caught it in the air. "Good boy." She held out her hand, giving him the second treat, already tired of the game.

Jinxi pulled her boots off, then lay down on the bed without bothering to get undressed. She pulled a soft throw over her legs, curling into a ball. Hot tears formed behind her eyes, but she bit her lip until they were forced back.

What should she do? Thoughts spiraled down into a dark place where doubt and fear turned rancid and sour. How could she go back to work? Everyone would suspect her since she was the only one seen coming out of the unlocked office.

If she didn't go to work, Skeeter would tell everyone who she really was. Then for sure they'd believe she'd taken the money. She'd lose her job, and Janice would kick her out. She'd be back on the street, hustling for money. Or she'd be forced to go back and be Skeeter's delivery girl. She'd probably end up in jail. Again. Her life was one big hot mess.

Every word her mother had said came back.

"Your dad wouldn't have left me if I hadn't gotten pregnant with you."

"My life would be easier without you to take care of. You're my burden to bear."

"You were a mistake. You shouldn't have been born."

You shouldn't have been born.

Words assaulted her, male and female voices.

Worthless, scarred, broken.

Dirty, stupid.

Hopeless.

CHAPTER TWENTY-TWO

Jinxi heard the steady thud of someone coming up the stairs. She recognized Janice's tread but didn't turn when Janice reached the open door of the bedroom. The bed sagged as Janice sat on the corner.

"How are you feeling?" Her voice was soft, motherly with concern.

Jinxi shrugged, still curled into the fetal position.

Janice patted her on the leg.

"I remember when you first showed up here. When I saw you step out of Dean's truck, I wondered who that strange child was he was bringing home. He's always had a soft spot for people in trouble. In high school, he'd bring home friends whose parents kicked them out of the house. They'd stay for a few days, and then Tom would drag them back to their homes and have a talk with their parents. He was good like that."

Jinxi shifted on the bed. Janice's voice took on a faraway quality. "But you were like my daddy's winter garden, surrounded by a barbed wire fence. He built that fence to keep the cows from eating all our produce. They seemed to know what was in the garden was better than their feed, just like I knew there was something good inside you, behind all the prickliness."

Without knowing how it happened, Jinxi was in Janice's arms, holding her like a drowning child. Jinxi's tears, held in for too long, wet Janice's blouse.

"Want to talk about it?" Janice asked, rocking Jinxi back and forth like a mother with a fretful baby.

Jinxi shook her head against Janice's shoulder. It was enough to be comforted, even for a moment. If she started to tell the depths of her shame, she wouldn't be able to stop. Janice's comfort would be replaced by revulsion.

She pushed away before Janice could reject her.

Janice's forehead crinkled with concern. "Is there anything I can do?"

Jinxi shook her head as she used her sleeve to wipe her nose. "No. I have to figure it out."

"Goodness gracious. Everyone needs some help now and then. Are you sure?"

Jinxi didn't answer. She'd already swung her legs over the side of the bed and was heading for the bathroom for a tissue.

The mood was somber the next day at the food bank, as if the fog rolling in from the delta had permeated the walls, obscuring the light. Aneesa looked up as Jinxi entered the office to sign in, but her eyes skittered away. Dread settled heavy in Jinxi's stomach. Would this be the day she got fired?

Jinxi followed the aroma of frying onions and garlic to the kitchen. Connie stood on a low stool in front of the stove, stirring a concoction of what looked like the beginning of her famous enchiladas.

Connie saw her and pointed toward the counter. "Hand me the salsa, por favor."

Jinxi complied, using both hands to carry the industrial-size container. She leaned a hip against one of the counters, watching.

"How are you today, chica?" Connie asked.

"Okay, I guess."

"I not talk to you after our meeting yesterday."

Jinxi didn't know what to say. She stared down at the gold-flecked linoleum.

Connie set the spoon on a plate and turned toward Jinxi. "You still come to my house tomorrow, sí?"

Jinxi's head shot up. "You still want me to?" They'd planned to make tamales at Connie's apartment. Her husband was taking Miguel and Rosa to visit his sister, so they'd have the place to themselves. Tamale-making was an all-day process.

"Of course. Why not?" Connie's confusion seemed real. Maybe Padish was the only one who suspected her of stealing the money. "Come early. I make a special cake for us." She gave Jinxi a quick hug before returning to the bubbling mixture on the stove.

Jinxi's step was light as she headed for the storeroom to see what needed to be done that day. Her relief lasted only as long as it took to see Skeeter. The big metal doors were rolled up, and he stood outside in the alley talking to the driver of a delivery truck. They passed a cigarette back and forth, deep in conversation.

Jinxi had seen the driver before and avoided him. His belly hung over the waistband of his dirty jeans. He always leered at her when she told him where to unload the pallets of canned and dry food. What could he and Skeeter be talking about?

The door clanked behind her, and they both swung their gaze toward her. Skeeter threw the cigarette down and crushed it under his boot. He clapped the other man on his shoulder, then turned and headed toward her.

"'Sup?" he greeted her, with a toss of his head. His hands shook as he rubbed his scalp, fiddled with one of his ear gauges, then adjusted the waist of his jeans. He hadn't exhibited any of the symptoms of his ADHD since he'd been at the food bank, until today. His constant movements had inspired his mom to christen him with his nickname, Skeeter. She said he always buzzed around like a mosquito. Had he been taking his meds?

Her eyes narrowed with suspicion. "What were you talking to him about?" She indicated the departing truck with a wave of her hand as they went inside the building.

"None of your business." Skeeter shrugged out of his jacket, tossing it onto a shelf behind him. "The thing Saturday night is off."

"Off. What do you mean?" Relief flooded her, only to be replaced by dread a moment later.

Skeeter shrugged. "It's postponed, so to speak. But don't think you're off the hook. I'll let you know when it's going down." He put his hands in his back pockets and grinned. "But you could still come over Saturday night. Keep me company and all."

Jinxi stared at him in revulsion. How could she have ever thought she loved him? Her mind flicked to Dean. So different, so … clean. He would protect her, not blackmail her into doing something illegal.

"I'm busy." Her response was curt.

Skeeter's face darkened. "Don't forget. If you flake out on me, I'll tell everyone what you done."

"Unload the boxes," she told him, her voice quavering. She turned to head into the other storeroom and nearly bowled into Hank. How long had he been standing there? How much of their conversation had he heard?

He stepped aside to let her pass. "Everything ok-k-kay, Miss J-jinxi?"

"Fine," she muttered, pushing past him.

She stomped into the big storeroom, letting the door slam behind her. Her fingers dug into her pocket, seeking the comfort of nicotine. Oh, snap. Why did she ever quit smoking?

What was she going to do? How could she keep Skeeter quiet, even after she did what he asked? He was mean enough to tell her secret, just to stir up trouble.

Trust me.

The words dropped into her spirit. How could she trust someone she couldn't see? She'd always trusted in her ability to survive, no matter what happened to her. She'd managed pretty good on her own so far.

She'd survived the neglect of her mother, school bullies, her mother's boyfriends, juvenile hall, and Skeeter's abuse. She'd even made it through a night in jail, courtesy of Sac PD's finest undercover cops.

Of course, if she hadn't been arrested, she'd never have met Dean. Or Janice. Or God. Funny how things happen. Maybe God did know what was best for her. But why, oh why, did Skeeter have to come back into her life?

CHAPTER TWENTY-THREE

The sound of a dog barking drove Dean from the comfort of sleep. He pulled a pillow over his head, which did nothing to muffle the noise. It sounded like it was right outside his door. With a groan, he rolled off the futon and onto his feet. He grabbed for the end table to steady himself before shuffling to the door of his upstairs apartment.

He barely cracked open the door when it was forced against his hand. Ted pushed his way into the room. His coat was soaked, drops of water glittering like opals on his back. He shook himself before Dean could shout, "No!" Water sprayed across Dean's bare legs. He lunged for the dog to stop a second wave of drenching. Dragging Ted into the bathroom with one hand, he used the other to grab a bath towel from the rod and wrapped it around the shivering dog.

"How'd you get stuck outside in the rain, buddy?" he asked, vigorously rubbing the wet fur. "Where is everybody?"

He glanced at his watch. It was later than he thought. He'd lain awake half the night, tossing and turning, wrestling with his circumstances. He'd fallen asleep sometime after three a.m.

His mind shot to the upcoming interview with Freeman. His head ached with the thought of another grilling from IA.

Dean pulled a blanket off his bed and threw it on the floor in front of the furnace. "Lie down, Ted," he commanded, surprised when the dog obeyed.

First coffee. Then food. As the coffee pot gurgled, he threw two pieces of bread into the toaster and shoved down the plunger. The coffeemaker beeped just as the toast popped. He spread peanut butter on the toast, then searched for a clean mug. Finding none, he grabbed one out of the sink and rinsed it. He poured himself a cup of the brew, thinking about what to say to Freeman. He had three hours to come up with something.

The interview started much the same as the first one. Dean sat stiffly on his mother's sofa, while Freeman and his partner arranged themselves on the two chairs at either end. Dean's head swiveled from side to side as he glanced first at Freeman, then at the other man, unsure of where to address his answers.

"Do you waive your right to have your union representative in attendance?" Freeman asked.

Dean nodded. There wasn't much she could do to protect him from what was to come.

"Please answer verbally."

"Yes." Dean's hands clenched into fists between his knees.

"Let's go back and talk about the night of October 22, 2021."

"I already told you what happened," snapped Dean. Hammers pounded behind his eyes.

Freeman's voice dripped with condescension. "Humor me. Pretend I have short-term memory loss."

The other man snorted.

"Fine," Dean said, turning his attention back to Freeman. "My partner Raul Hernandez and I were headed back to the station after our last call. Our shift ended. A 415-F call came over the radio. We were within two miles of the incident, so I responded."

"Who was driving?" Freeman interrupted.

"My partner—"

"Officer Hernandez?"

"Yes. He drove and I—"

"What time was that?"

"Uh, I think it was around one-thirty." He squeezed his eyes shut, trying to picture the computer screen mounted on the dash. "Our shift—"

Freeman seemed determined to pick away at Dean's concentration. "Your shift ended at midnight."

Before Dean could continue, Freeman sucked all the air out of the room with his next question. "Why didn't you report your partner's drug use?"

The question hung between them like a hawk circling its prey. What should he say?

Raul's words came back to him. You have to have my back, bro. And the note on the back of the traffic citation. Watch your back, amigo.

The grandfather clock's rhythmic cadence calmed Dean's agitated spirit. He thought of his dad and knew without a doubt what he needed to do. He rubbed the back of his neck as he began.

"Raul and I had been partners for just a few weeks before the incident. Before that night, I'd never seen him use any illegal substance—"

"But that night?" Freeman leaned forward in his chair.

Sweat broke out on Dean's upper lip. He swiped it away with the back of his hand. "As we drove to the 415, Raul, took something from his pocket and put it in his mouth."

"Did he offer you any?"

Dean nodded. "He said it was something to keep him awake."

"Have you ever used drugs?"

"No." Dean exploded. "Never." He shot to his feet, fists clenched.

"Sit down, Officer Rafferty."

Dean blew out a breath, then sank onto the couch, head down. When the silence lengthened, he looked up to find both men staring at him.

"What?"

"Are you willing to take a drug test?" Freeman asked, a sly smile on his face.

"Of course. I have nothing to hide." As soon as the words left his mouth, he remembered the pain meds he'd been taking for the headaches. Would they show up in his urine? Would he be able to explain them? A granite slab settled into his gut. *My career is over.*

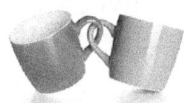

Dean slouched on his mother's sofa long after the men were gone. He clutched the card for the drug testing facility with numb fingers. His thoughts spiraled down into darkness. He should never have gotten transferred to patrol duty. He should have been content to work in the jail for the rest of his career. No one would believe he wasn't a druggie. His friends would abandon him, and he'd be fired from the police force. He'd have to try to find a job as a rent-a-cop in a mall.

Then there was that girl. Katie. If it turned out her kid was his, he'd never be able to pay child support without a job. He'd lose his driver's license. Probably go to jail. Everything he took for granted would disappear.

Loser.

The walls of the living room seemed to close around him, tamping down on his lungs. He sprang up from the sofa and grabbed his phone off the coffee table. Jabbing in a number, his foot tapped impatiently while he waited for the call to be answered.

"Big D!" Damaris's voice boomed.

"Hey. I gotta get out of here. You up for some pool?"

"I'm just finishing my shift. Meet me in thirty, and you're on. Bring your wallet, loser."

Dean's teeth ground together at Damaris's jibe. Loser. He was referring to their last pool game when Dean went down in flames. But the jab struck home. If he wasn't a loser now, he was about to become one.

CHAPTER TWENTY-FOUR

The autumn sky faded from blue to gray to purple as Jinxi trudged from the bus stop toward Janice's house. Her feet hurt from standing all day in Connie's kitchen. They'd prepared over fifty tamales.

Jinxi had arrived at Connie's apartment as Natividad was herding Miguel and Rosa out the door. The children greeted her with a hug, chirping excitedly about their upcoming visit with their cousins. Like a gust of wind, they swept out, led by their father.

"I didn't know if you would come," Connie said, handing Jinxi an apron.

Jinxi shrugged. "Why wouldn't I?"

Connie's shrug mirrored Jinxi's as she turned toward the sink where the corn husks soaked in cold water.

"Come. Let us enjoy some coffee before we begin." Connie poured two cups of coffee into mismatched mugs, dumping a liberal amount of sugar in her own.

Jinxi grimaced as Connie laughed. "I not know how you drink it so," she commented, handing Jinxi's black coffee to her. "Go, sit. I bring some cake."

When they'd eaten their fill of Connie's special chocolate cake, they worked in silent rhythm, mixing the masa for the outside of the tamales in two large bowls. While Jinxi spread the masa mixture into the corn husks, Connie stirred the savory meat and sauce that would fill the tamales. She watched a moment or two in silence at Jinxi's attempts.

"Remember to spread it evenly, chica," Connie admonished. "Like this." Connie's nimble brown fingers were faster than Jinxi's.

Jinxi groaned in frustration. "I'll never get it right." She bit her bottom lip, moving the stud around with her tongue.

Connie laughed. "You are getting it. Do not worry." Connie bumped Jinxi good-naturedly. "Remember when you first came to the food bank? You were like a little frightened pájaro. Now you are cooking as good as me."

Jinxi rolled her eyes. "I'll never be as good as you."

"No, chica, I think you are wrong. When Norma went back to the drugs, and Padish invite you to stay after your community service, he do a good thing. He see something in you."

Jinxi' face grew warm. "Thanks," she mumbled. "But what's a pájaro?"

Connie laughed and pointed to the kitchen window. A tiny bird sat on the fence, its bright yellow feathers in stark contrast to the dull gray fence.

They went back to work, filling the husks with the spicy meat.

"You never told me how you come to Sacramento," Connie said.

Jinxi's hands froze. How much could she tell her only friend, not counting Dean, of course? Should she tell Connie about her life with Skeeter, hopping from motel to campground to dumpy apartments? How they tried to stay one step ahead of the police, until Skeeter's luck ran out and he was busted for possession? Connie knew Jinxi had been arrested and had to work forty hours of community service at the food bank. She'd never asked why, and Jinxi had never told her.

"I, um, needed a change of scenery, so I left Bakersfield and came here."

"You have family in Bakersfield?"

"Yeah. My mom." And her creepy boyfriend.

"And your papa?"

"I don't really, like, know where he is. He left when I was little." Her last memory of him was him crouching down to wipe the tears from her face. I'll be back, Princess, he'd said. But he never came back.

Connie clicked her tongue. "That is not good. A little girl need her papa." Her fingers deftly filled a corn husk with meat, wrapping it like a burrito. As she set it aside and reached for another, she said, "And God provide you with a new family. Señora Rafferty, Dean, and all us."

Family. The word was both comfort and fear, wrapped together as tightly as Connie's tamales.

"Could I ask you something?" Jinxi ventured. Her stomach twisted, anxious to hear the answer.

"Of course, chica." Connie's nimble fingers worked the masa mixture into perfect amounts inside the corn husks.

"Do you think I stole the money?" Jinxi held her breath.

Connie's hands stilled. She turned her head and met Jinxi's gaze. "No. I do not."

Jinxi exhaled, her breath caught halfway in a sob. "Everyone else thinks so."

"No, chica. They do not. Mr. Padish wants to find the truth. That is all."

"But it looks like I took it. I was in the unlocked office."

Connie scraped the corn mixture off her fingers, then touched Jinxi's sleeve. "You would not do such a thing. I saw you give money when you did not know I saw. You have a good heart, chica."

Jinxi's face grew warm again. A few times when they'd run out of food before the end of the line, she'd slipped a ten-dollar bill into a mother's grateful hand. Against the rules, but she did it anyway. Jinxi knew what it was like to be hungry and cold. She couldn't imagine what it would be like to have a kid to feed too.

Janice's house loomed in the twilight as Jinxi neared the chain link fence surrounding the yard. Only one light shone through the living room windows, but it was enough to guide her to the safety of its walls. The gate clanked behind her, and she turned to make sure it closed all the way. It wouldn't do for Ted to escape the yard. He'd gotten out once before. She'd chased him several blocks before catching him, dragging him back by his collar. She'd arrived at the house winded, shaking to think he could have been hit by a car.

His familiar woof didn't greet her as she climbed the porch steps. She unlocked the front door and pushed it open, dropping her backpack onto the piano bench.

"Anybody home?" she called. The silence was broken only by the ticking of the grandfather clock. Where was Janice?

Shrugging, she grabbed her backpack and trudged up the stairs, anxious to take off her boots. She returned downstairs in pajama pants and thick socks, heading straight for the kitchen for a snack.

The pantry yielded a sleeve of Oreo cookies. She looked longingly at the coffee maker. If she made a pot of coffee, she'd only have to clean it afterward so it would be ready for the next morning. Too much effort. She settled for a cup of instant hot cocoa. She grabbed her favorite mug from the bottom shelf, filled it with water, and put it in the microwave.

While it heated, she headed down the short hall and around the corner to Janice's office and craft room. The computer started up soundlessly, the desktop waiting for her fingers. She returned to the kitchen to retrieve the hot cocoa, then back to the desk to look for some new recipes.

Jinxi paused in her search to sip some of the hot liquid. Her gaze dropped to the bottom drawer of the desk, the one containing Janice's household files. It was cracked open several inches. She sat up straight in the chair, fingers twitching around the mug.

The *tick-tock tick-tock* of the grandfather clock echoed through the silence. Should she? What would it hurt, just to have a little peek. She edged the drawer open a little further with her stocking foot. The chair rollers squeaked as she pushed back from the desk to look down.

It wasn't going to work. The files were all labeled, but unreadable from her seat. She set the mug on the desk, then leaned over to look.

Appliances. Birth certificates. Car information.

What a minute. Birth certificates? This should be interesting. She'd just take a quick look at how much Dean weighed when he was born. He was such a big guy, he must have been a huge baby.

She pulled the file out, set it on the desk and began to read. Dean Michael Rafferty. Born March 19, 1988. This couldn't be right. Six pounds seven ounces? No way. She shook her head in disbelief. The certificate listed Tom and Janice's full names as well as their occupations.

She flipped it over to the other side of the folder and glanced at Robin's birth certificate. Robin Grace McCloud.

What? Why wasn't her last name the same as Dean's? And why weren't Janice and Tom listed as her parents? She quickly set it down and read through Brian's information. Sure enough, his last name was Rafferty, and the listing for his parents mirrored Dean's.

Intent on the mystery before her, Jinxi jumped at Robin's voice.

"What are you doing?"

Jinxi started, dropping the certificate from electric-charged fingers.

"Were you snooping in my mom's desk?" Robin's voice, more strident than usual, was incredulous.

Before Jinxi could answer, Robin snatched the file folder and the three birth certificates off the desk, eyeing the certificate on top. Jinxi watched as myriad emotions played over Robin's face. The skin across her cheeks grew taut, and her freckles stood out in relief. Her hand shook as she waved the paper in front of Jinxi.

"Where did you get this?"

"In the desk." Jinxi's heart thundered against her rib cage.

A voice called out from the kitchen. "Hello, I'm home. Did I see Robin's car out front?" Janice came around the corner and skidded to a halt outside the office door. "Hi, sweetie. What are you doing here?"

Robin turned, her face a mask of fury. "I'm adopted?"

Janice's neck suffused with color. Jinxi wanted to crawl under the desk and hide. She'd seen too much confrontation in her life. Situations like this ended up coming to blows after a lot of shouting.

"Come into the living room and let's talk about it." Janice did her best to soothe Robin's wrath. She turned and headed into the living room, Robin following.

Jinxi got up too, hoping to sneak upstairs when they weren't looking.

"Don't think you're getting out of this," Robin said, grabbing Jinxi and pulling her down the hall. "This is all your fault."

Her fault? Jinxi wasn't the one who never told her daughter she was adopted. That should have been a conversation between her and Janice a long time ago. Now she was to blame? It figured. Jinxi slumped onto the piano bench, hoping to fly under the radar.

"How could you not tell me I was adopted?" Robin's words were sharp blades hurled toward Janice. "All these years ... all this time. What were you thinking?"

Janice tried to speak, but Robin continued to rant. "Did you ever think how I would feel? Did you consider me at all?" Robin paced pack and forth in front of her mother. "How could you—"

"Robin, sit down. Let me explain." Janice sank into her favorite chair. Robin sat stiffly on the edge of the sofa, legs bouncing. Her face was red and splotchy.

Janice took a deep breath. "First of all, you're right. I should have told you a long time ago. Your father and I made the decision not to tell you the circumstances of your birth because we didn't want to upset you."

"By that, you mean you didn't want to answer any questions I might have."

"Yes."

"So who are these people on my birth certificate, anyway? And why did they give me away?"

Janice took a deep breath and told her a story that shocked even Jinxi.

CHAPTER TWENTY-FIVE

Sunlight forced its way through the wood blinds in Janice's bedroom. It would be a perfect Indian summer day in Sacramento—a crisp, cool morning followed by warm afternoon temperatures. As the leaves on the trees turned from green to gold and red, they belied the change of seasons.

Janice lay on her back, the sun warming the top of her head. Too bad she wouldn't be appreciating the beautiful day. She rubbed her sandpaper eyes, dry and itchy after a sleepless night.

The confrontation with Robin had ended with her daughter storming out of the house, hand clutching the accusing birth certificate. Jinxi had slid out of the room like a vapor. Janice didn't blame her. She'd rather have been anywhere else too.

She supposed she should be angry with Jinxi for forcing the issue out in the open. But it was bound to happen sometime, so she couldn't really blame the girl. After her conversation with Emma, it seemed God wanted her to tell the truth to Robin, so much so that he made it impossible for her to keep silent.

Janice exhaled, wincing at the soreness in her lungs from sobbing into her pillow during the night. For the millionth time, she wished Tom were here. He'd been her rock, always knowing what to do in every situation. He'd had a better relationship with Robin, anyway. It seemed she and Robin had always fought for alpha female status. After Robin went away to college, then got married, their relationship slipped into a rhythm. Robin demanded, Janice complied. It was easier that way.

Robin's anger had turned to hysteria. Janice cringed, remembering some of the things her daughter had said to her. How difficult it had been to say Robin's birth father was in prison for sexual abuse of his daughter that spanned years, and that Robin was the result of that abuse. How painful it had been to tell Robin her birth mother had disappeared after he went to prison.

Janice's heart ached over having to explain all that to her beautiful, headstrong daughter. She was a fool for not telling Robin when she was young, so she could grow into the truth and gradually accept it. Merciful heavens, what was she going to do?

She dragged herself out of bed and slipped on a robe. She padded out to the kitchen in her slippers, tying the robe around her waist. Jinxi sat at the kitchen table, sipping a cup of coffee. She looked up as Janice entered.

"You look like heck," Jinxi commented.

The edges of Janice's mouth turned up. "Good morning to you, too." She pulled a mug down from the cupboard and poured herself a cup of coffee.

"Sorry," Jinxi mumbled.

Janice sank down onto the other wooden chair after adding cream and sugar to her mug. "I don't think I slept at all last night."

Jinxi's eyebrows flicked upward. "No doubt."

"I'm sorry you had to witness that. It got way too ugly."

Jinxi raised a shoulder. "I'm totally sorry. It was my fault she saw her birth certificate."

Janice shook her head. "It was bound to happen sooner or later." She stirred her coffee absently. "I should have told her a long time ago."

"She didn't know anything?"

Janice shook her head.

"Her dad is really ... her grandfather?"

Janice nodded.

"That's messed up."

"I'm not going to church today," Janice announced, anxious to change the subject. "But if you want to take my car and go by yourself, that's fine with me."

"That's cool. I don't really feel much like going either."

Janice watched her over the rim of her mug. What was going on with Jinxi? Ever since her decision to give her life to Christ, she'd been a regular attendee at church.

"Want me to make us some breakfast?" Janice offered.

Jinxi's smile lit up her face. "You better let me do it. If you feel like you look, who knows what your cooking will taste like?" She scooted her chair back from the table and walked to the fridge.

Janice watched her pull ingredients and set them on the counter. Jinxi reached for bowls, utensils, and pans, perfectly at home in Janice's kitchen. Janice sat back, sipped her coffee, and thanked God for the transformation in Jinxi from a scared, pointy-edged girl to a confident young woman in the span of a few months.

"How's everything at the food bank?"

"It's good."

Janice continued to probe. "How's Padish? And Aneesa?"

"Fine."

"Looks like you and Connie made another batch of tamales."

"Uh-huh."

Jinxi beat some eggs with a fork, then tore a tortilla into strips and pushed it down into the egg mixture. She added some shredded cheese, then moved to the stove to heat up a frying pan.

Janice pursed her lips in frustration. How to get the girl to open up? Something was going on. Especially since she'd cried on Janice's shoulder a few nights ago. That had never happened before.

She tried another tack. "Now you know my deepest, darkest secret."

Jinxi glanced at her over her shoulder, then turned back to the stove. "Yeah, I guess."

Goodness. This wasn't going well at all.

"Well, now that you know my secret, maybe you should tell me yours."

Jinxi's shoulders stiffened. "What?"

"Why don't you tell me what's bothering you? Did something happen at work?" Janice's eyes focused laser-like on Jinxi's form. The room was silent except for the sound of the spatula scraping the frying pan.

Jinxi's shoulders sagged. She didn't turn as she spoke. "It's no big deal. Some money went missing from the office and everyone was, like, questioned."

"If it's no big deal, why were you crying?" Janice probed.

"Padish thinks I stole it. Someone saw me leaving the office. A little kid."

Janice's mind flashed to her missing earrings. "Remember when my earrings disappeared? And Dean thought you took them?"

Jinxi nodded.

"Remember how it was really Hannah playing Pirates' Treasure? She put them in your nightstand."

"So what?" A shrug.

"Sometimes perception has little to do with reality. I'm sure they'll find the real culprit," Janice said, sipping her rapidly cooling coffee.

Jinxi dumped the egg mixture onto two plates.

"Whatever." She set the plates down on the table, then brought the coffee pot over and refilled both their cups. Her hand shook as she poured Janice's coffee.

They ate their breakfast in silence. Janice brooded over Jinxi's situation, grateful to not think about Robin for a little while. Maybe she'd ask Dean if he could help. He wanted to be a detective someday. Maybe he could do a little investigating into the theft. Why, that would be just the thing to keep him occupied until he could return to work.

Janice breathed into her mug. Dean would get to the bottom of this. Now, if someone could fix the situation with Robin, her life could go back to normal.

CHAPTER TWENTY-SIX

Insistent knocking drove Dean from dreamless sleep. Someone was banging on his front door. Sheesh, can't a guy get some sleep? Yesterday, Ted. Today, who knows? He rubbed the sleep from his face with both hands before rolling over and climbing out of bed. Ted was already at the door, curly tail wagging like a flag in a ninety-mile-an-hour wind.

Dean yanked open the door to find Jinxi standing at the top of the steps.

"What?" he demanded.

Her smile was tentative. "Hey. Thought you might like some company."

"What time is it?"

"I dunno. Maybe ten?"

"Aren't you supposed to be in church?" He didn't budge from the doorway.

Jinxi crossed her arms and frowned. "Open the door and let me in. Maybe I'll tell you why I'm not."

"Fine." Dean flung open the door and stepped aside. Jinxi stepped over the threshold and wrinkled her nose.

"Your place is a mess."

Dean shut the door with more force than was necessary.

"Maybe I like it like this." He glanced around at the empty fast-food wrappers dotting the counters. A pizza box stood open on the coffee table with a lone piece of pizza still in it. Dirty dishes filled the sink.

"Whatever." She leaned down to pet Ted, who had finished his sniffed inspection of her jeans. "Traitor," she told him. "You're supposed to sleep in my room."

Dean smiled for the first time. "He's more at home in the man cave." He sat on one of the stools in front of the bar. "What's up?"

"It's a long story." Jinxi sank onto the other stool.

"Why don't you put on some coffee, and I'll jump in the shower." He stood and headed to the bathroom, then backed up, gathered up clean clothes, and returned to the bathroom.

Jinxi stood as she heard the shower. She grimaced as she dumped yesterday's coffee grounds into the overflowing garbage can. This was way too reminiscent of her childhood. After filling the pot with fresh water and pressing the ON button, she cleared a spot on the counter. She laid a clean dish towel on the counter, then squirted dish soap over the dishes in the sink and filled it with hot water, grinning when she heard Dean's yell from the bathroom as his shower ran cold.

As she scrubbed, she thought about her conversation with Janice over breakfast. What had possessed her to tell Janice about the money? How could Janice not suspect her, especially after Jinxi had taken money from Janice's investment account? Once a thief, always a thief. Would she have taken the money from Aneesa's desk if she'd had the chance? She wasn't sure about herself anymore. At one time, she wouldn't have hesitated to snag it. But since her experience with God, well, things had changed. She'd changed.

Dean emerged from the bathroom as she finished drying the last of the dishes.

"You didn't have to do that," he said, dumping his dirty clothes in the closet and closing the closet door.

"You need to empty your trash." Jinxi flung the dishtowel over the faucet and pulled two clean mugs toward the coffee pot. She filled both of them, leaving enough room for Dean's milk and sugar. "Here." She shoved the mug across the bar toward him, followed by the carton of milk and two sugar packets.

Dean sniffed the milk before pouring a liberal amount into his coffee. "Thanks."

"No problem." Jinxi leaned back against the counter and raised her mug to her lips.

"So why aren't you in church?"

Jinxi squirmed under what Jinxi called his 'cop look.'

"Well, your mom wasn't feeling well, so I stayed home with her." It was only a tiny lie, after all.

"What's wrong with my mom?"

Jinxi pulled the stud against her teeth and clicked it back and forth. "She isn't really, like, sick or anything. She didn't sleep very good."

"So? That's never kept her from going to church before." He set his mug down, looking at her with laser-like focus.

"Did you know your sister is adopted?" The words flew out of her mouth before she could stop them. Deep inside, the urge to hurt Robin for all the times she'd been snubbed, for every rude comment, or every time she'd pulled Hannah away from her, had festered into an open sore. If telling Dean would stir up trouble for Robin, she was ready to start the battle.

Dean nearly spewed out a mouthful of coffee. "Robin? No way."

"Yeah way. I saw her birth certificate."

"Okay, first off, my parents would have told her and us by now. Second, how did you happen to be reading her birth certificate?"

Jinxi felt her face grow hot. She turned her back to him, refilling her mug to buy some time. "I was working on your mom's computer, and it was on the desk." Another tiny lie.

Dean sat up straight. "Seriously?" He stood and paced back and forth. "Unbelievable."

Jinxi watched him over the rim of her mug.

"Although that does explain a few things," he said.

"Like what?"

"Like why Robin has red hair, and Brian and I have dark brown. She's a lot shorter than Brian and me and my mom and dad."

"Right," Jinxi responded, exhaling the breath she'd been holding.

"She's always been a rebel. Her temperament is totally different from Brian and me." Dean rubbed the back of his neck, a gesture she recognized.

He sank back down on the stool, a faraway look in his eyes. "Wow." His attention swung back to Jinxi. "What does this have to do with my mom not sleeping good?"

"Your mom told Robin last night."

"Whoa."

"Robin was like, you should have told me. Your mom was like, I'm sorry, I'm sorry."

"So let me get this straight. You found Robin's birth certificate on Mom's desk, then my mom just happened to tell Robin she's adopted?"

"Well, not exactly." Jinxi wrapped her hands around the mug, absorbing its warmth. "Robin showed up at your mom's, then she saw the birth certificate on the desk. When your mom got home, she, like, threw it in her face and went off." She held her breath, waiting for Dean to respond.

"How's my mom doing?"

Jinxi shrugged. "She went back to bed, so I came over here."

Dean stood and came around the corner of the bar. He opened the refrigerator and leaned over to stare at its meager contents. "There's nothing in here to eat."

"Looks like you've been surviving on Mickey D's and pizza."

Dean swung around. "Come on, let's get out of here." He grabbed his keys and wallet off the counter.

Jinxi set her mug down and shoved her hands into the front pouch of her sweatshirt. "Where're we going?"

"Let's go grab some breakfast. I'm starved." He headed toward the door, turning to whistle to Ted. "Come on, boy, time for you to catch some fresh air."

Jinxi sat in front of the television, her attention elsewhere. Dean had gone on and on about Robin's adoption. Jinxi told him what she'd heard the night before. Dean was shocked by the story, even after all the things he'd seen while working for Sac PD.

Uneasiness sat in her gut, a hard rock of regret for telling him. It wasn't her story to tell. It was Janice's.

She'll be really ticked off when she finds out.

She'd blown it again. When would she ever get things right?

CHAPTER TWENTY-SEVEN

For the first time since the accident, Dean woke up without a headache. He stretched, savoring the sweet relief from pain. Maybe he'd be able to go back to work soon. The memory of Sarge's accusation slapped him back to reality.

He sat up and swung his legs over the side of the futon. Time to get some things done today. He'd been procrastinating for too long.

Once the coffee started to brew, he sat at the counter, pulling a scrap of paper toward him. Before starting a list of things to do, he mentally rehearsed what needed to be done. Send in the DNA test. Empty trash. Finish cleaning the apartment.

The coffee pot beeped to signal the brewing was finished. He grabbed a clean mug off the counter, mentally thanking Jinxi for doing his dishes. He thought about their conversation the day before. His sister was adopted? Unbelievable.

Forget the list. He knew what needed to be done. Before anything, he needed to have a conversation with his mom.

"Hi, Son," his mom greeted him. She sat at the kitchen table, sorting through a pile of mail. Her eyes were red-rimmed. She seemed to have aged several years in the last two days.

Dean sat across from her, sipping from the mug of coffee he'd brought from his apartment.

"Morning. How're you feeling today?" He watched closely for her response.

"Fine." Her smile didn't make it to her eyes.

He tried another tack. "Jinxi and I went out to brunch yesterday."

"Did you have a good time?" Janice stood and walked to the recycle bin, tossing in a stack of advertisements.

"She said you weren't feeling well. That's why you didn't go to church."

His mom went to the pantry and brought out the cookie jar. She put several cookies on a plate before returning to her seat.

"These are homemade. Jinxi made them last night." She took one and broke it in half, then in half again.

Dean reached over, placing his hand over hers. "Mom, I know about Robin."

She inhaled sharply. "How?"

"Jinxi."

Emotions played across his mom's face. Anger, relief, sadness. "I should have told Robin years ago." Her shoulders slumped.

"Why didn't you?"

"Your dad and I thought it would be for the best if we didn't." She brought her gaze up to his. "Did Jinxi also tell you the circumstances?"

Dean nodded.

His mom pulled her hands away, stood, and began to pace the kitchen. "After Brian was born, I was told I couldn't have any more children. His birth was difficult, and I was on bed rest for six weeks before he was born. Your dad and I wanted more children, so we looked into foster care, with the hope of adopting. Right after we got licensed, we took on the foster care of a little baby."

"Robin?"

"Yes. At that time, we didn't know anything about her, other than her mother was a teenager and couldn't take care of her. Not until her father's parental rights were terminated were we able to adopt her. The social worker told us everything—how her father was in prison and her mother disappeared." She stopped, wiping her eyes with a dish towel. "Your dad and I didn't want her to have to deal with all that ugliness. We should have known—I should have known—she'd find out sooner or later."

Dean leaned the chair back on two legs. "How's Robin?"

"I don't know. She won't answer her phone." His mom's tortured look cut him to the core.

"Is there anything I can do?" Dean brought the legs of the chair down with a thump.

"Why don't you try calling her?"

"Will do." Dean stood to leave. The room was too small to contain his mother's grief.

"Wait. Before you go, I need to ask a favor."

Dean stifled a groan. "What?"

"Did Jinxi say anything to you about some missing money from the food bank?"

"No." He struggled to control his irritation.

"Apparently some money went missing from the food bank office. She thinks they think she took it. I was wondering if you could look into it?"

"What am I supposed to do?"

"Maybe see if you can find something out?" Her hands fluttered. "Gracious, I don't know."

Dean sighed in exasperation. "Fine. I'll look into it." He kissed his mom's cheek and headed out the back door.

He whistled for Ted, then tossed the rest of his coffee in the bushes. Ted raced around the side of the house, tongue lolling.

"Hey, buddy." Dean scratched Ted's ears, his eyes searching for the tennis ball. "Where's your ball? Huh? Where's your ball?"

Ted took off running, returning with the ball clenched in his jaw. He dropped it at Dean's feet, waiting expectantly for Dean to throw it.

Dean threw the ball over and over, thinking about how he'd be able to help Jinxi solve the mystery of the missing money. Something niggled at the back of his mind. Something about money or earrings. Or maybe he was imagining things.

He sat on the back steps, forcing himself to concentrate. Ted barked, wanting to resume their game. The tennis ball sat forgotten at Dean's feet as he emptied his mind of everything except the thought of gold and diamond earrings. His mom had a pair of earrings like that.

Like a camera shutter snapping open, the image clicked. A wave of dizziness hit him as he shot to his feet. His mom's earrings. In the drawer in Jinxi's bedroom. His mom's investment account, depleted by Jinxi.

He rubbed the back of his neck.

"Oh, my gosh." Jinxi had stolen from his mom. He remembered everything. Her tearful confession. His disbelief that she'd repented. He wasn't speaking to her before his accident. Now he was taking her to brunch. Confiding in her.

Jinxi's betrayal hit him like a punch to his solar plexus. She never said a word. She must've thought by pretending it hadn't happened, it would go away. Or maybe Jinxi hoped he wouldn't remember.

Dean stomped across the lawn to his apartment. He took the stairs two at a time, bursting through the apartment door, Ted at his heels.

He grabbed his phone, searched through his contacts and dialed the number.

"'Sup?" The man answered within two rings.

"I need a favor."

CHAPTER TWENTY-EIGHT

Janice watched Dean throw the ball for Ted from the kitchen window. If only her life could be as uncomplicated as Ted's. She turned away, shuffling into the living room. She picked the phone up from its charger before sinking down onto her chair. She dialed Robin's number, praying she'd answer this time.

Her stomach jumped as the call connected. There was silence at the other end, except for someone breathing.

"Robin?"

"Hi, Grammy."

"Hi, Princess. How are you?"

"Good."

"What are you doing today?"

"Playing."

Why did Hannah clam up when she talked on the phone, but was a chatterbox in person?

"Where's your mommy?"

"She's changing my baby brother."

"Can you ask her if she can talk to me?"

"Okay."

The phone clanked in Janice's ear. Hannah must have set it on the counter. A few moments later, she returned.

"Mommy said she can't come to the phone right now. Can I talk to Jinxi?"

Janice swallowed her disappointment. "No, Princess, she's at work."

"Can you take the phone to her?"

"No, I can't. She works too far away."

"When can I come over and see you? I want to play with Ted."

"Soon, Princess. Soon." Janice hoped she wasn't lying. "Tell your mom I love her."

"Okay, Grammy. I love you."

"You too, Princess."

She disconnected, holding the phone with numb fingers. She set it on the coffee table and pulled her Bible onto her lap. The prayers that used to come easily now felt stilted and awkward. Where had her faith gone? The circumstances of the past few months had tested her beyond endurance. How could she get relief?

Never before had she felt the overwhelming need to run away. Not even after Tom's death. Then, she'd been surrounded by comforting friends and family who helped support her during those first few weeks. Now everything was falling apart, and she was powerless to pick up the pieces.

Abandoning the Bible, she picked up the phone again and dialed a number from memory.

"Hello?" Her sister's voice was like a soothing balm.

"Hi, Debbie. It's me. I'm thinking about coming out for a visit."

Debbie laughed in delight. "Great! Are you coming out for Thanksgiving? What will your family do if you're not there to prepare the feast?"

"No, not Thanksgiving. I was thinking about tomorrow."

Janice stuck her head out of the bedroom door when she heard Jinxi's key in the lock. "In here," she called.

Jinxi followed her voice into Janice's bedroom. "What's going on?" she asked, spying the clothes piled on the bed in folded stacks.

"I'm taking a trip to see my sister in Iowa," Janice said over her shoulder.

Janice heard the thud of Jinxi's backpack hitting the wood floor. She turned to see Jinxi leaning against the doorframe.

"When?"

"Tomorrow."

"Isn't that, like, kinda sudden?"

Janice turned away. "I've been thinking about it for a while. Debbie's been after me for some time to come and see her. With everything that's happened, maybe it's a good idea to let Robin cool off a bit."

"Whatever. I'm going to start dinner."

For once, Janice was glad Jinxi was a woman of few words.

Over dinner, Janice went over the details of her trip. She handed Jinxi a list of reminders. Remind Dean to put the garbage cans out, pick up the mail every afternoon, how to get hold of her at Debbie's.

"I'll leave my car keys on the piano. You can drive it while I'm gone if you want."

"Okay. Thanks."

Janice snapped her fingers. "Oh, and I talked to Dean about your money situation at work. He said he'd look into it."

The corners of Jinxi's mouth turned down. "Do you really think he'll be able to do anything?"

"I don't know. But he said he'd try."

As Janice prepared for bed that evening, her thoughts tumbled like socks in the dryer. Running away had seemed like a good idea a few hours ago. Now she wondered if she'd made a huge mistake. Would she be better off staying and having it out with Robin? Her heart ached over the hurt Robin must feel. She loved Robin as if she'd given birth to her herself. They'd always had a difficult relationship, but her love never wavered. She hoped this wouldn't drive a permanent wedge between them. What if Robin never let her see her grandchildren again?

She slumped onto the bed, clutching the footboard.

Dear God, help me see clearly.

She turned off the light and climbed beneath the covers. She'd set a course. Now she was bound to see it through.

Raul lounged on the sofa in his apartment. He held the remote in his hand, idly tapping it against his leg as he watched a boxing match. The subpoena mocked him from where it sat on the scarred coffee table. Family of Justin Smith vs City of Sacramento Police Department. What a joke. The union rep had coached him on what to say, but it still angered him. That little punk got what he deserved.

His cell phone rang, and he reached to grab it. He glanced at the screen to identify the caller before answering.

"Bueno."

"He talked to IA."

"You know what to do."

CHAPTER TWENTY-NINE

Dean returned to his apartment after a twenty-minute jog on the treadmill downstairs. His strength was gradually returning. He grabbed a sports drink from the fridge, then sat down at his computer to answer a few emails.

After deleting the ads for prescription drugs and fast cash, he wrote a quick email to his Aunt Debbie, asking if his mom arrived okay, and if she was having a good time. He shook his head at her rapid departure. So unlike her.

One of his friends from college wrote, "When are you gonna get on Facebook?"

He wrote back, "Never. Too easy for the punks I bust to find me."

The last message, at the bottom of the screen, was from Katie. He hadn't responded to her email, thanking him for his willingness to take the DNA test. He stared at the computer screen for ten seconds, fingers poised over the keys.

Dear Katie, There's no way I could be the father of your kid. You had a relationship with John long before we hooked up that one night. Even if I am the father …

He paused. What could he say? That he wasn't willing to take on the responsibility of a child right now? That he had too much on his plate? He'd sound like a selfish creep. She had to deal with the kid by herself for the past five years.

His finger rested on the DELETE key until all that was left was "Dear Katie." He bit his lip, then wrote, "I sent the DNA test back yesterday. Dean." He hit SEND, then sat back in his chair. His hand went to the back of his neck, rubbing it back and forth.

Dear God, what if—

His cell phone rang, interrupting the negative flow of his thoughts. It was his friend Matt.

"Yup?" Dean answered.

"It's me. I did a little digging like you asked, and I found something you might find interesting." Dean's buddy worked for a computer security firm. His access allowed him to do background checks, discovering information not readily available to the general public.

"What?"

"She spent a year in Juvie, then transferred to California Girls' Ranch."

"What for?"

"Not sure. Gotta do a little more digging."

"See what you can do."

Dean stood and paced the small living area of his apartment. Jinxi spent time in Girls' Ranch. Why should he be surprised? He finally remembered about the money she'd stolen from his mom. She said she'd had some sort of experience with God, but maybe it was because his mom found out. Like the 'conversions' he'd witnessed while working at the jail. She probably did steal the cash from the food bank and was scared because she'd been caught.

Dean looked back over the past couple of weeks with disgust. How could he have thought he liked her? She was probably using him to stay close to his mom so she could take more from her. Wasn't his mom letting Jinxi stay there rent free? She was using his mom, and his mom was blind to it.

Now that his mom was out of town, this would be his opportunity to kick her to the curb.

Jinxi put her hands on the small of her back and stretched. She ached from unloading the huge pallets of rice that were delivered early that morning. Where was Skeeter, anyway? He was supposed to be helping her, but he hadn't shown up yet. Maybe he wasn't coming. Maybe he'd gotten arrested again. Good. One less problem.

She jumped when a voice spoke into her ear.

"Miss me?"

She spun around to see Skeeter grinning at her. His eyes were red-rimmed, and his pupils dilated.

"Where've you been?"

"You did miss me. Admit it." He shrugged out of his jacket and threw it on a shelf.

"You're on something." He wore a tank top despite the frigid temperature in the warehouse.

"So what if I am?"

"The rules—"

His voice mocked her. "The rules. Always the rules. You know what you can do with your rules." He grabbed a bag of rice from the pallet and flung it on top of a pile on one of the shelves.

Jinxi gritted her teeth. Just ignore him.

"When you're finished with the rice, pile the pallets in the alley. Someone's coming by to pick them up later." She turned to head into the kitchen.

"Yes, boss."

She forced down the urge to respond.

Volunteers had just begun to arrive by the time Jinxi wrapped her apron around her and pulled a hairnet over her head.

"I'm glad you are here, chica," Connie said. "You will make the salad, sí?"

"Sí," Jinxi responded. She retrieved the salad ingredients from the refrigerator, glad to have something to occupy her hands so her mind could wander. The end of the workday would arrive, and she'd have to take the bus to an empty house. Janice had only been gone a day, but she missed her already. They'd grown close in the past three months. Janice was her one constant, the one person who loved her unconditionally. At least she hoped so.

She couldn't blame Janice for wanting to run away. Jinxi herself felt the same way. What would it be like to escape her life for a week? Maybe two. Forget all about Skeeter, the missing money, Burn Boy. A week of lying on a beach—

"Yinxi! I am talking to you." Connie's voice shocked her back to the present.

"I—I'm sorry. What did you say?"

"That is enough lettuce, chica."

Jinxi looked down at to discover she'd torn enough lettuce to fill two industrial-sized bowls. Oh, snap. She'd blown it again.

Dry leaves crackled under her boots as Jinxi trudged along the sidewalk from the bus stop to Janice's house. An occasional dog barked as she passed, but most of them knew her by now. She remembered how they used to lunge at the chain link fences surrounding their yards, speeding up her heart rate and her steps. Seemed like everyone in the neighborhood had a fence, a dog, and barred windows. Anything to feel safe. Janice had told her the demographic of the community had changed over the thirty years since they'd first moved in. There used to be a neighborhood watch group and block parties. Now people were afraid to leave their homes. Many of the families had moved out to the suburbs into newer communities.

Jinxi's steps slowed as she reached the gate at Janice's. The house loomed dark and lonely. Where was Ted? He usually ran back and forth in front of the house as she approached. He was probably at Dean's. Maybe she'd go get him so she wouldn't have to be home alone.

The first thing she did after unlocking the front door was turn on several lights in the living room and dining room. She headed into the kitchen and turned on that light too before heading upstairs to her bedroom.

Off came her boots, replaced by a pair of slip-on canvas shoes. Then she unpacked her backpack, tossing the stained Tee shirt into the hamper. She'd splashed salad dressing on the front. She picked up the knife case and carried it down to the kitchen.

What to eat for dinner? Tapping her foot, she mentally went through a list of possibilities. The thought of eating alone didn't appeal at all. She should head over and see what Dean was doing. Maybe they could eat together.

She pulled up the hood of her sweatshirt before stepping out the back door and bounding down the steps. She was halfway across the lawn before noticing no lights shone through his apartment windows. His truck was gone too. Her shoulders slumped as she hiked back to the empty house. A frisson of panic rose inside her gut. Where was Dean? He was usually home around dinner time. Was he lying trapped inside his truck, overturned in a ditch?

She swallowed the fear inching up her back.

CHAPTER THIRTY

Jinxi changed into her pajamas and curled up on the couch with a soft throw draped over her lap. She'd managed to choke down a bowl of cereal, even though it tasted like sawdust. She'd checked all the doors and windows to be sure they were locked.

If only Ted was here, lying in his spot under the coffee table. At least there'd be another living being to keep her company. He must be with Dean, wherever that was.

Her heart jumped as the grandfather clock chimed. The old house creaked and settled. Noises she'd been used to now sounded ominous. Was that someone trying to break in? She muted the TV, cocking her ear toward the window. Probably just a bush, rubbing against the house, right?

She gave up trying to watch a show, turned off the TV, and tossed the remote on the sofa. Best to go to bed. Should she turn off the lights, or leave them on? If she left them burning, someone could see in. If she turned them off ...

Jinxi clicked the stud in her lip back and forth against her teeth. She switched off all the lights, double-checked the front and back doors, then headed up the stairs.

After an hour of rolling back and forth in the bed, she fell into an uneasy sleep. Several hours later, she was awakened by the sound of car tires screeching in the street.

They stopped, then she heard breaking glass, then more screeching.

Heart racing, she flew down the stairs, turning on lights as she went. She skidded to a stop at the entrance to the living room. One of the windows had been shattered, glass strewn on the rug and covering part of the sofa. A brick lay in the middle of the mess.

Jinxi hugged herself before racing back up the stairs to retrieve her cell phone. Her fingers shook as she dialed Dean's number. He'd know what to do. The phone rang twice before going to voice mail. Oh, snap. What should she do?

Like an icy finger, fear crept up her back, tensing her shoulders. Was there writing on the brick? She crept forward as far as she could without stepping on glass. She peered at the brick and could just make out the words.

You've been warned.

She dialed Dean's number again with the same result. She turned on her heels and fled upstairs. When she reached her room, she closed the door and pushed the nightstand in front of it. Grabbing a blanket and pillow off the bed, she crawled into the closet and pulled the door closed behind her.

Someone was licking his face. Dean turned over, trying to retrieve the last bit of the dream he was having. The licking moved to his ear.

"Wha—" He sat up with a start, bumping his head against Ted's nose. "Hey, buddy. Can't you let a guy sleep?"

Ted responded with a bark, then trotted over to the door, looking back at Dean.

"Okay. I get it." Dean pulled himself out of bed and opened the door. Ted trotted out and dashed down the stairs.

Sometime during the night, Dean decided he was going to confront Jinxi. She hadn't been completely honest, and that irked him. She'd tried to call him in the middle of the night, and he'd ignored the calls. He hadn't wanted to talk to her until he had it in his mind what he was going to say.

After splashing water on his face, he pulled a sweatshirt over his head and slipped on a pair of flip-flops. By the time he got to the back door of his mom's house, he heard Ted barking like crazy from the front yard. What was up with that dog? Had he treed a cat again?

The back door was locked, so he pounded his fist against it until Jinxi appeared, carrying a broom. Her face was whiter than usual. She stared at him with bloodshot eyes before turning around without a word. He followed her into the dining room, then stopped short when he saw the mess.

"What happened?" He grabbed her arm and spun her around to face him. "What did you do?"

"I didn't do anything." She pulled out of his grasp and faced him with sparks shooting from her eyes. "In the middle of the night, someone threw this brick through the window." Her voice rose an octave. "I tried to call you. Why didn't you answer your phone?"

Dean took a moment to process the information. "You're telling me you have no idea what this is all about?"

"Yeah, that's what I'm saying."

Jinxi started to shake, then she hurled herself at him. His arms wrapped around her as she cried.

"I was scared. You didn't answer your phone. I didn't know what to do."

A shaft of guilt pierced him. He'd seen her number displayed on his phone and sent the calls to voice mail.

He patted her back, murmuring comfort. "It's okay. You'll be okay. No one's going to hurt you."

When the tempest of her outburst slowed, he held her away with his hands on her upper arms. "Why don't you go get a tissue, splash some water on your face, and let me help you clean up."

Jinxi nodded dumbly. When she was out of sight, he took out his phone and snapped a few photos of the mess. He stepped gingerly on the glass to get a closer view of the brick. He crouched down to get a look at the words. When he saw what was written, he had to catch himself from falling backward.

You've been warned.

He took several photos of the brick before backing up.

He dialed a number, rubbing the back of his neck while waiting for it to connect. "This is badge number 9746255. I need a patrol car at 8001 Baxter Street."

Jinxi returned from the bathroom. "Where should we start?" She reached for the broom, but he stopped her with a motion from his hand.

"We need to wait for the police."

"You are the police."

"I want to make a formal report. This is serious. Did you see what's written on the brick?"

"Yeah. What's it mean?"

Dean thought back to the note on the back of his traffic citation. Watch your back, amigo. Was this part of the same warning? Or was it a coincidence and it had nothing to do with him? Maybe someone had something against Jinxi. That old boyfriend, or someone else from her past?

"Do you know anyone who would want to warn you about something?"

Jinxi shook her head, but not before he noticed her hesitation. He decided not to pursue that line of questioning ... yet. He still hadn't dealt with her lying to him. Well, not exactly lying, but not telling him the whole truth. Anger boiled inside, threatening to explode. What was happening to his world? He'd been on a path to fulfilling his life-long dream. Now everything he valued was being slowly chipped away.

"Make us a pot of coffee while we wait."

"I'm gonna be late for work."

"After you start the coffee, call and let them know you have a situation at home. Tell them you'll be in as soon as you can. I'll drive you to work."

He took a last look at the mess before following Jinxi into the kitchen. He wouldn't mention this when his mom called.

CHAPTER THIRTY-ONE

Things at the food bank were in their normal state of chaos. Jinxi stepped through the front door after Dean dropped her off.

He'd been moody and sharp while they waited for the officer to show up to take the report. He'd slipped outside to talk to the officer alone while she rinsed out their cups. She'd returned to the living room to see him gesturing toward the house, then the street. After the two men shook hands, the officer got in his car and drove away.

Jinxi couldn't fathom why someone would hurl a brick through Janice's front window. It couldn't have been Skeeter. Could it?

She dropped her pack in the food bank office, nodded a quick hello to Aneesa, who was in her usual position, ear glued to the phone, talking at the speed of light. She headed straight back to the storerooms, intent on finding Skeeter.

She found him smoking a cigarette in the alley. "Don't you ever work?"

He pushed himself away from the wall. "I'm entitled to a smoke break every once in a while." He took a last puff, then dropped the butt on the ground. "Where ya been?"

Jinxi eyed him with disgust. "Do you know anything about a brick thrown through the window of my house?"

"It's your house now?" He gave her a mocking smile.

"Whatever." She dismissed him with a wave of her hand. "Someone broke a window last night."

Skeeter held up both palms.

"Whoa. I don't know nothin' about it. I got better things to do than that." His voice took on a different tone. "That thing I asked you about? It's going down this weekend. I'll let you know when. Just be at my place when I say." He turned to head back into the storeroom. "Until then, I got work to do."

Jinxi thought about Skeeter's denial of the window. She knew him well enough to know he was telling the truth. If not him, then who? Could it have been meant for Janice? She immediately dismissed the idea. If not Janice, then was Dean involved in something? She'd have to ask him when she got home. Until then, she had other things to deal with. Like, how would she follow through with Skeeter's demand? Her stomach clenched with the thought of having to do something for him. Something illegal. When she'd left Bakersfield, she'd vowed never to let someone take control of her. Now it was happening again. If she didn't do what he said, he'd follow through with his threat to expose her. She couldn't let that happen.

The speed bag took the brunt of Dean's self-anger. His boxing gloves pounded it over and over, first his left hand, then his right. He'd worked up a sweat, despite the chill of the garage. He'd opened up the big rolling door to get some fresh air. Ted lounged on the driveway in the sun, belly exposed.

Why hadn't he said anything to Jinxi when he'd driven her to work?

pound pound

He should have confronted her.

pound pound

Was the brick meant for him? Was it Raul who threw it?

pound pound

Dean stopped punching, grabbing the bag to halt its momentum. Why couldn't his memory have returned sooner? He could have nipped a lot of his bad situation in the bud. He could have told IA about Raul and the shooting, then distanced himself from his partner. He would've known about Jinxi and his mom's account and could have kept her at arm's length. Or maybe not.

He resumed his assault on the speed bag. He hated to admit to himself how good it had felt to hold Jinxi while she cried. Like a syringe drawing blood, she pulled out the emotions he'd hidden since his father died. He remembered their verbal sparring, and how before his injury she'd challenged his narrow views time and time again. With a pang, he realized how much he missed their relationship.

Dean missed a punch, and the bag smacked him in the face. Reality check. He liked a woman who'd spent time in Juvenile Hall and the California Girls' Ranch? No way. He needed a plan to get her out of his mom's house before she did something worse than taking money from his mom's investment account.

His hands dropped to his sides. What about the warning on the brick? He'd better make some calls and see what the rumor mill had to say. He stripped off the gloves, dropping them on the floor. He'd text Damaris and Patrice. They were the most tied into squad room gossip.

After a quick shower, he hustled across the yard to his mom's house to meet the window repairman. The sooner the glass was replaced, the better. He didn't want his mom coming home to find her house violated. He'd done his best to clean up the glass, but it would take a professional to extract the tiny shards imbedded in the sofa. While the window was being replaced, he searched the web for a local company to come in and finish the cleanup.

His phone whistled the announcement of an incoming text.

PATRICE: Nothing yet. Send a pic.
DEAN: Here ya go.
PATRICE: Scary. You okay?
DEAN: Yeah. Must have thot I live w/ my mom.
PATRICE: Anything from D?
DEAN: He's on shift. He'll txt me when done.
PATRICE: K. Be safe.

Dean sat back in the chair at his mom's desk. A dozen or so recipes were spread across the surface, some with handwritten comments. 'Try this one.' 'Substitute port. mush. 4 meat.' Must be Jinxi's writing. She really knew how to cook, he'd give her that. Maybe he'd wait until just before his mom got home before making her leave.

Jinxi adjusted the strap of her backpack as she jumped off the bottom step of the bus. Skeeter's constant presence was getting on her last nerve. His favorite thing was to sneak up behind her, startling her. When no one else was around, he made suggestive comments, hinting they should get back together.

The missing money still hadn't turned up. Suspicion wrapped its tentacles around her. Padish's attitude toward her had changed. He didn't smile as often and spoke even less. Connie must be wrong. Jinxi was his top suspect.

Then there was Burn Boy. Every day his presence was a reminder, a silent accusation. Would she ever escape her past?

Someone had left a light on in Janice's living room. The soft glow welcomed her through the brand-new window. She stepped through the front door, relieved at the absence of glass. The fragrant smell of freshly cleaned carpet hit her. How'd he get it all done in one day? Must be nice having all those cop connections.

Jinxi dropped her backpack at the foot of the stairs, then headed into the kitchen to find something to fix for dinner. She opened the refrigerator door, then froze as she heard the floor creak above her head. Someone was walking around upstairs. Could it be the person who threw the brick? She struggled to hear over the pounding of blood in her ears.

After thirty seconds of standing with cold air flowing around her, the sound didn't repeat. Probably just the sound of the settling of an old house. She reached for a package of roast beef with a shaky hand.

Creak.

She threw the lunchmeat back on the shelf, slammed the refrigerator, and ran to the back door. She raced across the back yard and dashed up the stairs to Dean's apartment. Using her fist, she banged on the door until it was thrown open.

"What the—"

"Hurry. Let me in."

Dean stood aside as Jinxi pushed past him. She turned to see him stick his head out the door. "Is someone following you?"

"No." She took several deep breaths. "Give me a minute." She collapsed onto his futon.

Dean took a seat on one of the bar stools while he waited for her breathing to return to normal. "What's going on?"

"The house. I think someone's in there. You know, like, hiding upstairs." She clicked the stud in her lip against her teeth.

His voice was derisive. "Seriously?"

"I heard a noise."

"Right. You heard a noise. What do you want me to do about it?"

"Could you go check? Please?" Her voice took on a pleading tone. No way was she going back over there alone.

"Fine." He pulled on a pair of sneakers and shrugged into a sweatshirt.

After he left, Ted at his heels, Jinxi sat back to wait. The realization came slowly, growing with intensity, that she missed Janice. She'd come to rely on the older woman for security. She was the one constant in her life, a constant she'd never had before.

Sure, her mother had always been there physically. But as the drinking had increased, her mother's emotional connection had stretched like a rubber band, becoming thinner and brittle with time.

When Janice was bitten by a black widow a few weeks ago, Jinxi experienced real fear that the older woman might be taken from her. She couldn't imagine a life without Janice. She'd pointed Jinxi to church, to God, and to salvation. That was why Janice could never be allowed to know about Jinxi's past.

CHAPTER THIRTY-TWO

Dean trudged up the stairs to his apartment, shaking his head in disgust. Women and their imaginations. He knew he wouldn't find anyone hiding in his mom's house. He'd made sure all the doors were locked after the cleanup crew left. Although if Raul had tossed the brick, he might have found a way to get past his security measures. If it was Raul. Could be Jinxi's loser boyfriend. What a dumpster fire that was.

Jinxi looked up at him expectantly as he went through the door.

"Nothing," he told her. The relief on her face softened its sharpness.

"Thanks." She looked down, twisting her leather bracelet around and around. "Do you think you could, maybe, stay over at your mom's house tonight?"

"I don't—"

"Just tonight?" Her voice sped up. "It's just that I'm, you know, a little sketchy since the whole brick thing. Maybe you could sleep in your mom's room? Or on the couch?" Her eyes were like twin blue saucers as she gazed up at him.

He exhaled. "Why don't you stay here?" As soon as he spoke the words, he wished he could grab them back.

Her face paled as she looked around the one room apartment. "Where?"

Dean pulled open the closet door and hauled out a folding ladder. He walked past the futon, past his desk, and propped the ladder against the wall in the far corner.

"There's a loft up here. The bed's pretty comfortable. You can sleep up there."

"Why don't you sleep up there?"

"I, um, well ..." There was no way he would admit to her he was afraid of heights. "The bed's too short for me."

Her relief was palpable. "Sweet. Could you do one more favor?"

"What?" he asked with resignation.

"Come over to the house with me so I can get my PJ's and stuff?"

They shared a jumbo-sized bowl of popcorn for dinner while watching a mystery movie. They argued good-naturedly over who the murderer would turn out to be. Dean's thoughts strayed to how he would extract her from his mom's home. He pictured several scenarios, but none of them worked out to his satisfaction. He'd need his mom's cooperation, and that probably wasn't going to happen. She'd let Jinxi into her world, and she liked having someone else in her home. Just like him.

The thought hit him like a jolt of electricity. He liked Jinxi's company. His mind wandered to what a relationship with Jinxi would look like. She was a decent pool player, one of his favorite pastimes. She liked fast food as much as he did. They both liked dogs. He didn't drink, and it seemed she didn't either. His mom already liked Jinxi.

He'd have to find out about her incarceration as a juvenile offender. That brought his mental wanderings to an abrupt halt. Then there was the pending DNA test. What would

Jinxi think if he showed up with a kid? His personal life was a hot mess. Dean didn't need any more complications, like adding a girlfriend into the mix. Now that his memory had returned and the headaches had decreased, maybe his life could get back to normal.

Whatever normal was.

When the movie was over, Jinxi climbed up the ladder and disappeared into the loft. Dean hauled out his futon and grabbed a blanket out of the closet. He let Ted out for the last time, waiting until he heard Ted's toenails click on the wood stairs.

Ted settled into his bed with a sigh. Dean lay on his back on the futon, arms behind his head. A streetlight cast a soft glow into the room.

"Dean?" Jinxi voice called from above.

"Huh?" he grunted.

"It's dark up here."

"There's a night light on the far wall. Switch it on."

"Dean?"

"Go to sleep." He turned on his side and pulled a pillow over his head.

Jinxi woke early to muted sunshine from a skylight in the sloping ceiling. The loft was a cozy cocoon, safe and warm. What she wouldn't give to stay here all the time. Above anyone's reach. If she wanted to, she could pull the ladder up. No one would even know she was here. If only she'd had this hideaway as a kid.

Peering over the edge, she saw Dean still sleeping, one arm flung over his head and the other tucked near his chin, hand curled into a fist. The hair hadn't completely grown in over his head wound. With a grimace, she turned from the view and slipped silently down the ladder. When she reached the bottom, she glanced toward the futon. He hadn't moved.

An irresistible urge drew her to his desk. She sat in the chair, rolling it toward the laptop computer. A quick glance told her Dean still slept. After perusing the piles of loose papers, she wiggled the mouse to bring the computer to life. Dean's email appeared.

She scanned the senders and subject lines, intensely curious for any clues about his life. Hm, who was Katie Edwards? One more glance toward the bed.

Her hand hovered on the mouse as she scanned the email. Scrolling down, she started at the bottom to read the entire trail.

A DNA test. Dean might have a kid?

Oh, snap!

Dean woke to the smell of coffee. He smiled, despite his irritation from the night before. His eyes opened to Jinxi standing beside the bed, a steaming mug in her hands.

"Here. Just the way you like it." She waited for him to sit up, then handed him the cup.

Dean took the cup and inhaled deeply before taking the first sip. "Thanks." He squinted up at her. "Are you always up so early?"

She headed into the kitchen to pour herself some coffee. "Some of us have to work," she said over her shoulder.

"Don't remind me. I can't wait to go back to work."

She sat on one of the bar stools, bare feet tucked around the legs. "When's that gonna be?"

"Dunno. Gotta call my sarge." Now that he'd given his full statement to IA and provided a urine sample for the drug test, he hoped to clear everything up and get back on patrol. None of this was even his fault. Raul was to blame. If he hadn't ... well, it wasn't Dean's fault.

Jinxi finished her coffee and took the cup into the kitchen to rinse it in the sink. "Do you think you could come over to your mom's house with me while I get ready for work?"

"No. I have things to do."

"I promise I'll be quick."

"I said no." Dean stood and pulled the blanket off the bed so he wouldn't have to see her expression. After tossing it in the closet, he folded the futon up into a sofa.

"Can I take Ted with me?"

"Fine. Whatever." He knew he was being a jerk but couldn't help himself. He wanted to be left alone to wallow in self-pity.

Jinxi didn't glance his way as she gathered up her things. "C'mon, Ted." He trotted after her as she went out the door without another word.

After she left, Dean smacked his hand down on the counter. Dang. Why was everything so complicated?

After showering, he checked his phone and found a voice mail from his buddy Matt. The message was brief.

"Call me about your friend."

Dean pushed the call back button. "It's Dean. What ya got for me?"

Matt's voice bubbled with excitement. "You'll never believe this, dude. She was in for manslaughter."

The word was like a bomb exploding in Dean's head. "You've got to be kidding me." A murderer lived with his mom? Holy moly, this was serious. Was his mom in danger? Would she kill again?

"She started a fire that killed a kid."

"Can you send me the report?" Dean needed to read it for himself.

"No, I just got to read the trial transcript. I don't dare copy it."

"What else can you tell me?" Dean slipped into his cop role. He needed all the facts.

"She and some friends started a fire in a vacant lot. It spread to a nearby house. Before the fire department could get there, a toddler died of smoke inhalation. The mom was outside with another kid and didn't see the fire start. She tried to get inside, but it was too late. The other kid was hit by some falling shingles and was burned on his face and arm. It was pretty sad."

Dean's hand was sweaty on the phone. "Thanks. You did me a solid. I'll call you later." His finger left a wet smudge on the screen as he punched END. The coffee he'd drunk earlier churned in his stomach.

Unbelievable. He sat back on the futon and rubbed the back of his neck. With determination, he shot to his feet and headed for his desk. He fired up the laptop and began a search for newspaper articles about the incident in the Bakersfield newspaper. What he found was even more chilling than Matt's grim report.

CHAPTER THIRTY-THREE

Snow continued to fall outside Janice's sister's farmhouse. Wind howled around the corners, intent on penetrating every crack and crevice. Janice held a mug of tea with both hands and scooted her chair closer to the pellet stove.

"Now I remember why we moved to California," she said to her sister, as Debbie settled onto the sofa.

Debbie tucked her legs under her and smiled. "You watch. In a couple of days, the snow will all be gone."

They sipped their tea in companionable silence, broken only by the sound of the wind driving the snow against the windows.

"Remember that time—"

"How are the—"

They spoke at the same time, then laughed.

"You first."

"No, you first."

Debbie acquiesced. "What I wanted to ask is, how are all the kids? And how are your adorable grandchildren?"

Janice dropped her gaze to the rapidly cooling mug of tea. She set it aside with a sigh. "It's a long story."

"Honey, we have all the time we need. We're not going anywhere for a while." Debbie indicated the window.

Janice took a deep breath. She started at the beginning, reminding Debbie of Robin's adoption.

"You know I never agreed with Tom's and your decision not to tell her," Debbie commented, not unkindly.

Janice shifted in her seat, absently rubbing her aching knees. "I know. It just seemed like the right thing to do at the time." Janice told Debbie about her confrontation with Robin, and Robin's refusal to talk to her.

"Mercy, that must have been a real kerfuffle."

Janice laughed at her sister's reverting to using words from their Scottish upbringing. "Indeed."

"My dear, I'm sure Robin will come around." Debbie reached for Janice's hand and gave it a squeeze. "Give her a little more time."

"I hope you're right." Janice searched Debbie's face for any trace of doubt, desperate to believe her.

"In the meantime, let's pray for her."

While Dean read through the accounts of the fire Jinxi had started with her friends, his computer notified him of an incoming email. Grateful to take a break from the newspaper's sensational coverage of the incident, he toggled over to his email account. The photos of the charred remains of the home chilled him.

The email was from Family Ancestry DNA.

Dear Mr. Rafferty:

Thank you for using Family Ancestry. We have received your DNA sample and will notify you of the results. Please allow ten to fourteen days.

Dean released the breath he'd been holding. He'd expected to see something in bold print, announcing he either was or wasn't the father of Katie's son. How would he be able to wait until the results came back to him? This was worse than waiting to hear if he'd been accepted into the police academy.

His chin dropped to his chest. What had begun as an opportunity to move up in the police department had turned into a disaster. The accident, Raul's threats, and Sarge accusing him of drug use. Then finding out about Jinxi's past, just as he was beginning to think he might like to start a relationship with her. Learning of his sister's adoption. Then this whole deal with Katie, the DNA test, and possibly having a kid.

Dean shoved his hands into the pocket of his sweatshirt. His fingers landed on something square. It was the business card of the hospital chaplain, Mike Zannakis. How did that get in there? He turned it over and over before throwing it on the desk.

"Call me if you ever want to talk. Or pray." He'd shut the guy down quicker than the Lakers shut down the Kings that night.

One hand rubbed the wound on his head, while the other reached for his phone.

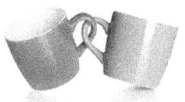

"I'm glad you called. I was wondering why God had given me the morning off." Chaplain Z dropped into the chair across the table from Dean. Removing the lid from his coffee, he blew on it before taking a tentative sip.

Uh-oh. This guy was a spiritual nut case.

"Yeah. Thanks." Dean sucked some of the whipped cream off his caramel macchiato.

"How're you feeling? Healing up okay?"

"Sure. Fine."

"Great. How's your memory? Any issues?"

"No. Well, a few things are sketchy," Dean conceded.

Chaplain Z regarded him with frank curiosity. "So what's up?"

Dean looked down at his drink, stirring it with the straw. This was a mistake. Why did he think he could dump on this guy? Sometimes his spontaneity got him in trouble. Like the day he literally ran into Jinxi outside the jail and took her to breakfast. Look how that turned out. He let a murderer into his mother's house.

The chaplain took another sip of his coffee. "Shall we play twenty questions?"

Dean looked up to see a twinkle in the other man's eyes.

"Chaplain Z—"

"Call me Mike."

"My bad. This was a mistake." Dean shoved back his chair, ready to spring up, but Mike grabbed his arm.

"Why don't you wait a minute? We're just two people having coffee." He gestured around the busy Starbucks. "Like everyone else in here."

After a moment of indecision, Dean scraped his chair back under the table.

"Why don't I start," Mike said, "by telling you why I became a hospital chaplain?"

Dean nodded.

"A few years ago, my wife and daughter were killed by a drunk driver. They were riding their bikes on Watt Avenue when this guy swerved to pass someone on the right. He went into the bike lane and plowed them down. My wife died instantly, my daughter a few days later. The hospital chaplain was amazing. Because of her, I quit my job and went back to school to learn chaplaincy."

"How do you get over something like that?" Dean asked.

Mike smiled. "You never get over it. You just learn to deal." He replaced the lid on his cup. "I never would have made it through the grieving process if I didn't have my faith in Jesus Christ."

Dean frowned. "I'm having a hard time reconciling all that 'God is love' stuff, when bad things happen like my dad's death and your wife and kid."

"That's the big question, isn't it?" Mike smiled. "God didn't take away my family, and he didn't take away your dad. Bad things happen because there's sin in the world. Sin made that guy drink too much at ten o'clock in the morning, then get into his car. Accidents are part of life. Everyone makes choices."

Dean looked down at his drink. "What if you've made bad choices?" He thought about how he'd deliberately taken advantage of Katie.

Mike leaned forward and rested his elbows on the table. "That's the beauty of an active, living faith in God. We can't escape the consequences of our choices, but he helps us through the mess."

Half an hour later, Dean shook Mike's hand as they said goodbye, promising to stay in touch. Dean climbed into his truck with a lighter heart than he'd had for a long time.

As he turned the corner to pull up to his apartment, a police cruiser drove by, slowing when it passed in front of his mother's house. A rock of tension settled in his gut. Was it a friend, checking on the house after the thrown brick? Or one of Raul's buddies, looking for a chance for more destruction?

He sat in his truck, drumming his fingers on the steering wheel until the car was out of sight.

CHAPTER THIRTY-FOUR

The door to the Sunday school classroom opened, releasing the dozen or so women in the addiction support group. Jinxi helped Aneesa rearrange the chairs into their correct positions. Aneesa locked the door behind them, and they walked to the parking lot and climbed into Aneesa's ancient Honda.

"Good group," Aneesa commented while she waited for the engine to warm.

Jinxi tucked her chin into the neck of her sweatshirt. "Yeah."

Aneesa glanced sideways. "You okay? You hardly said a word tonight."

The accusation of the missing food bank money hung over her.

"I'm fine."

She wasn't fine. She was suspected of being a thief, someone had lobbed a brick through Janice's living room window, and Skeeter threatened to expose her if she didn't accept a drug shipment for him. Yeah, life was just peachy.

"Are you mad at me?" Aneesa's voice cut through the dark silence.

"No."

"Is this about the money at the food bank?"

Jinxi shrugged.

"Oh, child, what are we going to do with you?"

Jinxi snapped her head toward the other woman. "What?"

Aneesa clucked her tongue. "Until we find out what happened to the deposit, everyone's a suspect, and no one's a suspect."

"But that kid said he saw me coming out of your office." Jinxi hated the whine in her voice.

Warm air trickled reluctantly out of the vent as Aneesa pulled out of the parking lot. "Were you in my office?"

"Well, yeah, but I didn't take the money. I'm not a thief." A pang of guilt shot through her as she remembered how she'd transferred money from Janice's investment account. She'd used some to get a new tattoo. The rest was stolen by you-know-who while she went to Bakersfield for a visit.

Aneesa turned down the street to where Jinxi lived. "The thing I've noticed, honey, is that in the end, the truth always comes out. One way or 'nother."

Jinxi hoped it was sooner rather than later.

Jinxi pushed open the front gate, happy to see Ted's dark form racing around the corner of the house. He barked a greeting, then ran to her for his customary sniff of her legs.

"Hey, Teddy, good boy." She wouldn't have to sleep alone in the house tonight. She let herself in, then turned on every light in the living room, dining room, and kitchen. She couldn't bring herself to walk down the dark hall to Janice's bedroom and the office-and-craft room opposite.

Dinner consisted of a grilled cheese sandwich and tomato soup, eaten in front of the television. She tossed the crusts to Ted, taking grim satisfaction that it would infuriate Dean. His voice echoed in her head. Don't give him human food.

He'd been nice enough to let her sleep in the loft last night, but he'd turned into a surly jerk this morning. Jinxi hoped it was part of the head injury and not something she'd done. Or maybe he found out she'd snooped in his email.

Her thoughts swung around to the image of Dean with a kid. Weird. That would totally change things, including her friendship with him.

She rubbed her sweatshirt-covered arms, grateful Aneesa hadn't asked her to push up her sleeves during the addiction group. The new cut hadn't healed up yet, continuing evidence of her inability to deal with all the drama in her life. Would she ever be normal? Probably not. Maybe if she could just get past this whole money mess, the Skeeter thing, and keep Burn Boy at bay, things might go back to normal. Maybe.

What about the email she'd seen on Dean's computer? Why hadn't he said anything last night? He used to tell her everything. Why was he keeping such a big secret? Maybe that's why he got all moody. She'd be cranky too if she found out she had a kid out there. Of course, that wasn't possible. She'd made sure of that. Her hand went involuntarily to her stomach. What would her life have been like if ...

No use going down that path. She'd be a terrible mother.

After setting the plate on the coffee table, she stood and stretched. Braving the dark hall, she slid toward Janice's office on stocking feet. She flicked on the light, sweeping her eyes around the room, checking for ... what? Monsters? Some brick wielding psycho?

The computer hummed to life as she logged on, searching for the next knife in the set she was building. She took her time, intent on finding a good knife at a reasonable price.

"What're you doing?" Dean stood in the office doorway.

Jinxi jumped, fists clenching. "Stop sneaking up on me!"

"I made enough noise coming through the back door."

"I didn't hear you." The shock left her feeling jangly. "What do you want?"

"I came to see if you were okay. No more brick incidents?"

Jinxi peered up at him. "I think the brick thrower likes the middle of the night. More shock value, know what I mean?"

Dean pulled the chair away from Janice's worktable and sat, one leg bouncing up and down. "What are you doing on my mom's computer?"

He wore his cop face, serious, piercing all the way to her soul.

"Looking for a knife."

When his eyes swung to her arm, she quickly added, "For work. You know, cutting vegetables and stuff."

"Sure."

Jinxi's jaw tightened. She didn't care if he believed her or not. Or did she? Resisting the urge to go into more detail, she turned to face the computer, her back to him. Silence lengthened between them. The back of her neck tingled as she felt his eyes boring into her. What was he waiting for? Why didn't he go away? She couldn't breathe.

Ted padded into the room, breaking the tension.

"Hi, buddy." Jinxi pictured Dean rubbing Ted's back. "What's this? Huh, Ted? What's on your face?"

Jinxi whirled in the chair. Dean was picking what looked like cheese off Ted's muzzle. He held it up, throwing Jinxi an accusing look. "What's this?"

She opened her eyes wide, hoping to look innocent. "I dunno."

"Looks like cheese. What did you have for dinner?" There was that cop thing again.

"Tomato soup." She resisted the urge to break eye contact.

"And?"

"Sandwich."

"Grilled cheese, maybe?"

Jeez, he was relentless.

"Maybe."

Dean grunted. Hadn't he told her not to feed people food to Ted? He couldn't remember. He had an urge to laugh at her attempt to look innocent. He remembered seeing that look before, usually after she'd played a trick on him. His brain flashed a memory of the time she'd put salt in his coffee along with the cream, after he'd teased her about something.

He'd had every intention of coming to his mother's house to confront her with what he'd learned about her past. His resolve leaked out when he saw her hunched over the computer, drowning in the oversized hoodie. His breath caught in his throat as he watched her hands, small as a child's, working on the keyboard.

He'd taken a psych class in college. They'd talked about why kids set fires. Many times, it was traced back to physical or sexual abuse. The cut marks on her arms revealed there was more going on inside her than she showed.

Dang. He really liked this woman. She challenged him like no one else. Why did she have to have so much baggage? How could he get her to talk about the fire?

So, you set a fire when you were fourteen? Not a great beginning.

How did it feel to know you killed a kid? Not much better.

Are you sorry you did it? Isn't that what he really wanted to know? Did she feel remorse? Why was it so important for him to hear her say the words?

CHAPTER THIRTY-FIVE

Sacramento International Airport buzzed with constant movement. Dean stood near the arriving gate while passengers swirled around him. How long could it possibly take for his mom to get off the plane? Glancing at his watch for the tenth time, he wished he'd taken time to eat lunch before he left home. Smells from the food court wafted over him. Maybe he could talk her into stopping for a burger on the way home.

His cell phone buzzed as he spotted his mom making her way toward him. Pulling it out of his pocket, he glanced at the text. His stomach growled with a different kind of angst as he read the message from Raul.

Think your girlfriend can protect you? Or your mama?

Dean pasted a smile on his face.

"Hi, Mom. Have a good trip?" He kissed her cheek, then took the carry-on from her hand.

Janice chatted away as they descended the escalator to the baggage claim area.

"It was so nice to see my sister again. It's been way too long. We talked about having a family reunion next year."

Dean let her words wash over him as he thought about the meaning of Raul's text. Was he planning another middle-of-the-night brick throw? Or something more ominous? How could he protect his mom and Jinxi without freaking them out?

"What do you think?" Janice touched Dean's arm.

"Huh?"

"I said, what do you think about all of us going back to Iowa next summer for a family reunion?"

"Okay, I guess." He was starting to sound like Jinxi. "What about Robin?"

His mom's face clouded over. "Maybe she'll be speaking to me by then."

Why did he have to go and bring up his sister? He felt a pang of longing for his little niece and nephew. It'd been way too long since he and Hannah had played hide and seek. A random thought struck his head like an arrow. Wonder what Mom would do if she found out she had another grandchild? Would she be ecstatic? Or embarrassed and ashamed of him for the way the kid was conceived? Better keep that in its compartment and concentrate on the problem at hand. Raul.

"Anything interesting happen while I was gone?"

Dean was saved from answering right away when he spotted his mom's suitcase inching toward them on the conveyor. He pulled it off with a grunt.

"What'd you pack in here? Rocks?"

Janice laughed. "Your Aunt Debbie couldn't let me leave without giving me some of her famous homemade soaps and bath salts."

"Did she send enough for the entire population of Sacramento?"

"Well, not the entire population."

Once they were in Dean's truck, Janice asked, "How did Jinxi do while I was gone? Was she scared to be in the house alone at night?"

What should he say? He couldn't mention the broken window. Neither could he tell her about Jinxi staying over at his apartment.

"I think she did okay." Not really a lie.

Janice settled back in her seat. "Good. I was worried about that. Considering what she's gone through."

What did she mean by that?

Janice sighed. "The first thing I'm doing when I get home is taking a nap."

"Good idea," Dean said absently. Maybe his mom knew more about Jinxi's past than she let on. Maybe it was time for a heart-to-heart chat with his mother.

Janice transferred the last of her clothes from the washer to the dryer. She turned it to the proper setting and hit the start button just as she heard Jinxi coming through the front door.

Hurrying into the living room, she embraced the younger woman. "You're a sight for sore eyes."

Jinxi was slow to raise her arms and reciprocate the hug. "Thanks, I think."

Janice laughed. "Whatever you put in the crock pot smells delicious. I'm starved."

Jinxi ducked her chin into her sweatshirt. "It's just some chicken and veggies and stuff." She picked up her backpack from where she'd dropped it and headed toward the stairs.

"Go ahead and get settled. We'll eat when you're ready. I made a salad."

"Cool."

Janice watched her tread up the stairs, dragging her pack behind her. It was good to be home.

They ate in the kitchen, knees bumping under the ancient table.

"I had such a good time visiting with my sister. Her name is Debbie, and she has two grown sons. Jack is Dean's age, and Preston is a couple of years younger. Jack works construction, and Pres helps his dad manage the farm."

Used to Jinxi's silence, Janice kept talking. "Dean said you were okay staying here by yourself?"

Jinxi choked, coughing and waving her hands in front of her face. After she took a sip of water and a few deep breaths, she asked, "Didn't he say anything about the brick?"

Janice set down her fork. "What brick?"

Jinxi was saved from answering by the sound of the back door opening, and Dean stepping into the room.

Janice shifted her gaze from Jinxi to her son. "What brick?" she repeated.

Dean froze as the blood drained from his face. His mother's eyes snapped back to Jinxi, who sat with her head down, hands in her lap.

"Will someone please tell me what's going on?" Janice shoved her plate away.

Dean pulled out a chair and dropped into it. He rubbed the back of his neck, then let his hands drop, resting them on the table. He shot an accusing look toward Jinxi before answering.

"Mom, it's nothing to get all worked up about. Just some kids vandalizing the neighborhood. A brick was thrown through your living room window. I didn't want you to get upset, so I had the window replaced and had a company come in to clean up the glass. That's why I didn't mention it at the airport."

Janice shifted her gaze back and forth between them. Why did she have the sense there was something they weren't telling her?

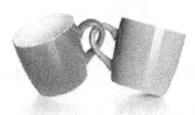

"Jinxi, come outside with me," Dean said. "I want to show you something Ted can do." He grabbed her arm, hauling her to her feet. "We'll be right back, Mom."

Dean whistled for Ted as they closed the back door and trudged down the concrete steps to the back yard. When they reached the bottom, he swung around. "Why did you have to say anything about the brick to my mom?" He rubbed his face, grimacing.

"How was I to know you didn't want me to say anything?" She stood with her hands on her hips, a defiant look in her eyes.

"You should have known she'd be upset. And worried."

"She has a right to know—"

"No. She doesn't need to have something else to worry about. You know how moms are."

"No, I don't."

Words ready to pour out stayed in his mouth, unsaid. There was still so much he didn't know about this strange young woman. Or did he, and he'd forgotten? Why was everything so complicated?

"Forget it," he mumbled, as he turned to walk across the yard to his apartment.

"Wait," Jinxi said, but he waved her off.

"Go back inside. I'm sure my mom has a ton of questions for you. Just don't mention the writing on the brick, okay?"

Dean didn't wait for her answer. His cell phone buzzed in his coat pocket. A fifty-pound weight settled on his chest as he fumbled for the device. With a breath of relief, Damaris's name appeared on the screen.

"Li'l D," he answered with their usual greeting.

"Big D, 'sup?"

"Not much," Dean lied.

"We gotta talk." Damaris's voice held an urgency Dean hadn't heard before. "I'm off shift. Let's meet at your place."

"Why? What's up?"

"I don't want to say over the phone, if you know what I mean."

Dean didn't know. "Uh, okay. I'm home."

"I'll be there in twenty."

Something must have happened down at the station. What was it this time? Dean climbed the stairs to his apartment, pondering the possibilities.

He sank onto the futon, resting his head against the wall. He tried to capture the feeling of peace he'd had after talking with the chaplain. Mike had given him a lot to think about. Dean told him something he'd never shared with anyone.

"Tell me about the day your dad died," Mike had asked.

Pressure in Dean's chest built, squeezing his lungs like a fist. "We fought that morning," he blurted.

"What about?"

"Dad wanted me to apologize to one of my friends, someone from high school. This friend was living with a girl, and they had a baby together. I told him it was sin, that they should get married." Dean huffed a humorless laugh. "He didn't like what I said."

"What you said was true—"

"Yeah, but Dad said I went about it the wrong way. He said God has a high standard of holiness, but a huge hand of grace. He told me I always look at things black and white, with no shades of gray."

"That must have hurt." Mike's look was sympathetic.

"He said I can't admit when I'm wrong. I told him he was a hypocrite. That's the last thing I said to him."

Dean's thoughts were interrupted by a loud knock on the door. He sprang to his feet, strode to the door, and yanked it open. Damaris pushed past him into the room.

"Broseph, what's going on?"

Dean stared uncomprehending at his friend.

"I heard you're involved in some drug deal going down next week."

CHAPTER THIRTY-SIX

"Everything all right?" Janice asked when Jinxi stepped through the back door.

Warmth spread through her, seeing Janice sitting at the table. How was it possible this place felt more like home than the house she grew up in?

Wonder how my mom's doing.

Where did that come from? Her trip to see her mom last month had been all kinds of bad. Jinxi tried to tell her mom about the change God made in her life, but her mom turned it into a joke.

Still blown away at the older woman's forgiveness, Jinxi wondered for the millionth time if Janice would be as forgiving if she knew about the kid she'd killed. If she could just keep it a secret a little longer, until she had enough money saved to move out. Maybe Skeeter would give her a little of his earnings after she did the deal for him.

Jinxi pulled the stud against her teeth, keeping her head down.

"Sure. Fine."

The temperature in the house dropped as Jinxi clomped up the stairs to her room after she'd washed the dinner dishes. Janice's husband, Tom, had added the second story bedrooms and bathroom when their family outgrew the two bedrooms downstairs. There was no central heat or air conditioning. Jinxi switched on the space heater.

Ted appeared a few minutes later, nudging Jinxi's hand for a rub before settling into his bed. Jinxi crawled into bed, leaning against the headboard, arms circling her bent legs. She ran through her conversation with Dean, wishing she'd reacted differently. Why did the words I'm sorry stick in her throat?

She pulled open the drawer of the nightstand, taking her Bible out with a guilty pang. It'd been way too long since she paid any attention to God.

The devotional guide Janice had given her pointed to Romans 8:1. "Therefore there is now no condemnation for those who are in Christ Jesus." Something dropped into Jinxi's spirit. Tentacles of warmth, immediately pushed back by fear. Wrestling. Doubting.

When she finally settled into sleep, the dream came without warning. She was in the burning house, desperately seeking the source of the child's screams. The ceiling in the hall behind her collapsed into a red heap of fiery plaster. As she neared the last bedroom, the screams turned into whimpers. Heat blasted her face as she stepped gingerly over pieces of burning debris, entering the room. Someone was lying on the bed, faced away from the door. Jinxi tried to call out, but her tongue refused to move. She touched the figure on the bed. When the person turned over, Jinxi was staring at her own face.

She woke with a gasp, heart thudding in her chest, Tee shirt soaked with sweat. She'd never be free of the nightmare. Just when it seemed her life was getting better, Skeeter bombed into her life and threatened everything. Every bad choice turned her fortune into brittle pieces, easily broken.

What she needed was a plan. Jinxi pounded her fist against her forehead. Think, think. There were only two choices to choose from. Go along with Skeeter's plan and risk arrest again, or let him tell everyone she was a murderer.

Trust me.

Her movements stilled. Was that God?

There is now no condemnation.

Right. Now she knew it wasn't God speaking. There couldn't be forgiveness for her.

Maybe she should just go back to Los Angeles with Skeeter. He'd take her back, wouldn't he? They could go back to the way they were before. He made the deals, she did the deliveries. Bouncing from motel to apartment to campground. Making a grip of money and spending it all.

A full moon slid across the sky outside Jinxi's bedroom window, casting the dark furniture into sharp relief. The bureau now held all the clothing she'd amassed in the past three months. A few items hung in the closet, including her white chef's coat, a recent purchase. Two library books sat on the nightstand, ready to be returned. The one photo of her mom and dad together, perched on the dresser, along with the worn stuffed bunny.

Her heart ached with the thought of leaving everything behind. She didn't really want to return to her old life. But it would be better if everyone thought of her as a deserter rather than a murderer.

She wiped the tears from her cheeks and thought about who she would miss the most. Dean, who was still mad at her? What about Janice, who'd let her into her home? Or Hannah, who first broke the cement block of Jinxi's heart? Maybe Ted, the first pet she'd ever known. A litany of people paraded through her head. Friends from work, from her support group, from church.

Clamping down on the tidal wave of emotion, she willed herself to stop before the dam broke and she drowned in sorrow.

"Hola, chica." Connie greeted Jinxi, minus her usual smile. Morale had sunk low since the theft. Aneesa barked at everybody more often. Padish lacked his bounce. Even Hank was affected, speaking even less than usual.

Maybe she should just confess and get it over with. They'd never believe she didn't do it. That'd solve the Skeeter problem. Better they thought of her as a thief than a killer.

Jinxi dragged herself into the warehouse, bracing herself for Skeeter's appearance. She tracked him down by the telltale smell of smoke drifting in from the alley. Moments later he ducked under the partially opened rollup door.

"Aren't you done with your community service yet?" Jinxi snapped.

"Hello to you, too," Skeeter answered, approaching her.

Jinxi backed up when he got within a foot.

She cringed as he raised his hand to rub his head.

"Still scared?" he sneered. He grabbed her arm in a vise-like grip. "You used to like it rough." He yanked her close, grabbing her hair with his other hand. Forcing her face close to his, he dropped his lips on hers.

Jinxi struggled to escape but was no match for his sinewy strength.

The door from the cafeteria snapped open.

"What is going on here?" Padish demanded.

Skeeter dropped his arms as if Jinxi was on fire. Skeeter grinned lazily at Jinxi, then turned to face Padish.

"What can I say? She thinks I'm irresistible." He spread his arms wide and shrugged.

Jinxi's face burst into thousand-degree heat. Eyes downcast, she wrapped her arms around herself.

"Come with me," Padish told her.

Jinxi followed him to the door, chin tucked into the neck of her hoodie. She thought she heard Skeeter snicker.

Head down, she followed Padish through the cafeteria, then down the hall to his office. Aneesa took one look at them before springing to her feet and heading out the door, closing it behind her.

Jinxi sat in the hard chair across from her boss. The sound of his fingers drumming on the desk matched the staccato pounding of her heart.

"I do not even know what to say."

Jinxi stole a glance, but his eyes were focused somewhere over her head.

"I can explain—"

"No. Do not say anything."

"But—"

"Stop." Padish sighed heavily. "Please collect your things and go home."

Jinxi's pulse stopped, then resumed its runaway speed. "Am I fired?" She held her breath, waiting for his answer.

"No. I want to think about this ... situation. You may return tomorrow."

Too ashamed to lift her head, she gathered her backpack with wooden arms, slinging it over one shoulder.

Words fought for release. Let me explain ... it wasn't my fault ... he's not really Jared ... he's bad ...

"You're bad too," the accuser said.

"Yes, I know," she answered.

CHAPTER THIRTY-SEVEN

The bus grunted to a stop. Jinxi stepped off, pulling the hood of her sweatshirt over her head. A slight drizzle wet the pavement and settled like jewels on her sleeves. She hunched her shoulders, catching the flashing neon sign in the window of the convenience store across the street.

A swift decision, driving her legs toward the store. Pulling a few bills from her wallet, she tossed them on the counter, receiving in return a pack of cigarettes and a lighter.

She sat cross-legged on the asphalt under the overhang from the store's roof. She set the backpack next to her, then began the ritual of pulling out a cigarette, lighting it, and taking the first deep draw. With each exhale of smoke, she rehearsed every insult, every imagined slight, every suspicion from the past three months at the food bank.

They didn't care about her. Padish didn't even trust her enough to let her explain. He probably still thought she took the money. That he'd believe Skeeter over her hurt the most. Anger burned as hot as the tip of her cigarette. They all hated her. Even Connie. They were probably laughing behind her back.

Look at the dirty white girl. She can't do anything right. What a loser.

A low-rider slid down the street, its bass thumping as loud as the voices pounding in her head.

She lit a second cigarette, using the first as a lighter. Why bother trying to be good? It didn't get her anything. Where was God? Why would he let all this stuff keep happening?

A police car cruised by windows down despite the rain. The officer gave her a hard stare. She stared back.

A few minutes later, he rolled by again, pulling to the curb across from where she sat.

Keeping his hands on the wheel, he leaned out the window. "Everything okay, miss?"

His words belied the intent. Move on.

Jinxi slowly stood, dropping the cigarette, and crushing it under her boot. "Yeah. Fine." She pulled the backpack over her shoulder and started to move toward the sidewalk, aware of the officer's stare.

The cruiser kept pace with her as she headed toward Janice's. Jinxi shivered, trying to decide whether or not to break into a run.

"One more thing."

She snapped her head toward the police car as the officer spoke.

"Tell your boyfriend it isn't over."

He stepped on the gas, tires squealing on the wet road.

Jinxi stood frozen until the taillights were out of sight. Then she broke into a jog, arriving at Janice's front gate, winded from the cigarettes and unexpected exercise. She bent over, resting her hands on her thighs, gulping in air. If only her heart would slow down.

After unlocking the front door, she dropped her pack on the piano bench, then slumped onto the sofa. What did that cop mean? Her boyfriend? Why did he think she and Dean were together? What wasn't over? Maybe he was behind the brick throwing.

It was time for a chat with Dean.

Jinxi headed into the kitchen, disappointed to see an empty space where he normally parked his truck. The microwave clock showed ten twenty. She should be at work, helping Connie get ready for the lunch crowd. What would Padish tell everyone? That she was some kind of skank, coming on to Skeeter?

The coffee pot was clean, thanks to Janice. Jinxi measured out enough for two cups, poured in water and hit START. She wandered around the kitchen while it brewed, opening and closing the fridge, pantry, spice cabinet, freezer. What should she do for the rest of the day?

Her gaze rested on the knife rack on the counter. It pulled her like a magnet until she was leaning against the counter, reaching for a blade. She jerked back as the house phone rang. That was close. Too close. She let it ring. The answering machine would pick it up. It wasn't for her anyway.

The coffeemaker beeped. Her hands shook as she poured a steaming cup. Maybe some cooking therapy would help. Anything to keep her away from another step toward self-destruction.

An hour later, she'd assembled a chicken casserole, mixing cooked chicken, broccoli, mushroom soup, noodles, and Swiss cheese. She covered it with foil to bake later. After washing and drying the prep tools, she tossed the towel on the counter. What to do next?

Rain dripped from the trees in the backyard. The world outside matched Jinxi's inside. Gray, drab, wet, sad. No matter what she tried, her past would always be there, a specter haunting everything.

She watched Dean's truck jerk to a halt at the curb outside the garage. He zipped his jacket up around his throat, scrunching down like a turtle. He walked around to the passenger side, opening the door to let Ted leap out. A pang of longing for Ted's comfort shot through her heart. How many secrets had she whispered in his scruffy ears? He didn't judge her past, didn't repeat her secrets, always greeted her with a sloppy tongue. His presence in her bedroom at night kept her from closing the door and shoving the nightstand against it. Even so, he was Dean's dog. He'd never be hers, no matter how many times she let him sleep with her.

Better for her to break the attachment. To Ted, Dean, Janice ... to everyone. She'd never be a part of this family, or any family.

She took a sip of her cold coffee. Yuck. She poured it down the drain, then turned her back to the window. The knife rack beckoned from the counter next to the refrigerator. One cut was all she needed to release the anguish inside. One stroke of the knife across the delicate skin of her inner arm. Redemption would come with the bright red spurt of blood.

Without hesitating to think through the decision, she strode across the kitchen and reached for the smallest knife in the rack. She waited for the familiar warmth of release after the first pinch of pain, just as she waited for the first draw of smoke into her lungs. But the release, the rush of satisfaction didn't come.

Blood dripped from her arm onto the floor, crimson spots on the yellowed linoleum. She stared, unblinking, as a Bible verse flashed across the screen of her memory.

His blood was shed for you.

With a cry, she crumpled to the floor, tears mixing with blood. She'd broken two promises to God in one day.

CHAPTER THIRTY-EIGHT

Dean's thoughts about his conversation with Chaplain Mike were interrupted when Damaris burst through his door.

"Drug deal?" Dean stared at his friend in confusion.

Damaris shrugged out of his jacket, threw it on the futon, then dropped onto a stool. He held his hands up in surrender. "I don't know, dude. All I know is what I've heard."

Dean sank onto the futon, rubbing the back of his neck. "And you believe the smack talk?" His eyes pinned his friend with laser-like focus.

Damaris held his gaze, then looked away. "I don't know what to believe."

A slow burn of anger ignited inside Dean's gut, bursting into white-hot heat. He slammed his fist down on the arm of the futon and shot to his feet.

"I'm sick of people talking about me. I haven't done anything wrong. I did my job, told my story to IA, and now I'm a drug dealer?" His voice rose in intensity. "You're supposed to be my friend, my BFF." Dean used his fingers to make air quotes.

To his surprise, Damaris started laughing. "Did you just say BFF?" His laughter rocked him back and forth as he struggled to keep his balance on the bar stool.

Dean spoke through gritted teeth. "This isn't funny."

"You're right. It's not funny, it's ridiculous. Mr. Clean Dean would never get involved in something as dirty as drugs, right?"

"You know I hate that nickname."

"Which only goes to prove I don't believe any of the trash that's going around."

Dean sank back onto the futon. "Then why'd you come running over here like one of the Gossip Girls?"

"We need to figure out who's trying to take you down. There's some crazy rumors in the cloud. Some people are starting to take notice."

"Like Sarge?"

"Yeah. Sarge." Damaris pulled a notebook out of his shirt pocket and flipped it open. "Got a pen?" He swiveled on the stool, searching the bar for something to write with. "Dude, your place is like, skankville." He shoved aside a plate of half-eaten pizza and grabbed a pen.

"What're you doing?" Dean watched as his friend turned a few pages in his notebook.

"You're the one who's jonesing to be a detective, right?" Dean nodded.

"So start thinking like one." Damaris pointed to his head, then to Dean's. "Let's figure out who's spreading crap about you."

Dean held up a hand to stop him. "I don't need to be a detective to figure it out."

Damaris barely glanced up from his writing. "Huh?"

Dean leaned forward. "Did I tell you about the brick?"

That got his friend's attention. Damaris sat stock-still as Dean told him about the brick through the window, the note on the back of the traffic citation, and the cruiser slowing as it passed his mom's house.

Furious knocking on the door broke the ensuing silence. Dean slapped his hands on his thighs, went to the door, and opened it to find Jinxi on his doorstep. Anxiety pinched her face.

"Not now, Jinxi. I'm busy." He tried to close the door, but she blocked him.

"Wait. I have to tell you something." Her breaths came in short gasps.

"Can't it wait?"

"No. Let me in. It's important." She put her hand on the door and shoved it back.

Dean sighed. "Fine. Whatever. But make it quick."

She skidded to a stop when she saw Damaris. "Sorry. I didn't know anyone was here."

Dean waved her forward. "Come in. Say your thing." Then leave.

Jinxi took a few deep breaths. "I came home early from the food bank, okay?"

"Why?" Dean's focus was now on her face, probing for anything she wasn't telling him.

Jinxi waved a hand in dismissal. "That's not important. I was at the convenience store—"

"Why?"

Jinxi placed her hands on her hips. "Would you quit interrupting me? Jeez. I was leaving, and this cop car came by. The guy—"

"What guy?"

Jinxi sighed. "The cop, okay? The cop. He leans out the window and says to me, 'Tell your boyfriend it isn't over.' Then he drives away."

Everyone was silent for the space of a heartbeat. Then Dean motioned toward the futon.

"You better sit down."

Jinxi clomped to the futon and sat, arms crossed. "What do you think he meant? Was it connected to the brick? It was totally creepy." She grimaced. "Who thinks we're, you know, together anyway?"

Dean and Damaris exchanged glances.

"What?" Jinxi asked. "Why are you two looking at each other that way?"

"Somebody's out to get your boyfriend," Damaris said, his attention on Jinxi.

"Not you too!" Dean exploded.

"Just kidding, Big D." Damaris turned toward Jinxi. "We think—well, Dean's convinced— his partner is trying to turn things around to discredit him. The question is, why?"

"And what's the chatter about some drug deal I'm supposedly involved with?"

Jinxi straightened. "What drug deal?"

"There's a rumor about Dean arranging a drug handoff next weekend."

"Next weekend?"

Dean turned to her, frowning. "What's wrong with you?"

"Uh ... nothing. It's just that ..." She stood. "I gotta go. I left something on the stove."

Dean watched her go, wheels in his head turning. "Hey, Jinxi—" But she was already out the door.

"What're you thinking?" Damaris asked.

Dean shook his head. "Nothin'. Let's figure out how we can turn things around on my so-called partner."

After Damaris left, Dean sat at his desk, hands poised over the laptop keyboard. He started writing out everything he could remember from the time of the shooting. As he got to the part about what Jinxi told him, a window popped up, telling him a new email had arrived.

Grateful for the diversion, he toggled over to his email account and found another email from Family Ancestry, subject line "DNA Results."

Fear gripped his stomach like a fist. He shoved back from the desk, staring at the unopened email as he stood.

Pacing around the small apartment, he tried to grasp the feeling of peace he'd had after telling Mike Zannakis about his sin with Katie when he was in college, her email, and the DNA test. Instead of peace, confusion and anxiety swirled, faster and faster until his head threatened to burst.

Dean grabbed his phone off the desk, and with cramped fingers scrolled through his contacts. He needed Mike. Instead, he got his voice mail.

"Hi, this is Chaplain Z, or Mike, if you prefer. Leave me a message. If this is a life-threatening emergency, hang up, drop to your knees, and pray." Beep.

"Uh, Chap—I mean, Mike. This is Dean. Rafferty. I need to talk to you. Call me, okay? Uh, thanks." Dean punched END, then tossed the phone over to the futon.

Where was Mike when he needed him? He said he'd be available any time Dean wanted to talk. Where was he? Dean's brooding turned to anger as he stomped around and around in the apartment. Finally, he sank onto the futon and grabbed the phone, pushing the redial button.

His foot tapped an impatient rhythm as he waited through the voice message.

"Hi, this is Chaplain Z, or Mike, if you prefer. Leave me a message. If this is a life-threatening emergency, hang up, drop to your knees, and pray."

Dean ended the call before the beep.

He dropped his head in his hands, resting his elbows on his knees. The words came from a deep chasm of hurt, forcing themselves past the serrated edges of fear and shame.

"God, I'm in a huge mess. I may lose my job. I possibly have a kid I've never met. Everyone's going to call me a deadbeat dad, or a date rapist or something. You probably don't even like me anymore. I said I hated you. But I don't. Can you please help me?"

Dean sat for several minutes, rocking back and forth. The heat of his anger cooled, morphing into a refreshing calm.

"Thank you, Jesus," Dean whispered, as the peace he'd experienced with Mike spread over him like warm chocolate.

He returned to the computer, clicking on the email from Family Ancestry.

Dear Sir:

Attached are the results from your DNA test. Please contact us if you have any questions. Thank you for using Family Ancestry DNA.

Dean took a deep breath and held it as he opened the attachment. The report was several pages long, filled with graphs, charts, and medical jargon. He scanned through it quickly, not seeing what he needed to know.

He read through it again, then sat back in the chair, exhaling his disappointment. He began a new email.

"Dear Katie," he wrote. "I have the results of the DNA test, but it's all scientific stuff. I can't figure it out."

Her answer came within minutes. "Forward it to me. I have someone who can decipher it."

He forwarded the email to her, regretting that he hadn't asked her how long it would take. Was he a father of a six-year-old? Or not?

Now to think about what Jinxi was hiding. Again.

CHAPTER THIRTY-NINE

Janice opened the blinds in her bedroom and peered out at the damp street. This was the coldest October she could remember. With Halloween coming, would children be able to wear costumes without a coat?

Her breath hitched as she thought about Hannah and Owen. Would she see them this year, all dressed up? Would Hannah's scrap book have a gap between last year and this? What if she never got to see them again?

Why did Jinxi have to find that file, anyway? She could have kept Janice's secret a little longer. Just until the grandkids were older. Or maybe forever. Now she had no relationship with her daughter, couldn't see her grandchildren. Janice rubbed her chest, tears building behind closed eyes. Was it possible to feel your heart breaking?

Everything comes to you through my hand.

Janice felt, rather than heard the words in her spirit.

"Yes, I know, Lord. I just don't understand. This hurts so much."

She sighed, recalling the familiar hymn, "Turn Your Eyes Upon Jesus."

Hours later, stiff from sitting in her chair, Bible in hand, she rose and shuffled down the hall to her office. She had two things she needed to do. First, write a letter to her daughter.

Dear Robin,

After your brother Brian was born, I was told I'd never have any more children. I was devastated because I always wanted a little girl. When your dad and I found out about you, we couldn't wait to bring you home. You had this beautiful head of red hair, so we named you Robin, like the bird. We loved you like our own flesh and blood.

I realize now it was wrong not to tell you the circumstances surrounding your birth. Please forgive me for hurting you.

You've given me so much joy. I don't regret for a moment adopting you.

I love you,
Mom

She addressed the letter, stamped it, and carried it out to the mailbox. That done, she returned to the house to wait for Jinxi to come home from work.

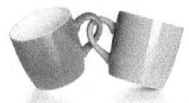

"Yinxi, Yinxi!" Connie's voice, shrill with excitement greeted Jinxi as she covered the distance between the front door and the dining hall. "Come, chica. I must tell you something." Connie grabbed her arm, pulling Jinxi into the dining room.

"What is it?" Jinxi sat on one of the tables, which was strictly forbidden. What did she have to lose, anyway?

"Natividad and me buy a house!" Connie fanned her face with her apron, visibly struggling to find the words to explain.

"What? That's awesome."

With her growing understanding of Spanish, she gathered Connie's family was in a lottery for a Habitat for Humanity house. They would be able to move in two months, when the house was complete.

"Is one bad thing." Connie's face fell. "Is farther from here."

"So? That's cool. You can do it." Connie's excitement infected Jinxi. The two of them talked in Spanglish until a cloud came over their fun.

"Miss Jinxi, you will come to my office with me, yes?" Padish stood unsmiling over the two women.

Jinxi sprang to her feet, happiness evaporating.

"Hasta, chica," Connie said, disappearing into the kitchen.

Jinxi followed Padish into the office, feet dragging. She sat across from him, staring down at the now-familiar stain on the carpet.

Padish steepled his fingers. "Jared will finish his community service this week. He will work in the warehouse with Hank in the afternoons only."

Jinxi's head swung up to meet his gaze.

"You will work in the warehouse until it is time to help in the kitchen. After lunch, you will come straight to this office and help Aneesa. You are to have no contact with Jared. Do you understand?"

Jinxi nodded dumbly. She wasn't fired. Not yet anyway. And she didn't have to talk to Skeeter. She heaved a sigh of relief as Padish waved her out of the office, like an annoying mosquito.

Mosquito. Skeeter. If she couldn't talk to him, how would she take care of his favor? Would her part be called off? What if he decided to tell everyone anyway? She couldn't trust him to keep her secret. She'd have to find a way to talk to him, rules or no rules.

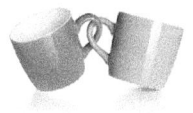

Janice paced in front of the living room windows, phone glued to her ear.

"I know, Emma, it's just that it's so hard not to see the grandkids."

Janice's best friend murmured assent. "When was the last time you tried to call?" Emma asked.

"A couple of days ago. I prayed all morning and felt like I should write Robin a letter."

"That's a wonderful idea, dear. What did you say?"

"I asked her forgiveness for hurting her." Janice recited the letter to Emma from memory. "Then I put it in the mail before I could change my mind." Janice pulled back the lace curtain to see if she could spot Jinxi approaching the house. What she saw almost made her drop the phone. Jinxi had stopped at the entrance to Janice's driveway and was puffing on a cigarette. She'd told Janice she stopped smoking a few weeks ago. What was going on with the girl?

"I'm sorry, Emma, I have to go."

"Is everything all right, Jan dear?"

"Yes. Fine. I'll talk to you tomorrow." Janice let the curtain drop, then set the phone on the coffee table. She looked heavenward and prayed a quick prayer for wisdom.

Jinxi stepped through the front door, Ted pushing past her.

"Hi," Jinxi said.

Janice watched her let the backpack slip to the floor. Jinxi bent down on Ted's level, letting him lick her face while they exchanged sloppy greetings. Janice rarely saw her let down her guard like she did with the dog.

"Would you like something to drink?" Janice asked, heading toward the kitchen.

Jinxi rubbed her arms. "Sure. Something hot, I think. Is there any coffee left?"

Janice turned on the kitchen light, Jinxi at her heels.

"No, but how about hot cocoa?"

Jinxi shrugged, still rubbing her arms. "Sure. I'm cold."

Janice filled the mugs with water and set them in the microwave. Jinxi moved to the pantry to take out two packets of cocoa, while Janice retrieved two spoons.

"Kitchen dance," Jinxi said.

"What?" Janice half-smiled. "What did you say?"

"Kitchen dance. It's what we do when we're in the kitchen together. Haven't you noticed we never bump into each other?"

Janice chuckled. "I never noticed."

Jinxi sank into a chair at the wooden table. "It's like ice skating or something." She blushed, red blotches starting at her neck and disappearing into her bangs.

"I never thought of it that way," Janice commented, taking their mugs from the microwave.

They stirred their cocoa in silence, until Jinxi said, "It's stupid. Forget I said anything."

"No, it's not stupid," Janice protested. "I think it's beautiful. It reminds me of what the Bible says about how the whole body works together, each one with their own part."

Jinxi nodded, holding the mug with both hands.

Janice took a deep breath. "I owe you an apology."

"For what?"

Janice took a moment to sip the hot liquid before answering. "When you had your ... encounter with God, I said I'd help you find your way. I feel like I've let you down. I've been so focused on me and my needs that I haven't asked you how you're doing."

Jinxi pulled the lip stud against her teeth, clicking it back and forth. The sound set Janice's nerves on edge.

"So how are you doing?" If Janice could get Jinxi talking, she'd stop that incessant clicking.

"Okay, I guess." Jinxi shrugged, a gesture Janice was familiar with.

"How is work?"

"Fine."

"Really? It looked like you were home early yesterday. Did something happen?"

"Not really." Jinxi twisted the hoops in her ears, avoiding eye contact.

"What about the missing money? Did they find who did it?"

Jinxi's face turned pale.

"No. Not yet."

Janice reached across the table, lightly touching Jinxi's arm. "Surely, they don't think you took it ..."

Jinxi sprang to her feet.

"I don't know what they think."

Jinxi carried her mug to the sink and turned on the water. Janice watched her slip off the dark hoodie. Jinxi had filled out in the past several weeks. From the back, she no longer looked like a twelve-year-old boy. Jinxi pushed up the sleeves of her Tee shirt before plunging her hands into the soapy water.

Janice pinched her lips together to keep the gasp in her throat. She saw the scabbed-over slash on the inside of Jinxi's arm. First the cigarettes, now a new cut? She needed to take a different tack.

"Want some help?" Janice asked to Jinxi's narrow back.

"No. I'm good."

Janice sent up a quick prayer for wisdom. "I wrote a letter to Robin today."

Jinxi swung around, dripping suds on the floor. "You did?" She stooped to mop up the mess.

"Yes. And I put it in the mail before I could change my mind." Janice waited, but Jinxi continued to scrub each utensil as if they'd been infected with Covid. "I realized that sometimes secrets shouldn't be hidden. Things need to be out in the open. I thought I was protecting Robin, but I was really protecting myself."

Janice got up and refilled her water glass from the spigot on the fridge. When she returned to the table, she continued, "I'm not sure what's going to happen, but I feel like a burden's been lifted, now that everything's out in the open."

Jinxi pushed a stray strand of hair out of her face with her shoulder. "What'd you say in the letter?"

"I asked her for forgiveness. I told her I was wrong to keep it hidden."

"Seriously?"

Janice wasn't sure which direction to go—now that she had Jinxi's attention. She took a sip of water, stalling for time while she prayed.

"I realized that no matter the consequences, God had everything under control. He's already forgiven me." It was a shot in the dark, and Janice hoped it resonated with whatever Jinxi was hiding.

CHAPTER FORTY

Dean lay back on his futon, feet on one armrest, head at the opposite end. The cell phone buzzed four times before it was answered on the other end.

"Hello?"

"Hey, Sis, it's me," Dean said.

Robin's voice turned flat. "In case you hadn't heard, I'm not your sister."

Dean sat up, swinging his legs to the floor with a thump.

"You're not gonna let a little something like DNA deny me the pleasure of hassling you." He walked to the window, pulling apart the blinds to see if the sun had made an appearance.

"You can hassle me all you want. It doesn't change the facts."

"C'mon, Robin, don't be like that." Dean missed the friendly banter they'd enjoyed before their mom's big revelation.

True to her personality, Robin responded, "I can be any way I want. Right now, I'm so mad at Mom I could spit."

Heartened by her use of the word 'Mom,' he continued. "It hasn't been easy for her, either."

Robin snorted. Dean changed tack. "How're my niece and nephew? When can I come over and see 'em?" He held his breath, waiting for her response.

She sighed into the phone. "Tomorrow. Hannah's been asking to see you. And bring Ted, okay?"

Dean smiled. "You got it. Peace out." He disconnected, grinning from ear to ear. As he set the phone down, it pinged. A text from Chaplain Mike.

MIKE: Sorry didn't answer your vm. Emergency last night. Will call u ltr.
DEAN: NP. It's all good.
Mike: ☺

Still craving outside contact, he scrolled through his address book and dialed his brother. As usual, Brian answered as if he was in a hurry.

"Hello?"

"Hey, big brother. 'Sup?"

Papers shuffled in the background. "Not much. Just working."

"Have you talked to Mom?"

"Yeah, she called me last night. Big surprise about Robin, huh?"

Dean paced the small apartment. "For sure. Never saw that coming. It doesn't change anything, though."

Shuffling got louder as Brian put his phone on speaker. "Sure, it does. It changes all kinds of things. What if her birth mother shows up someday, wanting a relationship? What if there are other siblings? Suppose Robin decides to drop us and go with them. Then what?"

Dean already regretted calling Brian. His brain didn't work like Brian's technical one. "Bro, there is no 'us' and 'them.' Robin's part of our family, end of story."

Brian heaved a sigh. "Look, I don't have time to talk to you right now. All I'm saying is there could be huge ramifications of something like this. Possibly legal implications too."

Dean rolled his eyes. "Whatever." He did it again. Jinxi was definitely rubbing off on him. "Talk to you later." He tossed the phone on the counter, resisting the urge to slam a fist into the wall.

Maybe he should go down and vent his frustration on the speed bag. Or run a few miles on the treadmill. What he really craved was human contact. He was used to working around people all day. This imposed isolation was slowly killing him. Maybe he'd text a few friends, invite them over for pizza, talk about a strategy to bring Raul down.

That done, he sat back at the computer, scrolling through what he'd written, organizing it into a chain of events.

- Raul tells him to tell Internal Affairs that the dad discharged his weapon before the responding officers.
- Raul becomes increasingly insistent about what he should tell IA.
- Raul is agitated when Dean tells IA he can't remember.
- IA asks him about Raul's alleged drug use.
- Someone throws a brick through his mom's front window (Raul?).
- His traffic citation has a threat written on the back.
- Police seem to be surveilling his mom's house.
- Cop delivers a threat to Jinxi.
- Rumor surfaces he's involved in a drug deal.

Dean worked the kinks out of his shoulders, fingers hovering over the keyboard. A headache, at first as small as a pinprick, worked its way up to his eyes, bursting into a bomb-sized explosion. He remembered the doctor telling him to avoid too much computer use.

He shoved the chair back, sending it crashing into the coffee table.

"Arrrggg!" Dean grunted, gripping his head with both hands. Would he ever be over the effects of the fall? He stumbled into the kitchen, tossing down two Tylenol with a half-empty can of Coke. He had to make some kind of sense out of Raul's behavior. He took the few steps to the futon and sank down. Or was it Jinxi he was supposed to be thinking about?

Thoughts moved sluggishly through his brain. Something about her ... what? His head fell back as he sank into slumber.

Jinxi let Janice's words sink in. With her back to Janice, she groped through the soapy water, searching for any stray utensils. She pulled out the sink stopper and let the water and suds drain away. What did Janice mean, God had already forgiven her everything? That he had everything in control? It sure didn't feel that way. Just when she thought she'd gotten her life together, it was unraveling.

What else should she expect? She'd gone from one disaster to another, usually her own fault. With no one to guide her, she'd made decisions based on what she needed at the time. As she swirled the faucet around to clear the sink, Jinxi thought back to the first time she'd been caught stealing. She'd been eight or nine years old. She hadn't eaten all weekend—her mom had been too drunk to fix anything to eat. Not that there was food in the house.

Jinxi had ridden her bike to McDonald's, waiting inside for the perfect moment to grab someone's to-go order when they were too slow to pick it up. The manager caught her at the door. She stiffened, remembering how he'd hauled her back to the counter and forced her to put the bag back. Then she had to apologize to the guy for taking his food.

She'd returned home and cried herself to sleep. The episode only strengthened her resolve to get better at the art of theft.

From there, she learned to pilfer, shoplift, steal, and manipulate to get what she needed. Food, clothes, whatever. Looking younger than her age totally worked in her favor.

When her acting out had escalated to arson, her life took a dark turn. Her friends took obscene pleasure in starting small fires in vacant lots. They'd enjoyed a sense of camaraderie, miscreants together. The camaraderie vanished like smoke when the house caught on fire, when only she was left to take the full blame. To carry the heavy burden of shame. To go to juvenile hall, then off to Girls' Ranch to pay her dues.

In one way, the Ranch was a blessing. Her grades improved because there wasn't anything else to do. She discovered a voracious love of reading. She learned some responsibility by having to help the younger girls with homework and chores.

The downside was the constant bullying. Her size invited bigger girls to pick on her.

Janice's voice jolted her out of her meanderings. "I think the sink might be clean by now."

With a start, Jinxi realized she'd been rinsing the sink for a while. She turned off the water. "Sorry," she mumbled, reaching for a towel to dry her hands.

"Don't you worry, honey." Janice stood and went to the pantry. "Want some cookies? I brought home a few from Brian and Courtney's house today."

Jinxi leaned back against the counter. "Courtney's?"

Janice's head appeared from out of the cupboard. She brought a plastic bag to the table. "I told Courtney I'd help her bake cookies for her church's youth group. Apparently, she volunteered to do it, then forgot. She called me in a panic yesterday."

Janice handed her the bag. Jinxi took three out and stacked them on a napkin on the table. Her sweet tooth began to ache. Chocolate chip was her favorite.

"Goodness gracious, sometimes that girl gets so involved in the creative process she forgets what day it is," Janice continued. "She's the exact opposite of Brian. His head is numbers and logic, and her head is always in the clouds."

"Courtney's nice," Jinxi said.

"Have you spoken to her lately?"

Jinxi shook her head.

"She's certainly been through some rough times. I'm sure she's told you about her parents." At Jinxi's nod, Janice continued. "For a long time, she carried a load of guilt for not being there when her parents died. She finally realized God's grace covers everything." Janice sighed. "I have to keep reminding myself it's true when I think about Robin."

Jinxi picked at a piece of food stuck on the leg of her jeans, head down. At least Courtney didn't actually kill anyone.

"Are you all right, honey?" Janice spoke to the top of Jinxi's head.

"Yeah. Fine." The urgency to flee set her feet on fire. "I'm going upstairs." She snagged two more cookies, then turned to go.

"How's your Bible reading going?" Janice called out.

Jinxi pretended not to hear as she escaped to the sanctity of her room.

CHAPTER FORTY-ONE

Dean gathered the empty fast-food containers off the counter, shoving them into the trashcan under the sink. As the sink filled with warm, soapy water, he hustled through the apartment, picking up bowls and cups. He flashed back to when Jinxi washed his dishes and straightened the kitchen. That was probably the last time it had been cleaned.

He glanced at his watch before plunging his hands into the sink. His friends would be here soon. He didn't want them to think he lived in a pigsty.

As Dean scrubbed the dishes, he wondered what Jinxi was up to. Was she hanging out with his mom, staying on her good side? He needed to have a talk with his mom. Soon. Jinxi might be dangerous. After all, she'd killed a kid.

As soon as the thought hit his brain, his heart rejected it. Had she ever exhibited violent behavior? No. Had she ever lashed out or made his mom uncomfortable? As far as he knew, no.

His cop brain kicked in, separating the knots of her story into logical threads. Just think about the facts.

She was arrested for attempted solicitation of a police officer. Her motive had been survival. She'd taken money from his mom's investment account. Again, survival.

He'd been wrong about his mom's missing earrings. All the evidence had pointed to her guilt, but the real culprit was his niece, Hannah, who'd hidden the jewelry in Jinxi's room. Dean's neck grew hot when he remembered how he'd gotten in her face, accusing her.

Aneesa told him Jinxi was a hard worker. Yet money was missing from the food bank. There was no real evidence, just circumstantial. Why would she risk her job for a few bucks?

He rewound to the report his friend had sent about the fire. Jinxi was fourteen when it happened. What did the report say?

Dean pulled the plug from the sink and let the water drain. He dried his hands, rushing to the laptop to retrieve the email from Matt.

The report said the fire had been started in a vacant lot. A gust of wind carried debris which landed on a house, causing the roof to catch fire. A child had been trapped inside and had died from smoke inhalation. Another child was burned, but he and his mother managed to escape. The house fire was ruled as accidental, the vacant lot, intentional. She'd been convicted of involuntary manslaughter, serving three and a half years at California Girls' Ranch, a kind of prison for minors.

He remembered from his psychology classes that one of the reasons kids set fires was if they'd been sexually abused. It was a form of acting out to attract attention, a sort of cry for help.

Dean slumped in the chair, chin in hand. What if the fire hadn't been Jinxi's fault? What if she'd suffered some horror that made her do what she did? And what about accomplices? The report said neighbors sighted more than one kid running from the scene. Jinxi had been the only one caught. She never ratted out her friends.

Maybe he'd been wrong about her. In the short time he'd been a cop, he'd seen what happened when women were abused. Drugs, alcohol, prostitution. He thought about his mother, risking everything to give Jinxi a home. Could he do the same thing?

A tender shoot of his renewed faith pushed its way through the tough shell of his heart. Maybe he'd been looking at her all wrong.

Fists banging on his door snapped him out of his reverie. His friends clamored to get in, pizzas and sodas in hand. The room burst with life as the guys jostled for the best seats, and the women searched Dean's cupboards for clean glasses.

Everyone was soon stuffing their faces with pizza. Laughter and chatter rose in intensity as the guys tried to outdo themselves to impress the women, talking about their latest pool and basketball games, Frisbee golf wins, and football conquests. Dean soaked it in, realizing what he'd been missing since his accident, jealous he'd been left out.

Patrice stood and tapped her glass with a plastic fork. "Sorry to interrupt all you Neanderthals, but we have a job to do."

"Is this an intervention?" someone quipped.

"Good question," Patrice answered. "As a matter of fact, you could call it that. D, I'm going to turn the floor over to you." She pointed her fork at Damaris, who licked pizza sauce off his fingers before speaking.

Damaris stood and began to pace the floor, rubbing his head.

"Let's talk about the rumors. We all know Clean Dean doesn't do drugs, has never done drugs, and would rather die than do drugs."

The group nodded in agreement.

As Damaris recounted the progression of events, Dean watched him pace. Four steps to the counter, four steps back to the chair. It was the same four steps he'd walked the day before, right before he prayed. The peace was still there, rooted in his spirit. Dean realized, for the first time since his fall, God had everything under control. No matter what Raul did or said, he couldn't arrest God's will.

If he lost his job ... the thought sliced through his heart. Could he still trust God? His dad would say so. Did he believe his dad? How was it God's will for his father to be killed?

A dull ache started behind Dean's eyes. It was too confusing to think about right now.

"So that's about it," Damaris concluded. He turned to Dean. "Did I get everything right?"

"Huh? Oh, right. Yeah." Dean swiveled his chair around to face the computer. "Let me check." He brought up the notes he'd written. Damaris approached him and looked over Dean's shoulder.

"Blah, blah, blah," Damaris read. "Brick, note, ticket ... yeah, I think that's everything."

The computer dinged, signaling an incoming email. A box appeared in the upper right corner. "New email from: Katie Edwards," it read.

"Who's Katie Edwards?" Damaris asked.

Dean's face prickled like he'd fallen into a porcupine. "Uh, someone I knew in college."

Patrice spoke from behind him. "Some college crush, hoping to re-fan the flame?"

Dean snapped the lid of the laptop down. "Okay, guys. Enough." He turned around to face the group. "And take those goofy looks off your faces."

"Thought you already had a girlfriend," Sommer commented.

"Yeah, the little hottie with the tats." This was from Sanjay.

Patrice smirked. "You know we have nothing better to do than gossip about your love life."

"Or lack thereof." Damaris laughed.

"At least you're keeping busy while you're off work," someone else commented.

Dean stood. "Stop. You guys are killing me."

Patrice agreed. "He's right. We've got work to do. I say we start our own rumor. About Raul."

Dean relaxed as the talk shifted away from the subject of him and women. Now there was an oxymoron. Dean plus women usually equaled … well, not disaster exactly. Usually just a lack of interest on his part. The few women he'd dated were either hot to sleep with him or shallow and self-absorbed. He hadn't met anyone who'd challenged him. Until Jinxi. She wasn't afraid to speak her mind with him, and she'd never hinted at any kind of sexual activity. He loved her snarky sense of humor. And she seemed to adore his mom. Too bad she came with so much baggage. If it wasn't for her dark past, she might be perfect for him.

As soon as that thought appeared, reality slammed him. What about the kid? If he ended up being the father of Katie's kid, his dating days would go from very few to nonexistent. Who wanted some guy with baggage? Oh, the irony. Who had more baggage—him or Jinxi?

His friends prepared to leave, gathering up empty pizza boxes and crumpled napkins.

"I'll take this down to the garbage," Patrice offered.

"I'll help," Sommer chimed in.

Damaris shook Dean's hand, then pulled him into a man hug. After some slaps on the back, they released each other.

"Looks like we have a plan," Damaris told him.

"A plan?" Dean asked.

"We'll take care of Raul, broseph. His rumors are about to backfire on him."

Dean nodded as everyone piled out. He sat back down on the desk chair, staring at the closed laptop, deep in thought.

Unease churned in his stomach. The group had a plan, but something wasn't right. They were going to fight lies with more lies. His dad's wisdom came back to him.

"Always tell the truth, son. The truth will set you free."

Yeah, Dad, or get you fired.

His friends had a plan, but Dean had a different one.

CHAPTER FORTY-TWO

"No, Teddie, you can't have some." Jinxi pushed Ted's nose away from her last bite of chocolate chip cookie. "They're not good for you." She patted the bed beside her. Ted jumped up and settled at her feet with a contented sigh.

Dean would be mad if he saw Ted sleeping on her bed. Somehow the thought didn't give her its usual grim satisfaction. She pulled her Bible from the nightstand drawer and laid it across her lap. It dropped open to where she'd stuck the devotional guide after the last time she'd read it. She'd highlighted Romans 8:1.

> There is now no condemnation for those who are in Christ Jesus.

She smoothed the page with her hand, rubbing it back and forth. She remembered Courtney telling her the story about the night her parents died. Jinxi had no idea Courtney had felt guilty. She hadn't mentioned that. She'd only said it was the turning point in her life.

The question came unbidden to her mind. Was it possible for God to forgive everything? Really? She flipped to the back of the Bible, looking for a dictionary or something to help her find the word forgive. What did Janice call it? Con-something or other.

There it was, in front of the maps. Concordance.

So many verses for forgive, forgiveness, forgiven. She picked the last one in the list. First John 1:9.

If we confess our sins, he is faithful and just and will forgive us our sins and purify us from all unrighteousness.

That day under the tree, sitting in the swing, she'd confessed everything. Even the fire. She'd felt clean for the first time in her life. How did things get so complicated? Where did the peace go?

What if other people didn't forgive everything? What if they changed their opinion of her? That wasn't something she was willing to face. If she did this thing for Skeeter, everything would go on as before. Well, except for the missing money.

Jinxi clutched her hand to her chest as something dropped in her spirit. Maybe Skeeter took the money. He could have had access to the office. He could have seen Aneesa leave, maybe when he was mopping the floor. She worried the lip stud back and forth, trying to make sense of the missing money.

After several minutes of her thoughts circling around and around, she dragged herself back to the problem at hand—the delivery of drugs for Skeeter. Her spirit rebelled against it, but her mind told her it was the only way to be free from him.

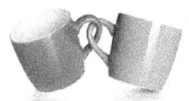

The bus ground to a halt in front of the food bank. Jinxi stood on the top step as the bus doors whooshed open. She stepped down to the sidewalk, adjusting the backpack over her shoulder, and trudged to the food bank entrance. Taking a fortifying breath, she pushed open the door, where familiar smells assaulted her—frying food, bleach, hopelessness. Standing just inside the door, she took in the freshly waxed floors, rows of tables and benches in the cafeteria beyond the entry, and the toddler play area. Hank waved to her across the space. She raised her hand in greeting, watching him methodically line each trash can with a fresh bag.

This was her comfort zone. The place where she finally belonged, with people who appreciated her hard work. How could she let Skeeter destroy all she'd gained? She stifled a curse, pushing open the door to the office.

Aneesa greeted her without smiling. Jinxi was clearly in disgrace. Her breakfast threatened to make an encore appearance at the thought of Skeeter kissing her. Anger rose at the injustice of being blamed for something she had no control over.

"What meaningless task to do you have for me today?" She glared at Aneesa, daring her to respond in kind.

Bring it on.

Aneesa's curls took on a life of their own, coiling around her head like Medusa. "Ooh, girl, don't take that attitude with me." She grabbed a pile of loose papers and shoved them toward Jinxi. "These need to be filed."

Jinxi swallowed her need to fight, grabbing the papers and dropping them on top of the file cabinet. She let the backpack drop to the floor, kicking it toward the cubbies where she usually stored it. Aneesa turned the radio on, cranking up the volume to squelch any further argument.

At least, Jinxi could see out the window while she worked. Jinxi's heart jumped when she saw Skeeter approach the building. Must be time for his shift. She kept her back to the office door, hearing him enter and speak briefly to Aneesa before leaving. She turned around and watched his back as he headed down the hall toward the cafeteria. She glanced over to Aneesa, who was watching her. Jinxi spun back around, turning to finish her work.

An hour and a half later, she longed to sit down and smoke a cigarette, but it was time to help Connie in the kitchen. Aneesa motioned her to go, waving a hand in dismissal.

It was only after lunch was served that she was able to slip away and head out the back door. She sat on the hard asphalt, fishing her lighter and a cigarette out of her sweatshirt pocket. How she'd missed this. The routine of pulling out the first one, snapping the lighter, then the first big inhale, instantly calming the nerves.

Why had she said she'd quit? Oh, yeah, because it was an addiction. Just like drinking, drugs, tattoos. And cutting her arms. Well, two out of four wasn't bad. She took another drag on the cigarette, jumping as the metal door clattered open.

"Thought you quit," Skeeter said with a smirk.

Jinxi looked at him in alarm. "I'm not supposed to talk to you."

"Since when did you start following rules?" Skeeter hunkered down next to her. "Gimme a smoke."

Jinxi dutifully handed the pack and lighter to him, then stood, taking the last few puffs in rapid succession as Skeeter used her lighter, then tossed it back.

"I gotta go."

"Not so fast." Skeeter grabbed her arm, blocking her access to the door. "We made a deal. Saturday night. Ten o'clock. Here's the address." He pulled a crumpled piece of paper from his back pocket.

Jinxi took it, holding it between two fingers.

He moved closer to her, his face inches away. "Unless you want to come earlier and do a little partying. Just like the old days, right?"

Jinxi's stomach rolled with disgust. She pulled against his grip. "No."

Skeeter's face turned ugly, and he shoved her away.

"Just be there. Or else." He took a drag from the cigarette and blew smoke toward her.

Jinxi scrambled for the door handle, yanking it open with such force that it crashed against the brick wall. She stomped into the cafeteria, colliding with Padish.

"Oof." She stepped back, glaring up at him.

"I told you not to have contact with Mr. Jared," he said, unsmiling.

"He followed me, okay? I didn't follow him." Jinxi's voice, already shrill with outrage, rose in intensity. "I'm sick of everyone blaming me for everything."

Connie emerged from the kitchen, drying her hands on a dishtowel. A few stragglers moved closer, drawn to the drama.

"I didn't take money from the office. I know you don't believe me. Maybe you should look in another direction." Her arm swept back toward the door where Skeeter stood, arms crossed, a smirk on his face.

Jinxi's voice shook as she shouted, "You're all supposed to be my friends, but you blame me for everything. Because I'm different? Because I don't fit into your narrow description of what a Christian should look like?" She used air quotes around the word Christian.

Jinxi was out of control, and she knew it. "You're all the same as everyone else, hating on me. Well, guess what? I hate all of you!"

Connie's mouth dropped open. Padish took a step back, dark eyebrows disappearing into his hair. Hank dropped the broom he'd been holding, the clatter as loud as a gunshot in the silent cafeteria.

With a sob, Jinxi dashed for the office and grabbed her pack, heading out the front door. Tears burst from her eyes, blurring her vision. Too hyped up to wait for a bus, she turned the opposite direction and started the long walk to Janice's house.

Half an hour later, she was walking under the freeway overpass, noting the makeshift homeless camp on her right. She rubbed her face with one hand, scrubbing the dried tears.

"Hey, you. Girl!" called one of the men lounging against the concrete abutment. "Got a dollar for a veteran?"

Grasping the strap of her backpack tighter, Jinxi hastened her steps.

"Hey, I'm talking to you, girl!"

Jinxi tried walking faster, but the heavy boots impeded her progress. She slipped the pack off her shoulder, grappling in an outside pocket, the pack bouncing awkwardly off her legs. Her fingers landed on the pepper spray. Holding it in one hand, she slung the pack over her shoulder. Feeling a bit more confident, she left the homeless camp behind. Ahead was the strip of X-rated movie houses, the Salvation Army headquarters, and the Gospel Mission.

More people loitered on the street, a human side show of the lowest of the low. She passed them, head down, ignoring any attempts to engage her. Just when she thought she was through the worst of it, two women pushed themselves from the brick side of a building and approached her.

"Whatcha got in the bag, honey?" one asked, while the other circled around behind her. She felt a pull as her backpack was grabbed.

"Wanna make a trade?" The woman could have been thirty or fifty, Jinxi couldn't tell. She clasped the strap more tightly.

"Yeah, you got something to trade?"

"Trade?" Jinxi turned so both women were in her line of sight.

The two women exchanged a look. "Yeah, you give us somethin' and we let you pass."

"I've got pepper spray," Jinxi warned.

One of the women laughed, revealing several missing teeth. "You don't want to do that, honey. Draw attention and all?"

"No, you don't," the other said, shaking her head.

"Cigarettes?" Jinxi offered.

"And twenty bucks."

"Ten," Jinxi countered. Fear leaked away as the basics of human exchange began. This was familiar, this negotiation of terms, establishing boundaries, determining rank.

Hearing no objection, Jinxi slipped the backpack off her shoulder and onto the ground, keeping an eye on the women. The cigarettes sat on top. She threw them across the space that divided them, the lighter following. While they scrambled for the tossed items, Jinxi quickly reached deep into her bag, opening her wallet, and slipping out some bills.

"Here," she said, not knowing if she was giving them fives, tens, or ones. She threw the money on the ground, then took off running. A few blocks later, she stopped, chest heaving. She sat on a bench under the cover of a light-rail stop, grateful it was deserted.

Those women could have been her, if it hadn't been for Janice's rescue. The women wore short skirts and high heels. Their skin-tight tops revealed emaciated stomachs. Their hair was lank and uncombed. What an idiot she'd been, trying to street-hustle an undercover cop. Was that how she wanted to end up? Living in a hovel at the mercy of some guy?

Jinxi shook her head at the irony. She'd been at Skeeter's mercy, acquiescing to be his drug-carrier, his mule. The only difference was they made a grip of money, spending it on partying, eating out, and gambling. Her prison wasn't too much different from theirs.

Dragging herself off the bench, she continued down the street, not sure how much longer she'd be able to walk. The pain in her feet throbbed in time with the pain in her heart. How could she have screamed at everyone the way she did? They must hate her for sure. She'd probably be fired. She wouldn't blame Padish for kicking her to the curb. She'd never be able to get another job.

Shoulder slumped, step after painful step, she clomped down the sidewalk. Toward what? Janice's house, where she stayed by Janice's pity. Jinxi's world teetered in a delicate balance, and it was about to come crashing down. Like standing under a falling meteor, she'd be crushed like an ant. After all, wasn't that what she deserved?

The streets began to look familiar. Maybe she'd be home before she passed out. She stepped out from behind a parked car to cross the street, jumping back with a muffled curse as a truck rolled by without slowing.

"Hey!" she yelled, more in fright than in anger.

The truck screeched to a stop, then backed up. When it reached her, the passenger window went down. "What're you doing here?"

Dean's dark head leaned over from the driver's seat.

"Forget I asked," he said. "Hop in."

She climbed up into the truck, spitting fire. "You nearly drove over me."

He grinned. "You're so small I couldn't see you."

"Stupid jerk. You could have killed me," she huffed, slamming the door.

"You going home?" Dean put the truck in drive and gunned the accelerator.

"Yeah."

She caught his sideways glance out of the corner of his eye.

"Why?"

"Cuz that's where I live now. Or did you forget?"

"Very funny. You know what I meant."

Sighing, she gave him part of the reason. "There was some drama at work, and I needed to bounce."

"Why didn't you just take the bus? Or call me?"

Jinxi shrugged, stalling for time. "I dunno. Just thought I'd walk."

"Seriously? Through the 'hood?" He shook his head. "You're nuts. We get service calls in that area you passed through every night. Knife fights, territory wars, drug stuff."

Jinxi looked up as he glanced over at her.

"Call me next time, okay? Or my mom. She'll come get you."

"Whatever. I'm fine. I can take care of myself."

Yeah, I've done such a good job of it so far.

"So, little Miss Sunshine, want me to drop you at my mom's?"

"Yeah." She wrapped her arms around her backpack, resting her chin on top.

Dean pulled up to Janice's house, stopping in front of the gate. She reached for the door handle, but he stopped her with a hand on her arm. "Hold up a sec, okay?"

"What."

"What's going on with you?"

"Why? You worried I'm gonna take more money from your mom?"

Dean made a disgusted noise. "No. I'm concerned about you. There's something going on, and I want you to understand you can talk to me about it. That's all."

Jinxi shifted toward the door. "Thanks. If I want someone to talk to, I'll let you know." She opened the truck door, sliding down to the sidewalk. As she swung the door closed, she thought she heard him say, "I'll pray for you."

She must have heard wrong. Either that, or his head injury did more damage than they thought. When she'd told him about her experience with God, he'd mocked her. Said he didn't believe in God anymore. She shook her head. Yeah, she must have heard wrong.

CHAPTER FORTY-THREE

Janice's car wasn't in the driveway. Jinxi rested her pack on her knee as she dug around for the house key. Ted ran from around the side of the house, trotting up the front steps to greet her with excited barks.

"Hold on a minute," she told him. Her fingers closed around the key. She pulled it and her cell phone out at the same time. Pushing the door open with her foot, she stepped through into the empty house. With one eye on the phone, she shut the door, dropped her pack, and sank down on the piano bench.

Three missed calls. She recognized the number as coming from the food bank. Several texts.

One from Connie. Chica, what happened? Why you yelling and mad?

Two from Aneesa. One from Skeeter. Her mouth turned down. How'd he get her phone number?

Putting the phone down next to her, she leaned over and began to unlace her boots. The phone buzzed again. Another text from Skeeter. Merciful heavens. Great, now she was sounding like Janice.

One more incoming text as she removed her boots. She grabbed the phone, tempted to throw it across the room.

Wait.

This one was from Dean.

DEAN: I meant it, you know.

Seriously? He'd pray for her? What happened to him?

Jinxi hobbled into the kitchen to find a snack. Just as she settled onto the sofa with a bag of chips and dip, Janice's house phone rang. Without thinking, she picked it up.

"Hello?"

Only breathing on the other end.

"Who is this?"

"Is my grammy there?" Robin's daughter.

"Hannah? Is that you?"

"Jinxi? Hi! Are you with Grammy?"

"No, she's not here. Did you dial the phone all by yourself?"

"I have Mommy's cell phone. Mommy showed me one time."

Jinxi was at a loss. "Cool."

"Can you get Grammy? I want to come over and play."

"I don't know where your grammy is. But I can tell her to call you the minute she gets home, okay?"

"Okay. Tell her I miss her very, very, very, very"— Jinxi heard a big inhale—"very, very much. Tell her."

"Okay, Hannah. I will. I promise."

"Okay. 'Bye."

That was painful.

With a sigh, Jinxi pulled her cell phone onto her lap. The texts from Aneesa were terse commands to call her, either at the food bank or on her cell.

With a sigh, she dialed Aneesa's cell with one hand, rubbing her sore feet with the other.

"It's me," Jinxi said, when Aneesa answered.

"What got into you, girl?" Aneesa demanded.

Several responses ran through Jinxi's head.

I had a meltdown.

I'm tired of being at fault.

I'm sick of everyone judging me.

"I'm ..." Why did the word sorry get stuck in her throat like yesterday's gum?

"You're what?"

"I can't explain right now."

Aneesa sighed into the phone. "You better explain, girlfriend, or you'll find yourself out of a job. Padish is pretty upset."

What about her? She was upset too. "Look, could we talk about this tomorrow? It's been a rough day."

"Okay. But we're talking first thing when you get here. Remember, honey, I'm your friend."

Right. She'd be one of the first to drop her like yesterday's trash.

Aneesa's words cut into her like shattered glass. If she was Jinxi's friend, why didn't she say something to Padish in her defense? Why couldn't anyone see that Skeeter was a low-life loser? Why was he above suspicion, and she was the suspect?

She pounded a fist into the sofa.

It's not fair!

"You look ticked off."

Electricity shot through her fingertips at the sound of Dean's voice. "Stop sneaking up on me."

Dean picked up one sneaker-clad foot and examined it, then the other. "I'm pretty sure these size tens make plenty of noise."

Jinxi crossed her arms and harrumphed. "Whatever."

Dean raised both palms. "I come in peace." He sat on the other end of the sofa, reaching over to grab some chips. He shoved a handful into his mouth and chewed noisily.

"You eat like a pig."

"Nice to see you too." He grinned. "Have a bad day?"

"You know I did." Anger that had died down to ashes and coals flamed into rage. "I'm so sick of everyone thinking bad about me. Money goes missing from the food bank, and bam! Blame the weird girl. Low-life guy tries to get cozy with me, and bam! It's my fault. I'm told to stay away from him, not the other way around. He talks to me, and I get blamed for breaking the rules." Her voice rose an octave. "Even your sister is in on it. I'm to blame for her finding out she's adopted." She turned to glare at Dean, jabbing an accusatory forefinger at him. "Bet you've got something you can blame on me."

Dean leaned back. "I, uh—" He swallowed, his Adam's apple bobbing up and down. "I just came over to see how you're doing."

"You've seen. Now leave." She sounded bratty even to herself, but she was beyond caring.

The growling in his stomach urged Dean from sleep to wakefulness. Before opening his eyes, he made a childish wish.

Please let Jinxi have coffee made and ready.

Opening one eye, he knew the wish hadn't been granted. That one morning of having coffee already made and brought to him in bed had been pure heaven. Was that what it was like being married? Having coffee brought to you every morning? If so, he'd have to do something about his unmarried state, and fast.

As the coffee brewed, he scoured the pantry for something to eat, turning up only a box of cereal that was down to crumbs. The milk carton was just as barren. He had a decision to make, milk in the coffee, or milk on the cereal? There wasn't enough for both.

As he pondered what to do, his cell phone buzzed.

"Dean, this is Mike. Sorry it took me so long to call you. What's up?"

"No problem. Do you have time to grab a quick cup of coffee?"

"Sure. Same place?"

"Yup. What time?"

"How 'bout an hour and a half?"

"Cool."

Dean pocketed his cell phone and grabbed a sweatshirt, then stopped. Was a sweatshirt appropriate wear when meeting with a clergyman? He shucked off the shirt, pulled a brown polo from the back of his closet and slipped it on instead. The tags still dangled from the sleeve. His mom had given it to him on his last birthday. She'd told him he needed to start dressing like an adult. He cast a longing glance at the sweatshirt, leaving it draped across the back of a chair. He'd rather freeze than wear a sport coat. His only other outerwear was police-issue. Probably not a good idea to show up at the mall with POLICE plastered across his back.

As Dean locked the apartment, he made a mental list of the errands he had to accomplish before meeting Mike. Out of habit, he glanced across the yard to his mom's house. Everything looked peaceful. No more bricks thrown, no more drive-bys.

Tomorrow he'd go see his sergeant.

Dean rubbed the two-day scruff on his cheeks. Today he needed to buy some new blades and shave cream, and fill up the fridge. He drove toward the retail area a few miles away. A sporting goods store loomed ahead. On a whim, he turned into the parking lot. Only a few cars in the lot.

An eager young associate greeted him as he walked through the door.

"Welcome to Big Sport. How can I help you today?"

Dean rubbed the back of his neck. "I'm looking for a football. For a kid. Maybe six years old."

"Of course. Follow me."

The associate was off and running. Dean pounded after the clerk, wondering what he was thinking, coming in here, buying something for a kid that might not even be his.

He was shown to an area displaying every kind of ball ever made. He hefted a miniature football, tossing it from hand to hand. What would it be like to teach his son to play football? What if baseball was more his sport? Dean pulled out a child-sized mitt, folding it over and then flattening it back out.

"I'll let you look around," the associate told him. "Yell if you need any help."

Dean wandered around the ball area, carrying the football under his arm. The next section displayed dozens of fishing poles. A big grin split his face. His dad taught him when he was four or five years old. He couldn't remember the last time he'd been fishing.

He hefted a fly rod, pretending to cast. He eyed the price tag and set it back down. Not today. He'd have to go home and see where his fishing poles were. Another thing to remember.

The child-sized rod was like a toy in his hands. He pictured long afternoons, taking his son out on a two-man raft, scouring the American River for catfish. He'd be just like his dad, teaching his boy life lessons through the art of fishing.

So lost in his daydream, he didn't hear the associate until he spoke.

"Finding everything okay?" the associate asked with a smile.

"Uh, yeah. I'm good."

"You a fisherman?"

"Yeah. Well, I used to be."

"We've got some new models in. I can bring a couple in from the stock room if you're interested."

"Uh, no thanks." Dean felt his face flame. "I'll just take the football."

The associate's smile flattened into a straight line. "Fine. When you're ready, I'll meet you up front."

Dean was tempted to hurl the ball at the associate's head.

Dean didn't blame him. He was an idiot. Buying a toy for a kid who might not even be his. He shrugged as he waded through the display racks toward the front of the store. He supposed he could always give the thing to Ted.

Chaplain Mike was already drinking coffee when Dean dashed in.

"Sorry I'm late. Traffic."

"No worries. Get yourself something to drink. I'll finish up this email." Mike barely looked up from his phone to acknowledge him.

Dean returned to the table with his coffee, pulled out the chair across from Mike.

Mike laid his phone on the table, giving Dean his undivided attention. "What's up?"

Dean stalled for time by pulling off the lid of his cup and taking a sip of the scalding liquid. Where to begin? Should he mention how stupid he felt about buying the football? Or should he start with his prayer of desperation the other night?

Mike reached across the table, laying his hand on Dean's arm. His lips moved in what Dean assumed was a silent prayer.

"You feel different," Mike said.

"Huh?"

"Remember the last time we got together? When we shook hands, I felt all your stress and anxiety through your hand. I don't feel it today."

Weird. This was definitely taking a different direction.

"Let me explain," Mike continued. "I visit a lot of people in the hospital. Some are just going into surgery and they're scared. Others are recuperating after some trauma, and they've received devastating news about their prognosis. I always touch them, hold hands, put my hand on their shoulder, as I pray for them. Many times, I can feel their anxiety melting away as I pray. Touch is powerful."

Dean pondered this for a moment, turning the cup around in a circle. "Did you have a good relationship with your dad?"

Mike sat back in his chair. "Not really. He was gone a lot, traveling for work. When he was home, he wasn't there, if you know what I mean."

Dean nodded. "My dad was the best. He taught me a lot of stuff. Fishing, football. I can't remember everything." He raised his hand involuntarily to the scar on his head.

Mike waited for Dean to continue, watching him over the rim of his drink.

Dean took a deep breath and blew it out through pursed lips. "I'm scared I won't be as good as my dad."

"You mean if Katie's child turns out to be yours?"

"Yeah." Dean stared down at the Formica tabletop, rubbing his fingers over someone's initials etched into the surface. "What if I can't be the man I need to be?"

Mike reached across the table, gripping Dean's arm again. "I have a feeling you already are."

CHAPTER FORTY-FOUR

After Dean and Mike had talked for an hour, Dean drove home lighter in spirit. Whatever the outcome of the DNA test, he was ready. He would let it rest in God's hands. Now he needed to figure out what to do about the Raul thing.

Dean pulled up to his apartment. After turning off the ignition, he checked his phone for any texts. Funny he hadn't heard from any of his friends. He wrote a quick group text asking if there was anything new.

By the time he unlocked the front door, there was a return text from Damaris to call him.

"What's up?" Dean asked, as soon as Damaris answered the phone, not bothering with their usual greeting.

"You sitting down? This is madness. The undercover unit's been following some Black Beauty movement. You know, amphetamines?"

"Duh. I wasn't born yesterday."

"Sorry. Well anyway, there's a shipment coming in this weekend. Some local guy is taking the handoff."

"Who is it?"

"That's what's weird. There's no history the guy existed before a couple of months ago, when he got busted for possession of a joint."

"So where does Raul fit into all this? And me?"

"Hold on."

Dean heard voices in the background, then traffic sounds.

"I stepped outside. This is ears-only stuff." Damaris's voice dropped to a whisper. "Raul's spreading the rumor the guy taking the handoff is you."

Dean's stomach clenched as he processed the information. Who would believe such a rumor? He'd been teased since he started in the police academy about being Mr. Clean Dean.

"That's bull."

"You know it and I know it, but rumors take on a life of their own. They're saying you've been hiding your drug dealing beneath a façade of innocence."

Anger propelled Dean to his feet. Pacing back and forth in the small space, his thoughts went from punching Raul in the face to standing in the middle of the squad room, shouting his innocence.

"Hey, I gotta go, Big D. Whatever happens, I got your back."

"Right." Dean disconnected and flung the phone in the direction of the futon. It landed with a satisfying thud.

Sinking down on one of the bar stools, he smacked himself in the forehead with the heel of his hand. He'd forgotten to ask Damaris the guy's name.

As Dean drove toward the police station to talk with Sarge, the sun shone bright in his rearview mirror, reflecting off the windshield of the car behind him. A stab of pain behind his eyes reminded him he wasn't back to a hundred percent. He pressed down on the accelerator as a wave of irritation overtook him. When would he finally be well? He was rudderless on a swift river, taking him further and further away from his career. He'd never wanted to be anything but a cop. If he couldn't do his job, what else was there? He shuddered at the thought of sitting at a desk all day.

Dean parked a few blocks away from the police department, frustrated over not having his badge. With the badge he'd be able to park in the employee parking lot, saving himself the walk.

Dean located the freestanding kiosk halfway down the block. He pulled his debit card out of his wallet and inserted it in the machine.

"Please enter your PIN," it instructed him.

He stared at the screen, mind whirling. PIN? What the heck was his PIN?

Someone behind him coughed. "Just a minute," Dean barked.

He hit the CANCEL button, pulling the card out, then reinserting it.

"Use as credit?" the machine asked.

His index finger twinged at the force he used to press YES. Wiping the sweat off his forehead, he stomped back to the truck, sticking the parking permit to the driver's side window.

He paused outside the police department to take a moment to let his temper cool. It wouldn't do to be in a foul mood when he talked to Sarge.

The door opened and two officers emerged. Dean recognized them and raised a hand in greeting. They didn't respond. Dean turned to watch them descend the concrete steps to the street, heads bent together.

Dean squared his shoulders and pushed through the door. The receptionist greeted him.

"Hiya, Dean. Long time no see." A pencil rested behind her ear, just below the massive beehive hairdo. Marsha was a fixture at Sac PD. She'd been there for as long as anyone could remember. No one dared to guess her age.

"Hi, Marsha. I'm here to see Sarge."

Gazing at him over her reading glasses, she asked, "He expectin' you?"

"Uh, I'm not sure."

She pushed her chair back, giving him a reproachful look. "Gimme a minute. I'll see if he's available."

Dean watched her back as she headed across the squad room toward his sergeant's office. His gaze shifted to the manic activity swirling around every desk. Phones ringing, handcuffed perps moaning or yelling, detectives trying to talk over the noise.

His heart speeded up in response. He missed this. He needed this. The rush from a call on the radio. The satisfaction of bringing in some low-life. Even the paperwork didn't bother him, as long as he had purpose.

Marsha motioned him across the room. He passed desks with half-empty coffee cups, remains of fast-food lunches, and perps hunched over, hands behind their backs. The fierce smell of dirty bodies permeated the room, a reminder of his months working at the jail.

A few uniformed officers nodded at him as he zigzagged between the desks. Others glanced at him, then averted their eyes.

"Thanks, Marsha," he said as he brushed past her to enter his sergeant's office.

"Rafferty," Sarge greeted him.

"Sir."

Sarge motioned him to sit. The chairs in his office were no different than the ones in the squad room. Metal, made to withstand abuse and bodily fluids, and hard as concrete. Dean always felt a little guilty, like he was the criminal, when he sat across the scarred wooden desk from his superior.

"What can I do for you, Officer?" Sarge asked, his brown face wrinkled in its perpetual frown. His jaw tightened as he chewed the ever-present gum.

Dean rubbed the back of his neck, unsure where to begin. He took a deep breath.

"Well, uh, since my, uh, accident, there's been some talk about me. I'd like to clear the air with you, sir."

Sarge steepled his fingers, staring unblinking at Dean. "Go on."

"I'm not sure you're aware of some incidents since I've been off work." Dean described the intensity with which Raul insisted Dean tell IA his version of the shooting, then the brick, the warnings, and the rumors about his alleged drug use. As he talked, Dean felt warmth spread through him. His voice grew stronger and more confident. He spilled everything, including the undercover sting operation.

When Dean finished talking, Sarge opened his mouth to speak. In the same instant, commotion broke out in the squad room.

"Everybody down!"

Dean dove for the floor, then crawled to the door to peek out. A giant of a man swayed from side to side, waving his arms. Every officer in the building had his weapon trained on the guy.

"Put your hands behind your head!" yelled the officer closest to him.

The giant mumbled something incoherent. Dean reached for his holster before remembering he wasn't armed. Sarge belly-crawled next to him.

"Somebody's gonna get shot."

Dean nodded his agreement. The officer again ordered the giant to put his arms behind his head. He'd barely finished his sentence when two uniforms pounced. The giant went down like a tree. There was a collective exhale of relief as the guy was overtaken, handcuffed, and dragged to a holding cell.

The entire room started talking at once. Shaky laughter erupted at the expense of the officer who was supposed to have control of the giant.

Sarge stood, brushing off his pants.

"Sorry, Rafferty. We'll have to pick this up at another time. I need to write an incident report and have a word with one of my men."

Dean pulled himself to his feet. The beginning of a headache stabbed behind his eyes.

"Sure." His shoulders sagged in disappointment as he shuffled out of the office. No one paid him any attention as he made his way to the front counter.

He should have been involved. It should have been him and his partner to take the guy down. His buddies should be clapping him on the back, congratulating him for being the hero of the day. Instead, he was the suspect. The dirty cop. Not trusted to have his partner's back.

He passed by Marsha, who patted her stiff hair. "That was close," she commented. Dean didn't respond as he shoved open the door.

The truck offered respite from the headache-inducing sunlight. He clenched his hands around the steering wheel.

I thought I did what you wanted. I thought you wanted me to talk to Sarge.

Dean's mood plummeted like a rock. What was he supposed to do now? He wanted some sort of resolution, or even absolution from his boss. He wanted to be told everything would work out, that he'd return to work, and everything would be the same as before.

Frustration grew as he worked the problem over and over in his head. Several minutes later, he banged a fist on the dashboard, then jumped out of the truck. His neck muscles tightened as he strode back to the police station.

Marsha wasn't at her post, so he skirted around the reception area and headed straight back to his sergeant's office.

Sarge looked up as Dean entered without knocking.

His frown deepened. "I'm busy, Rafferty."

"I just need a minute, sir."

Sarge sighed and threw down his pen onto a stack of incident forms. "Look, son, as you're aware, you're still a rookie until you successfully make it through six months of field patrol. That means you have six months to prove you have what it takes to be a Sacramento police officer." Sarge's gaze pierced into Dean's. "Are you sure this is the right job for you?"

The question hit Dean like an uppercut to the jaw. Of course, this was the right job for him. What else was there? This was what he'd worked for his entire life. He'd joined the Police Explorer program at fourteen, keeping up with the commitment despite football and academics. He'd worked as a volunteer security guard on his college campus, before graduating and being accepted into the academy.

"Sarge, I—"

"Son, not everyone makes it. Only a small percentage of academy graduates make it through the probationary period."

Dean clenched his fists, tension knotting his neck and shoulders. "As soon as I come back to work, you'll see I have what it takes. I can do this, Sarge. I can. I will."

Sarge sighed, as if he'd had the wind knocked out of him. He picked up his pen, tapping it quickly on the pile of papers.

"Bring me your doctor's release, and we'll see."

"What about the IA investigation?"

"Your drug test came back clean, so the investigation should be finalized by the end of the week. You'll be contacted if there's anything you need to know."

Dean was clearly dismissed. Turning on his heel, he strode through the squad room and through the front door. He reached his truck moments before Parking Enforcement got to it. With relief, he pulled out into traffic. His parking permit had expired.

Elation bubbled up at the thought of returning to work. After a mental fist pump, reality smacked him on the face. His memory wasn't a hundred percent. He was still plagued by intermittent headaches. What if he went back on patrol and forgot vital information? What if Internal Affairs held him accountable for the shooting? What if they found him negligent for not reporting Raul's drug use?

Groaning with the effort of working through all the possibilities, he steered through traffic, wondering what would happen if he couldn't work.

He arrived at his apartment, jerking to a stop at the curb. Ted dashed across the yard, greeting him with excited barks.

"Hey, boy, how ya been?" He took a moment to scratch behind Ted's ears, then turned to head up the stairs to the apartment. Just as he placed his foot on the bottom step, Ted returned with a tennis ball in his mouth and a hopeful look on his face. He dropped it at Dean's feet, then nudged it with his nose.

"Oh, all right." Dean stepped into the yard, throwing the ball while Ted raced after it, returning each time to drop it at Dean's feet.

Dean remembered the toy football in the truck. He'd shoved it under the passenger seat, hoping to avoid embarrassing himself again. Something wouldn't let him give the ball to his dog.

What-ifs swirled through his brain in a kaleidoscope of images. He imagined himself showing the kid how to toss the football through a hanging tire to teach him accuracy.

He saw them wrestling on the lawn, Ted in the middle of things. He'd be like his dad, imparting wisdom in every circumstance.

The vision came to a screeching halt. He wasn't his dad, and he didn't have the same integrity his father did. How would he be able to explain how the boy was conceived? Tell him his dad was a brute, forcing himself on the kid's mother? As if the conversation would ever come up. Dean was no worse than his sister Robin's father, taking advantage of someone weaker and more vulnerable.

Dean hurled the ball with such force that it bounced all the way to the edge of the driveway on the other side of the lot. He couldn't be a father.

You have a heavenly Father who will teach you all things.
Why did God have to sound like his dad?

CHAPTER FORTY-FIVE

Clouds obscured the moon as Dean barreled down Highway 80 toward West Sacramento. Wisps of tulle fog drifted up from the grassy berm on the side of the freeway, adding to the gloom. The darkness outside matched Dean's mood. He'd asked himself a hundred times why he was doing this. Why did he care how the drug deal went down? He'd hear about it tomorrow from Damaris and Patrice.

His friends had made a plan to spread rumors about Raul, deflecting the focus from Dean. But his newly sensitive spirit told him to counter lies with the truth. That's why he'd gone to Sarge. And that was what he was doing here tonight. If he was under suspicion for taking a drug shipment handoff, he'd at least find out who really was responsible. Of course, there was the possibility he was being set up. Again.

Maybe this is a bad idea.

Something in his gut urged him on. Pressing on the accelerator, he plowed through his doubts. The West Sacramento exit loomed ahead. He'd taken this exit dozens of times, heading to a River Cats game or an outdoor concert. Turning left instead of right off the exit felt foreign. The road led down a street with a billboard shouting 'Eighteen Motels on West Capitol Avenue!'

This area of West Sac used to be a thriving tourist area. Located right on the river, it offered lots of recreational opportunities for families. Now the recreational activities tended toward illegal gambling and prostitution. Thank God he wasn't on the West Sac PD.

Dean cruised past the Sands Motel, offering weekly rates. Someone had blacked out the E in rates. He huffed a humorless laugh, then made a U-turn two blocks down. Doubling back, he passed the motel, then pulled into the parking lot of a liquor store a few streets away.

Pulling on a beanie, he climbed out of the truck, locked it, and sauntered down the street like he belonged there. A bus bench sat conveniently across from the Sands Motel. He sank onto it, slouching, hands in his sweatshirt pockets.

Without checking his watch, he figured he had about twenty minutes to wait. He watched the traffic slide by. Seemed like every other car was a huge SUV, windows darkened, thumping what was called music. Surely the drug guys wouldn't be that obvious.

Dean's backside stung from the cold metal bench. He stood, twisting his shoulders right and left to loosen the tension, then sat down. A delivery van drove by, obscuring his view of the motel. As soon as it passed, Dean spied a familiar figure striding down the street. The hoodie pulled over her dark hair didn't fool him. He instantly recognized her from her size and gait.

He jumped up from the bench, dodging cars as he dashed across the street. "Jinxi!" he shouted, as she turned into the motel driveway.

He reached her a moment later, out of breath. "Jinxi, what are you doing here?"

Jinxi's eyes flashed fire. "What are you doing here?"

Repressing the urge to grab her arms and shake her, he gritted his teeth. "I asked you first."

Jinxi took a step back. She glanced around, then leaned toward him. "There's something I have to do. You wouldn't understand. You need to leave." Her voice, husky with emotion, tugged at his heart.

"No. You don't have to do whatever this is."

Her eyes pleaded with him, and her voice took a tone of desperation. "Look, I'll explain later. I promise. Right now—"

A nondescript sedan turned off the street, pulling into the motel driveway. Dean grabbed the sleeve of her sweatshirt, pulling her to the side.

"There's going to be trouble here. I don't want you involved. C'mon, let's go home."

"I'm already involved." Her head dropped.

Dean sent up a quick prayer for guidance.

What do I say, God? What's going on?

He opened his mouth to speak, with no idea of what he would say.

"Jinxi, whatever's going on, this isn't the place for you. Whatever this guy has on you, it's a lie." Dean lifted her chin with his finger and looked into eyes filled with tears. "Don't let him manipulate you into doing something you shouldn't. Trust me. I know what I'm talking about."

"But it's not a lie," Jinxi whispered.

Before he could say anything else, two police cars bounced over the driveway and jerked to a stop, blocking the motel entrance. Dean enveloped Jinxi in a hug, shielding her from their view, just a young couple in love.

In a flurry of movement, the officers jumped from their vehicles and disappeared into the motel courtyard. Dean heard shouting.

"Let's go." Without waiting for any argument, he grabbed Jinxi's arm and pulled her down the street, a dead weight behind him. He thought at first he'd have to physically throw her into the cab of the truck, but she complied.

As soon as he pulled out of the parking lot, several more cop cars sped by, heading straight toward the Sands Motel.

"What the—" Jinxi sputtered.

"Be quiet," Dean demanded. Thousands of questions hammered in his head. What was she doing there? And why? How did she get involved in a drug delivery?

He pulled off the freeway into the parking lot of an all-night chain diner. Too bad Starbucks wasn't open this late.

"We're going inside. We're going to order coffee. And you're going to tell me what's going on. Got it?" He pinned her with his best cop stare. She nodded wordlessly, then opened the door and slid onto the concrete.

In the restaurant, Dean ordered coffee for both of them, along with a large order of French fries, though he doubted he'd be able to eat.

They sipped their coffees in silence until the fries arrived. Jinxi hadn't once made eye contact with him. She clicked her lip stud back and forth against her teeth, setting his nerves on edge. He shoved the plate of fries closer to her.

"Here. Eat. I know how much you love fries." Anything to get her to stop that blasted clicking.

He waited until she'd dipped a fry in ketchup.

"First question. Why were you going to the Sands Motel?"

"What makes you think that's where I was headed?"

Good, she had some of her spunk back. He smiled to himself. "Let's assume you were. Why?"

He watched her swirl a fry in the pool of red, around and around, without speaking.

"Fine. How about I go first?"

Her gaze shot to his, her blue eyes wide.

Dean continued. "My friends told me about a drug handoff happening tonight. There were rumors going around saying I was involved."

Jinxi shook her head. "No way. You?" She pointed a fry at him, ketchup dripping off the end.

"Yeah. Rumors spread by my former partner Raul. He has some sick idea that I'm to blame for him being on administrative leave."

"That's crazy."

"Seriously."

"Doesn't explain why you were down there tonight," Jinxi said, her mouth full.

Dean leaned back in the booth. Now who was asking the questions?

"I think Raul's involved somehow, and I wanted to see for myself. Otherwise how would he know all the details?"

Dean shoved a handful of fries in his mouth and crunched. Speaking around them, he said, "Your turn."

Jinxi pushed the plate across the table toward him. She licked each of the fingers on her left hand, then wiped them on the napkin. Her hand shook as she lifted the coffee cup to her lips.

Dean waited.

"Remember that guy I told you about? The community service guy at the food bank?"

Dean nodded. "Jared?"

"Uh-huh." She pulled the napkin from one hand to the other, sliding it from palm to palm. "Well, his name isn't Jared. It's Skeeter."

Dean searched his memory, trying to make the connection. "Who's Skeeter?"

"My ex."

"Okaaaaay." This was getting more confusing. "If his name is Skeeter, why did you call him Jared?"

Dean sat nonplussed as Jinxi told him about Skeeter's identity change, and why. And how he coincidentally landed at the food bank. Dean didn't believe in coincidences.

"Okay, so I get that. But why involve you in some drug thing? Why not just tell him no?"

Jinxi looked down at the table, rubbing the fingers of one hand over the beveled edge. "He knows something about my past. Something he threatened to tell everyone."

Dean was dumbfounded. She'd agreed to do something illegal so her ex-boyfriend wouldn't tell that she'd been sentenced to time in what was basically a prison for minors. For accidentally causing the death of a child? Had she carried the guilt all these years? Hadn't she learned anything about grace from going to church, or from his mom?

He examined his own heart, realizing he hadn't shown her grace. Not at all.

Reaching across the table, he placed his hand over hers and took a deep breath before he spoke.

"I know your secret."

Jinxi flinched. Dean's hand tightened on hers. Somehow the pressure didn't make her feel trapped. The warmth was comforting. He knew? Her brain struggled to comprehend what he'd just said. Dean knew about the kid dying. And jail. She shook her head, hardly able to choke out the words. "How long have you known?"

Dean shrugged. "A few weeks."

"But how? Why? I mean, how?"

He looked away, redness creeping up his neck and onto his face. "It's stupid. I shouldn't have done it."

"Done what?"

"I asked a friend to investigate your past."

"Those records are supposed to be sealed." Jinxi jerked her hand from under his, clenching her fists in her lap.

"Apparently neither you nor your mom completed the paperwork to have them sealed."

Conflicting emotions swirled through Jinxi's heart. Pain, betrayal, exposure. Shame.

Grace.

"You knew all this time about the fire, the kid who died, my time at the Girls' Ranch? And you never said anything. Why not?"

Dean's brown eyes searched her face. "I was waiting for the right time to use it against you. To get you out of my mom's house. Then something happened. Some of my past reared its ugly head, and I realized I'd also done things I was ashamed of. Things with bigger consequences that I ever thought possible."

Jinxi nodded. "You mean, like the kid you might have?"

Dean braced himself against the booth, arms straight against the edge of the table. "You know about that?"

Warmth suffused her face. "I did a little snooping too. Do you have the results yet?"

Dean shook his head. "No, but if the kid is mine, I'm ready to take on the responsibility for him. I'm not the man my dad was, but with God's help I can try."

Wait a minute. Dean didn't believe in God. "God's help?"

Dean signaled the waitress for a coffee refill. "Looks like we both have a lot to talk about." He leaned across the table toward her, his hand fisted except for the little finger. "No more secrets between us, okay? Pinkie swear."

Jinxi smiled, intertwining her little finger with his. "Pinkie swear."

After a couple of hours of tossing and turning, Jinxi woke with a killer headache and a sense of doom. She and Dean had talked into the early morning hours. He'd convinced her to go back to the food bank and come clean with everyone. She didn't share his confidence they'd be willing to forgive and forget. She still had trouble believing God had forgiven her. She'd felt more sure last night, after talking to Dean and his recommitment to the Lord. But in the light of day, reality hit with the destruction and carnage of a seven-car pileup.

She'd felt something when their pinkie fingers entwined. That strange jolt of electricity, like the time she put her tongue on a nine-volt battery. Not unpleasant, just surprising. Did Dean feel the same thing?

No more secrets—they'd agreed on it. Did that mean she had to tell him about the electric shock? It had been so easy to talk to him after everything was wide open. Like they were finally on the same page. They'd discussed God's forgiveness, his grace, how he intercedes in people's lives.

Strangest of all, they'd agreed to be good friends. Dean jokingly reminded her of their first meeting, how she'd told him she didn't want to be his BFF. Jinxi told him he had selective memory, only remembering her at her worst. Dean promised to try to remember her good side if he could find it. Seemed like they were back the way they were, way before any of the stuff hit the fan.

Jinxi hurried to get ready, forgoing the black eyeliner. She pulled a beanie over her hair, shaking her head at the blonde roots growing more evident. She'd have to do something about that soon. Go back to blonde or stay with the black? Something to decide later. Right now, she needed coffee before she let Dean drive her to face the gang at the food bank.

CHAPTER FORTY-SIX

Groggy with too little sleep, Dean groaned when his cell phone chirped its wake-up alarm. He dropped his face down into the pillow, silencing the annoyance with one hand. He'd have to get used to a whole new schedule once he went back to work. If he went back.

A jolt of adrenaline reminded him of last night's incidents. Flipping over on his back, he brought his phone close to his face to check for texts from Damaris or Patrice. Nothing.

He dropped the phone on the bed, rubbing his hands over his face. Why did he set the alarm so early? He shot up, remembering he'd promised to take Jinxi to the food bank. Muttering to himself, he dashed for the bathroom to shave and shower.

The cool spray of water washed some of the cobwebs away. The events of the previous night turned over and over in his mind. Waiting for something to go down at the motel, spying Jinxi there, dragging her away, their heart-to-heart talk. Had he really been that vulnerable?

No more secrets, they'd said. He'd promised to tell her when Katie's email arrived with the DNA results. She'd promised to confess everything to her coworkers and apologize for her outburst.

Dean frowned, remembering their pinkie swear. Had he really felt something when their fingers joined? Jinxi hadn't reacted, so it must've been his imagination. Maybe some lingering effects of his injury.

Dean dressed quickly, hoping to have time to down a cup of coffee at his mom's before they had to leave. He dashed across the lawn separating the apartment from his mom's house, Ted at his heels.

"I don't have time to play right now, buddy." Dean spoke over his shoulder, as he bounded up the concrete steps two at a time.

"Morning, sweetie," his mom greeted him as he burst through the door.

"Coffee?"

"Help yourself," Janice answered. "You know where everything is."

"Is Jinxi up?"

"Mhm. I heard her moving around, but she hasn't been downstairs yet. Usually, the first thing she does is get a cup of coffee."

Dean filled a mug with coffee. "Maybe I'll just take a cup up to her."

"How thoughtful." His mom returned to reading the morning paper.

Dean trudged up the wooden stairs, pounding on each step to make enough noise so Jinxi wouldn't accuse him of trying to scare her. He really wanted to talk to her alone before they left.

By the time he reached the top, she was standing in the door of the bathroom, the light behind throwing her face into shadow. She'd pulled on a black beanie.

"I brought coffee," he said, waving the cup around, like he was trying to pacify an angry zoo animal.

"Sweet! Just what I need." She grabbed the cup out of his hand, sniffing in appreciation before taking a sip.

She turned toward the bedroom. The morning sunlight pouring in through the dormer windows revealed the paleness of her face and the dark circles under her eyes, like she'd been in a fight and lost. Mouth set in a grim line.

Dean tried for humor. "Guess next time I shouldn't keep you up so late." He caught a flicker of something in her eyes. "Do you want to eat before we go?"

Jinxi shook her head. "I'd hurl if I ate anything."

"Set the mug down for a minute."

"Why?"

Dean let out an exasperated sigh.

"Can't you just do something one time when you're asked? Sheesh." He took the mug from her hand and set it on the nightstand. Gathering her into his arms, he held her loosely. "Look, I know you're scared. It's gonna be okay. I promise."

Jinxi stood stiffly at first, and then he felt her relax. Her arms went around him to return the hug. Her voice was muffled as she spoke against his shirt. "You better be right."

He threw his head back and laughed. "I'm always right."

Jinxi pulled away and shoved his chest with force. "Whatever. Now leave me alone so I can finish getting ready."

Dean grinned as he turned to leave, half expecting to feel her coffee mug hitting the back of his head.

He headed back downstairs and into the kitchen. He filled his own mug with coffee, adding a liberal amount of milk and two spoonsful of sugar.

"Having a little coffee with your milk?" his mom asked.

"Aw, Mom, not you too. Jinxi always gives me a hard time about destroying my coffee." He took a hearty slug. "See? It's not too hot to drink now."

Janice folded the newspaper and laid it on the table. "To what do I owe the pleasure of your company this morning?"

"He's taking me to work," Jinxi answered for him, stepping into the kitchen. She pulled a sweatshirt over a white tee. A look passed between them, which didn't escape his mom's notice.

"Really?" Janice asked. Dean felt the weight of her unasked questions.

"Yeah," Jinxi said, "he offered to drive me today, so I didn't have to take the bus. Wasn't that sweet?"

Sweet? Did she just use the word sweet to describe him? The world must have tilted on its axis.

"Yeah, that's me. Sweet." Dean stood and carried his mug to the sink. "Ready?"

"Aren't you going to eat breakfast, Jinxi?" his mom asked.

"No, I'm good. I'll just grab an apple and put it in my backpack." Jinxi reached for the fruit bowl, grabbing an apple from the assortment.

"But you can't go to work on an empty stomach," Janice protested.

"Mom, it's fine." Dean went to her and kissed her cheek. "Let it go," he whispered.

Placing a hand on Jinxi's back, he ushered her out the door and into the crisp October sunlight.

"Seems like I'll be doing some early raking this year," Dean commented, looking up at the trees which had already begun to shed their leaves. They walked in silence the rest of the way across the yard.

As he opened the gate, Jinxi stopped. "Wait. We can't leave yet. I have to feed Ted." She turned, taking a step back toward his mom's house.

"Already done. I took care of it when I got up."

"What about clean water? You know he hates day-old water. I better do that."

Dean opened the gate, indicating with a wave of his arm that she should go through. "Did that too. And I shook out his bed. Anything else?"

Jinxi appeared to be thinking.

"Stop putting this off. Get it over with, like ripping off a Band-Aid." He touched her arm, giving her a gentle nudge toward the gate, and beyond it, his truck.

Her shoulders drooped. "Okay."

They climbed into the truck. Once it warmed up, Dean shifted into drive, and they pulled away from the house.

"Stop looking like you're being taken to Death Row. I told you it'll be fine."

Jinxi looked across the divide of the truck's cab, her blue eyes fixed on his. "Will you still tell me that after I've been fired?"

Dean supposed that was a real possibility. To lighten the mood, he said, "Let's play a little game. Peanut butter and jelly, or peanut butter and honey?"

"What?"

"C'mon, play along. Which do you like better?"

Jinxi tucked her chin into her sweatshirt. "Umm, PB and J."

"Chocolate chip or snickerdoodles?"

"What's a snickerdoodle?"

"You've never had a snickerdoodle? It's like the best cookie ever. Okay, how about chocolate or vanilla ice cream?"

"Vanilla."

"McDonald's or Burger King?"

She looked at him sideways. "Seriously? McDonald's."

"Now you ask one."

After a few seconds of silence, she said, "Dogs or cats?"

Now it was his turn to say, "Seriously? Dogs."

"Sci-fi or murder mystery?"

"Murder mystery. My turn. Coke or Pepsi?"

By the time they pulled up at the food bank, both were laughing, each question becoming sillier. The minute he pulled into a parking spot, Jinxi's laughter died. The tension that had melted away returned like a live electric wire shooting sparks.

"Want me to go in with you?"

Jinxi shook her head.

"Then at least let me pray for you." Dean launched into a prayer, his words uncertain and halting after so many years. He reached for Jinxi's hand, hoping his touch, along with the prayer, would give her strength.

He gave her hand one last squeeze. "Amen. I'll wait here. Let me know if I need to take you home, okay?"

Jinxi nodded, then took a deep breath. "Okay if I leave my backpack here?"

"Sure." He watched her slide off the seat, onto the sidewalk. She patted her right front pocket, then rubbed her hand across her lips. This time his prayer was silent.

Jinxi eased open the front door of the food bank. The lights to the cafeteria were off, typical of early morning. She closed the door behind her with a feeling of finality. Would this be the last time? The familiar smell of Connie's cooking wafted through the entry, prompting a visceral response. Meat, onions, bell peppers. Chili. Three months ago she wouldn't have known about any kind of food that didn't come from a can or a fast-food place.

A sob worked its way up her throat, burning to be released. Jinxi swallowed it back down. This was no time to get all weepy. She needed to get this over with, face the consequences, and get out.

Clenching her fists inside the pockets of the sweatshirt, Jinxi mentally rehearsed what she would say. First, the apology. She couldn't remember the last time she'd uttered the words I'm sorry. Next, the explanation. The fire, the kid, all of it. Laid bare, opened up for everyone to see. Like taking off all your clothes and lying naked in the middle of a crowd.

Picturing their horrified faces, she almost turned around and walked out. Padish, who'd offered her a job after she completed community service. Aneesa, who shared her propensity to relieve pain by cutting. Would Hank understand what she was about to confess? Would his gentle soul turn away, not understanding how someone could carelessly murder?

Her friend Connie who'd given her the precious gift of learning to cook. Connie would gather Miguel and Rosa against her plump body, keeping them away from Jinxi the child-killer.

Jinxi's hands were behind her, already pushing the door back open.

"I thought I heard someone come in." Aneesa's voice stopped Jinxi in her tracks.

Jinxi raised her eyes, an inch at a time, until she faced the other woman. Aneesa's head was totally covered by a dark scarf. The scarf matched the somber look on her face.

Jinxi pulled her sweatshirt up over her chin, shoulders hunched. "Yeah, I thought I better come in and talk about yesterday."

"You're right, you better talk. That was some meltdown, girlfriend. What's got into you?" Aneesa stood with her arms akimbo.

Another shrug. Jinxi's insides swirled like clothes in a washing machine. "Do you think I could maybe talk to everyone at the same time?"

"All right. Let's see if I can find Padish."

Jinxi braced herself against the door as Aneesa returned to the office to call Padish's cell phone. She heard Aneesa's voice rise and fall but couldn't distinguish the words. A few moments later, Aneesa reappeared in the office doorway.

"You gonna stand there all day?"

The door rattled as Jinxi pushed herself away. She shuffled toward the cafeteria, head down. Aneesa turned on one set of lights, illuminating half the room. She left Jinxi standing alone, as she headed through the door to the storeroom.

Connie peeked out of the kitchen, squealing when she saw Jinxi. Connie rushed to her, enveloping Jinxi in a hug.

"Chica, I'm so happy to see you. I was worried." A torrent of Spanish tumbled from Connie's lips. Jinxi's head swam with the effort to understand what she said.

When Connie released her, she held Jinxi at arm's length. "Talk to me, hija."

"I need to tell everyone something."

Connie made the sign of the cross, kissing her thumbnail when she was done. "You are not leaving, sí?"

Jinxi shrugged. "It's not up to me."

Aneesa reappeared through the door, Padish and Hank behind her.

Buzzing in Jinxi's ears warned her she might pass out. She leaned over, pretending to adjust the laces of her boots, giving the blood a chance to trickle back into her head.

Taking a deep breath, she said, "Could everyone sit down, please?"

Benches creaked and groaned as everyone took a seat except Padish.

"I want—" Padish began.

"Please. Sit down. I have something I need to say." Jinxi's fists clenched inside her sweatshirt pockets.

"I'm ..." She gulped. The word stuck around the razor blades in her throat. "Sorry. About what I said yesterday. I don't hate everyone." Tears blurred her vision. She used the heels of her hands to stop the flow. By the time her hands fell back to her sides, she was surrounded by her coworkers, crowding in to gather her into their arms.

Jinxi pulled the truck door open and stuck her head in.

"Can I have my backpack?" Raw with emotion, she almost giggled at Dean's look of surprise.

"What happened? You've been crying."

Jinxi touched her swollen eyes. She must look a mess. Climbing into the truck, she pulled down the passenger side visor to peer at herself in the mirror. Blotchy face, puffy lips, red eyes. Yes, she'd been crying. So had everyone else. Wet spots on her shoulders testified to that.

"I didn't get fired."

"That's great! What about the other stuff?" Dean waved his hand, anxious for a full report.

She shook her head. "I never got the chance."

Dean sat back against the seat, deep in thought. "Maybe it's for the best."

"I dunno," Jinxi answered, swinging her backpack over one shoulder. "I just know I gotta go to work."

Slamming the truck door, Jinxi waved to him one final time before heading back inside.

Business as usual. Jinxi, Connie, and a phalanx of volunteers danced around the kitchen, readying for the tidal wave of hungry people. Connie had whipped up some soup concoction of vegetables, bits of meat, and potato in a tomato base. Jinxi tucked a stray hunk of hair up under her hairnet. She'd have to ask Connie for the recipe, if there was one. Most of the time, Connie took inventory of the fridge and freezer, then made something wonderful. Jinxi had years to go until she was as good as Connie. Until then, she'd watch and learn. She closed her eyes, relieved she hadn't been fired.

Jinxi shifted her weight from one foot to the other as the crowd lined up. The human snake of people wound down one side of the cafeteria and up the other. Padish waited until the doors were closed before he said grace. After a resounding 'amen,' the noise increased as food was served.

After all the drama of the past few days, Jinxi had forgotten about Burn Boy. Then he was in front of her, holding out his plate for the garlic bread. Jinxi picked up a piece with the tongs, setting it on his plate. Behind him, his mother balanced two bowls of soup. Without speaking, Jinxi took another piece of bread and laid it on the boy's plate. His lopsided smile revealed a gap in his front teeth.

"Thank you." His mom prodded him forward. Jinxi watched them find a place to sit at one of the long tables.

After everyone was fed, the volunteers began the process of cleaning up the kitchen. Connie sighed and rubbed her back.

"I am tired today. Rosa was not well last night. I didn't sleep very much."

"I'm tired too. I stayed up too late talking with Dean."

Connie took on a sly look as she smiled. "He is a good friend, no?"

Jinxi rolled her eyes. "He's a friend, okay? That's it."

Connie handed her a bowl of soup. "Here, you eat. Dean would not like such a skinny novia."

"I have no idea what a novia is, but I don't think I'm it."

Connie winked, then dished up a serving of soup for herself. They moved together toward the door leading into the cafeteria, leaving the volunteers.

Everyone jumped as the metal door leading to the back of the building crashed open.

"Fire!" someone yelled.

Dark smoke poured through the open door. Yellow and orange flames curled over the top of the entrance, advancing into the cafeteria. Jinxi froze. Images from the past poured over her like the black smoke billowing into the room.

Boom!

The explosion propelled everyone into action. Men and women sprang to their feet, knocking over benches and spilling their bowls. Women screamed and grabbed their children's hands as they ran for the door.

"Quick—everyone this way!" Padish opened the fire door to the side of the cafeteria and ushered the frightened crowd out of the building. People jostled around Jinxi, shoving their way to safety.

Jinxi's bowl dropped to the floor as her fingers went numb. Unaware of the hot liquid soaking her jeans, she stared transfixed at the encroaching fire. A lone figure stumbled through the flames and into the building, collapsing on the floor. Burn Boy? This was her chance to redeem the past. Spurred into action, she ran into the kitchen and wet a towel, then dashed to the person lying on the floor.

She coughed, and her eyes burned and watered at the thick vapor surging through the door and filling the room with an acrid smell. The person's clothes, singed and blackened, gave off choking smoke. Embers smoldered through his shirt. Not Burn Boy, but an adult male figure.

Her first thought was Dean, who'd somehow come into the building through the back door. The closer she got, the more she noticed. Tattoos, bald head, skinny frame.

Skeeter.

Jinxi pressed the wet towel to the still-burning places on his torso. The heat intensified, blistering her bare arms and neck.

She was going to die. This was God's payback for the kid she'd killed. She redoubled her efforts to tamp out the burning places on Skeeter's body. At least she could tell Jesus she'd tried to save the creep who'd made her life a living hell.

"Jinxi!"

Her head jerked up at the sound of someone calling her name through the roar of the fire. With a sudden realization of where she was, Jinxi shot to her feet, then leaned down to grab Skeeter's arm to drag him to safety.

Burning gas filled her lungs. Darkness dotted the edges of her vision, slowly closing until only a pinprick of light remained. Then she was falling. Someone tugged her arm, but her feet refused to respond. She landed hard on one shoulder. Her cheek came to rest in a puddle of fire retardant.

CHAPTER FORTY-SEVEN

Jinxi gagged as something smelly assaulted her nose. Struggling to open her eyes, her vision sharpened on the concerned male face hovering over hers.

"Atta girl. Just some smelling salts."

"Wha ..." She licked her lips with a tongue as dry as a two-day old tortilla. "What happened?"

The face moved back, and Jinxi saw his paramedic uniform. She struggled to sit up, but her arm wouldn't cooperate.

"Relax. Don't try to move. You've broken your collarbone, and we're taking you to Mercy Hospital."

Jinxi lay back, clamping down on the nausea that threatened to bring up the contents of her stomach. Before closing her eyes, she took in her surroundings. She was in the back of an ambulance. Tears leaked out of the corners of her eyes.

"I'm going to give you a little something that'll help take the edge off."

She felt the pinch of the needle in the back of her hand, then the sting of something going into her vein. She began to cry in earnest.

"Can somebody go with me?" she asked through her tears. Would anyone want to go with her? Maybe they'd be glad to get rid of her. Shame washed over her as she remembered the fire and her inability to move. Wait, that wasn't right. She'd tried to help someone.

The paramedic laughed. "I think all your friends are doing *ro-sham-bo* to see who gets to ride in the back with you."

Jinxi heard Connie's voice, speaking rapid-fire to someone in Spanish. Someone responded in kind.

"Your little round friend is telling my partner to take extra-special care of you—or else."

A moment later, the rig dipped and swayed as someone else climbed in the back. Jinxi opened her eyes, peering at Aneesa through her lashes. Warmth spread through her limbs as the narcotic took her away from the pain.

"I gueshh you won," her words slurred. "Or loshhht."

Aneesa took Jinxi's hand in both of hers. "Hush, child. We're going to get you fixed up."

Jinxi drifted on a cloud of warmth. She heard a door slam, resenting the sharp interruption. A man's voice rose and fell as the ambulance was set into motion. Why couldn't everyone just be quiet?

She was jostled awake by movement. The stretcher was wrestled out of the rig, jarring her shoulder with a stab of pain.

"Hey, that hurt!"

No one paid her any attention. Had she actually said it out loud? Whatever that guy put in her vein was stronger than anything she'd ever taken.

Jinxi closed her eyes to the sun's brightness. Someone squeezed her hand. Cracking her eyes open, she saw the hand that held hers was dark. She turned her head to see Aneesa keeping pace with the rapidly moving gurney.

"Aneesa," Jinxi said.

"I'm here, child. You're gonna be okay."

"I need to tell you something." The gurney bumped over the threshold leading into the hospital emergency room. It came to a stop in a wide hallway, pushed up against the wall.

"You can tell me later."

Jinxi forced herself to form the words. She struggled up on one elbow, pushing against weariness. "It's important."

Aneesa patted her hand. Jinxi took it as a sign of encouragement. "You know Burn Boy? I killed him. In a fire." There, she'd done it. She'd broken open like a raw egg and spilled out her guts. Somebody else could clean up the mess.

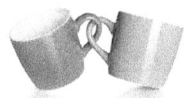

"Miss? We're taking you for an X-ray now." Jinxi forced her eyelids open enough to see a competent-looking nurse. A rolling sensation, then a turn, a bump, and more moving. The pain meds were wearing off, leaving her shoulder with a dull throb. Her arms felt hot. The back of her neck too. Her Tee shirt had a bunch of holes, like someone had put it through a food processor.

"Am I broken?" What she'd meant to say was *Did I break something*. Why weren't her words making sense?

"Your clavicle appears to be broken, but we'll know more once you've gotten x-rayed. After that, you'll have an MRI."

"MRI? Why?" Jinxi resisted the urge to giggle at the rhyme.

"Apparently you hit the floor pretty hard when you fainted."

Jinxi searched her memory. Fainting, falling, breaking bones. Things were coming back to her. She'd tried to help Skeeter.

"Why did I faint?" Probably when she'd realized she'd tried to save Skeeter's life.

The nurse chuckled. "It doesn't say in the report."

Jinxi was about to tell her to ask someone when the technician began the work of positioning her for the set of X-rays.

Dean charged into the emergency room waiting area, quickly scanning the room for a familiar face. He sagged with relief to find Aneesa dozing in a chair. She woke the minute he plopped down on the chair next to her.

"What the heck happened?" Dean demanded.

Aneesa's black curls bounced crazily as words poured out of her mouth.

"It all started with a fire that someone set in one of those big barrels we keep out back. The fire got out of control and spread to the propane tank. When the back door was opened, the flames came inside. The next thing I knew, everyone was racing for the door except Jinxi. She stood there a minute, then ran into the smoke. Apparently, one of our volunteers, Jared, came through the back door. Jinxi tried to help him. "

"Did she pass out?"

Aneesa nodded.

"She broke her collarbone when she fell?"

"She must have hit her head, too. She was talking crazy. Something about killing Burn Boy."

Dean's stomach dropped. He knew exactly what Jinxi was talking about. Should he tell the whole story to Aneesa? No, it wasn't his story to tell. But this new information made him pause. Deathly afraid of fire, yet she rushed in to save her ex. He was struck with a stab of jealousy. Last night, she'd tried to do something illegal for that loser, and today she overcame her fear to help save his life. His jaw tightened.

"What about the volunteer? This guy Jared?"

"The firemen were able to drag him out. He has significant burns on his body and in his lungs."

A sudden thought slammed Dean in the gut. "Do you know who caused the fire?"

Aneesa frowned. "No. It's pretty suspicious, though."

Suspicious would be the word for it, all right.

A guard approached them. "Are you here for Ms. Lansing?"

Dean and Aneesa answered in unison. "Yes."

"You can go back now. She's ready to go."

Dean jumped to his feet, anxious to see for himself she was okay. The guard led them through a locked door and down a hall.

Jinxi sat on the edge of a stretcher, legs dangling. Her head was down, face hidden by the unruly mop of black hair. He reached her several strides before Aneesa.

"You ready to go home?"

Jinxi grimaced as she raised her head. Her right arm was hidden by a blue sling. Her left hand held a sheaf of papers, which she thrust at Dean.

"So ready," she mumbled.

Jinxi slid off the gurney and would have fallen if Dean hadn't grabbed her good arm.

"Whoa. Not so fast, princess." He pulled her to her feet, then to his side, wrapping his arm around her uninjured shoulder. Aneesa tagged along behind as they stepped down the hall toward the door.

Outside, Dean helped Jinxi down onto a concrete bench. "Wait here with Aneesa while I get my truck." He jogged toward the parking lot, keys jingling in his hand.

He was back within minutes, pulling into the passenger loading zone. He left the engine running. "C'mon, let's get you out of here."

Jinxi's face was white as new snow, her blue eyes hazy from either pain or the meds they'd given her, Dean couldn't tell which.

"I'm gonna need your help getting her into the truck and sliding her over," Dean told Aneesa. "I can put her in the middle, then I can give you a ride back to the food bank to get your car."

Aneesa's curls whipped around as she shook her head. "Someone's coming to pick me up. Just get our girl home."

"You sure?" Dean hoped his face didn't reflect his relief.

"I'm sure. You go on now." She shooed him off in the direction of his truck.

Jinxi didn't protest when Dean picked her up and carried her to the truck, gently setting her inside. He reached across to buckle the seat belt, acutely aware of the heat radiating off her body and the acrid smoke smell clinging to her hair and clothes. Greasy-looking salve covered the red blisters on her good arm and her face and neck.

"You okay?" He straightened, peering at her intently.

Her head was thrown back against the seat, eyes closed. "Fine."

Something was different. He searched her face for what had changed. Then it dawned on him. All her piercings were gone. "What happened to all the metal?"

Jinxi's eyes cracked open. "MRI. They made me take everything out." Her eyes closed again.

Dean closed the truck door, walked around to the driver's side, and got in. Hmm. Maybe she'd leave out that dang lip stud. That clicking got on his last nerve.

Just let me lay my head down. That's all I ask.

Today's trauma had left her limp. Jinxi felt her

temperature spike when Dean picked her up and carried her to his truck. She didn't dare open her eyes when he leaned against her to fasten the seatbelt. What a hot mess today had been. She fainted. Fainting was for wimps. But there she'd been, in a puddle on the floor, with a broken collarbone. And she'd tried to help Skeeter.

Jinxi was pretty sure she'd told Aneesa about the fire incident, but she couldn't remember clearly. That was some strong stuff the EMT gave her. Another dose of whatever that was would be sweet. At least she had a prescription for pain meds.

Turning her head against the seat, she watched Dean drive. The muscles in his jaw clenched like they did when he was ticked off. His knuckles stood up like tree stumps as he gripped the steering wheel.

He must have felt her gaze. His head swiveled around to face her. "You okay?"

"Yeah. You?"

Dean released one hand from the death grip on the wheel, using it to rub the back of his neck. "You scared the you-know-what outta me today."

"Now we're even."

Dean laughed. "I guess that's one way to look at it."

Jinxi smiled despite herself. "At least I didn't lose my memory."

"True that."

Dean let his hand drop to the seat between them. Jinxi reached over, resting her hand on his. She nearly laughed at his look of surprise. Those pain meds were definitely making her loopy.

Jinxi winced at the raised blisters on her arm. "Looks like my arms will have even more scars now." Still reeling from the reality she'd actually rushed toward the fire and not away, she said, "I thought it was you."

Dean glanced over. "Who?"

"I thought it was you, lying on the floor."

"Is that why you ran into danger, instead of the other way to safety?" A look crossed his face, but Jinxi was too exhausted to decode it.

"Yeah. Too bad it was Skeeter. I shoulda let him die."

"You don't mean that."

Jinxi shrugged. "Prob'ly not. Woulda served him right, though. I'll bet you all your mom's money he started it." She giggled. Definitely the pain meds.

Did everyone know Skeeter was Jared, and they'd been together? Then there was the whole Burn Boy thing. Her brain swirled with jumbled thoughts. Once the truth about everything came out, she'd be out of a job for sure. Especially if Jared—no, Skeeter—

Started the fire.

Jinxi let her head fall back against the seat. So tired.

They arrived at Janice's house as the late afternoon sun was changing from yellow to orange. Once Jinxi was settled on the couch, Janice fluttered around her like a moth.

"Can I get you anything to drink? Eat? How's your pain level?"

Dean kissed his mother's cheek. "She's fine, Mom. Let her rest. I'm going to get her prescription for pain meds filled." He jingled the car keys and was gone.

Janice sat on the coffee table across from Jinxi. "Honey, I'm so sorry about your accident. Can you tell me what happened?"

Jinxi's eyes cracked open. "I'm an idiot. That's what happened."

Janice reached over and patted Jinxi's unbandaged shoulder. "I'm sure you aren't. Dean said you fell."

"I fainted. Like a wimp."

"Why?"

Jinxi's chest rose and fell as she took a deep breath. Her eyes remained closed as she spoke. "There was a fire outside the cafeteria. It reminded me of something terrible that happened when I was fourteen."

Janice waited, anxious to know, but concerned about tiring Jinxi out.

"My friends and I started fires in vacant lots. We thought it was fun, watching the fire department roll up, all serious and stuff." She huffed out a humorless laugh. "One time the game got out of control. The fire spread to a nearby house. You wouldn't believe how fast a house can burn." She cracked open an eye. Janice patted her shoulder again.

"Go on," Janice urged.

"So, anyway, the bottom line is, a kid died in the fire, another kid got burned, and I went to jail."

A giant fist squeezed Janice's heart. Jinxi killed someone? A child? Merciful heavens. She looked at Jinxi's face, devoid of makeup and metal, and wondered who she'd let into her home.

CHAPTER FORTY-EIGHT

Dean pulled up to his mom's house, Jinxi's prescription on the seat beside him. He'd also picked up some of her favorite junk food. Oreos, potato chips, Pepsi. Anything to make her feel better. She'd been through hell and back these past couple of days. What was she thinking, doing some drug thing with her loser ex? Would she have done it if her secret wasn't on the line?

Jealousy burned, unfamiliar and hot. Had that guy touched her ... kissed her? The urge to smash his fist into the guy's face rose up. Dean gripped the steering wheel, knuckles white. After everything that loser had done to her, Jinxi had tried to save his life. And had almost died in the process. Still, he had to admire her guts, charging into the smoke despite her terror. Gutsy. Brave.

He'd thought he wouldn't get there in time. When Aneesa called him, Dean had been halfway home. He'd broken every speed limit to get to the hospital. From Aneesa's breathless report, things had sounded a lot worse.

I almost lost her.

The thought made him pause. Life without Jinxi would be inconceivable. She'd woven herself into the fabric of his life—Mom's too. She'd changed them. She'd helped him find the faith he'd lost after his dad's death. If the DNA results came back from Katie that he was the father of her little boy, he'd have to find a way to convince Jinxi to stick around. Once the whole Raul thing was over, he'd come up with a plan.

Dean tossed the prescription bag into the grocery sack and hopped out of the truck. Ted raced around the side of the house, barking his greeting.

"Hey, fella." Dean set the bag on the porch and stooped to rub Ted's coarse fur. "What a day. You're lucky you're a dog."

He stood and went through the front door, Ted pushing ahead. The couch was empty, a wrinkled throw and the scent of smoke the only evidence Jinxi had lain there.

"Mom?" Dean called.

Janice appeared in the hallway. "Oh, hi, honey. I was just lying down."

"Where's Jinxi?" Dean set down the bag and indicated the empty sofa with a wave of his arm.

"Upstairs, I think. Sit down, Dean. We need to talk."

Dean sank onto a chair. "Sounds serious. What's up?"

"Did you know Jinxi killed a child?" Janice's words hung between them, a knife suspended in air.

Dean rubbed the back of his neck, sighing. "Yeah. I knew."

"How long have you known?" Janice asked, the accusation sharp.

"Only a few days. It wasn't intentional, you know." Dean recognized the irony of defending Jinxi, after he was so ready to pry her out of his mom's house. Things were changing, and Dean struggled to keep up.

Janice pulled a tissue from her sweater pocket and dabbed her eyes. "I just don't know what to do anymore."

Dean looked around the room, desperate for something to say. Women and tears. He was unequipped to deal.

"Mom—"

Janice sobbed in earnest.

"I'm so confused. First your accident, then Robin, Jinxi's accident, and now finding out she killed someone. Am I safe? Should I tell Jinxi to leave? Will you ever get back to work?" She dabbed at her eyes again. "I keep waiting for something else bad to happen."

"Mom. Stop. Didn't Jinxi tell you anything about what happened at the food bank? She could have died, Mom." Dean shuddered, remembering her holey Tee shirt and the burns on her arm. "She overcame her fear of fire and tried to save someone."

Janice sat in stunned silence.

"I think you're safe having her here, Mom. No more drama, okay?" Dean bit his lip, holding back the urge to tell his mom about the DNA test, Katie, the boy who might or might not be his son. What a relief it would be to get it out in the open. But how much more could his mom take? His spirit longed for relief, but his flesh told him to keep silent.

Dean escaped into the kitchen, setting the grocery bag on the table. He snagged the prescription and headed up the stairs to Jinxi's room. Her door was partially open. He found her sitting on the edge of the bed, head down. She wore a pair of plaid jammie pants and a shapeless Tee shirt. Her bare feet dangled several inches off the floor.

"You okay?"

Her head jerked up. "*Snap!* You scared me."

The sling sat on the bed beside her. "I was trying to get the sling back on, but I can't do it one-handed." Her face was pinched and white.

Dean shook the bag at her. "I brought drugs."

A brief smile lit her face. "Sweet. Let me get a cup of water." She made as if to rise, but he held out a hand.

"I'll get it. You stay put." Dean filled a cup from the bathroom sink and returned to the bedroom. Jinxi hadn't moved. He shook out a pill and handed it to her, along with the water. Jinxi guzzled it down and sighed.

"Thanks. I should be good in about twenty minutes."

Dean reached for the sling. "Let me help you with that."

Jinxi watched him while he worked on reattaching the sling around her arm, careful to avoid the worst of the blisters.

"Your mom hates me."

Dean didn't meet her eyes. "She doesn't hate you."

"Yes, she does. I told her everything, and now, she hates me. I knew that would happen. You said it wouldn't, but it did."

Dean fastened the last of the straps. "She's just confused, that's all."

Jinxi shrugged, then winced. "Yeah, right."

Dean wandered to the dresser, hoping to change the subject. "Are these your parents?" he asked, pointing to the faded picture.

"Yeah." Jinxi's voice was low.

"Cute bunny," Dean commented. He picked up the one-eyed stuffed rabbit, running his hand across its nubby surface. She wasn't as tough as she liked to portray. Who kept a stuffed animal as ratty as this?

Dean glanced over his shoulder. Jinxi still hadn't moved. Something shifted inside him at the sight of her bare feet. She needed to be kept safe. She shouldn't have to do something unlawful just to hide her past. People loved her and accepted her for who she was, baggage and all. Even him.

What? Did he just say *loved*? His thoughts came to a screeching halt. He tucked that bit into a compartment to be opened later.

"Hey, Jinxi, come downstairs. I bought some chips and stuff for you."

She looked up with a faint bit of interest. "Food?"

Dean grinned. "Junk food."

"Sweet."

Jinxi woke the next morning with a mouth like cotton and an incessant throbbing in her shoulder. She raised her head and sniffed. Yup, somebody'd made coffee. Awesome.

She struggled to sit up, then swung her legs over the side of the bed. She grabbed the prescription bottle with her good hand, adjusted the sling, and headed downstairs for the day's first bracing cup of life's magic elixir.

Pouring with her left hand was awkward, and she ended up spilling a good portion of the first cup on the counter. Stifling a curse, she grabbed a wad of paper towels to mop up the mess. Janice came into the kitchen just as she carried the dripping mess to the trash.

"I thought I heard you up. Mercy, you slept a long time."

"What time is it?" Jinxi glanced at the clock on the microwave. "Nine?" Holy smokes, she'd slept almost twelve hours. Pain meds were her new best friend. Speaking of ...

She popped open the bottle and downed a pill with a sip of scalding liquid.

Jinxi sank onto one of the kitchen chairs, carefully setting her cup down with a shaky left hand.

"How about I toast you a bagel?" Janice offered.

"That'd be great. Thanks." How long until Janice told her she'd have to leave? Would she give Jinxi's collarbone a chance to heal before she lowered the boom?

When the bagel was done, Janice prepared it just the way Jinxi liked it—lots of cream cheese and a touch of jelly. Jinxi took an appreciative bite.

"You know—"

The doorbell rang, interrupting whatever Janice was going to say. "My goodness, who could that be?"

Jinxi shrugged, then regretted the move when a sharp stab reminded her of the injury.

Janice turned, headed out the kitchen door and through the living room. Jinxi heard her exclaim in surprise at whoever was at the door. She bit into the bagel, holding it between her teeth so she could carry her coffee cup with her good arm. She hoped to scurry around the corner and up the stairs before anyone saw her in her PJs.

No such luck. Padish and Aneesa barged into the living room, followed by Connie.

"We had to come see you."

"Are you all right?"

"Chica! *Pobrecita!*"

Jinxi winced at the cacophony of voices, expressing their concern. Dean was there too, adding to the mayhem, along with Ted prancing around everyone's legs.

She froze, a bagel-eating, coffee-carrying statue. In her jammie pants. Bed hair and all.

"Merciful heavens," exclaimed Janice. "Come sit down, everyone. Dean, get Jinxi a throw. And help her with her cup. And put that dog outside!"

Jinxi sat on the couch, listened as the conversations swirled around her.

"And then the fire started—"

"Everyone was yelling and running—"

"It was a frightening experience, yes?"

"Yinxi fell on the floor—"

"I thought the girl had died—"

Jinxi glanced at Dean to find him watching her. He winked before turning back to the group. She stifled a smile.

Padish stood and patted the air. "Everyone, please be quiet. I have some things to say that cannot be said with all this talk." The room became silent.

"First of all, I speak for all of us when I say we are so happy our little Jinxi is all right." There were nods around the room. "However, due to the fire, the food bank is closed temporarily until repairs can be made. We shall work at the main food bank in South Sacramento, except for Jinxi, who will fill out the papers for State disability."

Padish's face grew somber. "We have discovered the culprit of the missing money. We believe it was the community service volunteer, Jared. One of the children saw him coming out of the office, putting the money in his pocket."

It had to have been Burn Boy.

"But why didn't the child tell someone?" Aneesa asked.

"Mr. Jared threatened to hurt his mother if he told." Padish turned to look straight at Jinxi. "Mr. Jared is not a good person. I am sorry I doubted you."

Tears sprang to Jinxi's eyes. She blinked rapidly to keep them at bay. Sure, he was sorry now, but what if he knew the truth about her? What if he knew 'Jared' and she had a history? Would he still believe she was resistant to his moves?

"We have preliminary information from the fire department that the blaze was intentionally set. Mr. Jared has been questioned." Padish's mouth formed a straight line. "He is the number one suspect."

Hm. Maybe 'Jared'—or Skeeter—would be arrested, and she'd never have to deal with him again.

Padish's face broke into his habitual smile. "Let us all celebrate. Jinxi is on the mend, and so is the food bank."

Janice stood. "I think I'd better make more coffee."

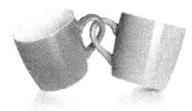

Later, after everyone had gone, Jinxi reflected on their conversation while she showered and dressed. It seemed like everything was forgiven. Her bad attitude, her meltdown, the Skeeter thing. Did it take a broken collarbone to get everyone to feel sorry for her? Or was it more than that? Maybe her friends really did care.

Jinxi sank down on the edge of the bed as the enormity of it hit her. They truly cared about her. Warm tears flowed down her cheeks.

"Thank you," she murmured. She looked down at her scarred arms and realized she had no desire to cut herself to relieve the dual-edged feeling of pain and joy.

Should she dare try to tell her secret to her friends? Or would they react in horror like Janice did? Maybe now that Skeeter was gone, she should just let it go. Keep the past in the past, nice and neat. Forget it ever happened. Right. Like that would work.

Janice busied herself around the house, putting away coffee cups and wiping crumbs off the sofa. Encouraging as the visit from Jinxi's friends at the food bank had been, Janice still held on to a thread of fear. It was one thing for Jinxi to intentionally set a fire, and another for her to try to help someone when the fire wasn't her fault.

"Hello?" Janice answered the phone on the second ring. "Oh, Emma, I'm so glad you called. I really need some advice." Janice carried the portable phone to her bedroom and closed the door.

"I found out something disturbing about Jinxi. I don't know what to do."

"More disturbing than the other things you know about her?"

Janice sank onto the bed. "Mercy, yes." She lowered her voice. "She told me she started a fire, and it spread to a house. A child died, Emma, and it was her fault." Janice plucked at the patchwork quilt covering the bed.

"My goodness, Jan. When did this happen?"

"I—I'm not sure." Janice wracked her brain to recall the conversation. Had Jinxi said when? "I think she was fairly young. Early teens? I can't recall. It was such a shock."

Emma was silent for a few moments, and Janice knew she must be praying. Janice stood and paced around the bedroom, pausing before the photo of Tom. He'd know what to do. He'd have some wise counsel. She was adrift in unfamiliar waters.

"Tell me more, Jan. How did she seem when she told you? Contrite? Defiant? Proud?"

Janice sank back down on the bed. "She was still heavily medicated, but she seemed relieved to get it off her chest."

"Do you have any idea why she would tell you?"

"I think it was like a confession."

"So maybe she's been carrying the guilt for so long, she needed to confess to you?" Emma probed. "Do you think she might have told you because she cares what you think about her?"

That hadn't occurred to Janice. "Merciful heavens, Emma. I've been thinking the worst since she told me. I've been frightened she'll do something like that again."

"A perfect foothold for the enemy."

Janice bowed her head, sending up a silent prayer for forgiveness. She'd been so focused on her own safety, she hadn't given a thought to what Jinxi had been through. Jail? At fourteen years old? What might that do to a child?

"Emma, thank you. What would I do without you?"

Emma chuckled, her voice raspy with age. "I'm sure you'd do just fine. Turn to the Lord, dear."

Janice sighed as she disconnected the call. Tom was gone, but there was one who was always with her.

She'd been so quick to condemn Jinxi's past, even after all her talk about God's forgiveness. Would she ever get it right? Was God's grace big enough to cover an old woman like her?

"Hey, Mom. Got any coffee left?" Dean barged into his mother's house at nine o'clock the next day. He headed straight for the coffee pot.

"Good morning, Dean. To what do I owe the pleasure of your company this beautiful morning?"

Dean did a double take. The last time he'd spoken to his mom, she'd been terrified Jinxi would start a fire in the house and kill them both. He pulled a mug out of the cupboard and filled it. As he reached into the fridge for milk, he answered, "You're in a good mood this morning."

Janice smiled. "It's a beautiful day, the sun is out, and my youngest son is having coffee with me."

Dean leaned against the counter, stirring the sugar and milk in his mug. What was going on? The sun was out, but a brisk wind rattled the forty-year-old windows. "Is Jinxi up?"

"I'm not sure. She hasn't been downstairs yet. Why?"

"She called me last night and asked me to take her to the food bank."

"I thought it was closed for repairs."

"It is, but the staff is meeting there this morning to pack up the kitchen and dining room. They're taking home their personal items for the duration of the remodel."

Clomping on the stairs indicated the object of their conversation was coming down to the kitchen. Dean pulled another mug from the cupboard and filled it with coffee. He held it out just as Jinxi turned and entered the kitchen.

"Mmm, thanks." She took it in her left hand and brought it to her nose, breathing deeply before taking her first sip.

Janice jumped to her feet. "Goodness me, I've got to run, or I'll be late to my class."

"You still volunteering at the elementary school?" Dean asked.

"Yes, and the children get restless when I'm not there on time."

"Have fun."

"Always." Janice smiled and swung around, rushing down the hall toward her bedroom.

Dean indicated the now-empty hall with his mug. "What's going on with my mom?"

"What do you mean?"

"Last night, she was freaked out, and today it's like she drank some happy juice or something."

Jinxi shrugged, then winced. "I dunno." She swallowed a liberal swig of coffee. "What was she freaked out about?"

Oops. Better change the subject, and fast. "Never mind. Ready to go?"

Jinxi refilled her cup. "Can I take this in your truck?"

Dean eyed her sling, his gaze sliding over to the too-full mug. "Uh ..."

"Oh, good grief. Get me a travel mug then."

Dean grinned. Good, her fall hadn't dampened her feistiness.

They pulled up to the food bank twenty minutes later. Dean threw the truck into park. "Do you need help getting out?"

"I think I can manage."

"And you'll get a ride home?"

"Yes, mother. What time is my curfew?"

"Smart aleck." He watched as Jinxi slid from the passenger seat, using her left hand for balance.

"Good luck with your doctor's appointment," she said, a second before she closed the door.

Dean checked the clock on the dash. He had just enough time to get to his doctor's building, park, and head to the third-floor office.

Three hours later, Dean was headed home with a piece of paper declaring him fit to return to work the following Monday. Exhilaration and exhaustion filled him in equal measure. He needed to tell someone. He reached for his cell phone just as a police cruiser pulled even with him. He glanced over, keeping his hand low. The officer on the passenger side held up his hand, thumb and index finger in the shape of a gun. He pointed it at Dean, pretending to take a shot.

Dean slammed on the brakes, adrenaline surging. The cruiser accelerated, disappearing into traffic.

CHAPTER FORTY-NINE

Jinxi slammed the truck door and strode across the sidewalk toward the food bank. She felt naked without the weight of her backpack. She'd left it behind when she'd been carried out on a stretcher. A sudden stab of pain in her shoulder was a sharp reminder of the fall.

She fumbled with the door, using her left hand to negotiate the handle. Familiar sounds poured through the hall, pulling her toward the cafeteria. Connie's quick chatter, Aneesa's slow drawl, and Hank's deep chuckles. Pots and pans clanging. The only thing missing was the aroma of Connie's cooking. Jinxi's stomach growled. She should have eaten breakfast.

"Yinxi! Come here. We have Mexican doughnuts and coffee."

Sweet. Just the thing to take the edge off her hunger. Everyone gently hugged her, mindful of the sling.

"How are you feeling?"

"How did you sleep?"

"When can you come back to work?"

The questions swirled around her like a kaleidoscope of joy.

Padish appeared in the doorway and the room grew still.

"You are good, yes?" Padish's smile, warm and inviting, drew Jinxi close. He put an arm around her and led her to a seat at one of the tables. "Sit, little Jinxi, and we will bring you some coffee and sweets."

Most of the tables were covered with flame retardant, but someone had wiped off this one. Everyone gathered around, coffee and doughnuts in hand. Jinxi glanced to where she'd run to Skeeter, then looked away.

"Some volunteers will be here soon," Padish began. "We will pack up the kitchen first, yes? The main food bank will send a truck to remove the food from the warehouse later today." Padish's face turned sad. "This is difficult for all of us. I am sorry—"

"What is *she* doing here?"

Every head swiveled to see who had interrupted Padish's speech. Jinxi's stomach clenched. Burn Boy's mother stood in the doorway, literally quivering with anger.

Advancing toward Jinxi, she shook her finger in Jinxi's face. "Now I know who you are. I wasn't sure until I heard about this fire here, but now I know, and I'm sure. You're the one who murdered my baby!"

Janice pulled into the driveway and parked. Ted raced back and forth against the chain link fence, barking his greeting. Janice smiled. She'd never been a dog person, but it was nice having such an exuberant greeting.

She walked around to the front of the house and pulled the mail from the box. Flipping through the stack as she walked back toward the side gate, her steps froze when she came to the letter she'd written to Robin.

Unable to deliver
No such address

The words, printed on a yellow label, screamed up at her. What in the world happened? A sick feeling settled in the pit of her stomach. She barely acknowledged Ted's demand for attention as she hurried to unlock the door. She scurried down the hall to the office and quickly pulled her address book from the desk drawer. Setting the envelope down, she thumbed through the book until she came to Carlos and Robin's information.

Goodness gracious, she'd written down the wrong address. She slumped onto the chair and dropped her head in her hands. Robin never got her letter. The words spun round and round like an eggbeater.

Desperate for some consolation, she reached for the phone and dialed her sister, Debbie.

"Hi, Sis. How lovely to hear from you." Debbie's cheery voice was like a balm to Janice's aching heart.

"Oh, Deb, you'll never believe what happened. You know that letter I sent to Robin? She never got it. I wrote down the wrong address. So stupid of me."

"That's certainly a bumble, isn't it?"

Janice was near tears. "I was so hoping she'd call me, and everything would be back to the way it was."

"Apparently God had other plans, sister mine."

"What should I do? How can I fix this? I should have told her she's adopted years ago. I'm so mad at Tom right now for insisting we not say anything."

Debbie laughed. "Easier to blame him, since he's not here."

Janice chuckled in spite of herself. "Right. Because I had nothing to do with the decision."

"Honey, you know what to do. Pray."

Janice murmured her agreement.

"Now tell me what else is going on," Debbie said.

Janice told her sister all about Jinxi's accident, the fire, and her own quickness to go to a place of fear. Twenty minutes later, Janice disconnected the phone with a lighter heart.

She booted up the computer, praying while she waited for it to come to life. She glanced through her emails, then clicked 'compose' and began to type.

Dear Robin ...

Dean barged into his mother's house, waving the doctor's note like a white flag. "Mom! Guess what?"

His mother sat in the living room, Bible on her lap. "Goodness, you look happy."

"I can go back to work," he exclaimed, excited as a five-year-old with a new toy.

"That's wonderful, dear. Praise the Lord."

"Amen."

Janice's forehead wrinkled. "Did I just hear you say 'amen'?"

Dean grinned and walked over to give his mom a hug. "Let's just say your prayers have been answered."

At that moment, Dean's phone chirped. A text from Jinxi.

JINXI: Pick me up from the FB. NOW!

Uh-oh. Wonder what happened. "Gotta run, Mom."

"What is it, dear?"

"I'll explain later," Dean called over his shoulder as he dashed for the back door.

What in the world? Jinxi was going to the food bank, picking up her stuff, and catching a ride home with Aneesa. How could something so simple have gone south so quickly?

Dean pulled up in front of the food bank, grateful to find a spot near the front. He jumped out of the truck and hustled to the door, pausing in the hall. The eerie silence raised the hair on the back of his neck. Where was everyone?

The office door opened, and Aneesa peered out.

"I thought I heard someone come in," she said. She motioned for him to go into the office. Jinxi was hunched over in a chair in front of Padish's desk. Connie stood in one corner, wringing her hands and muttering in Spanish. An African American woman and child crowded the room, along with Padish. Dean estimated the kid to be about ten years old. The skin on one side of his face was white and puckered, indicating a burn of some kind.

Jinxi looked up as he entered. Her eyes beseeched him to ... he wasn't sure what. The tension in the room radiated like heat waves. The boy started to cry. His mother shushed him.

Padish rubbed his hands across his face, weariness expressed in the slump of his shoulders.

"Ah, Mr. Dean. Welcome to our little party." Padish's attempt at humor fell flat.

"What's going on?" Dean looked at everyone in turn, stopping at Jinxi's huddled form.

The African American woman's voice shook with anger. "This monster killed my baby." Her bony finger pointed at Jinxi, who shrank even more into her hoodie.

"Mrs. Jackson, perhaps Officer Rafferty can shed some light on this situation." Padish's Indian accept deepened. "I have explained to Mrs. Jackson that Miss Jinxi served her time for a childish incident, which quickly went out of control. She insists that we terminate Miss Jinxi's employment because of the terrible outcome. As you can see," he motioned toward the boy, whose silent sobs shook his body, "this young man did not escape unscathed."

Dean settled his hands on his hips, unconsciously assuming his cop's stance. "Ma'am, I'm sorry for your loss. It's unfortunate that you and Miss Lansing have crossed paths after all this time. However—"

"Unfortunate?" the woman screeched. "I'll tell you—"

"Let me finish." Dean stared her down until she dropped her eyes. "Miss Lansing was barely a teenager when your son died. She paid her dues in California Girls' Ranch, and I believe I speak for her when I say she is very sorry."

Dean looked at Jinxi, whose eyes pooled with tears.

The mom exhaled on a sob. She sank down and wrapped her arms around her son. The tension in the room released like a pressure cooker blowing off steam.

Padish clapped his hands together. "I think this is a very good time to pray."

Dean bowed his head as Padish began a prayer of thanksgiving. His eyes popped open when something brushed his arm. It was Jinxi, slipping quietly out of the room.

When Padish was done praying for restoration, forgiveness, and healing, Dean echoed the amen.

"Excuse me," he murmured, as he opened the office door and stepped into the hall. He checked the kitchen and the cafeteria, but Jinxi was nowhere to be seen.

The restroom.

He slapped his open hand on the door. "Hey, you in there?"

"Go away," came the muffled reply.

Dean leaned his forehead against the door. She would be the death of him. What was he supposed to do now? His cop training, sluggish from nonuse, rose grudgingly to his brain.

"Jinxi, if you don't come out, I'll be forced to come in." His command was met with silence. He inhaled, then pushed against the door. His movement was met with resistance.

"Hey," Jinxi yelped. "Give me a minute, jerk."

They stood face-to-face in the open doorway.

"My bad," Dean said. He stepped to the side and motioned for her to pass. When they were both in the hall, he put a hand on her good shoulder and turned her to face him.

"What's going on?" he asked.

Jinxi's shoulders slumped as she tucked her chin into her hoodie. "Everybody knows."

"So? Sounds like Padish was defending you."

"Yeah, but that was just for show. I know they hate me. I'm a kid killer."

Dean dropped his arm to take her hand. "We talked about this, remember?"

Jinxi's black hair swung back and forth as she shook her head.

"Everything in our past is forgiven, gone. Like it never existed," Dean continued.

Jinxi glanced up, her eyes full of wary hope.

"I know what you're thinking. Can it be true?" He rubbed the back of his neck with his other hand. "When I talked to Chaplain Mike, he helped me see that what I did with Katie was in the past. I still have to deal with the consequences, but I asked God for forgiveness, and he gave it to me. Same with you. The truth is still that you were responsible for a child's death, and the scarring of another, but you don't have to carry that weight around anymore."

Dean pulled Jinxi to him, wrapping his arms around her slight frame. It felt right. They stood that way for a few moments, before Jinxi pulled away. Dean stared down at her until her eyes rose to meet his.

Pressure rose in his chest. Dean leaned forward, compelled to rest his lips on hers. He lowered his head, watching Jinxi's eyes widen. When they were a breath apart, the office door banged open, and the hall was suddenly filled with noise.

"That's not the first time that's happened, you know," Jinxi whispered. "Getting interrupted like this."

"You'll have to remind me," Dean whispered back.

They turned in unison to see the mother and boy slam out the front door of the food bank, the mother saying something over her shoulder as they went. Padish and Aneesa were talking at the same time, insisting she return.

"Everything okay?" Dean asked.

Aneesa stood with hands on her hips, legs apart. An aggressive stance. Padish rubbed his hands together, head bent over as if in prayer. Connie made the sign of the cross and kissed her thumb.

"No, everything isn't okay," Aneesa answered, looking toward Dean and Jinxi. "But it will be soon enough. As soon as that girl leaves town."

CHAPTER FIFTY

Jinxi froze, resisting the pressure from Dean's hand. They wanted her to leave town. They hated her. She knew it. Hot tears filled her eyes. Everyone turned against her. So much for their fake acceptance. Forcing her legs to move, she stomped toward the door.

"Just where do you think you're going?" Aneesa's voice cut through the air. "You come on back here and let us love on you, girlfriend."

"Wh—what?" Jinxi turned halfway toward the little group.

Everyone moved toward her, gathering her into a group hug.

"Hey, what about me?" Dean demanded, forcing his way in.

Tears ran freely down Jinxi's cheeks. "But I thought—"

"You thought wrong, girl," said Aneesa. Padish's smile was a white expanse against his brown skin.

"*Te amo,* chica," Connie murmured.

"Yes," Padish echoed. "We love you."

Jinxi glanced up at Dean. The expression in his eyes said, *See, I told you so.* She'd deal with him later. She struggled to be free of everyone's embraces so she could breathe again. Stepping away, she said, "You don't hate me?"

Padish laughed, a welcome sound to Jinxi's ears. It had been weeks since she'd even seen him smile.

His smile faded, and his forehead creased. "Something very bad happened to you many years ago. It is a terrible tragedy that childish carelessness caused such a thing. But you are not the same Jinxi now as you were then." Padish brought his hands together, resting them under his chin. "We all have things in our past that bring us shame. But God has removed the shame, so we don't have to carry it."

Connie and Aneesa murmured their assent.

Tension drained from Jinxi's body, leaving her spent. "I need to go home." She turned toward the door on quivering legs.

Dean beat her to the door by a second, pushing it open.

"Don't forget your backpack, girlfriend," Aneesa said. She rushed into the office, returning with the pack dangling from one hand.

"Thanks," Jinxi mumbled. Her shoulder throbbed, an insistent reminder she was past due for a pain pill. "And thanks for everything," she said to the trio still huddled outside the office door.

Once they were outside, Dean helped her into the truck.

"When are you going to get something easier for me to get into?" Jinxi used her right hand on the armrest to push herself onto the seat.

"If you were taller ..." Dean commented.

"But I'm not," she snapped.

Dean had to have the last word. "Maybe if you hadn't smoked when you were a kid, you wouldn't have stunted your growth." He slammed the door before she could smack him.

They rode home in silence. Jinxi gritted her teeth against the knife stabbing her collarbone. She should have put her lip stud back in. Anything to distract her from the pain.

Dean pulled up to the side street next to his garage apartment. Jinxi barely registered the unfamiliar car parked a few feet in front of Dean's pickup. Dean opened her door, supporting her weight until her feet were solidly planted on the sidewalk. Keeping his hand under her good arm, he guided her through the gate.

"C'mon, I'll walk you to—"

"Stop!" The word snapped in the air like an order.

"What the—" Dean turned toward the man's voice. *Raul.*

Jinxi slipped her right hand into the sling, gripping her hands together. Her stomach roiled at the sudden tension in the air.

Raul advanced toward the open gate, then stopped. He held a gun in his hand, pointed toward Dean. Dean slid his arm away from her and slowly raised both hands.

"Hey, partner," Dean said. "What's up?" He took two slow steps to place himself between Jinxi and Raul.

"Don't move. And don't 'partner' me. You betrayed me, amigo." Raul spit on the ground. "Everything was going along just fine, then you turned it into *basura*."

Basura. Garbage. Jinxi remembered the word from working with Connie.

Dean lowered his arms a few inches. "I'm sure we can work this out. Put down the gun and let's talk."

Raul stepped through the gate. He and Dean stood no more than three or four feet apart. Jinxi could see sweat beaded on Raul's forehead. So far he hadn't noticed her. She turned her cell phone around in the sling so she could use her right hand. She pressed the side button to silence it, then felt for the numbers, dialing 9-1-1. Then she prayed.

"No need to talk," Raul said. "There's only one way this will end."

Just as he raised the gun, Ted raced toward them, barking like a rabid dog. Raul jerked the gun toward Ted and fired. Ted went down with a yelp.

Dean lunged toward Raul, knocking him onto his back. The gun skittered away. Both men scrambled to grab it.

The wail of sirens pierced the air above the sounds of Ted whining, Raul and Dean grunting, and Jinxi screaming.

Just as Raul was about to wrap his fingers around the gun, Ted sank his teeth into Raul's wrist with a ferocious growl.

"Aaaah! Get him off me!" A string of Spanish burst from Raul's lips.

Two police cars pulled up. Dean sat on Raul's chest, pinning his arms to the ground.

The rest was a blur. Adrenaline surged through Jinxi, deadening the pain from her broken bone. She watched as Raul was dragged roughly to his feet by two cops, handcuffed, and thrown into the back of one of the cars.

Dean crouched by Ted as he continued barking and struggling to reach Raul.

It could have been minutes later—or hours later, Jinxi couldn't tell—when an officer approached her and asked her to give a statement. She shook her head, then turned and threw up into the bushes at the side of the garage.

"She needs to go inside," Dean told the cop. Dean bent down to briefly examine Ted's leg. The bullet had grazed him, and the blood was already congealing on the wound. "I'll be right back, buddy," Dean said. He turned to the cop. "Let's go to my mom's house."

He took hold of Jinxi's arm, the warmth of his hand a welcome pressure. She shivered, huddling down in her sweatshirt. Dean led her across the lawn to Janice's house. Once inside, he settled her on the couch, wrapped her in a throw, then disappeared upstairs.

He returned with her prescription bottle. Jinxi shook one out and swallowed it with the water Dean brought from the kitchen.

"I'll make you some hot chocolate," he said.

"What about Ted?" Jinxi's stomach threatened to explode again when she remembered the sound of the gunshot and Ted crumpled on the ground.

"He'll be fine for a little while. One of the guys is calling the vet."

Jinxi nodded, then lay her head against the back of the couch.

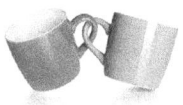

Dean carried the mug of hot cocoa and set it down next to Jinxi. Her head rested against the back of the sofa, eyes closed. Tension sharpened the angles of her face. Torn between staying with her and returning outside to the action, he chose the latter.

Dean sprinted across the lawn to where one of the uniforms was crouched, petting Ted.

"Vet said bring him in when you're done here."

Dean nodded, then turned his attention to the other cop who tapped his pen on his notebook, looking annoyed. The cruiser carrying Raul blocked half the street, forcing traffic to swerve around it.

"Let's get started," said the annoyed cop. He opened his notebook, found a clean page, and stood with his pen poised. The other uniform pushed himself to a standing position.

"That's quite a mutt you've got there."

Dean grinned. "Yup. Might just have to deputize him."

They laughed, releasing some pent-up energy. Dean knew the guy from his training days. He was a good cop, respected and liked by the others. His blond surfer looks made him a target for all the single women around headquarters. His name was Loffman. Dean didn't recognize the other guy.

Dean gave his statement to the two officers, then gathered Ted up and gently lay him in the truck.

They returned home, Ted sporting a bandage on his back leg and a cone around his head. Dean chuckled at Ted's woeful look.

"It's okay, buddy. You only have to wear the cone of shame for a few days."

Dean slumped onto his futon. He clenched and unclenched his fists, wishing he could have done something more to protect Ted from Raul. His brain replayed the scenario with several different outcomes.

What if he'd rushed Raul and taken him down?

What if he'd been able to grab the gun before Raul got off a shot?

What if ...

So many regrets. Chaplain Z told him he could regret the past or he could learn from it.

Speaking of the past ...

Dean pulled himself up from his reclining position and trudged the few steps to his desk. Opening his laptop, his heart sped up to see a new email from Katie.

"Dean, I should have the results either later today or tomorrow. Stay tuned. Katie."

He breathed a sigh of relief. Now to check on Jinxi.

CHAPTER FIFTY-ONE

The word exhaustion couldn't adequately describe the weight pressing Jinxi into the sofa. The pain pill was working its magic. No throbbing in her collarbone, just lovely numbness in her body.

She'd gone to the food bank to pick up her stuff, then was blindsided by Burn Boy's mom, who was intent on bringing her down. Only to receive the one thing she never thought to have—absolution from her friends. How cool was that? Even Dean didn't blame her. Maybe now she could stop blaming herself.

"You look tired." Dean's voice interrupted her thoughts.

"Thank you, Captain Obvious," she retorted. She forced her eyes open to squint at him. "All done with your buddies out there?"

"Yeah. You must have fallen asleep. I've already been to the vet and back. Ted's gonna be fine. Just a flesh wound. Oh, and by the way they're sending over a female uniform to take your statement."

"A female uniform? Not a whole person?" The meds were muddling her brain.

"No. A woman cop, druggie."

"You'd have drugs too, if you'd broken your collarbone." She closed her eyes again.

"I want to talk to you about something," Dean said.

"Sounds serious. Am I going to like this?"

"Prob'ly not. But I have to ask. Why did you think it was okay to do a drug handoff with your ex? What were you thinking?"

Great time for a lecture, Dean. Thanks a lot.

Jinxi sighed. "I didn't want him to tell everyone at the food bank about the kid, okay? Everything was going so good, and he would've ruined it all."

"But he didn't."

She didn't respond.

"So you were wrong," Dean pressed.

Jinxi rubbed her face with her good hand. "I guess."

"Just admit it. Say you were wrong." She heard the smile in his voice. "Repeat after me. I. Was. Wrong."

"Never," she said, biting back a grin. "Not to you, anyway."

The doorbell rang.

"That must be the uniform," Dean said. Jinxi forced her eyes open and watched Dean walk to the door. Was it the meds, or did he look especially good in his white Tee shirt?

When the policewoman was finished taking her statement, Jinxi was more than ready to crash. Dean offered to fix something for them to eat.

"Don't set the house on fire," she told him, as he headed into the kitchen.

"No worries. About the only thing I can make is PB&J. No open flames will be used in the making of our sandwiches."

"Don't forget the potato chips," she called.

Dean brought their sandwiches into the living room several minutes later. He held a plate in each hand, and the chip bag hung from his teeth. He set everything down on the coffee table, then returned to the kitchen to retrieve two bottled iced teas.

They ate in silence for a few moments. "Have you heard back on the DNA test yet?" Jinxi asked.

Dean shook his head. "Not yet. Soon, I hope."

"What're you gonna do if it turns out positive?"

Dean shrugged. "Dunno. Man up, I guess."

"You going to tell your mom?"

"Not unless it's confirmed I'm the father."

"Why not? Don't you think it's fair to give her a heads-up?"

"I don't want to disappoint her. She'll be pretty upset when she hears how the boy was conceived."

"You mean she might think bad of you?"

"Something like that."

Jinxi went for the kill. "What if you're wrong?" She took a huge bite of sandwich, and mumbled, "Like I was."

Dean cocked his head. "Care to repeat that last statement?"

Jinxi smiled and took a sip of tea. "Nope."

Jinxi's words were like a stab with a hot poker. How would he even begin to tell his mom about Katie? She'd be horrified at what he'd done. Like he'd been, when he first heard about the fire Jinxi inadvertently started.

"I'm going upstairs." Jinxi struggled to stand. "Thanks for lunch."

Dean watched her as she adjusted the sling. She was so cute. He had the sudden urge to grab her and squeeze her in a bear hug. She'd probably jab him with one of those pointy elbows if he did. Better save it for when she felt better.

He thought about what she'd said. When he'd confessed what he'd done to the chaplain, Mike hadn't judged him. Jinxi knew before he told her, and she didn't condemn him. Could it be she was right? He sat back in the chair and smiled to himself. Who would've thought a little Goth girl could have captured his heart and made him look at things differently?

Dean heard a car pull up. His mom climbed out of her Prius, reaching inside for her purse and a grocery bag. He stood and walked to the side door, opening it up as she climbed the steps onto the porch.

"Any more bags to bring in?" Dean asked, taking the sack from her hand.

"No, just the one," she answered. "I didn't expect to see you here, but I'm glad you are."

They walked together to the kitchen. Dean set the sack on the counter. "You would not believe the day I've had."

"My goodness, that sounds serious. You left here in a rush after telling me about your release to go back to work."

"A lot has happened between then and now."

Dean told her all about the incident at the food bank as she unloaded the groceries. She poured herself a glass of water, then sat at the table as he moved on to the story of Raul. She interjected several times with "Goodness me" and "Merciful heavens."

When Dean wound down, his mom asked, "What are you going to do?"

"I have to figure out whether or not I want to press charges against Raul." He rubbed the back of his neck. "But that's not the worst of it, Mom." He sat down and looked into his mom's eyes, so trusting, so full of love. What he was about to tell her would test the depth of that love.

Dean took a deep breath. "I did something a long time ago that could have consequences. Lasting, serious consequences."

CHAPTER FIFTY-TWO

Janice reeled from Dean's words. She didn't know whether to cry over the guilt he'd carried for the past six years, or laugh at the thought of having another grandchild.

She thought back to the previous summer when she'd told God she was bored with her life. In his sovereign sense of humor, he brought Jinxi to her. Having her around had been anything but boring. Then Dean's accident, and all the subsequent drama. And the situation with Robin, and now this. What she wouldn't give to go back to boring.

Janice reached across the table and laid her hand on Dean's arm. "I need some time to process this, Dean."

"Sure, Mom. It's a lot to take in."

"You'll let me know as soon as you hear from Katie?"

Dean stood. "Of course."

Janice watched with a heavy heart as Dean left. If he indeed was the father of a child, his life was about to drastically change. She was confident he'd do the right thing and be involved in the child's life. At least she'd have contact with *one* of her grandchildren, since Robin still hadn't answered her email.

Janice stood and walked to the refrigerator. What to fix for dinner for herself and Jinxi? She'd gotten spoiled with the girl living here. Janice wondered how long she'd be out of commission, then chided herself for being selfish.

Maybe she'd fix a nice, old-fashioned Sunday dinner tomorrow and invite everyone over. Dean, Brian and Courtney, Emma, the folks from the food bank. It had been a month of Sundays since she'd seen Padish's family. And she'd never met Connie's husband. She'd extend the invitation to Robin and Carlos, too. Even though they wouldn't come.

The doorbell rang, interrupting her musings about what to cook.

"Now who could that be?"

Janice closed the refrigerator and limped into the living room. She made a mental note to call the doctor Monday for a new arthritis prescription.

She swung the front door open. The first thing she saw was Robin's ashen face. Her eyes traveled down Robin's frame, noticing she'd lost a significant amount of weight.

"Mom, we need to talk," Robin said, pushing past Janice.

"Wait."

Janice grabbed her only daughter and wrapped her in a tight embrace. They stood together, swaying, as Janice patted Robin's back. Tears filled her eyes and overflowed to wet her cheeks.

"I've missed you so much."

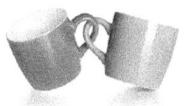

Dean walked back to his apartment with a lighter heart. He'd confessed to his mom. She was disappointed, but he felt better by knowing he no longer had to keep it a secret. As soon as the DNA results came in, he'd be able to deal with it. Hopefully.

What a week this had turned out to be. He was released to go back to work, Jinxi's loser ex would probably be arrested for arson, and Raul was in custody.

Even a positive DNA report wouldn't be enough to rock his world.

His cell phone pinged with a new email notification. Something about reading emails on his phone didn't work. Dean jogged up the stairs and sat at his laptop.

Another email from Katie. Subject line: *DNA Results!*

The exclamation point looked ominous. Dean clenched his jaw. Time to man up.

He quickly scanned the email, then read it more slowly. He leaned back in the chair to ponder what Katie said. He didn't know whether to laugh or cry.

Jinxi woke slowly from her nap. She sat up and swung her legs over the side of the bed. What she needed was a gigantic glass of water. Those pain meds made her mouth feel like she'd been on a three-day party spree, a feeling that was too familiar.

When she reached the top of the stairs, she paused. Voices drifted up to her, Janice and ... *Robin*? She crept halfway down, her bare feet soundless on the wood steps. From there she could eavesdrop without being seen.

It sounded like they were making up. After all the nasty things Robin said, Janice was going to let it all go. Unbelievable. Jinxi was filled with grudging admiration. Maybe one day she'd be as good at forgiving as everyone around her.

She heard the back door slam. Loud footsteps sounded in the kitchen. *Snap*! It was Dean. Now she'd be busted for sure.

"Mom, I got the results ..."

Jinxi heaved a sigh of relief when he passed by the open door at the bottom of the stairwell without looking up.

"Oh, hi, Robin," Dean said.

"Come on in, sweetie. Robin and I were just getting caught up."

Jinxi wished he'd finished his sentence. The results from the DNA test were ... what? She sat on the step, using her bottom to scoot down toward the open door. Just as she reached the last stair, Dean appeared.

"I thought I saw you."

Jinxi jumped to her feet. "One of these days you're going to give me a heart attack."

"Maybe you should stop snooping and you won't get caught."

"Is that you, Jinxi?" called Janice. "You might as well come in too."

Jinxi stuck out her tongue at Dean, then followed him to the living room.

"Come sit down, honey," Janice said, patting the sofa beside her. "You're practically part of the family, anyway."

"Yeah, and you're the one who started this whole adoption discussion." Robin's thin smile took some of the bite out of her words.

Jinxi ducked her head, waiting for the accusations that were sure to come.

Janice spoke to her and Dean. "Robin was just telling me she had a revelation of sorts. Do you want me to tell it, Robin?"

"Go ahead," Robin said with a wave of her arm.

Jinxi looked up to see Janice's broad smile. "Robin decided that it didn't matter what her birth circumstances were. The important thing is that she was raised by a loving family, and if she'd been brought up somewhere else, she might not have met Carlos, and had two beautiful children"—Janice laid her hand across her throat—"and I might not have two beautiful grandchildren."

Robin put her hand to her stomach. "Three," she said with a grin.

"Mercy! Already?" Janice clapped her hands.

"Uh, four," Dean said under his breath.

CHAPTER FIFTY-THREE

Jinxi looked around the dining room with satisfaction. Dean had set up extra tables for all the dinner guests. Jinxi had painstakingly set the table, making sure all the silverware lined up perfectly. She smiled to herself. She never would have known about something as simple as making a table presentable if she hadn't met Janice. She'd learned so much from Janice, but there was still a lot more to learn.

People were arriving, and the house filled with voices and laughter. Everyone gently hugged her, asking how the collarbone was healing. Jinxi's heart expanded to include their love.

After Dean said grace, Jinxi looked up to see Robin staring at her. For the first time Jinxi could remember, Robin smiled. Jinxi gulped down a sob.

"What's going to happen with your loser ex-partner?" Brian asked, as he handed the platter of meat to Dean.

"Rumor has it he's going down hard." Dean stabbed several pieces of roast and slapped them onto his plate. "He's got so many charges against him they'll need a wheelbarrow to bring 'em into court."

Robin leaned across Owen's highchair to address Brian. "Has our little brother told you about his drama?"

"Thanks, Sis. Like that's something I want to discuss in front of everybody." Dean's face flamed. That was Robin, always the drama queen stirring stuff up.

Dean spoke low to Brian as Padish and Aneesa started talking about when the food bank would reopen.

Jinxi let the conversations swirl around her. She wished she'd been born into a family like this. One where love wasn't given and taken away on a whim. She was here now, though. She warmed to the memory of Janice saying *You're practically family*.

Dean turned from his brother, leaning into her. "You and I have some unfinished business." He winked.

Jinxi hid her smile behind her napkin. "What might that be?"

"I think you know." Dean's cop stare was back, but this time instead of making her uncomfortable, she was filled with pleasant shivers.

"Does it involve talking?"

"Nope. There will be no talking."

As Dean leaned closer, Hannah stuck her head between them. "What are you talking about, Unca Dean?"

Jinxi snorted a laugh at Dean's expression.

"Nothing that concerns you, Little Bit," Dean answered.

"Looks like you were going to kiss." Hannah made an 'ugh' face.

Dean's face flamed as everyone laughed. He shoved his chair back from the table and stood. "I have an announcement to make."

Jinxi gaped up at him as everyone grew quiet.

"This has been a difficult few weeks for everybody," Dean said. "There's been a lot of drama, and we've all been touched in some way by circumstances beyond our control." His gaze touched everyone before landing on Jinxi.

"I want everyone here to know, so there's no question. I am in love with this woman. She brings out the best and the worst in me. I hope she will be part of my life for a long time."

Jinxi's throat grew thick with unshed tears.

"I hope she will help me navigate the world of parenthood. I don't know how to be a father, but I know a Father who will be there to guide me. And I want Jinxi to be by my side."

Dean extended a hand. Jinxi took it. The silence was absolute as everyone focused now on her, their faces expectant, their eyes alight.

She managed to choke out one word.

"Yes."